Frances Martin

Angelique Arnauld

Abbess of Port Royal

Frances Martin

Angelique Arnauld
Abbess of Port Royal

ISBN/EAN: 9783337156275

Printed in Europe, USA, Canada, Australia, Japan

Cover: Foto ©Andreas Hilbeck / pixelio.de

More available books at **www.hansebooks.com**

ANGELIQUE ARNAULD

ABBESS OF PORT ROYAL.

BY

FRANCES MARTIN.

SECOND EDITION.

London:

MACMILLAN & CO

1873.

than disobey the dictates of conscience; and she bequeathed to a small band of faithful followers, not certainly freedom from errors of dogma, but a love of truth and a holy zeal and courage in the cause of truth, which enabled them to endure persecution, affliction, and death rather than sin against it.

She differs from us in creed, ritual, and observance; but there is no diversity in the object of her worship and of ours, nor in the faith and love which lead us to cast ourselves, as she did, at the feet of Him who is the source of all virtue.

We shall gain something, nay, we shall gain much, if we learn to look upon her with sympathy and love, if we acknowledge that she was faithful, earnest, and devout, and strive, in the fuller light of a purer faith, to emulate the virtues which make Angélique Arnauld so noble and so great.

LIST OF SOME OF THE PRINCIPAL WORKS REFERRED TO IN THIS VOLUME.

"Histoire générale de Port Royal." Par Dom Clémencet. 10 vols. 1755-1757.

"Mémoires historiques et chronologiques sur l'Abbaye de Port Royal des Champs." Par l'Abbé Guilbert. 9 vols., 1755-1759.

"Mémoires touchant la Vie de M. de Saint-Cyran." Par Lancelot. 2 vols., 1738.

"Mémoires pour servir à l'Histoire de Port Royal." Par Fontaine. 2 vols., 1738.

"Mémoires pour servir à l'Histoire de Port Royal." Par Du Fossé. 1 vol., 1738.

"Mémoires pour servir à l'Histoire de Port Royal." Utrecht, 3 vols., 1742.

"Recueil de plusieurs Pièces pour servir à l'Histoire de Port Royal." Utrecht, 1 vol., 1740.

"Lettres de la Mère Angélique." Utrecht, 3 vols., 1742-1744.

"Lettres de la Mère Agnès." 1858.

"Vies intéressantes et édifiantes des Religieuses de Port Royal." 4 vols., 1750.

"Port Royal." Par Sainte-Beuve. 6 vols., 1867.

PREFACE.

ANGÉLIQUE ARNAULD is separated from us not only by the manners, habits, and customs of her age, but by her position and religious opinions. She was a Roman Catholic Abbess who lived more than 200 years ago, at a time when Pope and priest stood between the people and a God whom they feared but did not love. The religious rites and ceremonials of her Church formed then, as now, an almost impenetrable barrier between the human soul and the supreme object of its worship, and she was not free from the theoretical errors incidental to her condition. The struggles and suffering of her life were crowned, not by victory, but defeat. Her work was incomplete, and it is doubtful whether it could have been completed or whether she realized the direction in which her efforts were tending.

All these facts are patent and are readily brought to light by a superficial inquiry. But if we look beneath the surface we find that sublime virtues are associated with her errors, there is something admirable in everything that she does, and the study of her history leads to a continual enlargement of our own range of thought and sympathy. Her devotion was sincere, habitual, and profound; her life was strengthened by self-denial and sweetened by love, and we admire alike her self-dependence and her self-distrust. Moreover, at the last she dared to incur the disapprobation of her Church rather

CONTENTS.

ANGÉLIQUE ARNAULD

ABBESS OF PORT ROYAL.

INTRODUCTORY CHAPTER.

In the year 1202 Mathieu de Marli, of the noble house of Montmorency, joined the crusade preached by Foulques de Neuilly, and left France for the Holy Land. He gave in charge to his wife, Mathilde de Garlande, a sum of money to be devoted to some work of piety by which he hoped to obtain Divine favour, and ensure the success of his undertaking. Mathilde, after consulting her kinsman Eudes de Sully, Bishop of Paris and relative of Philip Augustus, King of France, determined to establish a monastery—for the word 'convent' was not then used—for nuns.

She purchased in 1204 the fief of *Porrois*, or, as it was afterwards called, Port Royal, situated in a narrow valley near Chevreuse, about eighteen miles west of Paris. A chapel dedicated to St. Laurence, which attracted a large number of devout worshippers on the Saint's day, already existed there.

Some of the later historians of Port Royal claim Philip Augustus as founder of the monastery and originator of its name. They say that one day during the chase he wandered away from his companions and was lost in the woods, but was at length discovered in this secluded valley close to the chapel of St. Laurence. He made a vow to build a church there because the place had been a Port-Royal or royal refuge to him. This story belongs to an age when royal founders were in fashion, and cannot be reconciled with what we know of the actual history of the monastery. The derivation given by the Abbé Lebœuf is most probably correct. According to him Port Royal has nothing to do with any royal visit, but comes from *Porrois*, which is derived from the corrupt Latin *Porra* or *Borra*, namely, a hollow overgrown with brambles, in which there is stagnant water. The monastery erected by Mathilde de Garlande stood in a hollow, surrounded by hills covered with brushwood; a pool of water on a higher level than the bottom of the valley often overflowed and converted the place into a stagnant marsh. The filling up of this pool was from time to time advocated and discussed, but it was not done. The health of the nuns of Port Royal was always more or less affected by the miasma of the valley, and from time to time fever carried off many of them. The locality chosen indicates the religious order which Mathilde had selected. Old Latin verses tell that—

> 'Bernard loved the valleys and Benedict the hills,
> St. Francis the towns and Ignatius the great cities.'

Accordingly, in 1208, we find that a few nuns of the Cistercian order, which had recently been reformed by St. Bernard, entered the newly completed building. Their numbers increased rapidly; that which was at first a priory became an abbey, and as early as 1233 was able to receive and support sixty nuns. By that time also the church built by Robert de Luzarches, architect of the cathedral at Amiens, was completed, and included in its precincts the sacred chapel of St. Laurence already alluded to. We know very little of those early days, but since this was a Cistercian monastery, in a wild and secluded spot, established about fifty years after the death of St. Bernard, and when the reform inaugurated by him had reached its fullest development, we are justified in assuming that the attractions which it offered were poverty, and the humiliation and unbroken penance which those who measured sanctification by suffering were anxiously seeking. The necrology of Port Royal gives the names of fifteen ladies of noble birth who joined the community in those early days. There were numerous monasteries at that time in which they might have found wealth, ease, and comfort; but they were doubtless among the more ardent spirits who could be satisfied with nothing short of absolute and total self-sacrifice. In the poverty and solitude of Port Royal they hoped to attain Christian perfection, and to procure by their prayers for those they loved what their influence and example had been powerless to effect.

Port Royal was under the jurisdiction of three abbots: the Abbot of Citeaux, who was the head of the Cistercian order; the Abbot of Vaux de Sernai, who was what is called the *immediate* father, namely, that Abbot of the Cistercian order who lived nearest to Port Royal; and the Abbot of Savigny, because Vaux de Sernai was an offshoot of Savigny. The confessors of Port Royal were chosen from among the monks of Vaux de Sernai, an abbey which was between four and five miles distant. Saint Thibault, the illustrious Abbot of Vaux, and grandson of Mathilde de Garlande, was for twelve years ecclesiastical superior of the nuns, and visited them constantly. In later times a small isolated building was shown in the outer court, which was known as St. Thibault's Lodge. It was the oldest building there except the church, and it was the poorest.

St. Louis and his Queen, Marguerite of Provence, were among the benefactors of Port Royal, and before the King started for the Holy Land, in 1218, he confirmed, at Aigues-Mortes, grants which had been made to the nuns; and bestowed on them an annual stipend, which was paid as late as the seventeenth century.

Popes also increased the fame of the abbey by granting it considerable privileges. Honorius III. by a Bull dated January 3d, 1223, permitted the nuns of Port Royal to celebrate Divine worship, even although the whole of France was lying under an interdict. He forbade the Bishops to interfere with the election of an Abbess or to depose one duly elected, and he declared all excommunications against the nuns or their dependants to be null and void, and excommunicated all those who should trouble the monastery and seize its goods or retain them. A more important privilege, as we shall hereafter see, was the permission granted to the nuns to offer a retreat to persons who were disgusted with the world and wished to do penance for their sins in a monastery without binding themselves by vows. Moreover, when a nun took the veil, the Bishop who celebrated mass and administered the Holy Sacrament con-

secrated a large wafer, which he divided into eight portions.
She received one, and the other seven he placed in her right
hand and covered with a dominical, or small linen cloth, so
that she might partake of one daily for the first week after
her benediction.　In a similar manner, priests administered
the Holy Sacrament to themselves during the first four days
of their ordination.

In those early times the community of Port Royal excited
extraordinary interest, and its rapid growth and development
indicate that it supplied a need which was strongly felt.
Mortification of the flesh and harsh penance were not only
endured but sought after, and the abbey gradually acquired
a reputation which attracted to it noble ladies who endowed
it with their wealth.　But as soon as the fatal element of wealth
is allowed to find its way into a monastic community, a gradual deterioration sets in, and poverty and self-denial give way
to ease and self-indulgence.

We have no means of tracing the history of the abbey from
that first impulse which led so many to flock thither and pray
for the safety of those whom they could help in no other way
than by prayer, to the point of degradation which it had
reached at the close of the sixteenth century.　During the wars
with England in the fourteenth and fifteenth centuries, and the
so-called religious wars of the sixteenth, the discipline of abbeys
which were too far from the great towns to receive protection,
was completely destroyed.　Dom Clemencet says that in the
sixteenth century Port Royal was merely a secular institution ;
the Cistercian rule, which the nuns ought to have followed,
was unknown, and order and regularity were banished from
within its walls.

The annals of the monastery give a list, probably incomplete, of the names of abbesses, and of benefactors.　Only two
of the former are in any way remarkable, and they are aunt and
niece, both named Jehanne de la Fin.　The aunt was at the
head of the community from 1468 to 1513, and the niece from
1513 to 1558.　They did nothing for the moral or spiritual
condition of the abbey ; but the aunt recovered alienated lands
and acquired new possessions, whilst the niece repaired and
rebuilt cloisters, dormitory, church and belfry, and placed
richly carved stalls in the choir.　A document of the period
shows that she did not attempt any religious reform ; no doubt

she did not think that it was necessary. But her work seemed to her contemporaries to merit the flattering epitaph found upon her tomb, ending in a manner characteristic of that century, with a pun upon her name. The edge of this is however lost in an English translation :—

'Finis coronat opus.'
[La Fin (The End) crowns the work.]

Guilbert in his historical memoirs of Port Royal has preserved certain documents which show the condition of the abbey at the beginning and end of the sixteenth century. They are *cartes de visite* or reports made by the ecclesiastical superior, the Abbot of Citeaux, after an inspection of the abbey, and in a certain way they do give a portrait of it at that time.

Port Royal was inspected in 1504, during the life of the first Jehanne de la Fin. In his *carte de visite* the Abbot advises the nuns to recite the services slowly and carefully, pausing between the verses, so that one may be distinguished from the other. They are also told to pronounce all the words and syllables distinctly, and not to drawl out unmeaning sounds as they had done when chanting before him. They are requested to provide a clock, so that Divine Service may be performed at stated and regular hours. The condition of the dormitory is spoken of as unsatisfactory, rendering the seclusion of the nuns impossible. The Abbot expressly desires that the confessional shall in future be so arranged that the father confessor does not enter the cloistered part of the monastery. He is to be in the church, and the penitent in the oratory, with a wall of partition between them. The aperture in this wall, through which the nun speaks, is to be filled by a closely fitting trellis, covered with waxed cloth. The Abbess is forbidden to receive or lodge male visitors in the guest chamber adjoining the sleeping chamber of the nuns, and she is advised to erect a building for such visitors outside the monastic precincts. Many precautions are also suggested with regard to doors in the outer walls, which sufficiently indicate the actual abuses as well as possible dangers which had been brought under the Abbot's notice. He reprimands the nuns severely because the love of property had taken the place of the spirit of renunciation. They no longer held all things in common, but every nun had her own furniture, her own little stock of money and silver plate. They are informed that this is a great and execrable vice, and are warned never again to make use of such a wicked and *damnable* phrase as '*my* robe,' '*my* knife,' but always to say *ours*. They are also forbidden to write or receive letters or send messages without the knowledge of the Abbess, and are requested to keep away from the kitchen, and not spend so much time in it as they had been in the habit of doing.

It appears from this *carte de visite* that Abbess and nuns had adopted the wide hanging sleeves which were fashionable in the sixteenth century, and were ridiculed in the sermons of popular preachers. The Abbess is bidden to reduce these sleeves, and to have them narrowed from the elbow downwards so that they shall not be larger below than above. There is every reason to suppose that this injunction was not obeyed. Guilbert says that the second Jehanne de la Fin was represented in effigy on her tomb as wearing a cowl or very large hood which completely covered her arms, and it is supposed that this had been adopted in order to conceal the prohibited sleeves.

The second *carte de visite* contains the report of a later Abbot of Citeaux, after an inspection of Port Royal made by him in 1572, when the second Jehanne de la Fin had been succeeded by Catherine de la Vallée. The irregularities complained of at the beginning of the century had increased instead of diminishing, and the disapproval of the Abbot is very strongly expressed. The nuns are requested to perform Divine Service in a decent and becoming manner. They are to partake of the Holy Sacrament every fortnight after confessing to the father confessor of the abbey, and not to anyone else. The Abbess is commanded to lock the door of the dormitory at night, and she is very strictly forbidden to leave the monastery herself, to allow the nuns to leave it, or to admit any male person within the cloistered precincts on any pretence whatsoever. The attention bestowed on dress and the manner of arranging the hair are strongly censured, and the Abbess is requested to pay more attention to the sick nuns, who seem to have been neglected and insufficiently fed.

By this time the scandals of Port Royal must have been notorious, for the Abbot took a very unusual step and returned in sixteen months. He found that his previous admonitions and injunctions had been unheeded, and thereupon issued a supplementary *carte de visite*, in which special reference is made to the presence of a man named Blouin, whom the Abbess on various pretexts insisted upon keeping in the abbey. She is now threatened with excommunication if she does not obey the commands of her ecclesiastical superior, which are sharp and strict. She does not appear to have submitted, but shortly afterwards she left Port Royal and retired to another monastery.

In 1575 she was succeeded by Jeanne de Boulehart, who did not attempt reform, but neither did she give occasion for scandal. Her epitaph states that she never left the monastery, that she took good care of her nuns, and fed them well. We shall find sufficient reasons for supposing that, even on these points, she deserves a moderate amount of praise, whilst the very nature of it shows that the spiritual functions of an abbess were at that time forgotten or ignored, and that she fulfilled her whole duty if she maintained an orderly and well-regulated household.

Jeanne de Boulehart died in 1602, and was succeeded by Angélique Arnauld, a child of eleven years old. The decadence of religious houses was at that time an established fact, and one that had even ceased to excite surprise. The Roman Catholic Church had never before occupied so low a position in France. Calvin and the Reformers seem not so much to have purified as to have exhausted it, drawing off all that was earnest and devout, and leaving a residuum of immorality and irreligion. Faith and good works were hardly to be found in the Church, and there seemed little possibility of leading a holy life in the monasteries. The scandal of the monks' lives had become almost too great to be endured, and that of the nuns, if more carefully concealed, was none the less a terrible reality. They arranged the hours for religious services so as not to interfere with the night's rest or the day's pleasure; they modified and adjusted their dress so as to make it becoming and as far as possible fashionable; they paid visits to their friends, received their lovers at home, and educated their illegitimate children in the convent schools.

But the profligacy of priests, monks, and nuns was only a faint reflex of a far deeper and more wide-spread national profligacy; whilst the national character had been degraded by civil wars in which religion was a party cry and a watchword.

It is true that in the sixteenth century St. Theresa in Spain and St. Charles Borromeo in Italy had done good work, but it was partial and limited, and perhaps its most striking result had been to show the necessity for the general reform of the Roman Catholic Church.

Ignatius Loyola, in the same century, desired to lead the whole world into the Church, but his followers, the Jesuits, had failed in the attempt, and were now trying to take the Church into the world. Their efforts in that direction were more successful, and they made religion easy and popular by dragging it down to the lowest level of immorality, dishonesty, and vice.

At this time, to which we cannot look back without a feeling akin to despair, the degeneracy of monks and nuns was suddenly arrested. There was a movement in favour of reform which attracted to itself so much that was good, true, and noble, that at one time it seemed possible to hope for the regeneration of the Catholic Church as well as of the monasteries. And this attempted reform, which was only crushed out and trodden under foot after a century of heroic struggle, was inaugurated by Angélique Arnauld, shows its brightest lustre in her life, and is associated with the name of the Monastery of Port Royal.

CHAPTER I.

NEARLY three hundred years ago, two little French children stood by their grandfather's side and listened to his plans and wishes for their future life. They were only five and seven years old, and yet he was gravely telling them that they would have to enter a convent, whilst their eldest sister would marry and go into society. Angélique Arnauld, the older of the two, was a high-spirited child, ardent and eager, and her grandfather saw that the prospect of being a nun did not please her, so he explained, 'I shall make you an abbess, the *mistress of all the others*.' She was somewhat consoled by this promise and said:

'Grandpapa, if you wish me to be a nun I will be a nun; but not unless you make me an abbess.'

'And I,' said Agnes, the child of five, 'I will be a nun, too, Grandpapa, but I don't want to be an abbess.'

And then they left their grandfather, and Angélique ran off alone into a long gallery, crying with anger and vexation, and saying to herself: 'Oh, how unlucky I am to be the second daughter, for if I had been the eldest I should have been the one to be married!'

A few days later the children again visited their grandfather in his study. Agnes spoke first:

'Grandpapa, I have quite made up my mind not to be an abbess, for they say that an abbess has to answer to God for the souls of her nuns, and I am sure that I shall have quite enough to do to save my own.'

'But,' said Angélique, eagerly, 'I want to be an abbess,

and I shall take good care that my nuns do their duty and behave well.'

This conversation has been preserved in the voluminous memoirs of the Arnauld family, and the discussion was not so premature as it now appears to us, for Angélique entered upon her noviciate a few months later, and became Abbess of Port Royal at eleven years old ; whilst little Agnes, in spite of her protest, was Abbess of St. Cyr at six.

These little girls were the daughters of M. Arnauld, *Pro-* *cureur-Général* to Catherine de Medicis, and of Catherine Arnauld, his wife, who was the only daughter of M. Marion, the French *Avocat-Général*. Angélique was born in 1591, and Agnes in 1593 ; and at the time of which we speak they had a sister and a brother older than themselves, and two brothers and two sisters younger.

Even at the close of the sixteenth century the Church of Rome would not have openly sanctioned such a breach of ecclesiastical discipline as the appointment of a child to the important post of abbess. But Mdme. Arnauld's father did not find the difficulties in his way insuperable. He was in high favour with the King of France, and had great influence at court. He wished to provide, during his own lifetime, for some of his daughter's numerous children ; and when he had obtained the presentations, he procured the requisite bulls from Rome for the appointment of the little abbesses by means of false certificates of age. We shall see that this matter gave him some trouble, and that the bulls had to be renewed from time to time ; but there is no reason to suppose that it was looked upon in any other light than as a pious fraud, at which the King of France and the court of France were very much amused, and the court of Rome not greatly shocked.

Mdme. Arnauld, the mother of the two little girls, was born in 1572, and at twelve years old she was betrothed to M. Arnauld, a young advocate whose ability and eloquence had made such an impression upon her father, M. Marion, that one day, after hearing him speak, he took him home to dinner, and, before long, promised him his only daughter in marriage.

M. Arnauld belonged to the old *noblesse* of Provence, and the family from which he was descended receives honourable mention in the annals of the twelfth and thirteenth centuries.

His branch of it had settled in Auvergne, and, in 1340, one of his ancestors, Gracieux Arnauld, fought bravely in the army of Philip of Valois. Another, Michael Arnauld, lived to the age of one hundred and four; and had a soldier son, Henri, whose courage was only equalled by his loyal devotion to the Connétable de Bourbon.

Antoine Arnauld, Seigneur de la Mothe, or, as he was called, M. de la Mothe, was the paternal grandfather of Angélique and Agnes. He was a soldier as well as a lawyer. In time of peace he was *Procureur-Général* to Catherine de Medicis, and in time of war he commanded a company of light horse. In the former capacity he opposed, on behalf of the Queen-mother, the claims of one of the French nobles to lands said to have been granted by the king. He gained his suit, and the king's gift was not confirmed. As he was about to leave the court of justice the claimant asked him if he was M. de la Mothe, and said that he was surprised he had ventured to oppose him, and would take good care to make him repent the course he had adopted.

'I think you mistake the person whom you are addressing,' answered Arnauld.

'How so? Did you not tell me that you were M. de la Mothe?'

'Yes; but I wear a soldier's coat as well as a lawyer's robe, and you dare not speak to me outside the court as you have done here.'

By this time a gentleman in attendance had recognized Arnauld de la Mothe, and reminded the angry nobleman that he was the same whom they had so often remarked at the head of his company during the civil wars. Whereupon followed apologies, explanation, and reconciliation. The story is characteristic of the Arnaulds and also of the French nobles of the sixteenth century. It shows the steadfast courage of the one, and the contempt of the other, not only for those who were not soldiers or nobles, but for right and justice also.

Arnauld de la Mothe was a Huguenot, though how or when he became one we do not know. His descendants acknowledge the fact, but do not enlarge upon it. 'He was led away into the error of Calvinism,' say the family annals, 'but after a time God opened his eyes, though this cannot be said with regard to several members of his family.'

As a matter of fact his eyes were opened by the massacre of St. Bartholomew, when, whatever he may have thought of the truth of his religion, he certainly found that it was unsafe. However, his courage and ability made him so valuable to the Queen-mother, that she saved his life on that terrible night. His house was surrounded and attacked, and at the head of his servants he attempted to defend himself and his children. Defeat and death were before him, when a safe-conduct arrived from the Queen, and the whole family was spared. Immediately after the massacre, Arnauld de la Mothe and several —but not all—of his children 'abjured the errors of Calvinism,' so say the annals, and returned to the Church of Rome. The fact is stated without comment or explanation, and at the present time it is in vain to seek them.

His youngest son, Pierre, was a soldier. He was present at the siege of Rochelle, and had to defend an unfinished fortress. He completed it almost entirely at his own expense and in such an admirable manner that he was afterwards known as Arnauld *du Fort.* His soldiers did not approve of being employed as bricklayers, carpenters, and masons, and took no pains to conceal their discontent. Pierre Arnauld was well aware of it, but he was silent and bided his time. One day a good-natured civilian, the body servant of an officer in the garrison, joined the working party, and had a hod on his shoulder when M. Arnauld passed by. He stopped and asked who this strange man might be, and on hearing that he was a servant struck him with his cane, saying: 'Do you mean to tell me that you are nothing but a valet, and yet you presume to undertake the work not only of a soldier, but of a prince, for no prince would be ashamed of a soldier's work!'

This story was repeated throughout the fortress, and so kindled the enthusiasm of the garrison that there was no more grumbling at hard tasks, and the building went on apace. All the Arnaulds had this fervent zeal, and whether their mission was to build a fortress or reform a monastery they devoted themselves entirely to the work, thought it the noblest in the world, and had the power of calling out the same enthusiasm of devotion in others.

Pierre Arnauld *du Fort* was Agnes and Angélique's uncle. Their father, Antoine Arnauld, was born in 1560, and was twelve years old at the date of the massacre in 1572. He

was one of those who 'abjured his errors,' and so apparently
did his younger brothers. But there were ' Protestant aunts '
of whom we shall hear afterwards, and who must have been
very young, if not unborn, at this time. The Arnaulds were
always suspected, and often accused of a leaning towards Protestantism, and doubtless there was some influence in M. de
la Mothe's family favourable to it. We must bear this in mind,
since it modified the conduct of his children and grandchildren ;
but it seems impossible now to trace it to its source.

Antoine was remarkable as a boy for his ability and industry, and his progress was so rapid that at seventeen he
began the study of law. He was sent to Bourges, where he
was a pupil of the learned Cujas, whose esteem and affection
for him led to the formation of a lasting friendship. At Bourges
he studied fifteen or sixteen hours a day, and for fear of not
waking early, hired a man to call him every morning at three
o'clock.

On his return to Paris when he was nineteen, it was arranged
that he should travel in Italy with friends carefully chosen by
his father. He had two hundred crowns for a six months' tour,
and was as diligent about his pleasure as he had been in his
work. He never wasted an hour, saw all that was remarkable,
and kept notes of all that he saw, so that he was said to know
Italy better than most Italians. He managed his money so
well that, although he was liberal on the journey, and brought
home a number of curiosities, he had cash to spare at the end
of his tour, which, as his biographer justly remarks, was a very
extraordinary thing for a man of his age.

He was successful at the bar, as in most other things that
he undertook, and the favourable impression produced on
M. Marion won him his wife.

His father had often urged him to marry, but he was not
attracted by any of the wealthy brides suggested to him, and
said he would marry no one but the daughter of the *Avocat-
Général.* He had not seen her, but a friend of his father's
offered to propose him to Mdme. Marion as a suitor for her
daughter. When the matter was broached, that lady, however,
put an end to the conversation by saying that her daughter was
only eleven years old, too young to marry ; and probably
Arnauld's name was not even mentioned at this time. A year
later Arnauld, a young man of good family, already popular,

and sure to make his way in the world, attracted the notice of the *Avocat-Général* and seems to have lost no time in urging his own suit, for when he was twenty-four and Mademoiselle Marion twelve years old they were betrothed, and in the following year, 1585, they were married. During the interval between the betrothal and the marriage, M. Arnauld's father died suddenly, leaving one son by his first marriage, and seven sons, of whom the young advocate was the eldest, and four daughters by his second wife. He left also an unfinished lawsuit, involving no less a sum than 100,000 francs, his whole fortune, and at that time a very large one. M. Arnauld did all in his power to comfort and console his mother, and he worked day and night until he had brought the lawsuit to a successful termination.

Friends suggested to M. Marion that as the burden of so large a family had fallen upon M. Arnauld, the marriage had better be broken off; but he answered, that he was glad of the opportunity of showing his future son-in-law that he esteemed him for his own merits; and that this esteem was not diminished but increased by his present position, so that he should give him his daughter's hand with even more pleasure and confidence than if Arnauld de la Mothe had been alive.

And so they were married; and in 1587, when Mdme. Arnauld was fifteen, her first child was born, and in 1612, when she was thirty-nine, she gave birth to her twentieth and last, Antoine, known as the *Great* Arnauld. Ten of these children died young, but four sons and six daughters lived to make the name of their family illustrious, and to immortalize it by their earnest faith, great courage, and undying constancy.

French marriages in the sixteenth century were not unlike those of the nineteenth, and were based upon other motives than the love of the contracting parties; but in this case there was esteem on both sides which ripened into affection, and the virtue and discretion of the young wife ensured her husband's respect. From the first he did not treat her as if she had been a child; whilst her behaviour towards him, his mother, and the numerous brothers and sisters, was that of 'a person of five and twenty.' Her biographers say that even in her earliest youth, which one is rather puzzled to look back for, she had never had any trace of levity or affectation. At eighteen she discarded all superfluous ornament, and from that time wore none but simple and plain dresses. Her household was a model of purity and sobriety, and in the forty years during which she was its head no scandal ever attached to any member of it.   She was especially strict with the women, and as a matron of thirteen years old she boxed the ears of a maid of twenty, who had allowed a man to kiss her.

Mdme. Arnauld was a woman of large heart, and her love and charity extended far and wide round the sacred centre of home.   Her husband and children were the first objects of her solicitude; after them came her household, then the poor of her husband's estate of Andilly, in which none needed to beg their bread, all who could work were well paid, and the old and sick were provided for; next followed the poor of the neighbouring village of St. Merri, and lastly the indigent and sick wherever she found and could help them.   Her husband approved of her good works, and was always ready to promote them by helping the poor with loans or gifts of money on unfinished work, and by forbearance and consideration in all his transactions.

'My wife does not make a brave show,' he used to say, 'but I would much rather she gave her money to the poor than spent it on gewgaws.'

After her marriage Mdme. Arnauld passed her spare time with her invalid mother, taking no interest in the pleasures to which her age and position would have entitled her.   Her own health was not good, and even if it had been we can well believe that the mother of twenty children had not much opportunity or inclination for the pleasures of society.   When she was twenty-five she had eight children living, four sons and four daughters; and it was this which caused her father to decide that Angélique and Agnes, the third and fourth, must take the veil, so as to weed out the family, and leave the way clear for the marriage of Catherine, the eldest girl.   Mdme. Arnauld regretted this decision, on the ground that young children could not have a vocation for the convent; but she did not venture to oppose her father's wish, more especially as her husband, though with some repugnance, had also consented to part with his children.

M. Arnauld succeeded his father as *Procureur-Général* to

Catherine de Medicis, a post which he held until the Queen's death in 1589. After that he devoted himself entirely to the bar, at which he achieved great success. Princes, princesses, and nobles came to him for advice, and in return offered him patronage and promotion. He might have succeeded his father-in-law, the *Avocat-Général*, or even have held the great seals of the kingdom and become Chancellor of France, but he was faithful to his first choice, and would seek no greater honour than that which his profession offered ; perhaps it would be more correct to say that he believed no greater honour was to be found.

He was looked upon as one of the most eloquent speakers of his time, a very Demosthenes of France. The eloquence of that age is not appreciated, one might almost say not appreciable in our own ; and the speeches by which M. Arnauld obtained his reputation are very dreary reading. They are pompous and pedantic, with an occasional outburst of violence and objurgation, 'sound and fury, signifying nothing,' as we are apt to think ; but we must not forget that in the sixteenth century classical allusions had a freshness and interest which they have now lost. At that time when a learned member of the bar conducted the prosecution of a man accused of theft, he would cite the siege of Troy and quote the oracle of Apollo, appeal to Telephus the son of Hercules, allude to the wounds of Achilles, and compare his own words to the unheeded shrieks of Cassandra. And the judges who listened to him 'vibrated with emotion,' and 'could not restrain their murmurs of admiration and astonishment.'

M. Arnauld took part in one trial, which must not be overlooked. Pierre Barrière made an attempt on the life of Henri IV. in 1593, and M. Arnauld, on behalf of the University of Paris, asked the *Parlement*[1] to expel the Jesuits from France on the ground that they had instigated the crime. Witty French writers have called this the 'original sin' of the Arnaulds, and we shall see that it was remembered against them by the Jesuits and avenged in the next generation. The Jesuits possessed sufficient interest to ensure the case being heard with closed doors, but there were crowds outside trying

---

[1] The French *Parlement* at this time was not a representative assembly but a court of justice, attended on important occasions by the royal princes, and the dukes and peers of the realm.

in vain to listen, and waiting eagerly for the report of those who had been fortunate enough to secure admission. M. Arnauld does not appear to have begun nearer home than Pharsalia; he discoursed largely of Catiline, of the Arsacidæ, of Satan in hell, and of Henri III. in heaven, but he was intelligible to everyone when he accused the Jesuits of being the authors of every assassination in Europe, either attempted or executed, during the previous forty years. Many of his contemporaries, and even those who shared his views, thought that the violence of his attack helped to defeat its aim; and indeed it was not until some months later, and after the attempt of Jean Chatel to assassinate the king, that the Jesuits were expelled from France. But it is certain that they always attributed their banishment to Arnauld's influence, and that the University of Paris considered him as its triumphant champion, and offered him a large sum of money, which he declined to accept. An extraordinary meeting of the members of the University was then convened, and a vote of thanks passed unanimously, expressing their gratitude and obligation towards M. Arnauld. Nine years later, in 1602, we find him addressing 'a frank and truthful discourse' to the king, in which he urges that the Jesuits shall not be permitted to return to France.

On the whole it seems that his early Protestant training and the massacre of St. Bartholomew were not without effect on him, although he was too much a man of the world to allow his feelings to lead him in one direction if his interests appeared to indicate another. Here, however, they coincided, and when he urged the expulsion of the Jesuits he advocated the popular cause.

Wealthy, prosperous, and popular he seems to have been throughout his whole life; he had influence at court, and royal as well as noble patrons, so that he had no fear that the little children who came year after year would lack suitable provision. He was a good husband and an affectionate father, and his wife was a pure, noble, unselfish woman. We can judge of their home by the love which the children felt for it, and the influence which home life exercised over them.

The Arnaulds passed the summer and autumn in the country at Andilly. In the winter they lived in Paris, where their house adjoined that of Mdme. Arnauld's father. There was a door

of communication between the gardens, and the children used
to run to and fro between the two houses. Angélique says
that she was no favourite with her mother, and was sent daily
to her grandfather in order to be out of the way. To avenge
herself on the sisters and brothers who were, as she imagined,
preferred by her mother, she always locked the garden door
after her; she was resolved that they should have no share in
her grandfather's affection, and if they got in she would drive
them away, saying : 'Go home about your business, this is my
house, and not yours.' She spent the day in her grandfather's
bed-room and study, and followed him wherever he went, holding by one of the long loose sleeves of his dressing gown. It
was the knowledge of her character which he acquired at this
time which made him say, ' You shall be an abbess, *the mistress
of all the others.*'

There seems to be nothing to justify us in assuming that
her mother disliked her; but she was a high-spirited child,
ardent and eager, not easily ruled, and she must needs be first,
so that the mother would find it a relief to send her to the
shrewd kindly grandfather, whom she interested and amused.
In later years she often lamented the death of a brother of three
years old, a child of remarkable beauty and intelligence.
' His affection was a great support to me at that time,' she
says quite gravely. Another of her childish reminiscences
relates to her first confession at seven years old. When she
had recounted her faults she was told by the father confessor
to go and ask God's pardon for them. She understood him
literally, and having heard that God is in heaven she went out
to the court-yard of the house, knelt down in the midst of it,
and with clasped hands, looking up to the sky, she asked God's
pardon so earnestly, and with such reverence, that in after-
times she regarded this as her first intelligent action. Not
long after, she went to Vespers on Whitsunday. During the
service she was giddy and inattentive, and on her return a certain Mdme. Pichotel, who had charge of her, whipped her,
saying : ' I intend to call your attention to your fault, and to
make you remember all your life that you were whipped on
Whitsunday for inattention and irreverence in church.' Fifty
years afterwards she told the story, and said that she had never
once forgotten the whipping when the day came round.

When it was decided that Angélique and Agnes should enter

a convent their grandfather determined to provide handsomely
for them.   He had no difficulty in finding friends to further
his views.   The Abbot of Citeaux was glad to oblige the
Avocat-Général, and in 1599 persuaded Jeanne de Boulchart,
Abbess of Port Royal, who was elderly and infirm, to accept
Angélique Arnauld as coadjutrix.   The Abbess had two nieces
who were nuns, but she had refused to nominate either of
them.   It is related as a prophecy that after she had consented to make Angélique her successor, for the coadjutrix
succeeded the Abbess in her charge, she said that the nuns
did not know what a good thing she had been arranging
for them.   It is not necessary, however, to fall back upon
prophetic insight as having dictated this speech.   The Abbess
was an invalid, but she did not know and others did not think
that she was dying.   She preferred, however, the prospect of the
ultimate succession of a young child, to that of a niece who
was, to say the least, quite ready to step into her shoes at any
moment; and she justified her choice, which was open to criticism, by an allusion to prospective benefits which no one was
in a position to disprove.

In the same year, Agnes became Abbess of St. Cyr, and
took the veil before she was seven.   It was arranged, however,
that one of the nuns of St. Cyr—Dame des Portes—should
take the title and perform the duties of abbess until the child
was twenty.   No similar provision was made in the case of
Angélique, because, although the Abbess of Port Royal was in
ill-health, she was expected to live for many years.

The two abbeys were, no doubt, selected by M. Marion in
order that he might keep his grandchildren within easy reach
of home, their parents, and each other.   Port Royal was at no
great distance from Versailles, and St. Cyr about six miles from
Port Royal.

Angélique entered upon her noviciate before she was eight
years old.   The ceremony took place in the church of St.
Antoine at Paris, the Abbot of Citeaux presiding; it was very
brilliant, and the child's vanity was fully gratified when she
found that the gay party was in her honour.   The friends and
the child novice returned to her father's house where there were
festivities and rejoicings.   The step taken was not considered
at all a solemn one for girls with such prospects as the Arnaulds,
and relations and friends thought that the children were now

sure of making the best of both worlds. Angélique remained for a few days with her parents, and then, after six weeks spent in the convent of St. Antoine, she joined Agnes, who was already at St. Cyr, and they passed eight months together. It was a happy time for both, and we find frequent references to it in their memoirs. Agnes did not resemble Angélique. She was delicate and sensitive, and shrank instinctively from any prominent position, she did not wish to be an abbess just because it would make her mistress. As a woman she mourned over the faults of her childhood with the keen sorrow which St. Augustine shows in his confessions; and she attached what we are inclined to think an exaggerated importance to them. Angélique was ardent, strong, and practical. Agnes was a spiritualist and mystic even from childhood. Angélique asserted, and easily maintained, her ascendancy over Agnes; sometimes, however, Agnes would remind her that St. Cyr was her abbey, Angélique had no business in it, and she could send her away if she liked. But repentance for these outbursts came quickly, and lasted long, and Agnes never recalled her petulant speeches without keen sorrow. She was a studious and pious child, delighting in religious ceremonies and divine service, and before she was nine, she knew the whole Psalter and all the chants by heart. No doubt it had been the intention of their parents that Angélique and Agnes should not be separated during childhood; but the abbeys belonged to different orders, Port Royal to the Cistercian, and St. Cyr to the Benedictine, and it was found necessary to educate Angélique in a Cistercian abbey. As there were no companions of her own age at Port Royal, she completed her noviciate in the neighbouring Cistercian abbey of Maubuisson, of which Mdme. Angélique d'Estrées, sister of the celebrated Gabrielle, was at that time abbess. Here she was confirmed and took the veil, and with it the name of Angélique,[1] chosen in compliment to her abbess. As the requisite papal bulls had been refused to so young a novice, those which appointed her coadjutrix of Port Royal were asked for under a new name. When she took the veil there was a brilliant assembly at Maubuisson,

---

[1] Her name was Jacqueline Marie and her sister Jeanne Catherine, but as they entered the convent and took new names at such an early age, it has been deemed unnecessary to retain the Jacqueline and Jeanne of their infancy.

and Angélique, radiant with delight, overheard the compassionate whispers of those around her :—

'Poor child, she little knows what she is doing!'

'It made me so angry,' she exclaims in telling the story, 'for I said to myself, "they must think me quite silly, if they suppose I don't know what I am doing; indeed, I know perfectly well!"'

She stayed more than two years at Maubuisson. When she was ten years old, Jeanne de Boulehart died suddenly, and the coadjutrix became Child-abbess of Port Royal.

Fresh intrigue and deception were necessary before she could be installed, for by the decree of the Council of Trent an abbess must be forty years old. The bulls that were requisite were on this occasion asked for a young lady of seventeen. Even this was an exceptional demand, and they were not granted and the abbess installed until after long and tedious negotiation.

As soon as her parents heard that the life of Jeanne de Boulehart was in danger, Angélique had been despatched to Port Royal, so that she might be on the spot to assert her rights. When everything was arranged for her succession, she went back to take formal leave of the nuns of Maubuisson, whom she had left so hastily. They were very fond of her, and parted from her with great regret. They did not foresee a day on which she would return once again, take the place of their scandalous abbess, and purify and reform the convent.

CHAPTER II.

ANGÉLIQUE was installed Abbess of Port Royal in 1602, before she was eleven years old. She had previously spent eight months at St. Cyr with her sister Agnes, and nearly two years and a half at Maubuisson, so that she had passed direct from the nursery to the convent.

It would be natural to suppose that as she was dedicated to the service of the Church her parents had endeavoured to prepare her for a life of self-denial and religious observance, but she cannot have even heard them spoken of at Maubuisson. The Abbess, Angélique d'Estrées, was a woman of most licentious life. Her sister, the notorious Gabrielle d'Estrées, resided with her, and the nuns of Maubuisson had no more respect for morality or religion than their Abbess.

Angélique was too young and of a nature too pure to receive any taint from the influences around her. But the bright, clever child, who was everybody's pet and plaything, could not fail to perceive that her vocation offered many opportunities for self-indulgence and pleasure. The King of France, Henri IV., was a frequent visitor at Maubuisson. Convent life was enlivened by music and dancing, and long moonlight walks with gay cavaliers, and there was no sense of wrongdoing to overshadow its pleasure. If the parents wished to make a nun's life attractive to their child, and this is the only motive which we can attribute to them, they succeeded. But at this point Mdme. Arnauld paused. She had no desire to see the immorality of Maubuisson repeated at Port Royal. Angélique, from whose memoirs we derive the accounts of these early times, tells us that her mother loved the world, but she also feared God. She had not learnt to love Him, but the fear of God made her very anxious that her children should not fall into sin. In addition to this it seems probable from what we know of Mdme. Arnauld's life and character, which were free from shadow of suspicion or blame, that she was not aware of the profligacy of Maubuisson when she placed Angélique there, and that her subsequent precautions arose from abhorrence of the evils which she could not fail to discover. M. Arnauld was a kind and affectionate father, but a man of the world. He accepted society, morality, and religion as he found them, and was not prepared to attempt any modifications. He could not give adequate dowries to all his daughters; therefore, though he regretted it deeply, some of them must enter a convent. It was a hard necessity, and he would have preferred to see children and grandchildren around him; still he could keep the little nuns near home, obtain comfortable establishments for them, watch over their interest, and secure their welfare. Mdme. Arnauld accompanied Angélique to Port Royal, to look after the temporal affairs of the Abbey, superintend the repairs which it required, and regulate the household of which her child was to be the head. There were twelve nuns in the abbey, three of whom were insane. In later times, when Angélique knew more about the condition of religious houses than any other woman in France, she speaks of it as quite an exceptional circumstance that only the eldest of these nuns, who was thirty-three, had been guilty of gross immorality, though all had been exposed to great temptation. The time had gone by when such sins were punished, but Mdme. Arnauld insisted on having the offender removed to another monastery. She also obtained permission to place Port Royal and its young Abbess under the supervision of Mdme. de Jumeauville, a discreet and trustworthy member of the community of St. Cyr, who had previously acted as Angélique's governess. When all necessary arrangements were made to secure order and comfort, Mdme. Arnauld returned to Paris. She was well aware of the necessity for constant vigilance, and used to visit Port Royal frequently, at unexpected times, in order to ascertain that all was going on well.

In spite of the laudatory epitaph on Mdme. de Boulehart,

her nuns had been poorly fed and badly lodged. They appreciated therefore the care of M. and Mdme. Arnauld for their comfort, and forgave the restriction of their liberty in consideration · of the kindness by which it was accompanied. The parents gained the hearts of the nuns by their liberality, whilst Angélique's nature and disposition attracted them, and she not only easily won, but was able to keep their love. We hear of her at this time buying candles in secret for the maid who waited on her, because Mdme. de Jumeauville, from economy, would not allow her to have them; she gave her own white bread to this girl who did not like brown, and in all things found her pleasure in pleasing others. A story is told of her at twelve years old which recalls the anecdote of Mdme. Arnauld boxing the ears of her maid. It was the custom at Port Royal for the sacristans to go into the sacristy, a room behind the altar, after mass was over, and fold and put away the linen which had been used. Angélique was informed that a monk who lived in the house was in the habit of meeting the nuns there and gossiping with them, and that he was at that time in the sacristy. She went thither immediately, turned the key, and locked them all in. After a time she opened the door and allowing her prisoners to pass out, reprimanded them in such a grave and earnest manner that they said she spoke like an Abbess, not a child.

Another anecdote has its place here.

In 1602 Henri IV. was hunting in the neighbourhood of Port Royal, and as he knew that M. Arnauld was on a visit to his daughter, he alighted, and entered the abbey. He was received by the child-abbess at the head of her nuns, bearing in her hands the crozier which bespoke her dignity, and mounted on such high pattens that the king remarked she was very tall for her age, and he had been told she was very short. He left with a promise to come again which he did not fulfil; but on the morrow as he rode through the high grounds overlooking the abbey he called out merrily, 'The king kisses the hands of the Reverend Mother!'

There was a carriage at Port Royal which had belonged to Jeanne de Boulehart, and from time to time Angélique sent it to St. Cyr, to fetch Agnes and their younger sister Anne, who had been placed in the convent school as a companion for her. The Abbesses were very happy together, and little

Anne was a favourite with both of them. When it was time to recite one of the services of the Church, Agnes would leave her sisters and go through it in a grave and earnest manner. She was greatly troubled to find that Angélique neglected her religious duties, and one day she ventured to say very gently that this made her unhappy, and she thought Angélique was not doing right. The elder child begged her not to give herself any trouble, for as she was not a nun but an Abbess, she had nothing to do with such things. But whatever Angélique may have thought of her duty to God, she did not neglect her duty to her neighbour. In the midst of the merriest games she would pause and say, ' I must go and say good-night to Dame Prieure (the Prioress), I shall be back directly.'

The General of the Order inspected the abbey in 1605, when Angélique was fourteen. He states in the *carte de visite* that all the rules are observed, and the only suggestion he makes is that the number of nuns shall be increased from twelve to sixteen. Angélique in after time used to point out how little there was to deserve his commendation, since they were merely a well-ordered secular community, reciting the services at due hours, with the exception of *matins*, which were said at four o'clock in the morning, so as not to disturb the nuns too early.

In this same year, 1605, M. Arnauld's eldest daughter, Catherine, was married to M. le Maître. She was only fifteen, one year older than Angélique, and her marriage which at once took her into society and the world from which Angélique was debarred, would naturally call the attention of the young Abbess to the very different position which she occupied.

Years passed on, and Angélique spent her time in occupations and amusements suited to her age. Childish sports gave way to social pleasures ; she was permitted and even commanded to walk with the nuns in the abbey grounds, and enjoyed these long rambles with her friends and companions. On wet days she read Roman history and novels, and every summer her parents came to Port Royal, bringing with them some of the little brothers and sisters ; and her grave young sister the Abbess Agnes visited her and talked of St. Theresa, of fasts, and visions, and religious austerities. But her happy childhood, her innocent enjoyment, her unconsciousness of the contradiction between her actual life and the ideal of her vocation were drawing to a close; with dawning womanhood she began to see that a yoke was fastened upon her, and she hated it. For a time she attempted to conceal her feelings; but some part of the truth must have been discovered, for she tells us it was suggested to her that she might renounce her calling if she chose, since it was impossible she could be bound by vows which she had taken before she could understand their meaning. To this suggestion coming we know not whence unless from Protestant relatives, she replied that nothing could release her from her obligation to God, and that he had done her a great honour in accepting her for His service. She tells us that she does not know how she acquired a notion of the sanctity of her vocation, for she had never heard anyone speak of it, nor how she learnt that the daily routine through which she passed was not a fulfilment of her duties. And yet she began to think that perhaps some day there ought to be a change, and that possibly it might be necessary for her to repent and lead a new life; but she tried to put away these reflections, and to still the aching of her heart, and silence the voice of conscience. She distrusted her present life with its ease and pleasure, but she shrank still more from that future in which she discerned duties that she did not dare to recognize and did not wish to fulfil.

She endeavoured to divert her mind by the amusements in which other abbesses indulged. Accompanied by two or three of the nuns, she paid visits to her neighbours, and even went so far as to receive friends at home. Mdme. Arnauld was immediately informed of this by Mdme. de Jumeauville, and she knew that it was the first step in a wrong direction. She hastened in great distress to Port Royal, and Angélique was deeply moved by her mother's earnest entreaties and tears. She saw that two paths were open to her; one, so far as she could see, was pleasant and bright enough, but her parents disliked it, and would be deeply grieved if she persisted in following it. The other, of which they approved, seemed to her dreary and lifeless. But she had that instinctive preference for self-denial over self-indulgence which is characteristic of a noble nature. Her mother was urging her to give up her own pleasures, not because they could not be reconciled with her duties, but from far lower motives; and Angélique yielded; asked pardon for the anxiety she had caused, promised amendment, and resolved to follow the course which her parents approved.

Her mother went back to Paris, and the Abbess turned, in her sorrow, to *Plutarch's Lives*, and tried, by a course of hard, steady reading, to stifle all longings for life and interest outside the walls of Port Royal.

In vain! The old craving came back again stronger than ever. She was now sixteen years old, handsome and clever, with boundless energy, aspiration, ambition, ability. The world would have appreciated her, and she would not have been contented with a mere life of pleasure and self-indulgence, but would have found work to do for others in whatever station she had been placed.

She considered herself bound by the promise to her mother, and resolved not to seek consolation, as other nuns did, in the disregard of her vows; she would be faithful and resign herself to the prison in which she was not to end life, but to begin it.

And then came a new form of temptation. There were Huguenot aunts at Rochelle, sisters of M. Arnauld, who had escaped conversion after the massacre of St. Bartholomew: should she run away from the convent and join them? She was at that time in correspondence with her aunts, for she says that they begged her to read the Epistle to the Romans, in which she would find a condemnation of the Roman Catholic faith. She read it, and found 'quite the reverse;' but then she had no misgivings as to the truth of her religion, and was not tormented by any spiritual doubt or distrust. She was pining for the free life of the outer world, from which she found that she was shut out for ever; and when the temptation came to escape from Port Royal and go to her aunts at Rochelle, it was not strengthened by any scepticism as to the doctrines of her Church. Very probably the earlier suggestion that she could not be bound by vows imposed upon her in infancy came from these aunts, and her certainty that they would befriend her, shows that, although they may not have interposed on her behalf, she had no doubt as to the course they were likely to adopt. Angélique knew that they would not give her up if she could but reach them, and that she would then be free, could marry, and the world, with all its interests, occupations, and enjoyments, would be open to her. We hear the echo of the child's cry: 'Oh, how unlucky I am to be the second daughter, for if I had been the eldest, I should have been the one to be married.'

For two months the struggle lasted, and then in the summer of 1607 the poor girl fell ill of fever. Her parents, who cannot have been ignorant of the cause of her illness, were greatly alarmed. M. Arnauld could not bear to think of his sick child so far from home and friends, and sent a litter to Port Royal in which she was conveyed to Paris. A bed was placed for her in Mdme. Arnauld's room, and Angélique says that if she asked for anything, her mother was always the first by her side, although the nurse sat close to the bed. When she was somewhat better, numerous friends and relatives visited her in her sick room. She says: 'I had no thought of God in my illness, and there was no one who spoke a single word to me about Him. But all the news of Paris and the court were discussed at my bedside, for I had usually a great many visitors.'

It seems that the fine dresses, the velvets and satins of her mother's friends, and the pleasant talk of her uncles, among whom we must not forget Arnauld *du Fort*, were not without effect upon her; as soon as she began to recover, she had a 'whalebone corset' made secretly, in order to improve her figure.

Mdme. Arnauld wished to rouse her daughter from the extreme depression and listlessness which had preceded her fever, and to give her what she doubtless considered an innocent interest in society. But she was alarmed at Angélique's extreme vivacity, and the eager interest which she displayed in all that concerned the life from which she was excluded. She was afraid that a love-affair was the cause of her illness and dislike of her vocation. It was not at all improbable, for among the visitors to Port Royal who had excited Mdme. Arnauld's apprehensions, there were gentlemen from Paris and the neighbourhood of the abbey. Moreover, the monks from the neighbouring monasteries used to amuse the young Abbess and her nuns with foolish talk, and many stories of what they called 'the good old customs' of their order.

M. Arnauld had more confidence in his daughter than her mother had, or he may have wished to soften an impending blow; one day, sitting by her bedside, he told her that she was so young, open-hearted, and free that her mother was rather alarmed about her, and had gone to Port Royal to search her papers for love-letters. Angélique laughed, and said: 'Then she will have her journey for nothing.' She adds that as a girl her fear of death and of God preserved her from great sins, and that she had an instinctive reverence for honour and purity which was strengthened by the example of all her family. She never was tempted through her affections; and although she wished for a married life it was not for the sake of any particular partner with whom she desired to share it, but because of all that belonged to marriage—dress, society, and above all, liberty.

M. Arnauld's fears pointed in another direction. He was afraid lest his daughter should abandon her vocation, and throw away the position and dignity he had taken so much pains to procure. One day he took a badly written paper to her bedside, and said carelessly and as if it was a matter of no consequence :

'My child, just sign this paper.'

She took the pen and did as she was told.

'Obedience and respect' forbade her to ask any questions, but, as she was writing her name, she caught sight of a few words, and saw that the paper contained a voluntary renewal of her vows ! She was 'ready to burst' with anger and disgust, and yet she thanks God that affection and respect kept her silent, and even enabled her to find excuses for her father's conduct.

'My illness,' she says, 'was of great use to me. The tenderness and affection of my parents made me resolve to carry out their wishes—to remain a nun, and live soberly as a nun ought to live. But my thoughts did not go beyond this, and never once turned towards my duty to God. However, I went back cheerfully to Port Royal, and the sisters received me with great joy. They showed more affection for me than they had ever done before, and I felt more for them.'

When Angélique returned to Port Royal, M. Arnauld sent with her Marie, his fifth daughter, born in 1600, and at that time seven years old. He expected that the pleasure and importance of this charge would soften the regret of the young Abbess at leaving home, and that the education of her little sister would occupy her time and thoughts. Angélique was still weak in consequence of her recent illness, and for a time Marie's presence and the affection of the nuns soothed and comforted her. But with returning strength came back the old trouble, the old discontent with her lot and craving for a change. At the same time she recognized that she was and must always remain the Bride of Christ; that her vows were not a gift which she had offered to God, but an honour which He had conferred upon her and which she dared not reject.

An incident which occurred at this time called her attention to the duties of her position. The vow of poverty taken by a nun was understood to mean not that she was forbidden to have money, furniture, plate or jewels of her own, but that she must not keep them *without the permission of the Abbess*, to whom she was bound to give an account of all that she received and the manner in which she employed it. A certain nun spent money without the knowledge of her Abbess, and when she confessed at Easter the priest refused absolution until she had complied with the rules. The nun would not submit, and as she had not received absolution, she could not partake of the Holy Sacrament at Easter. When she found that the confessor would not overlook her fault, she began to feel some compunction for it, and took an opportunity of explaining all the circumstances to her Abbess. Angélique heard the story, and it filled her with horror to think that 'an immortal soul had been placed in such peril;' to her practical mind it was clear that if the vow of poverty had been literally obeyed and the nun had possessed nothing of her own, she would not have been exposed to this temptation.

Carnival was a time of rejoicing in all monasteries, and in some convents the nuns acted plays before a mixed audience consisting of friends, abbots, monks, and their own community. But Angélique was faithful to her resolution, the carnival of 1608 was kept privately at Port Royal, and no secular friends were admitted to the abbey. When Lent came, the young girl's health was almost re-established; something beyond the mere dull routine of conventual life she must have; and she bethought herself of her unfinished course of study and *Plutarch's Lives*. But alas! she could not now read a secular book in Lent, for she intended to live as a nun ought to live, and in Lent a nun must read nothing but books of devotion.

Now books of devotion Angélique did not like. She talked the matter over with one of the nuns, who told her that a Capuchin monk who had preached at Port Royal had left a volume of *Meditations*, which she had read and thought very beautiful, would the Reverend Mother look at them?

Angélique took the little volume; she does not tell us what it was, says it was unlike any other book she had ever seen, very simple and direct, it touched her heart, and she found comfort in it.

A few days later, as the evening was closing in, she was walking in the abbey gardens when she was informed that Father Basil, a Capuchin friar, had arrived, and wanted to know if she would allow him to preach to the sisters of Port Royal. At first Angélique said that it was too late, she could not grant permission at that hour; but she repented of the refusal almost as soon as it was given, and recalled it; for she liked sermons. In those days preaching was a novelty, and during the previous thirty years not more than five or six sermons had been heard at Port Royal.

So in the twilight the Abbess and her nuns entered the church and sat listening to the friar as he told them of the Saviour's humility and self-denial. Even at the time when the impression produced by the sermon was strongest, Angélique used to say that she could not remember much about it. But as she listened, that great and apparently sudden change which we have learnt to call conversion came upon her. 'By God's mercy,' she says, 'I felt more happiness at the thought that I was a nun than I had ever before felt unhappiness, and I knew there was nothing I could not do for the love of God, if He did but continue to grant me the grace I then felt.' The conversion of Angélique was a change of direction in all her hopes and aims. She had longed for active life in the world, and she sees that active life in the cloister is her portion. Her rebellion ceases, and she is reconciled to her lot when she finds there is something she can do for the love of God.

When the service was ended, she thought for one moment of appealing to the preacher, opening her heart to him, and asking his help and advice. But even the early ardour and excitement of new feelings did not destroy the discrimination and power of self-restraint, for which she was afterwards so remarkable. She distrusted the preacher who was a young man, and remembering that she was not yet seventeen, she withheld her confidence; accompanied by a nun she went to thank him, and then retired. She had great reason to be thankful for her prudence; as she learned afterwards that he was a man of dissolute habits, and had been the cause of grave scandal in many convents.

Once more she is alone, the sermon ended, the *Meditations*

finished, and the dull conventual life going on as usual. But
to a noble nature there is no turning back from a contest once
entered upon or work once begun. Angélique had seen as in
a vision another world and a new life ; she could not return to
the old and beaten track, the cold external devotion, the
twilight walks in the abbey gardens, the gossip of the nuns,
and a course of Roman history. It was not enough to renounce
the world merely because it was the wish of kind parents whom
she did not desire to grieve. Those words that came to her
out of a gloom like the darkness of her own soul had shown
her in the life of Christ all that her own life was and might
become. A long period of mental struggle commenced,
through which she gradually made her way from fear to faith,
and from doubt to certainty. She had begun by thinking that
perhaps there might be such a life for a nun as had never
seemed possible in any convent that she had seen or heard
of ; a life of good works, a devout and religious life of the kind
that had faded out of view altogether at that period. She
now saw that such a life was not only possible but imperative,
and that she must lead it. At first it was not the reform of
her monastery that she was aiming at, it was her own reform,
for it was her own defects which troubled her.

We stand, however, on the threshold of a change, not for
Angélique and her little community only, but for monasticism
in France. We can measure the strength of her influence by
the opposition she called forth and the reaction against her teaching, and we shall see that she exercised it in the manner we
think highest for a woman and most womanly. It was no
intellectual difficulty which tormented Angélique, and made
rest impossible whilst work remained to be done. She eluci-
dated no dogma, and was not prepared to take any part in
a strife of words. Even in the contest which is so closely
allied with the name of Port Royal, her part is negative, and
she declines to enter into a theological discussion with which
she considers that nuns have nothing to do. The one thought
which gradually becomes clear to her is that her own life and
the life of every nun must be pure, holy, and occupied with
good works.

All that was noblest in her nature was kindled by the words
of the sermon she listened to in the twilight. Self-renunciation,
obedience, poverty, humility, these were realities, and not mere

words. The Son of God had shown them forth in His life, and she was called to follow in His steps. Hitherto she had groaned under the burden of His cross laid upon her, now we shall see her take it up and bear it, not with resignation, but with gratitude and exulting joy. We shall follow her through difficulties which are inseparable from her position ; uncertainty in her own heart, hesitation in the hearts of those around her, and opposition which is strongest from those who are dearest to her.

CHAPTER III.

ANGÉLIQUE's task was a very hard one. There was no consciousness of wrong in those with whom she had to deal, and she was trying to bring not sinners, but those who were righteous in their own esteem, to repentance. We can follow her efforts almost in her own words, for her autobiography is clear and full, and any gaps in it are supplied by the memoirs of nuns who either lived with her at this early period of her life or had often heard her speak of it.

She desired to serve God but had very little light to guide her efforts, and could only pray 'as well as she could and as much as she could.' She would often rise in the night and go up to an attic to pray, so as to escape the notice of the nun who slept in her room. Gradually she learnt to feel a great horror of her position as Abbess, in which her awakened conscience showed her that there were three crimes : 'first, the ambition of my grandfather, who desired to see two of us abbesses ; secondly, I had taken the veil at nine years old, and had been consecrated at eleven against all the laws of the Church ; and thirdly, a lie had been told to the Pope to induce him to grant the bulls, and I had been represented as seventeen.'

At Whitsuntide another Capuchin preacher visited Port Royal, Father Bernard, a very grave and stern old man. Angélique thought he was the guide she needed, and opened her heart to him. Years had not brought the old man discretion, for he not only encouraged her fasts and vigils, but he lectured the nuns, and attacked them with such severity that all the well-disposed rose up against him. At the head of these was the Prioress, a good and prudent woman, who had always obeyed the rules of the house, and did not therefore acknowledge that there was any special need of reform in the abbey. She remonstrated with Angélique, saying that Father Bernard was inducing her to undertake work for which she was too young and inexperienced. She would fail, or grow tired of it, and then the community would fall into greater irregularities than ever. Angélique urged that they were not keeping their vows; there was the vow of poverty for example, which no one obeyed, for every nun had her own private property. But the Prioress answered that their interpretation of the vow was a very good one, as nuns were careful of what was their own, whilst they were wasteful and extravagant with the common property; and that in this and other cases if one fault was removed two which were greater would be introduced.

Angélique was not convinced, but she acknowledged the force of the objections urged against her, especially of those that referred to her own unfitness for the task which had devolved upon her. She was beginning to hate her position as Abbess, and the influence and authority which it gave her, and to long to escape from it and hide herself from parents, relations, and friends, so that she might live a humble, hidden life, with no other witness of it than God, and no one to please or think of except God. She does not seem to have been oppressed by any sense of personal unworthiness; on the contrary, she writes: 'After my conversion I thought that I should never go to the confessional again because I should never do wrong, and therefore I should have nothing to confess.'

Sanguine and fearless as she was, we cannot, however, wonder that in so difficult a position her first impulse was to throw up her post as Abbess, and become a nun, or even a lay-sister, in some other community. She had not yet discerned what her work was to be as a reformer, but she saw that her actual life must be made to harmonize with her convictions. 'I said to myself, I know my duty well enough now, and although I may go into an ill-regulated convent that will not prevent me from doing what is right. I shall continue poor and obedient and patient, and there will be the more merit in it because I shall meet with great opposition and have few good examples.' At this time, when she was so young and ardent that fasts and vigils were a pastime to her, and the intense consciousness of her rectitude of purpose made her think that she could never sin again, at this very time there fell upon her a great fear of *delusions*, so that she used to pray to God by day and night to deliver her from them. At seventy years old she was able to add that her prayers had been heard, and that she had never seen any vision or heard any voices by day or when she was awake, and that as to what she might have seen or heard in the night she knew they were dreams.

Meanwhile Father Bernard was so much elated with the success of his visits to Port Royal that he took with him Father Pacifique, who was also greatly interested in Angélique. No doubt the worthy fathers would have been delighted if they could have educated the young Abbess into a saint ; but when they found that she was very much inclined to take her own way, and was already contemplating the renunciation of her abbey, they were alarmed, for M. Arnauld was not a man to be trifled with. The more practical Father Bernard said that he should at once make known her plan ; and as obedience to her parents was the first and highest duty which Angélique recognized she was frightened at the threat. She used to express astonishment in later years that although Father Pacifique was more spiritual than his companion, and had more sympathy with her views, yet it was the more worldly Father Bernard who spoke the will of God when he told her to remain where she was and try to do good to those around her.

Father Bernard appears to have drawn up a strict set of rules for tuᵢ guidance of Port Royal, which he submitted to the Abbot of Morimond, Grand Vicar of the Cistercian order. The Abbot took them to M. Arnauld, and asked his opinion of them. M. Arnauld did not approve of strict rules and projected reform, nor did the Grand Vicar, and they decided that the visits of the Capuchin friars should cease, and Angélique should see no more of Father Bernard. The Grand Vicar's decision is not surprising. A few years previously, in 1594 or 1595, he had been a well-pleased spectator of a tragedy performed by nuns known as 'The Ladies of Saint-Antoine,' whose Abbess was Mdme. de Thou, sister to the First President De Thou, and aunt of the historian. They performed a tragedy of Garnier's, called *Cleopatra*, in which

all the male characters were played by nuns in suitable costume.   The Abbot of Citeaux was present, and also the four
principal abbots in the Cistercian order, namely those of Clairvaux, Morimond, Pontigny, and la Ferté.

The summer of 1608 passed on, and in the autumn Angélique
was again attacked by fever, which was endemic at Port Royal.
M. Arnauld had heard from Mdme. de Jumeauville a full and
somewhat alarming account of his daughter's condition, and
was glad to have an excuse for taking her to Andilly, where
he hoped that all these troublesome cobwebs would soon be
swept from her brain.   Her younger sisters, Agnes and Anne,
came from St. Cyr to join her.   She took little Marie with
her, and the four girls went home together for the vintage.
At Andilly Angélique was placed under close supervision ; for
rumoured asceticism had reached the parents' ears, with which
they had little sympathy.   It was obvious enough that lace and
fine linen and the ' whalebone corset' had been abandoned, and
before long the maid who waited upon her reported that the
Reverend Mother wore no stockings, that she slept at night in
the woollen dress and cloth boots which she wore throughout the
day, and swarmed with the vermin so dear to mediæval saints.

This was too bad !   The whole household assailed her !   Did
she consider that dirt and devotion were synonymous ?   Could
she not see that she was too young to attempt any innovations,
and was only being led into foolish extremes !

M. Arnauld had a great horror of the Capuchin friars : he
pointed out to his child that she would destroy her health and
weaken her faculties by the austerities which they advocated,
and that this was precisely what they were aiming at in order
to obtain influence over her and gain a footing in the monastery.
They would then exact incessant contributions, and make Port
Royal an excellent farm for themselves.   M. Arnauld was ill at
the time, and in his anger he told his daughter that if he died,
his death would lie at her door.

Angélique felt that she was very unfortunate, and that the
world was cruel and unjust.   When she was too young to be
capable of choice, she had been placed in a position in which
her parents must surely have known that she could not be
happy.   And now that God in His mercy had made amends
for their fault and given her a love for her vocation, they opposed her and would not allow her to do her duty.

But once again filial affection triumphed. She found it impossible to grieve her father, and therefore she resolved to wait and see if God would show her any way out of her troubles.

All her hopes were shattered. The beauty of Andilly and the pleasant home life could not compensate for the loss of high aims and aspirations. Still in after years, when she spoke of her summer visits, she used to wonder how people could build houses in the country and scarcely ever live in them, saying that she thought Andilly so delightful and beautiful that she would have been glad never to leave it.

M. Arnauld liked to have his children with him, and his eldest daughter Catherine lived at home for three years after her marriage. She was at Andilly this summer with her first baby Antoine, who had been born in the spring. Magdalen, the youngest of the six Arnauld girls, was twelve months old, and there were boys of all ages; noticeable among them are Robert, the eldest, then nineteen ; Henry, who was afterwards Bishop of Angers ; and Simon, a clever little fellow of five, the pet and plaything of his elder sisters.

It is no wonder that home life seemed bright and happy to the young girls home from the convent, and that *the world* attracted them when it was represented by a generous, affectionate father, and a woman of such large sympathies and universal benevolence as their mother. Anne did not return to St. Cyr with Agnes, but was told that she was to stay at home and go into society. M. Arnauld was sorry to separate the sisters who had passed their childhood happily together, but Anne was now fourteen, and it was time to think of providing a suitable settlement for her.

Angélique's disappointment and the prospect of a blank and dreary future brought on another attack of fever, and when she had somewhat recovered she was sent back to her monastery, accompanied by little Marie. She returned with a heavy heart, determined to serve God as well as she could and not vex her father. At the festival of All Saints, M. Arnauld and the Abbé de Morimond sent a preacher of their own choice to Port Royal, a perfectly safe man as they thought. It was a vain precaution, for all fuel feeds the flame of an awakened conscience.

By this time the whole convent was interested in the condition of the Abbess, and when the text was given out : ' Blessed are they who suffer persecution for righteousness' sake,' it impressed all who heard it. After the sermon was ended, a girl who waited on Angélique said: 'Madam. if you like, you may be one of those who suffer for righteousness' sake.'

The Abbess rebuked her maid for the presumption of this speech, nevertheless the words sank into her heart, and from thenceforward she began to consider seriously whether she ought not to place duty to God above duty to her father.

One day a nun asked her if the Capuchin friars would come again, assigning as a reason for her question that she should like to see Port Royal reformed. Angélique was so touched by this mark of sympathy that she threw her arms round the Sister's neck and kissed her, and from thenceforward to the end of her life she loved her dearly, and never forgot how her heart leapt up when she heard this question.

Advent was at hand, and she prepared for it by a general confession such as she had never yet made, resolving henceforward to lead a new life. But how was it to be done, and how was she to induce others to join her?

Help came from whence she least expected it. Carefully as she had tried to conceal her fasts, vigils, and flagellations, and the scars left by burning wax which she had dropped on her arms, they had been discovered. In after time she opposed similar practices, and refused either to sanction or tolerate them; and when she was reminded of her own example she smiled and answered, 'Ah! yes; anything seemed good in those early days.'

The nuns of Port Royal were convinced that she was in earnest, and had discovered that no selfish desires had power over her pure, brave nature. Their hearts were touched by the sorrow of the grave, pale girl, who went about amongst them watchful and anxious. 'I was very unhappy,' she says, speaking of this time, 'for I did not know how to win over the Prioress, and the elder nuns.' And then one day in Lent, 1609, the good and prudent Prioress, who 'loved Angélique and feared God but did not see any necessity for a change,' asked for an interview with her and told her that it grieved the whole sisterhood to see her so sad, and they begged to know why it was. Angélique replied that she could not reform the monastery. The Prioress answered there was nothing they would not do rather than see her unhappy; she was commissioned to speak for the community and to offer to do whatever their Abbess might desire.

Angélique, with that marvellous tact, that combination of self-restraint and sympathetic insight which we shall hereafter see as the secret of her influence, did not pour out all her griefs and all her hopes, but asked merely that a day might be fixed when their vow of poverty should be fulfilled, and they should have all things in common.

Her own attention had been called to the neglect of this vow by the case of the nun who was refused absolution because she would not acknowledge the right of her Abbess to control her expenditure. No doubt the subject had been already discussed among the Sisters; some of them would side with the Abbess when she said that if the nun had possessed nothing of her own she could not have fallen into sin, and others with the Prioress, who urged that if they had all things in common nuns would be wasteful and exacting. When the Prioress, therefore, whose influence was only second to that of Angélique, had yielded, the first step was made very easy. A meeting of the Chapter was held, and the nuns decided in favour of the literal interpretation of their vow of poverty. They appointed a day on which they would surrender their little treasures, everything that they had been accustomed to consider their very own. One amongst them was deaf and dumb, but she understood by signs what was going forward, and brought all that she possessed to be added to the common stock. Angélique was radiant with joy, and when the nuns gave up their pretty beads and little ornaments, she thanked them for the act of renunciation as if it had been a personal gratification.

But there was one who stood aloof from the movement. She had been compelled to take the veil against her will, and in spite of all the efforts of her companions, she maintained an attitude of stubborn resistance. The Abbess reasoned with her, and showed great tenderness and forbearance, but could not bring her to a sense of duty. She remained cold, hard, and unyielding, and was ultimately removed to another monastery, where she died.

The oldest nun in Port Royal was Sister Morel. She submitted reluctantly to the innovation with regard to her property, and finally drew back, and would not give up the key of a little garden which she allowed no one to enter. Her companions were grieved, and tried to remonstrate with her; but this threw her into a violent passion, so they desisted, and she kept her key. The Abbess did not reprove or punish the refractory nun, she waited patiently, and before long her gentleness and sweetness prevailed. Sister Morel repented, and one day she put the key of her little garden into a letter and sent it to the Abbess. There was great rejoicing at this act, for, with the exception alluded to, Port Royal was now united, and we shall henceforth follow them in the path which the Abbess had sought from conviction, and along which the nuns consented to follow her though not without reluctance.

As they had agreed to have all things in common, Angélique was specially anxious to provide everything that was necessary, and to let them see that she took upon herself the care of their well-being and comfort. She abounded in deeds of kindness, and often carried wood with her own hands to the dormitory fire when the weather was cold. Meanwhile she had but one rule for herself—to take the worst of everything, the shabbiest gown, the poorest food, and the meanest accommodation. There was nothing in the house that she considered her own, and no work which she acknowledged to be menial. Her room was shared with the sick and infirm, and her own bed given up to them whilst she slept on the floor. Every moment which was not occupied by other duties she passed alone on her knees in prayer. Only one companion knew all the secrets of this time, for in after years she never alluded to them, and neither encouraged in others nor justified in herself the austerities which she then practised. She fasted so strictly during the whole of Lent, that, weakened as she was by intermittent fever, her health suffered severely. Meat of course was forbidden, but she would not touch fish, and, in spite of the permission of the Church and the commands of her doctor, she refused to eat eggs. Mdme. de Jumeauville became anxious, and wrote to her father, and, as he had no intention of allowing his daughter to starve herself to death, he sent an apothecary from Paris, M. de Sainte-Beuve, with orders that the Abbess was to eat an egg in his presence. She could not disobey her father, and immediately complied with his command. She discovered with regret, that whereas she had generally such a dislike to eggs that it was something of a penance to eat one, this egg seemed particularly nice, and she couldn't help enjoying it.

The incident, however, opened Angélique's eyes to the fact that Mdme. de Jumeauville was a spy, and reported to her parents everything that transpired in the abbey. She made no complaint to them, but asked aid of Father Basil the preacher, whom M. Arnauld and the Abbé de Morimond had sent to Port Royal at Advent.

Father Basil was about eight and twenty, and his antecedents had not led M. Arnauld to expect that he would adopt Angélique's views; but her influence was beginning to make itself felt by all around her, and the man who was sent to discourage her desire for reform remained to foster it. With his help Mdme. de Jumeauville was recalled to St. Cyr. He first of all remonstrated with her for leaving her convent in order to act as governess to a nun, and then represented to the Abbess of St. Cyr that she ought not to allow a member of her community to be absent for so many years. The result was that the Abbess recalled Mdme. de Jumeauville, almost at her own request and certainly in accordance with her wish.

CHAPTER IV

THE young Abbesses of St. Cyr and Port Royal were friends and companions, and although Agnes did not pass through the same spiritual conflict as Angélique, she sympathised deeply with her sister. When they left Andilly together in the autumn of 1608, and returned to their respective abbeys, Agnes was alone, but Angélique still had little Marie. Before long the two elder sisters wished to be together. Angélique longed to have Agnes with her, and told her father that she was sure Agnes, who was ill, was pining for Port Royal. Angélique's health and mental condition were causing her parents great uneasiness, and there was no Mdme. de Jumeauville to watch over her. They doubtless thought that as Agnes was quite resigned to her position, her influence over the more active and ardent temperament of Angélique would be very valuable. It is difficult to follow the tangled threads of the transaction and to find how far compassion and affection and to what extent worldly motives influenced M. Arnauld, but the result was that he permitted Agnes to give up the Abbey of St. Cyr, and become a novice of Port Royal. Probably he did not at that time suspect that he was carrying out Angélique's plan, and that it was her influence and not that of Agnes which he ought to take into consideration. The elder sister writes :—

'Agnes went with me to stay at our father's house, and I left her at St. Cyr on my way home. Soon afterwards she came to stay with me at Port Royal, for she was quite ill. I had grown more and more anxious to do the will of God, and

He had inspired me with the wish to draw her to Him also. I found this very difficult, for she was warmly attached to the Benedictine order, and still more, I fancy, to her future position as Abbess. I tried to win her heart, and by degrees the love of prayer, for which she was always remarkable, increased so much that though she was weak and ill, she contrived to crawl to church, where she would remain in prayer for hours together. She was drawn in opposite directions by her love for me and her love for the Benedictines and her own abbey. My father came to see us, and found her ill and out of spirits. I told him that it all arose from melancholy, and that she would be quite happy if he would allow her to give up St. Cyr and come to me. I said that because I was very anxious that my father's conscience should not be burdened with the responsibility of holding that abbey in charge for her. My father was convinced that her illness arose from the cause I had assigned, so he said that he only wished to see her happy, and that if she desired to remain at Port Royal she might do so. Agnes was surprised, but she would not contradict what I had said.'

Angélique disarms criticism by her frank confession. She did not tell the whole truth, but she acted as she thought for the best, and secured an end that was desirable by means that were unjustifiable. She saw her sister undecided and unhappy, and having no doubt as to the best thing to be done, she does it. Agnes is surprised, but she acquiesces. Henceforward, though for some years she wears the dress of a Benedictine novice, she belongs to Port Royal. She did not like the rough serge worn by the Cistercians, and was fond of her little white cape, which was always clean and carefully arranged. She retained also a small gold cross attached to her chaplet, which was a mark of her office as Abbess. Angélique did not interfere, and her toleration for things which she believed to be faults but saw that it was not the time to remedy, gained over many of those who were most opposed to her.

She was very gentle with Agnes, allowing her to follow her inclination and give up all her time to her devotions. Both sisters felt that they were called by God, both were trying to serve Him. Agnes was contented with her position so long as it afforded facility for the development of her own personal piety; but the more active intellect of Angélique could not rest satisfied with this. She also was converted, but her practical nature made her ask what were her duties towards God and man, and how she could best fulfil them.

Perhaps our surprise that her inquiries did not extend somewhat further is legitimate. She had originality and power, great courage and no lack of intellectual vigour. She held to her convictions when she believed them to be right, though Pope and priests were against them. 'If we are right,' she said once, 'God is on our side, and we may trust Him to defend us against the Pope or anyone else.' We should expect such a woman to be led or driven from her Church, but she remained a devout Roman Catholic to the end.

She wanted at this time to find out what an abbess ought to *do*, and not what an abbess ought to *be*. She made herself familiar with the details of the Cistercian rule and the edicts that affected her position, and resolved to sweep away innovations and abuses, and realize the ideal of conventual life. No doubt if she had founded the order instead of reformed it, she would have asked herself of many things if they were right, wise, and desirable. She would have been saved from many errors and many blunders. But, with the characteristic loyalty of the Arnaulds, having accepted a position she accepted all the duties that it entailed.

She was like her uncle *du Fort*, and would have thought it quite as much the duty of her soldiers to plaster a wall as to defend a fortress. As a girl she protested that her fate was hard and unjust; but after her conversion her vocation was her own choice, and she preferred it to anything and everything that the world could offer. She was the 'bride of Christ,' she was the chosen of God, she had attained the highest honour that could be conferred upon woman.

Agnes took the same view of her vocation, but she was absorbed in the contemplation of religious mysteries, whilst the conversion of Angélique had more practical results. It opened her eyes to her actual condition. She was a nun, bound by certain vows, everyone of which she was neglecting, or might neglect. She was an abbess, responsible for her nuns, and she and they violated all the rules which they had solemnly vowed to obey. She could know neither peace nor rest until she had reconciled their profession with their actual life. She looked back to the *cartes de visite* of the preceding century, and saw there protests against abuses which had now become customs of the order. She remarked the absence of religious feeling, and saw that the spiritual life of the community must have been even then extinct. With an awakened conscience she read the *rules* of her order, and resolved that poverty, chastity, obedience, humility, self-denial, and charity, should be realities for herself and her nuns. We cannot fail to recognize and regret her many mistakes, but we must also acknowledge that she did train to the full exercise of these virtues a very brave and noble band, not only of women, but of men also.

In order to estimate the difficulty of her task we must glance backwards to the origin of the Benedictines and Cistercians, and turn our attention to the strict rules which had long ceased to be obeyed, and which she now attempted to re-establish.

The rule of St. Benedict was written about the year 530, and it shows what monastic life was at that time in the West. St. Benedict did not consider it a perfect rule, but only a feeble attempt towards attaining the perfection of preceding centuries.

It is enough for our purpose to state that the three virtues which constituted the sum of the Benedictine discipline were : Silence, Humility, and Obedience.

Silence could only be acquired in solitude and seclusion, and the Benedictines were isolated from their fellows, although they were members of the same community, ate at a common table, and slept in the common dormitory.

Humility implied self-renunciation and poverty. The idea and even the name of separate or exclusive possession was to be abjured, and they were forbidden to use such expressions as *my* book, *my* cloak, *my* sleeve.

The Obedience required was absolute and unquestioning, and was shown by blind submission to the commands of the Abbot or Abbess, even if they were ridiculous or wicked.

The three duties which were inculcated by the rule were the Worship of God, Reading, and Manual Labour.

The early Benedictine monks and nuns led in absolute silence a life of the most abject poverty. They were poorly lodged and clad, and worse fed. Abstinence from meat was perpetual, and their ordinary food was vegetable broth, with bread and a small measure of wine twice every day, but they were allowed the occasional use of fowls and fish. The nuns never left the cloistered precincts. The monks were strictly forbidden to partake of food outside the convent walls, and when a monk was compelled to be absent during the whole day he was enjoined to fast rather than to eat abroad. The monks laboured in the fields, and during harvest-time or whenever there was any particular work to be done, they did not return to the house at the hours for divine service, but knelt and performed it out of doors. They were roused at midnight for prayers, retired again, and then rose at 2 A.M. for matins, after which they did not return to bed, and the long day was divided between labour, meditation, reading, and prayer.

Between three and four hundred years later, the Benedictines found that they were very far from an exact observance of their rule. Their monasteries were spread all over the west, were independent of each other, and had insensibly acquired different customs as to food and clothing, whilst none of them obeyed their rule with regard to manual labour. It was true, they said, that Benedict had set apart seven hours in the day for it, but this was to avoid idleness, which they escaped by occupying themselves in prayer, reading, and singing psalms. Wealthy benefactors and large bequests of land and money had banished poverty from their houses. They lived in luxury and ease, the abbots travelled in grand equipages with many horses and a great retinue, and it was a Benedictine abbot who said, 'My vow of poverty has given me 100,000 crowns a year, my vow of obedience has raised me to the rank of a sovereign prince.'

The letter of the Benedictine rule, however, remained unchanged; and as it was read aloud daily in Chapter, from time to time, some monk remembered that it had a meaning and he had sworn to obey it. Such a man would inaugurate reform, in the order if possible, if not in his own monastery. The foundation of Clugni in the year 910 owed its origin to an attempted reform of the Benedictine rule, and Clugni gained the esteem and affection of kings, princes, and emperors. In their gratitude they overwhelmed it with wealth, and then the rich monks grew proud, and despised poor communities and mendicant orders. Each monk wanted to have his share of the wealth of the house, and to be as well fed, clothed, and lodged as his order would allow, and sometimes better.

Two hundred years after the foundation of Clugni, the founders of Citeaux (in Latin Cistercium) again attempted to reform their order, and bring back the spirit of the Benedictine rule. It was St. Bernard, Abbot of Citeaux, who rendered the Cistercian order famous.

Bernard approved of manual labour and re-established it; but he introduced a novelty which grew into an abuse, namely, the distinction between monks and lay-brothers. His reason for this was that laymen, namely all those who had not been educated for the priesthood, were unable to read, and ignorant of Latin. As they could not read they could not learn the psalter by heart, and as they knew no Latin they could not profit by Divine service.

These uneducated lay-brothers were therefore to perform all the manual labour connected with the monastery, whilst their religious duties were confined to reciting a number of Paters at the canonical hours. In order to assist their memory, they carried grains threaded on a string, which are the earliest form of chaplets.

Before long there were lay-brothers in all religious orders, and as every change made by the monks was reflected faithfully by the nuns, this innovation reached them also. They had lay-sisters and choir-sisters, although there was no reason for the distinction, as the latter knew no more Latin than the former. This became a fruitful source of evil; monks and nuns looked upon lay-brothers and sisters as ignorant inferiors, destined to serve them. With a sense of their own superiority, and the wealth of their order, for Citeaux was soon as rich as Clugni, all the worldliness and vice which Bernard had tried to banish crept back again.

In the thirteenth century the Cistercian order had degenerated so much that the monks left their monastery without permission, stayed with secular friends in the towns, they took their meals with them, had their own property, borrowed money for themselves, or became security for others in their own names, ate meat, wore linen, and had separate apartments.

The degeneracy extended to the nuns, just as the reform of the Cistercian order had also affected them.

In 1148 Gilbert of Sempringham asked the Chapter of Citeaux to take charge of a congregation which he had formed, consisting of seven nuns. They were shut up in the church of

St. André, and were to live in perpetual seclusion, receiving their necessary food through the windows. Before his death Gilbert had formed thirteen similar monasteries, four for monks, and nine for nuns. In the same year another reformer, Stephen of Obasine, converted many men and women of noble birth. At first the women lived apart from the men, but were not strictly secluded. When, however, their number reached a hundred and fifty they were removed to a monastery that had been prepared for them, and which they were never on any account to leave. The east end of their church, containing the chancel, was walled off, and had an outer door, by which the monks entered to say mass. The wall which separated priests and altar from the congregation had a window in it, with a grating, which was covered by a thick curtain. Through this window the nuns received the communion, and even those who were sick and dying had to be carried to it, for the monks were to render them all kinds of spiritual service, but never to enter the cloistered part of the monastery. The rule for the seclusion of nuns in Cistercian monasteries was more strict than that of monks. They were never to leave the cloistered part of the monastery, to be seen in public, or to have any intercourse with the world. Their rule prescribed coarse woollen clothing, no meat, scanty food of poor quality, and hard labour ; silence and seclusion until death, and after death burial without the ministration of a priest. The Abbess possessed supreme power over her nuns, and they addressed her kneeling. The Council of Trent ordained that she must be forty years old, and must have been a professed nun eight years, and that under no circumstances should an abbess be elected who was not thirty years old.

But the monasteries for nuns relaxed the severity of their rules as much as those for monks. In the beginning of the fifteenth century there were abbesses in Spain, who gave the veil to their nuns, received confessions, and preached and read the Bible in public. In the sixteenth century, Gregory XIII. tried to check the abuses which were attributed to the perpetuity of the offices of abbess and prioress, and issued a bull in 1585, by which he ordained that these offices should be triennial, according to the decrees of the Council of Trent. He gives as a reason for this, that if the superiors knew that after three years they would be called upon to give an account of their administration, they would be more careful in the government of their houses. This measure applied only to Italy and Sicily, and would have been too revolutionary for France.

A French convent at the close of the sixteenth century was a place in which unmarried and unmarriageable women of noble and gentle birth lived together, wearing a distinctive dress, and obeying within what seemed to them reasonable limits the rules of certain religious orders. Their Abbess administered considerable funds, and often managed large estates. It was desirable that the lives of these ladies should be outwardly decorous, and that there should be some security for such defenceless communities in stormy and unsettled times, and therefore certain traditions of the past which reflected upon them the self-denial and sanctity of a previous age were still adhered to, and were not altogether without effect upon the people whom they were intended to influence. But upon the nuns themselves their vows sat very lightly; in the majority of cases they had been placed in a monastery without any reference to their own wishes on the subject. They were the superfluous women in a family; this fact at least was patent, and they must submit to the consequences of it. It was soon found that, after all, the life of a nun was not of necessity a complete sacrifice of all enjoyment and pleasure. Founders' wishes grew obsolete, and no one imagined them to be binding under changed conditions and in a different state of society. The religious aspect of conventual life was gradually lost sight of, and its social aspect tended to change with the views of the age. If society was dissolute, so were the religious communities; in fact they did not lead or stand apart from the world around them; they followed it, represented all its crimes and all its vices. We look into them as into an old-fashioned mirror with a border cut in many facets, in each of which you see an image of the room and all the persons in it, only they are infinitely little. The lives and the quarrels of the nuns were the infinitely little repetitions of all that was going on around them. The Abbess, if she was of royal or noble birth, kept her state in a small way, and snubbed her neighbours whenever she had the opportunity; and the nuns intrigued for the high places of the convent, and had disputes and quarrels within their own walls and their feuds with other religious houses. They made friends at court, and got as much of this world and its good things as they possibly could. A *good* abbess meant one who had not impoverished her house by receiving portionless women, who had always looked after the loaves and fishes, had taken care that money should come to the convent, but should not go from it ; that her nuns ate and drank every day of the best, and dressed as well, that is, as fashionably as they could, in spite of those absurd sumptuary regulations by which they were bound. These were not so absolutely stringent that they could not be evaded ; lace and fine linen and soft cloth, material of the best and most expensive could be chosen ; and cap and hood, collar and sleeve, could be so adjusted that the dress was made very becoming if not absolutely fashionable.

And thus the convents became luxurious homes in which kind parents were contented to know that their daughters were settled, and brothers who had been enriched by the portions of their sisters saw that they had not lost the good things of life, but only taken them under peculiar and sometimes irritating conditions ; whilst kings looked upon the monasteries as an appanage of the crown, and bestowed them upon whomsoever they would. Louis XIII. gave the Abbey of St. Germain des Près to the widow of the Duke of Lorraine, which is ' much as though the mastership of Trinity College, Cambridge, had been given to the widow of the Elector Palatine.'[1] The morality of these houses was the morality of the age, and if to the public it seemed somewhat higher, it was because the concealment of immorality was very easy. And the religion was the religion of the age ; that is to say, it was banished altogether from this world and this life, and relegated to the next. But throughout the whole of France there was at that time a strong and almost unquestioning belief in the life of the world to come. The most profligate and irreligious did not doubt that a time would certainly come when they must make amends to God for the past, and prepare for a new order of things in the future.

The Catholic Church had laid down an elaborate map of the next world. It was not only definite and distinct, but its accuracy was undoubted. The Church asserted that communication between earth and heaven had been unbroken for many

[1] Essays in Ecclesiastical Biography, by Sir James Stephen.

centuries; saints and martyrs were constantly showing that their interest in this world was undiminished, and their influence in the next was never questioned. Some time then before death these potentates must be propitiated. They were not inexorable; certain rules had to be observed, certain forms to be gone through, there was a certain manner in which they must be approached, and certain persons through whom they must be appealed to; provided this was done the forgiveness of sins and the life of the world to come were open to all men. Thus in spite of the degradation of the priesthood and the monastic orders in France, they were looked upon as valuable machinery which might be set in motion for the public good.

CHAPTER V.

ANGÉLIQUE was now free from restraint. The vow of poverty was fulfilled, but when she looked back to the *cartes de visite* she saw that the vow of chastity involved obedience to many rules now neglected, and that it necessitated the strict seclusion of the nuns in the cloistered part of the abbey. In fact, fulfilment of this vow implied closing the doors of the abbey against father and mother, relations and friends. Angélique did not, so far as we know, ask herself whether this was right; but when her conscience was awakened, the practical bent of her mind led her to resolve that she would obey literally all the rules of her order, and she believed this to be the only means of avoiding the flagrant immorality of other convents.

She told the community, many of whom now sympathised warmly with her, that she proposed to re-establish strict seclusion of the nuns and strict exclusion of all friends and relatives from the cloistered precincts; that for the future the Sisters would communicate with the outer world through a small window opening into a parlour built outside the abbey walls. She added that there would be no exception to this rule, and that it would apply to her own family as well as to others. This stopped the mouths of all who were inclined to object, or rather they said: 'Wait till M. and Mdme. Arnauld come, and then we shall see.'

The first opportunity for enforcing the rule occurred when a novice took the veil shortly after Easter. Many friends were present at the ceremony, and they were all entertained outside the cloistered precincts instead of inside, as formerly. Several of the guests protested against this *innovation*, and those who knew M. Arnauld said that his daughter would never dare to refuse him admission.

The charge of *innovation* was now often heard. The Cistercian monks said Angélique was a schismatic and an innovator, who was destroying all their good old customs; they called her an infatuated girl, and tried to induce the nuns to rebel against her rule. There is no doubt that strict exclusion and seclusion did introduce many changes, and the nuns in their ignorance thought that Angélique was inventing new rules, when she was merely re-asserting the old. As the nuns were neither to pay visits nor receive them, there was not much difficulty in inducing them to give up the use of starch and gloves and masks, although they had hitherto taken as much care of their muslins, their hands, and complexions, as young ladies in society. They ceased to do so when, in addition to being reminded that it was contrary to their rules, no one saw the result of their attention bestowed upon their personal appearance. That elaborate dressing of the hair for which they had even endured ecclesiastical reproof, their fashionable sleeves and the dainty material for their robes—all were renounced. The monks who still had access to the parlour protested, for they knew that modesty and simplicity were not virtues which they had much interest in cultivating.

But Angélique had Father Basil on her side. His zeal was that of a new convert, and fanned the flame which Angélique had kindled, so that she met with no open opposition within the abbey walls. Her parents received no reports now that Mdme. Jumeauville had left, and they did not know that there was anything to call for their interference.

M. Arnauld was, as usual, applying to the Pope for fresh bulls. There was always danger lest it should be convenient to discover and punish the fraud by which they had been obtained for Angélique when she was nine, and again when she was eleven years old. She was now nearly eighteen, and her father thought that the time had come for telling the truth, asking pardon, and securing her future position. He experienced some difficulty in this matter, for it was concluded that he had been farming the abbey for his own advantage,

and restitution of all the proceeds was demanded from him.
He was, however, able to prove that far from receiving anything, the house was so poor and dilapidated that it had cost
him large sums to repair and support it. And then he pleaded
the reform undertaken by his child, and urged that although
she was so young, the blessing of God had rested upon her
work, and would no doubt prosper it. It is said that the
Pope expressed great satisfaction at Angélique's conduct, and
granted the bulls without further expense to M. Arnauld. Her
first profession was declared null and void, and in order to
remain nun and Abbess she was to renew her vows within six
months. She heard of this, and prayed that her father might
forget the time, and then she would be free, and could join
some strict society or even become a lay-sister.

Meanwhile summer was drawing on. When term time was
over and the vacations came her father would visit her; what
was she to do?

'Obey your rule literally,' said Father Basil; 'write and
inform your father that your conscience will not allow you to
receive him, and that if he should resolve on visiting you after
receiving this your humble prayer, you must exercise your
authority as Abbess and close the doors against him.'

These were hard words. Hitherto the love of parents and
her sense of duty towards them had influenced Angélique more
strongly than any other motive. In later years she used to
regret having followed Father Basil's advice, because she
thought she might have attained her object without causing
her parents so much pain, and with far less suffering to herself.
But in this early stage of her life she saw no other way than
literal obedience to advice when it pointed to the path of duty.

Still when the time came she could not write this terrible
letter either to father or mother; so she addressed her sister,
Mdme. le Maître, and asked her, at a fitting opportunity, to
explain to her parents that, by the grace of God, she had
begun to reform Port Royal and had re-established the strict
seclusion of the nuns. She implored them not to put any
obstacle in her way, and if they proposed to honour her
with a visit during the ensuing vacation, she hoped they
would not be offended if she received them in the parlour,
as she did other visitors. If they would not consent to this
exclusion she must beg them to deprive her of the honour

of their presence, for she thought it right to inform them that her conscience compelled her to refuse to admit them.

Mdme. le Maître showed the letter to her mother, and asked what they should do about telling M. Arnauld. His wife replied that she knew Angélique, and was not at all afraid she would play her father such a trick, and that it was of no use to speak to him and make him angry about a thing which would never come to pass.

Meanwhile Angélique, and those who were aware of her intention spent much time in prayer for a good issue to the undertaking. At length the impending visit was announced, and on the appointed day the large travelling carriage of the Arnaulds left Paris for Port Royal. It contained the parents, with their eldest son Robert, or d'Andilly, as he was called, who was twenty-one; Mdme. le Maître also accompanied them, and Anne, the fifth in the carriage, who had been at home for a year and was now fifteen.

Angélique appears to have known her parents rather better than they knew her; and she asked for the keys of all the cloistered parts of the monastery and took them into her own charge.

The Arnaulds arrived at dinner-time. The nuns were in the refectory, but the Abbess was in the church alone, kneeling before the altar, and asking help for the trial that was at hand. She heard the carriage arrive, and went to the cloister door and waited whilst they all got out. Her father knocked, and she then opened a wicket, and begged him to go into a small parlour near the gate, where she could speak to him through the grating.

If ever man was surprised it was M. Arnauld. He argued, persuaded, commanded, and at length growing angry knocked louder and louder, insisting that the door should be opened. For all answer Angélique continued humbly to beg him to enter the parlour, where she would have the honour of explaining her conduct to him. Mdme. Arnauld now came forward and addressed Angélique as her ungrateful child; whilst d'Andilly, whose anger knew no bounds at seeing his father, and indeed the whole family, set at defiance by a girl of eighteen, addressed her with passionate invective, called her a monster of ingratitude, a parricide, who would have to answer to God for the death of her father, and entreated the nuns not to allow their benefactor to be driven with insult from their doors.

The sound of angry voices reached the refectory, and those who were on Angélique's side looked at each other in silence and prayed God to strengthen her heart. But good old Dame Morel, who had probably not then given up the key of her little garden, went into the courtyard to find the nun who kept the key of the gate, saying angrily that it was a shame to keep out M. Arnauld. Many nuns said the same, and even the men and women at work in the abbey and employed and fed by the Abbess's bounty, exclaimed that she must have a hard unfeeling heart since she treated her father in such a manner, and a father who was so generous to the poor and had done so much good in those parts for her sake.

Before long there was a tumult on both sides of the Abbess, but she had the keys in her own keeping, and her resolution did not falter. Her father saw this, and, changing his tactics, he demanded his two daughters, Agnes, who had not yet taken the veil, and Marie, who was nine years old.

Angélique divined his intention. He had a right to claim them, and when the door was opened for their exit, he expected to force his way in, and settle the difficulty by taking his usual place in the abbey. Her presence of mind did not forsake her. She assented to his demand, and gave the key of a side door in the church to a nun on whom she could rely, bidding her send the two sisters out that way. It was done so quietly that M. Arnauld suspected nothing, and so quickly that his daughters were at his side before he knew from whence they had come.

Their brother assailed them with bitter complaints of Angélique's conduct, but Agnes, in her grave and yet simple manner, replied that her sister was not wrong; she had done what her conscience dictated and the Council of Trent approved.

Whereupon d'Andilly angrily interrupted her, 'Come, come!' said he, 'this is too much. Here is another with her Canons and her Councils!'

Mdme. le Maître and Anne Arnauld stood aloof and said nothing. They felt for their father, but they knew how much Angélique must also be suffering, and compassion for her, not unmixed with admiration, kept them silent.

When M. Arnauld saw that Angélique was not to be moved,

he gave orders that the carriage should be prepared for immediate return to Paris.

He consented before his departure to grant the request that his daughter urged with such persistent humility, and to enter the little parlour built outside the abbey wall. Angélique went into the corresponding parlour on the inner side and opened the wicket of communication, so that they saw each other for the first time that day. M. Arnauld was deeply agitated ; he spoke in a low tone and as briefly as possible; reminded Angélique how tenderly he loved her, how dear her happiness and her welfare had been to him, so that everything which concerned her had taken precedence of his own affairs. She had now made it impossible for him to give her any further proofs of his affection, but he should never cease to love her. He should not see her again, but at this last meeting he made one request, urged one petition, and it was that for his sake she would not sacrifice health and life in her indiscreet zeal.

Up to this time Angélique's courage and fortitude had not failed. Her father's reproaches, the anger of her mother and brother, had affected but not overwhelmed her. But her father's grief and the half-broken sentences which he had difficulty in uttering were too much : she could bear no more, and for all answer to his tender words she fainted and fell insensible to the ground. In a moment everything was changed. M. Arnauld only saw that his child was dead, for so he thought when he saw her still white face, and that he could not get to her. He shouted for help, but the nuns ran from, instead of towards, his voice. Her mother and brother knocked at the convent door and implored the nuns to come quickly, but they thought this was a last attempt to force an entrance, and kept out of the way. At last some one distinguished d'Andilly's words, and heard that he was entreating them to go to their Abbess, who was dying or dead in the parlour.

They hurried in, and found her rigid and insensible. When they had succeeded in restoring her to consciousness she slowly opened her eyes and turned them to the wicket through which the poor father was watching her. With great difficulty she spoke and asked him 'just one favour'—that he would not go away that day.

He was ready to promise whatever his child cared to ask,

and the Abbess was carried to her own room until a couch was prepared for her near the wicket. When she was somewhat better they brought her down and placed her on the couch; and father, mother, brother, and sisters, who were all now in the outer parlour, watched her through the small opening.

The whole family was united by such strong bonds of love that their anger was but transient; and in their hearts there was a considerable amount of admiration for the young girl's courage. They talked quietly, and listened calmly and even respectfully whilst she explained her conduct and motives; and M. Arnauld was convinced, or at any rate he yielded in every particular to her wishes.

And now Father Basil, who had prudently kept out of the way whilst the storm was raging, thought this was a favourable moment for coming forward to acknowledge and justify his advice, and give his reasons for it. Never was man so mistaken. They all assailed him, and if he did not regret his conduct he had good reason to regret his attempt to justify it.

Angélique was very sorry for him; she respected him, and believed that his advice had been conscientiously given, but she could not help seeing that his judgment was at fault. He had told her that she would be guilty of mortal sin if she did not obey him and exclude her parents; she obeyed, and yet obedience did not satisfy her conscience. She thought the end she had attained was right, but regretted the means used, and felt that her own judgment, directed by filial affection, would have been a safer guide than the priest. No doubt it was of great advantage to her to learn this lesson so early, although what she suffered on that day very nearly cost her her life.

M. Arnauld and his family stayed at Port Royal until the following morning, and were entertained in the guest chamber outside the cloister walls. Agnes and little Marie were quietly sent back again without any explanation on either side. It was arranged that henceforth M. Arnauld was free to enter all except the cloistered parts of the convent, and to visit outbuildings, chapel, and gardens, and give orders concerning them as he had hitherto done; whilst Mdme. Arnauld and her daughters were to be received whenever they wished to stay at Port Royal.

But the breach between mother and daughter was not so
easily healed. Mdme. Arnauld in the first moment of anger
had taken an oath never to revisit Port Royal, and she did
not dare to break it. More than a year afterwards she heard
a sermon in which it was stated that oaths evil in themselves and taken in anger were not binding. She was greatly
excited, went home, ordered the carriage immediately, drove
to Port Royal, and had a happy interview with her daughter.
Angélique was so delighted that she never forgot the anniver-
sary of this day on which the reconciliation with her family
was completed.

In November 1609 M. Arnauld received the bulls from
Rome, which had been granted on condition that his daughter
should renew her vows within six months. He thought it
desirable to be silent about them, and as May approached
Angélique hoped that the limitation as to time had been forgotten, or else that her father intended to grant her wish and
allow her to resign her charge. This was not the case. M.
Arnauld's plan was once more to surprise his daughter into
acquiescence. He heard that the Abbot of Clairvaux was in
the neighbourhood of Port Royal, and begged him to go unexpectedly and request the renewal of his daughter's vows.

The Abbot arrived in the evening, and Angélique, seeing no
way of escape, prepared to obey. She sat up all night making
herself a new dress, for the nuns protested that it was impossible their Reverend Mother could wear her old, shabby,
every-day gown on such a solemn occasion. She yielded to
their wishes, but selected the coarsest serge for her new dress
which could be procured.

On the 7th of May, 1610, she renewed her vows, but
she thought it permissible to do so with considerable mental
reserve. She resolved to keep the three important vows of
poverty, chastity, and obedience, but not to bind herself to
her own order or her own monastery, for she intended to
leave them at the earliest opportunity.

CHAPTER VI.

IT is impossible to follow the memoirs in their diffuse details of the years that follow this memorable 1609, and we must be contented with an outline of the work done and the progress made, until we reach another important landmark.

Angélique saw that although her father submitted to her views, he did not adopt them, nor did he approve of her design of thorough and complete reform in the monastery. She resolved therefore, for the future, not to ask him for the supplies which he had hitherto so willingly granted, but to be contented with what the abbey provided. The poverty of the nuns became at once a reality, they saw that there must be restrictions in the matter of food and clothing, and that with a diminished income they must find means of giving more instead of less to the poor. Angélique sold all the silver vessels belonging to the abbey and spent the money, but even then they were pinched. By degrees furniture, clothes, and food were reduced to the barest necessaries of life. The nuns bore all privations cheerfully, nay joyfully. Their numbers increased, and the accommodation which the house afforded was necessarily more and more restricted. There were only twelve cells in the dormitory. The infirmary was low, and as damp as a cellar, *and it was always full*. 'The new-comers,' says Angélique simply, 'were nearly always ill, but even that did not disgust them.' Many good and pious nuns, hearing of the movement set on foot by Angélique, obtained permission to join the community at Port Royal; for good is contagious like evil, and attracts also that which is of its own nature. They were seldom wanted in their own monastery, and an abbess attached to the 'good old customs of the order' was glad to send away dangerous innovators. At Port Royal they doubtless experienced many discomforts ; but in these early days there was an ardour and enthusiasm of charity, submission, and faith, which lifted them into new and higher regions of existence.

Port Royal was poor; but the poverty of the nuns was nothing compared to the poverty they saw on all sides among peasants who found no demand for their labour, no means of tilling the ground or obtaining food. Angélique's practical mind had already decided that she and her nuns must fast, not on account of some benefit to accrue to themselves from fasting, but that they might have something to give away. She also resolved to find work for the poor and pay them for it, as she feared that alms would make them idle mendicants, who would no longer give themselves any trouble to obtain work. No doubt in this she was guided by what she had seen of the management of the poor on her father's estate. He gave employment to all, but alms only to the sick and aged. Probably by his advice, and certainly with his assistance, a few years later a large number of poor men, women, and children were employed to rebuild the cloister walls, which were in a very dilapidated condition. They received small wages and their daily food. Soup, meat, and bread were prepared in the kitchen of Port Royal, and taken in barrows to the garden, where they were served out with a measure of wine to each person. The Abbess and some of the Sisters presided and distributed the food, and the labourers were very well behaved whilst they were eating. Angélique, to whom all that related to the body was but a type of the far higher needs of the soul, used to set up a little boy in their midst who had been taught by the nuns, and he read aloud from 'a spiritual book suited to their capacity, so that body and soul might derive benefit at the same time.' One day when the child was reading, a labourer made some irreverent remark : the Abbess could not answer, but she looked at him and burst into tears.

She used to say that the troubles of this life only affected her on account of their influence over the soul, and because they induced rebellion against God. No doubt she did always look beyond the immediate present to a future life and an unseen world, but she had a warm, tender heart, and sympathetic nature, to which her own words do scanty justice. She could never look unmoved on human suffering, but must try to relieve it at any cost to herself; her helpful charity was a matter of instinct, which was encouraged by reflection, and justified by her convictions.

When she entered the infirmary the sick seemed to grow suddenly well, and even believed that they were cured of disease, because the joy of seeing her made them forget their sufferings. Her charity was not merely lip-service, but was ready to show itself in performing the most menial acts for the poorest and meanest in the community.

In order to be of more use she added surgery to her other acquirements, and was especially expert in blood-letting. It was a favourite remedy in the sixteenth century, but cannot have been well suited to the ailments of women enfeebled by ague and low fever. Angélique seems to have used the lancet with considerable vigour. We hear of a nun with a sore foot which defied the unguents of Port Royal, and had to be treated by a surgeon from Paris. He said the cause of her suffering was that the membrane surrounding the bones had been punctured when she was bled.

On another occasion we hear of Angélique kneeling before a nun whom she is trying to bleed, and holding the foot in warm water for two hours until she is weak and weary, and the great drops of perspiration start from her brow.

Or we find her in the infirmary where there is a nun shivering so violently in a fit of ague that she cannot keep the bed-clothes on her narrow couch. The Abbess says 'merrily' that they are not heavy enough, and lies down across the bed over the sick woman's feet; and there, after some hours' search, she is found consoling and comforting her.

Very often when she was wanted in the parlour or for important matters she would be found in a corner of the kitchen, sitting on an upturned basket and talking to a lay-sister who had asked for her, and whom she had gone to seek so as not to interrupt her work. A novice once told her with many tears that she had a wound in the leg, which she had not spoken of, because she was afraid that if the Sisters knew it they would not receive her into the community. It had now become so much worse that concealment was no longer possible.

Angélique's compassion and sympathy were at once aroused. She said the matter should remain a secret which they would both keep faithfully. She undertook the surgical treatment of the case, and as one of the nuns was suffering in a similar manner was able to obtain the necessary remedies without applying for them in the dispensary. The sore leg was soon made sound by her care and judicious treatment, the novice took the veil in 1613, and as Sister Garnier was one of the most devoted nuns in Port Royal, ready to follow her Abbess whithersoever she might lead.

The memoirs of the nuns of Port Royal abound in anecdotes which show that it was at this time that the foundation of Angélique's influence was laid, and that she obtained it by her love and tender care for the bodies as well the souls of those around her. We see growing up under her hands the frugal, well-ordered household, in which there is no waste and no extravagance, something to spare for the poor and needy, and above all peace and goodwill. She was very open-handed, and always wished the abbey guests to be treated hospitably, but with the simplicity that befitted their entertainers. She gave the best fare to the Capuchin friars and poor monks who were not accustomed to receive it ; when it was urged that they did not get such good living in their own monasteries, she replied that as they had plenty of opportunities for mortifying the flesh, it might be well for them sometimes to receive thank-offerings. Nevertheless she was by no means pleased when these same guests, as was often the case, asked for and expected the best of everything.

Her first care had been to set her house in order, to remove abuses which had crept in, to re-establish the rules of poverty and strict seclusion, and to prepare her nuns for that absolute surrender of self, which the Cistercian order requires. She said that every tie, every affection, every appetite ought to be shaken off by those who had renounced the world, and could not therefore understand the true monk or nun thinking of what they should eat, what they should drink, or wherewithal they should be clothed. She desired to see their souls enriched by Divine love and sacred poverty, by humility and ardent charity, and thought everything around them should be poor and mean, so that they themselves might be living temples for the most High God. Churches and vestments she considered as the mere externals of religion and matters of no importance.

By degrees she induced the nuns to make all the changes required by the Cistercian rule. Silence was enforced, fasts were observed, matins were chanted at 2 A.M., and nuns shared with lay-sisters the menial work of the infirmary, the garden, and the kitchen. The ardour of those early times affected even the young children in the convent school. They also tried to find opportunities for mortification and penance, and for overcoming their likes and dislikes. It occurred to two of these children that an excellent method of attaining this end would be to gather something very nasty out of the garden, make it into tisane or herb tea, and drink it. So they collected their materials, taking, among other things, a number of berries of the deadly nightshade, which, doubtless, they had been told were very nasty indeed. In accordance with the example of the Sisters they felt that the 'act of mortification' must be accompanied by an 'act of charity'; so they told Marie Arnauld, who was then between nine and ten years old, and gave her permission to drink with them.

She was a very dainty little creature, whose fanciful appetite occasioned her sister, the Abbess, considerable trouble, and she would certainly not have discovered this form of mortification if left to herself; but she was quite as eager as her companions to follow the example of the nuns, and acceded at once to the proposal that she should drink the tisane. As she sat watching the others whilst they concocted it, a nun fortunately entered the room and saw that something was amiss, for little Marie was pale and trembling. She would not at first tell what was going on; but finally yielded to the persuasion of the Sister, and was immediately dispensed from the fulfilment of her promise, whilst her companions received a slight reprimand for their indiscreet zeal.

Before the renewal of Angélique's vows, and when her whole thoughts were occupied with plans for leaving Port Royal and retiring to the solitude of some remote monastery, she used constantly to talk to the children, especially to little Marie, of this life in the desert, where she would spend all her time in prayer to God. Indeed throughout the whole of her active and useful life the contemplation of this impossible future of solitude and prayer gave her the greatest joy. Little Marie was very fond of her sister, and made Angélique promise to take her into the desert also. Angélique, with her practical turn of mind, at once took advantage of this to check the child's dainty habits, telling her that she could not think of taking her where there would be nothing but roots and vegetables. And thus she taught the little one to overcome her likes and dislikes, and in later years to surpass all others in self-denial and contentment with the humblest and poorest fare.

The story deserves mention as explaining the secret of Angélique's success. Visionary and impossible as some of her aims may have been, there was always a practical application of them, and she seized on every sign of grace, every touch of relenting in those around her, to lead them onward in the difficult path of self-denial and self-sacrifice.

We have said that she did not think it right to accept assistance from her father until he approved of her design of reforming the monastery, and that in consequence of the supplies being cut off, which were at that time necessary to supplement their income, she and her nuns often suffered privation. She taught them to bear it joyfully, saying that poverty does not deserve its name unless it make us suffer. She had moreover an absolute certainty of conviction that God would provide all things necessary. It cost her no effort whatever to leave the future in His hands, and in the present she accepted everything, either privation or plenty, as from Him.

At that time it was very difficult for a portionless woman to obtain admission to a convent, for the *dowry* of the nuns increased the wealth of a rich house, or paid the debts of a poor one. Angélique always had a great dislike to the bargaining which went on between an abbess and the friends of a candidate, in which each tried to overreach the other, the abbess to get as much, and the friends to give as little as possible. She attributes this to her pride—*courage humain* —as she calls it, which made her think the traffic shameful and mean.

A Capuchin friar who preached at Port Royal found that only one or two of the nuns had been confirmed, and that not one of them knew the meaning of Confirmation or understood that it was one of the Sacraments of the Church. He explained it to them and begged the Archbishop, M. d'Auch, to go to Port Royal and confirm them. This was done; and the prelate, in his conversation with the young Abbess who was so anxious to learn her duty as well as willing to do it, told her that it was simony, the crime of Simon Magus, to exact payment for the reception of a nun. She had always felt it was disgraceful, and now she found it to be a sin. Many reverend fathers tried to convince her that this very inconvenient doctrine was a mistake; but her instinctive dislike to what was mean was strengthened by religious principle, and she was inflexible in her resolve never again to entertain the question of dowry, but to receive or refuse a candidate according to her fitness for the vocation. She would neither accept nor reject any one on account of money.

In those early days, when the poverty of the community must have sorely tried her father's kind and generous heart, many girls, daughters of wealthy parents, applied for admission to Port Royal. M. Arnauld may have used his influence in the matter, and have hoped indirectly to remove the pressure of poverty; but the Abbess very rarely approved of any of the candidates. She had suffered so much herself that she understood how grave an evil it is to compel a person to enter a monastery who is not attracted to the life.

A friend of her father's had, in spite of protests and entreaties, compelled his youngest son to enter the Church at twelve years old. One day when the poor boy was hunting, he was thrown from his horse and killed. Angélique was told of this and said: 'God.loved his mother too much to let her fault go unpunished. She had allowed her son to hold benefices, and he had no vocation for the Church.'

One day she was sitting in the parlour with a nun, when four candidates were ushered in. They came from Chartres; three of them had wealthy parents, who were prepared to give each daughter a handsome portion; the fourth was the daughter of an advocate, a man of good family, but very poor and with many children. He had nothing to give his girls, and therefore no chance of placing them in an ordinary monastery, but had been advised to send his Marie with the other three to Port Royal. As they entered the room the Abbess watched them closely, and whispered to the nun who sat by her: 'That little one at the back is the only one that will stay.'

And she did stay, whilst the others after due probation were sent home to their parents. She was Sister Marie des Anges, of whom we have more to hear. Angélique used to say : ' I saw at a glance her piety, modesty, and sweet humility ; her face showed them, and indeed on that first day she was in those respects exactly what she is now.'

It so happened once that a Sister who had taken the veil, brought with her a dowry which paid all the debts of the household and provided for their immediate wants ; just at the same time Angélique received payment for the sale of timber belonging to the abbey. She did not know what to do with so much money, and laughed at herself for her uneasiness, saying, God had done well to keep her poor, since a little money gave her so much anxiety.

The Cistercian rule enjoins the use of serge under garments, and Angélique desired to substitute them for linen, but the Prioress objected. She said that serge was dirty, and fostered vermin ; it would be far better to have coarse linen, so coarse that it would be even rougher than serge. Angélique replied that the want of cleanliness could be remedied by frequent washing, and as for linen, however rough it might be at first, it became soft with age. When her father heard of the proposed change he thought it arose from poverty, and therefore made her a present of linen for under garments. but she would not use it. And gradually by persuasion, enforced by that strongest of all arguments, her own example, she induced all the household to consent to this ' mortification of the flesh.'

On the point of total abstinence from meat she knew that she would have to encounter far more serious opposition. Already fast days were observed strictly, and meat was eaten only three times a week. Many of the Sisters strongly protested against any additional restrictions, and M. Arnauld, who feared for his daughter's health, offered to supply all the meat required if she proposed to give it up on the score of economy.

But this was not the case. The Abbot of Charmoye told her in 1612 that abstinence from meat was still wanting to complete the reform she had inaugurated. She saw at that time that such a step could not be attempted with any chance of success, so she waited for two years, and then with her usual unselfish zeal tried the experiment first of all upon herself. Every day a small portion of omelette covered over with a thin slice of mutton was served in the refectory, so that the good Prioress who came at that time to pay her respects to the Abbess, discovered no change in her diet; Angélique ate the omelette and left the mutton. Night and morning this was her repast for some months, until she had convinced herself that she required nothing more. When she had done so she found no difficulty in establishing abstinence from meat throughout the monastery. The Prioress reproachfully said that she had been imposed upon, but Angélique replied that she could not ask others to consent to a thing which she had not tried fairly for herself, and that she would have had great difficulty in making the experiment if the Sisters had disapproved of it. The rule of total abstinence in regard to meat was never broken after 1614 except by the doctor's orders, and in consequence of failing health or advancing age.

One of the chief difficulties of this time was that of finding a resident confessor and priest for the abbey. The old man who had acted in that capacity for many years left as soon as reform was established, saying that he was no longer fitted to direct the nuns. As he could not translate the *Pater* into French, opened no book except his breviary, and spent his time hunting, he was doubtless right. He was succeeded by Father Basil, who was young and rash, and who, after the memorable scene with M. Arnauld already referred to, was withdrawn from Port Royal. After that an aunt of Cardinal de Retz told M. Arnauld of a certain Englishman of the house of Pembroke, Father Archangel, a refugee who had become a Capuchin monk. He was now an old man, wise, good, and of great repute. M. Arnauld consented to his appointment as director, and Angélique was well pleased with him.

She says that if he had not been 'imbued with the writings of the casuists' he would have been a perfect monk, but these works had done him much harm. He gave her, however, 'the most useful advice she ever received,' namely, never, on any consideration, to allow the nuns to speak to a monk, not even to a Capuchin, and not although he preached like an angel. Father Archangel rarely visited Port Royal. When he used to appear riding on an ass, the only manner in which he would consent to travel when he grew old and infirm, there was great rejóicing in the community. Angélique and the old man were very good friends, and he appears to have told her many scandalous stories of Queen Elizabeth, which go far to prove the wisdom of his own advice that nuns and monks ought not to gossip together. When he was travelling from place to place Angélique often sent him supplies of bread and meat; and on one of these occasions he said, ' It is a misnomer to call you Madame de *Port* Royal, your true name is Madame de *Cœur* Royal, *royal hearted;* ' and the old Englishman was right. He asked Angélique to ally with him Father Gallot and Father Eustace de St. Paul, which she did; and these three visited Port Royal, preached there, and in those early days guided and directed the Abbess. She was too young, ardent, and practical to follow them in their casuistry or to be much affected by it, but they explained to her the rules of her order, told her of holy lives and bright examples, and unfolded to her the possibility of leading a pure, useful, and unselfish life. She and her nuns were all equally ignorant; we have already seen that they did not know the meaning of Confirmation; neither did any one of them know their Catechism. From time to time therefore M. Gallot went to Port Royal ostensibly to teach and explain the Catechism to the pupils in the convent school. The Abbess and nuns were present, and derived great advantage from these lessons.

Still the difficulty of finding an ordinary resident confessor was not solved, and Angélique says that she was always inquiring for a good confessor, and whenever she heard of one she applied at once to her ecclesiastical superior and he was despatched to Port Royal. But monks who were weak and foolish, and monks who were wicked, wrought her constant disappointment. Their immorality was well known, and had to be guarded against; or rather a scandal in one monastery was the signal for removing the confessor from it and placing him elsewhere, whilst he was replaced by another as depraved as himself.

It will be remembered that at Port Royal Angélique gravely reproved the monk and nuns when she was twelve years old, and that she was on her guard against the young preacher whose sermon had so greatly excited her when she was seventeen. When she was twenty the community was exposed to

great danger from the confessor, but his intrigues were discovered, and she dismissed him with a stern rebuke.

'Ask God to forgive your sins,' she said, 'and know that
so long as you live you shall never enter within these walls.
We know you now. Go, I will never see you again.'

She found that what she calls that 'curious' passion, avarice,
which was characteristic of nuns as well as monks, was encouraged by the priests. They spoke of 'spoiling the
Egyptians,' and said that it was a service done to God to
obtain wealth for Him which would otherwise be squandered
in extravagant living and the keeping of dogs and horses. But
Angélique could not see that the wealth of religious houses
was spent in any better manner, or that rich vestments and
lavish expenditure in the monastery was a more legitimate
excess than that practised in the world. She discovered that
there was as much emulation in the Church with regard
to ornaments and vestments as there was in society as to
dress and jewels; abbots and abbesses were as anxious to
obtain new chants and keep them for the exclusive use of
their own convent as art collectors were to obtain a
masterpiece.

Angélique says that she cared nothing for any of these
things, and that her indifference did not arise from religion
or piety, but because they seemed to her so trivial. But she
saw that the priests profited by them, and had every reason to
promote the relaxation of rules which she was striving to
restore to their primitive severity, and to foster the spirit of
self-indulgence and self-gratification which she was trying to
subdue. She therefore opposed them upon principle and in
practice, and they were bitter in their denunciations of the
'infatuated girl,' and the nuns whom she had 'bewitched.'

Some years later, she wrote : ' I want to show what assistance
and advice nuns may expect to receive from monks, and I
will only point out where they fail to lead us aright, choosing
to be silent as to those darker ways by which they lead us to
evil. When an abbess is proud the confessor is her lacquey.
I have seen one at work in the garden of an abbess, laying
out the beds and borders in devices to represent her monogram
and arms. I have seen another bearing the train of a proud
abbess's robe as a lacquey bears that of a great lady. And
then if an abbess is humble and respects the priestly office,

the confessor becomes a master and tyrant, so that she dare do nothing without his orders, which are *dis*-orders.'

She goes on to say how anxious the monks are to involve monasteries in lawsuits, as it is a sure means of gratifying themselves by a journey to Paris, which is as pernicious to their own souls as it is to the welfare of the monastery ; how they ridicule all notions of reform, and laugh at the nuns for giving up the use of masks and gloves and starched frills ; how they have their own private *peculium* or property, buy and sell, rent farms, spend their time at the chase, and so on.   She continues : ' I will not speak of the expense which they entail, for although their theory is that priests whom they call *secular*, receive much higher salary than monks who ask for nothing but food and clothing, my own experience is quite the reverse.   Because not only does the food and clothing of the confessor amount to just whatever he pleases, but there is a continual influx of monks to the convent, so that dozens at a time come to partake of our hospitality, and the confessor's table is a very good *table d'hôte*.   Bachelors of art are sent to us, and we must bear the expense of procuring their degree as doctors of divinity. And then there are the confessor's nephews who must be provided for, and in short so many other things that if they were written down they would astonish all honest people.

'There is a celebrated abbey belonging to our order in Flanders, and when the babies in that neighbourhood cry, their mothers say, " Hush, baby, hush, and you shall be a Pater at Flyne." . . . A person who had been there assured me that in the confessional he had counted as many as seventeen little pillows, with which the confessor made himself comfortable.'   She proceeds to tell of a certain wicked old abbot who always shed tears at the benediction of an abbess if the sum of money presented to him on the occasion was less than he expected, and who was such a miser that he died with his purse in his hand.

We must bear in mind that Angélique could not discover an abuse without trying to remove it, and we shall not be surprised to find that the experience gained in her youth influenced her strongly and made her ultimately resort to the only measure which seemed to offer a remedy for all these evils.

CHAPTER VII.

THE SISTERS.

WHEN Agnes resigned the Abbey of St. Cyr in order to join Angélique she retained her dress as a Benedictine novice, but in 1612 she took the veil at Port Royal, and thus became a member of the Cistercian order. She had desired to take this step sooner, but Angélique would not accede to her request, for she thought that although her sister's nature was pure and good there were no signs of grace about her.

Agnes was devout, but she was also proud and ambitious. She asked God why she had not been born a Princess of France, and despised as well as disliked the humiliations and penance which were deemed essential in the training of a novice. Before she entered on her probation Angélique asked her whether she could submit to the punishment that would be inflicted upon her if, for example, she was late at church or in the refectory; she answered coldly and proudly that she should not be late.

The two sisters were very unlike in character; Angélique large-hearted, clear-headed, and strongly attracted by practical work. Agnes reserved, proud, and in these early years self-engrossed. Angélique, as we have seen, turned to Plutarch's Lives for interest and amusement, but Agnes to the Life of St. Theresa. She was deeply tinged with mysticism, longed for a life of prayer, and had a strong tendency towards asceticism. When she was fourteen Father Archangel said that she would become one of the most illustrious nuns in France; Angélique had faith in this prediction, and resolved to try and remove every defect which might mar the perfection of her sister's character.

One day when Agnes was carrying a can of oil to clean the choir lamps she spilt it over her dress and on the steps of the church. Any other novice would have been greatly troubled at such an accident, but to the lips of Agnes rose the words, ' Thy name is as oil poured forth ' ; for visible things were only an image of the spiritual truths on which she was always meditating. However she did what she could to remedy the disaster by wiping up the oil, and then she went to her abbess sister, and very gravely confessed a fault which did not particularly affect her. Angélique, who also looked beyond the immediate present, thought this an excellent opportunity ' to make the virgin's lamp burn the brighter for the loss of the oil,' so she said that the greasy dress must be worn unwashed until the due time came for changing it. She knew that this would be the severest punishment she could inflict on the young girl ; for she was very fastidious, and yet so scrupulous and attentive to all her duties that it had hitherto been impossible to check or punish what the Abbess considered a grievous fault in a nun. For six weeks Agnes wore the dress by day and slept in it at night ; ' it was a horrible mortification to her,' says Angélique, which we can well believe.

Angélique thought it an *imperfection* in Agnes that she had a tendency to work beyond her strength, for she saw that although this arose partly from the ardour of her nature there was also a touch of pride in it which made her shrink from the possibility of being rebuked for duty unfulfilled. She saw also that prayer and fasting were in danger of leading her away from the practical work for which they ought to have prepared her.

One day as a ' mortification ' the Abbess sent for her when she was in church, and she went out 'weeping bitterly.' Many years afterwards Angélique said, ' Ah, Mother Abbess, do you remember the day when I fetched you weeping from the choir, because you cared for nothing but prayer? It is forty years ago, but I am sure that if I were to keep you away from church now you would weep as bitterly as you did then. Certainly there is no cure for our old diseases.'

As she was a delicate girl Angélique would not always allow her to attend matins, which were chanted at 2 A.M., and this privation always cost her many tears.

She did not, however, neglect any duty assigned to her, and

looked upon all work as sacred, doing it 'with her might.'
She would scour the kitchen pans with such energy that her
fingers were blistered, and was so much respected by the
novices that she was appointed their Mistress whilst she was
herself a novice.   She fulfilled her duties admirably ; and
trained her pupils to habits of obedience, industry, charity, and
piety, so that not one of the nuns resented the appointment
or felt that it had been ill-bestowed.   In 1612, when she was
nineteen, she took the veil, and henceforward was a fellow-
worker with her sister.

When Mdme. des Portes was placed in charge of the
Abbey of St. Cyr, which she was to hold until Agnes was
twenty, M. Arnauld stipulated that she should maintain and
educate the little Abbess elect and one of her sisters ;
the sister chosen was Anne, born in 1594, and one year
younger than Agnes.   Anne is the little girl who used to go
with Agnes to Port Royal to play with Angélique; like Agnes,
she was brought up to the strict observance of forms and
ceremonies, and was shocked to find that their sister thought
that as she was an Abbess she need not pay any attention
to them.   Anne was attracted by monastic life, or rather
she says that she was very fond of her sister Angélique, and
at thirteen she expressed a wish to be a nun and live at Port
Royal.   Her father did not approve of this proposal, and said
that he would never consent to it.   He had yielded to the
wish of his father-in-law, M. Marion, with regard to Angélique
and Agnes, and was not sorry to see two of his daughters holding abbeys.   Matters, however, were not so prosperous as he
had expected they would have been, for at that time Angélique
had begun to cause them great anxiety.   When, therefore, in
1608, Anne went to Andilly for the vintage with Angélique,
Agnes, and Marie, she was not allowed to return to St. Cyr ;
indeed the pleasant country life very soon made the thought
of a convent distasteful.   She was at once introduced into
society, and at fourteen was amusing herself with the pleasures
and vanities of the world, and had forgotten the pious resolves
of her childhood.

Anne, like Angélique, had at one time some idea of becoming a Huguenot.   But the motives guiding the two sisters
were not alike. Angélique wished to escape from the monastery
and enter the world.   Anne, who was in the world, found her

Catholic friends most 'lamentably ignorant of all that concerned Christian piety,' and thought that her Huguenot relations had a monopoly of all the Christian virtues. This made her doubt which of the two could be the true faith, and she had almost come to the conclusion that it must be what was called the heresy, and had begun to reflect on what it would cost her to leave the Catholic Church ; but in 1613 she was attacked by small-pox, she expected to die, was tormented by fear of the wrath of God, and in her anguish vowed to serve Him absolutely and entirely in whichever was the true religion. She recovered, and seems to have thought no more of Protestantism. Probably it was at Port Royal, whither she had gone as soon as she was convalescent, that she learned to believe she had already found the true faith, and need make no further inquiry. Next there was a project of marriage with a gentleman for whom she seems to have felt some affection. But her father broke off the negotiation. Angélique told him she was sorry he had done so, for she believed Anne's affections were engaged. Upon this the father sent his eldest son d' Andilly to say that if Anne wished it the affair should go on; but she, weeping, begged that no further steps might be taken. The world, of which she had seen so little, was growing distasteful to her.

She returned to Paris in 1615 after a long absence, and found it in a panic because the Prince de Condé's army was expected to lay siege to the city, and reduce it by famine and fire. She thought then of the peace of those who had left the world, and who had no fear of death before their eyes.

Her father spoke to her again of marriage, but this time she answered :

' I assure you, dear father, that if your M. de Guise could and would marry me, who am only a *petite demoiselle*, I would not accept him. I must be the bride of a greater than he.'

Her mother first heard of her wish to be a nun from Angélique, and exclaimed: ' Impossible ! How will she ever make up her mind to obey you, when she finds it so difficult to obey her father and me? Truly one may say that religion works miracles if it ever comes to pass !'

Application was next made to M. Arnauld for his permission, which was refused. In his usual formal and roundabout manner he desired Mdme. le Maître to tell Anne that he would never give his consent to such a step whilst he lived, but that after his death she should be free to do as she pleased; that meanwhile he would not urge her to marry, but would simply inform her of the various suitors for her hand; neither would he compel her to take any part in the pleasures of the world if she disliked to do so, but would leave her absolutely free in every respect and at full liberty to see any of the religious ladies who did her the honour of taking an interest in her welfare.

Father Archangel was consulted, and he told Anne that, since her father demanded nothing that could be detrimental to her vocation, he should advise her to remain at home and follow her usual pursuits for twelve months. Anne accepted the advice, and acted upon it. For twelve months she remained 'in the world,' taking part in its pleasures, but longing for the time when she should join Angélique and Agnes and little Marie at Port Royal.

Still she said afterwards that it was a happy time, and she enjoyed this year very much. She visited convents and churches, and was a devout spectator of religious ceremonies and services, her heart dancing within her as she thought how soon these would be all in all to her. Before long whatever she saw or heard called up an image of this future life that filled her soul, and even a ballet which was performed before the Princesses of France transported her with joy, and seemed a foreshadowing of the ineffable beauties of Paradise.

Her father's opposition died out before this enthusiasm; but when he found that she had scruples about going to Port Royal because she feared the love of her sisters was drawing her thither, and that she had some thought of joining the Carmelites, he was very angry, and said if she must be a nun she should go to Port Royal and Port Royal only. Then she urged that the abbey was in the King's gift, and if Angélique died it would pass into other hands, and there would be an end of the reform, which was its great attraction. Numerous conferences ensued, at which Father Archangel was present; all the members of the family made long speeches, but they did not address any one in particular or say exactly what they meant.

One day Anne left the room, and joined Mdme. le Maître. Her father noticed it, and, thinking she would speak her mind more freely to her sister, followed her and *listened at the door.* Anne saw him there and showed herself equal to the occasion. She said at once that she had finally resolved to do whatever should be most pleasing to her dear father. Whereupon the proud and happy man rushed into the room and drew from his pocket a *Brevet du Roi* or deed by which, in case of Angélique's death, the abbey was secured to Anne.

Poor man, his business faculty never deserted him, but a more unsatisfactory set of children to plot and plan for no father ever had.

After many delays, for giving up Anne cost him a considerable struggle, she was allowed to go to Port Royal and commence her noviciate in October 1616. Her sisters and the nuns received her with great joy. Agnes, who was Mistress of the Novices, told her, laughing, that if they followed the rule of St. Benedict, they ought to greet her with insult and abuse in order to try if her vocation was real ; but still, although she had not called her a fool, she intended to treat her as one, and to teach her humility and implicit obedience.

On the following day her father left without seeing her, for he could not bear the pain of saying good-bye ; and then Anne bade farewell to her mother and eldest sister, Mdme. le Maître. Her father was told that she had shed tears at parting, and he returned instantly to seek her and beg her to go back to Paris with him. She entreated him to leave her, but was so undecided and agitated on that day that she was afraid she would not have courage to persevere.

When she retired to her bare little cell at night she covered the small table with a clean white cloth, and seems, as far as she was able, to have made such preparations for her toilette as she would have done at home. The Abbess, who entered and saw it, says that she 'laughed in her heart,' but said nothing that night. On the morrow all Anne's dainty little appointments were removed ; she did not know the reason of it, and when at night she again found her cell quite bare she spread a clean white handkerchief over the table. But Angélique was inexorable ; everything must go, and Anne must learn to understand 'the mystery of the poverty of Christ.'

Up to that time the postulants, or candidates who were upon approval, had retained their secular dress ; but when Anne came Angélique designed a simple garment for them, which was henceforward worn. It was a loose grey robe cut on the cross, fastened round the throat, and hanging to the feet. All kinds of work could be done in it, and this Anne found when she cleaned the fowl-house, the first office to which she was appointed.

She had not been long at Port Royal when Father Suffren came from Paris to see her. She was at work in the kitchen, and was told to go immediately to the parlour. So she appeared before him in her long straight gown, over which was tied a large black apron; a knife was hanging by her side, and she had such hands as might be expected from the fact that her last occupation had been to scour the saucepans.

The good father exclaimed: 'Verily, Mademoiselle, I never saw you so adorned; but don't you want some unguents for your hands?'

Now care of her pretty white hands, and procuring rare ointments and washes for them, had been one of Anne's chief vanities. But she laughed merrily, and said the water in which she washed the saucepans would do very well, and she wanted nothing more.

Among the numerous memoirs which form the material for a history of this period, there is one written by Anne herself, giving an account of the impression which conventual life produced on her at that time.

She says the first thing which struck her was the solitude of Port Royal; and that after Paris it seemed to her like the deserts of the Thebaid, and she liked it for that reason. And there was not only the solitude which it owed to its position, remote from towns or cities, there was also a solitude within the monastery, and God made them love this separation from the world, fulfilling His words: 'I will allure her, and bring her into the wilderness and speak comfortably unto her.'

And there was great simplicity in the community. Looking back upon this period after many years had passed, Anne writes:

'It was the simplicity of childhood. We loved the books that were given to us to read because they were given to us, and we received them as the gift of God.

'Sister Agnes taught us to pray, not in any set and fixed manner, but according to the way in which she saw that God had touched our hearts. She saw how much I longed to know God and to be near Him; and she taught me when I prayed, to say: "The meditation of my heart is always in Thy presence."

'When I first entered Port Royal I felt, as it were, a great void in my soul, which made me very unhappy. I told Sister Agnes, and she said that I must not be surprised at this, for I had given up everything upon earth and had not yet been consoled by God; so that I was, as it were, between heaven and earth. About a year afterwards I felt that this void was filled up.

'Also in the first year my mind was troubled by a great fear of the wrath of God, and by doubt and disbelief. Father Gallot advised them to let me read the life of St. Theresa written by herself, and this consoled and helped me, so that I knew the book had been sent to me by God.'

The last remark is characteristic of Anne Arnauld. She always prayed to God to help those from whom she asked advice, and entreated Him to guide them by His spirit; and she always returned thanks to God and not to man. She never said, 'I received great help from such a one;' but always, 'God helped me greatly through such a one.'

'All the novices,' she says, 'were very anxious to improve, and all were animated by love for the duties of their vocation. We rose at two to say matins, and did not go to bed again after that time. The church was very cold, but no one complained of it, and our clothing was not much warmer in winter than in summer. We used to go into the kitchen by turns for a week together. There we were placed under a lay-sister, whom we obeyed as if she had been a nun. We liked hard work of all kinds, and I was particularly fond of sweeping the floors, remembering that St. Theresa took great pleasure in it. In the summer mornings we used to go into the garden and dig in silence and with great zeal.

'Port Royal is situated in a deep valley, and might well have seemed desolate and lonely, but, instead of that, when I looked up at the sky through the dormitory windows I used to fancy that it was more serene than anywhere else. Everything consoled me. I remember once, when I was sad, that I was comforted by seeing the stars; and another time I was made glad by hearing our three bells chiming and making a sweet harmony.

'The nuns went into the refectory before entering the

church, and there began chanting the Benedicite and thanks-
givings, which they continued in procession and ended in
the church.   It was so beautiful that the first time I heard it
it made me think of Paradise.   Moreover, I especially liked
the reading aloud at meal-times ; and when one thinks of the
manner in which meals are eaten in the world, this seems to
me one of the most valuable of observances.

'Whilst I was a novice a lay-sister died.   M. de Charmoye
was present at her death and burial, and I think that the
funeral ceremony of Henri IV., which I saw, was not nearly
so beautiful or so devout.

''There was at that time a young nun named Claire Martine
at Port Royal, who was really perfect ; and when I heard the
lives of the saints read aloud I used to think that she had all
their virtues.   I was in the infirmary at the same time that she
was, and used to watch her, and she was so pure and good
that to judge from her life one would have thought that Adam
had not fallen. . . . She had a special love for the poor, and
delight in labour done for them ; and this love of the poor and
of almsgiving was characteristic of all the Sisters.

'After I had taken the veil I was filled with such gladness
to think I was a nun that once, when I was alone, I could not
help dancing for joy; and when I saw a nun with a sad
countenance, I thought she need only look at her black veil
to be sad no more.'

Henceforward Anne Arnauld is Sister Anne Eugénie de
l'Incarnation, and we leave her for the present and return
to her younger sister, that little Marie, M. Arnauld's twelfth
child, whom he allowed Angélique to take back with her
from Andilly, in the hope that the child would cheer and
console her.

Marie was born in Paris in 1600, and was a little prodigy of
wit and beauty.   We are told that she spoke distinctly ' before
she was weaned,' and that in society every one noticed and
petted the baby girl as the prettiest thing that could be seen.
She had been named after the Virgin, to whom she looked as
her protectress, and her biographers see the germs of her
later piety in the devotion to the Virgin which she showed as
a child of three years old.   In driving through Paris, whenever a picture or statue of the Virgin was passed, she insisted
on having the carriage stopped and her mask taken off—for

young children as well as nuns and fine ladies wore masks to preserve their complexion—and she would then stand at the carriage door and make a curtsey to the Virgin.

Her beauty was short-lived. She had the small-pox before she was four years old, and as her parents were very anxious that her face should not be marked, she was smeared with some kind of plaster which was supposed to be an infallible remedy against disfigurement. But a few hours afterwards she became delirious, and the fever ran so high that Mdme. Arnauld was afraid that in trying to preserve her beauty she ran great risk of losing her child, and insisted that, at any cost, the plaster should be removed. This was done, but the skin was terribly lacerated and the child's face not only marked but changed ; after she recovered whenever she passed a mirror the poor little coquette would put her tiny hand before her face, and say : ' *Ce n'est plus moi*,' ' That's not Marie.'

Perhaps the loss of her beauty may account for M. Arnauld's willingness to allow her to go to Port Royal.

When Angélique was sixteen and Marie seven, the little one was sent to *divert* the young Abbess, and, except for the few moments when he angrily demanded that Agnes and Marie should be given up, her father seems to have had no serious thought of withdrawing her from the monastery whilst she was a child, but he did not expect she would become a nun. He had witnessed Angélique's despair at finding herself chained to a vocation which she had not chosen; there had been good reason to fear that she might resign her abbey and even incur the disgrace of becoming a Huguenot. He had purchased obedience to his will and submission to her fate at a high price. It had cost the Abbey of St. Cyr, which he had allowed Agnes to resign so that she might be a companion to her sister, and he had also given up the younger child as a plaything. He was an affectionate man, who really loved his children, and tried to do well for them. He had procured for two of them the rank of abbess, state and power and an easy pleasant life. And they had renounced it all, had chosen hard work and poor fare, poverty and humiliation. He had provided for them the highest seats at the festival, and they had begun with shame to go down and take the lowest places. When other sisters wished to follow their example he hesitated; did not yield until he believed the vocation was freely chosen. At the last moment, as the reader will remember, he would have taken Anne back with him to Paris if she would have consented to return, and he now found it very difficult to give up all hope of having Marie home some day.

She spent three or four months every summer with her parents, but returned to Port Royal as her home. When she was eleven years old she began to have a taste for the world, and to enjoy the pleasant country life at Andilly; and that year for the first time she shed tears when she was going back to Port Royal. She was questioned about it, but gave an evasive answer, for if her father had discovered the truth he would not have allowed her to return.

Angélique soon found that an enemy 'had sown tares among the wheat,' but she was afraid 'lest she should destroy the good seed with the bad'; so she was patient, bore with Marie's peevish temper and changed manner and indifference to all that had formerly interested her, until the child's heart turned again to this noble, gentle sister with her high aspirations, saintly life, and tenderness to all around her.

Marie was always specially Angélique's child, trained by her to habits of self-denial and obedience. It was Marie who learnt to eat simple food in order that she might accompany her sister to the desert, and she was taught that she was not merely to receive but to *choose* everything that was poor and mean. With her natural love of neat and pretty things she is to be dressed in shabbier clothes than anyone else, and to be able to laugh when her schoolfellows tease her about her old gown and say she does not care. She must learn to like menial work, cooking and washing and scrubbing the floors, and this was easy enough to her as it is to most girls. She had also to go into the dispensary, which she particularly disliked. She undertook this office from obedience, and when she found that it was distasteful she devoted herself specially to that work for the rest of her life. Not that she was actually always at work in the dispensary, but she was very often there, superintended all the assistants and gave orders for everything that was prepared. The post was no sinecure, for as we have said the infirmary was always full.

She is the little child who waited trembling for the poisonous tisane, which she was ready to drink for a 'mortification;' and through life she often waited trembling, but she never shrank from any duty, or neglected any work because it was unpleasant. She learnt in early life that she was to overcome 'likes and dislikes,' and the lesson was never forgotten.

Angélique's love for the child was of the highest and noblest kind, and was shown in her efforts to make Marie pure and holy. At twelve years old she entered upon her noviciate, and in 1616, before she was seventeen, she took the veil. Young as she was, at this critical period she was the leading spirit among the novices. She had the earnest and enthusiastic nature of the Arnaulds and their power of influencing others. She had learnt to be obedient, humble, patient, loving, and silent. She was always striving to improve, and she led the other novices by her example. They followed her in a path along which she used to say no one could *walk*, for the feeble souls who thought they were getting on fast enough were already far behind. This again is characteristic of the Arnaulds. None of them can walk in the right path, they must all run.

There are now four sisters in Port Royal. The Abbess has begun to find that reform is no easy task; the world is against her, the priests are against her, and the nuns seldom yield without opposition and resistance. All her hopes therefore rest on the novices, who may be trained to become her fellow-workers. She has recruited largely from her own family. Agnes, having resigned her abbey, is Mistress of the Novices, and Marie is the novice whom all the others look up to and try to imitate; Anne, the fashionable young lady from Paris, is in the first fervour of her conversion, and at present is absorbed and self-engrossed, longing for communion with God, and attracted chiefly by the silence and solitude of monastic life.

Everything indicates preparation, waiting for work to be done and the girding on of armour for the fray.

CHAPTER VIII.

THE monks of Citeaux used to speak of the *Good Women* (bourgeoises) of St. Antoine des Champs, the *Ladies* of Maubuisson, and the *Nuns* of Port Royal. These *Ladies* of Maubuisson had as Abbess Angélique d'Estrées, originally Abbess of Bertancourt, in the diocese of Amiens. Her sister Gabrielle d'Estrées, who resided with her at Bertancourt, thought she was at too great a distance from Paris and Henri IV. She therefore induced him to bestow the Abbey of Maubuisson upon Mdme. Angélique, and he did so, after obtaining possession of it by a very disreputable trick. Maubuisson was only a few miles from Paris ; the King and the court passed much of their time there, and it was a fashionable retreat for women of good family who were compelled to take the veil and were not deterred by the flagrant immorality of the inmates of the convent.

In 1616 Gabrielle and her royal lover were dead. Henri IV. had been succeeded by his son Louis XIII. But Maubuisson was unchanged, and the scandalous lives of the Abbess and her nuns were beginning to be considered as an outrage upon public morality.

The Abbess had twelve children ; four grown-up daughters attended her as maids of honour ; doubtless in childhood they had been Angélique Arnauld's companions (it will be remembered that she passed her noviciate at Maubuisson, and took the veil there at nine years old). The Abbess was preparing her youngest child, who was the daughter of a nobleman, to succeed her as Abbess of Maubuisson. The others were educated and treated in accordance with the rank of their respective fathers.

It is said that it was Louis XIII. himself who desired the Abbot of Citeaux to investigate the charges brought against Mdme. d'Estrées and her nuns. The result of the first inquiry was to compel her to resign the Abbey of Bertancourt, which for twenty-five years she had held in addition to that of Maubuisson. The Abbot then sent word that he proposed to visit and inspect Maubuisson. It is scarcely necessary to say that there had been no inspection in Mdme. d'Estrées' time. She received the two monks who were the Abbot's messengers with angry reproaches, caused them to be imprisoned and kept without food, and added many further indignities. When she thought they had received a sufficient lesson she sent them back to their superior.

She relied on her influential friends and relatives to hush up the inquiry, and expected the matter to go no further. Very probably they suggested that it would be well to silence opposition by an assumed appearance of submission and reform. In 1616, when she was on her way to Chartres, she visited her former novice, Angélique, now Abbess of Port Royal, and asked her advice. She said that she should very much like to reform Maubuisson, but that it would be a difficult thing to do, and she should require the co-operation of some good and experienced woman to bring the matter to a successful termination. Angélique did not doubt her sincerity, and as she retained a warm affection for the house where she had been child-novice and nun she said that if she could be of any use she would gladly leave Port Royal and go to Maubuisson as Mdme. d'Estrées' prioress, and there do everything in her power to further her designs. Perhaps as the Ladies of Maubuisson had known her as a child they might feel more affection for her than for a stranger.

Mdme. d'Estrées did not close with this offer; but she had obtained all that she wanted. Her visit to Port Royal would be talked of by the Arnaulds in Paris and at court; the Abbot of Citeaux would wait in the hope that she would relieve him of the necessity of undertaking a difficult and painful task; and the Ladies of Maubuisson, for they were never spoken of as nuns, would rally round and support her at the mere suggestion of *reform* under the auspices of Mdme. de Port Royal.

No further steps were taken for two years, and then the Abbot was again assailed by remonstrance and protests, and he therefore despatched a Commissioner to Maubuisson to demand an audience in his name, and inquire into the conduct of the Abbess. But the Abbess suspected his mission, excused herself for that day on the plea of illness, and the Commissioner and his suite were conducted to one of the towers of the abbey, where doubtless they expected to be hospitably entertained. As soon as they had all entered the outer door was fastened, and they found that they were prisoners. They were kept for four days on bread and water, and very little even of that, and the Commissioner was flogged daily. They believed that the Abbess intended to starve them to death, and on the fourth day contrived to escape from a window and make their way back to the Abbot.

By this time he was convinced that he must resort to more active measures, so he went to Paris, and saw Cardinal de Sourdis, cousin of the Abbess, and Marshal d'Estrées her brother. He found that at length she had committed a fault which her relations could not pardon, and they were willing to withdraw their protection, and allow the Abbot to take such steps as he might see fit. One of her younger sisters was a novice at Maubuisson, and without the consent or knowledge of any other relative, she had given her in marriage to the Count de Sanzi, one of her own disreputable companions. The marriage had been solemnized in the abbey church, and it was considered so disgraceful that for a time Mdme. d'Estrées was forsaken by all her friends.

At the close of the year 1617 the Abbot commenced his journey to Maubuisson. He sent word that he was on his way, so that the Abbess might have time for consideration. He expected that she would now submit, and quite hoped to convince her of the necessity of adopting his advice and following his plans. She told his messenger that she would neither receive his visit nor listen to his proposals. The Abbot, however, had gone too far to retreat; he continued his journey, and on his arrival went to the chapter house, and there convened a meeting of the whole community. According to the custom on such occasions he then saw the nuns alone, one by one, questioned them, and afterwards re-assembled the Chapter and again summoned the Abbess.

She refused to attend, saying that she was ill.

He despatched a still more urgent message, imploring her out of consideration to her own interest to obey him. It was in vain; and so were the formal and peremptory commands which he next issued, and which she treated with contempt. In her absence, he drew up a report, or *carte de visite*, and returned to Paris, going, it is said, direct to the King and informing him of all that had passed.

The disclosures made by the nuns showed the existence of evils of such magnitude that they could not be hushed up; and the Abbess clearly was resolved to persevere in her wicked ways. It was therefore decided that she should be removed and imprisoned, and the monastery governed by commission. Early in February 1618 the Abbot of Citeaux was again on his way to Maubuisson, and this time he was armed with authority to convey the Abbess to the *Filles Penitentes* at Paris; and he had with him a company of archers, as they continued to be called, although they were armed with muskets and swords, and resembled the modern gens-d'armes.

As he still hoped that extreme measures would be unnecessary, he left the archers and their captain in the neighbouring town of Pontoise, and arrived at Maubuisson without military escort. The Abbess had been warned of her danger and urged to escape if she valued her liberty, unless she intended to comply with the demand of M. de Citeaux, and reform the abbey. But she laughed, and said there was no danger while she had such good friends to protect her, and again she prepared to set the Superior at defiance.

She refused to see him, once more urging the plea of ill-health; for two days he waited patiently, whilst first one and then another of her companions entreated her to submit, and come to terms with him. She was inflexible; so on the third day he sent to Pontoise for the archers.

When they arrived all the doors were closed against them, and, after a vain appeal for admission in the king's name, they broke open doors and windows, forced their way in, and two hundred and fifty men took possession of the abbey.

The Abbess was now convinced that matters were desperate; she hastily tore off all her clothes, rushed out of her own apartments, and concealed herself in the bed of a nun on whom she could rely. Throughout the whole day the archers searched for her in every part of the house. Each room was closely guarded, and towards evening it was discovered that something was moving in one of the apparently unoccupied beds; on examination this proved to be the Abbess. But a new difficulty arose; she was quite naked, and she refused to clothe herself. As she was absolutely unapproachable she seemed likely after all to remain master of the situation. The captain of the troop of archers was summoned, and he expostulated and argued, but with no result; at length he lost temper and patience, called four archers, told them to take each a corner of the mattrass, carry bed and Abbess into the courtyard, put them into the carriage which was waiting, and drive with all speed to Paris.

One of the nuns was sent with her, and she was safely lodged in the *Filles Penitentes.*

The Abbot had kept out of the way while the archers were at Maubuisson, but as soon as Mdme. d'Estrées had been removed he entered, summoned the whole community, informed them that the convent would now be governed by commission, and offered them the choice of three abbesses of the Cistercian order, of whom Angélique Arnauld was one.

They asked time for consideration, and passed the whole night in anxious thought. They had a pleasant recollection of the sweet bright child whom they had nearly all known, but were afraid of her reforms, which were already talked about. Still the elder nuns, trusting to their own influence to modify her views, were strongly inclined to select her; but the others would not consent, nor could they agree in the choice of any one to replace Mdme. d'Estrées. At length they hit upon what they considered a happy expedient, and in the morning humbly entreated the Abbot not to place a stranger over them, but to let them be governed by one of their own community, and to allow them to leave the selection of the fitting person entirely in his hands.

He complied at once, and expressed great satisfaction at their decision. He remembered what had escaped their minds, namely, that Angélique had taken the veil at Maubuisson, and was consequently one of their own community.

He returned well pleased to Paris, but found it no easy matter to persuade M. Arnauld to allow Angélique to undertake so difficult a task as the one that he had resolved to entrust to her. Her father knew the zeal with which she would throw herself into the reform of Maubuisson, but feared for her health, if not her life, in the labour and anxiety it would entail. Still father, mother, brothers, and sisters were all now on her side, were convinced of the value and importance of the work she had begun, and glad to promote it as best they could. M. Arnauld's objections were at length overborne; he consented, though with reluctance; and went himself to Port Royal to tell his daughter of the proposal. There was in Angélique's nature the ardour, love of adventure, true piety, and capacity for self-sacrifice which impel to missionary work; she said this was just what she longed for, a true labour of love, and if it entailed real hardship and great difficulty, why so much the better. Before her father left it was arranged that the Abbot of Citeaux should go to Port Royal on the 17th of February, 1618, that on the 18th Anne Arnauld should take the veil, and on the 19th the Abbess and those companions whom she might select should go to her father's house in Paris under the escort of the Abbot, and from thence to Maubuisson.

Port Royal was to be governed in her absence by the Prioress, whose fidelity had never wavered; whilst Agnes Arnauld was to fill the post of sub-prioress.

Angélique, who was now twenty-six years old, decided that three nuns should accompany her. Doubtless M. Arnauld had enlightened her as to the nature and difficulty of the task before her, and the character of Mdme. d'Estrées and her companions. Her choice shows her practical wisdom and tact.

She took the Mère de la Croix, one of the oldest nuns in Port Royal, who had accompanied her when she returned, after her consecration as Abbess, to say good-bye to the Ladies of Maubuisson. The Mère de la Croix had been her faithful ally at Port Royal, and had been instrumental in winning over the elder nuns to consent to the reformation of the convent. Her co-operation at this critical time would be most valuable; but Angélique saw also the necessity of zeal and enthusiasm to kindle the dull and darkened hearts of those with whom she would have to deal.

Her second associate was therefore her young sister Marie, not yet eighteen, or Marie-Claire as we must now call her, and the third was Isabelle-Agnes, nineteen years old, one of the portionless girls who had been rejected elsewhere and welcomed at Port Royal. Isabelle-Agnes had already been three years novice and nun, and Angélique had taken special pains to train her for future work; she was to be Mistress of the Novices at Maubuisson, the post which Marie-Claire had lately held at Port Royal.

Angélique told these two young nuns that when they had dedicated themselves to God they had offered to spend their lives in His service; that hitherto they had received no visible sign of the acceptance of their offering, but that now this mission was a sign; they must accept it with a determination to sacrifice health and strength and even life if they could hope thereby to help those who were in great need. Up to this time she said that she had imposed upon them a rule of discretion in all that they did, but now she removed it and imposed only a rule of extreme charity, which should make them forget themselves, their own interests, and their own wishes, so that they might be instrumental in promoting the salvation of souls. Then she turned to Marie-Claire and said that knowing the delicacy of her constitution, and not doubting that if she did not lose her life she would certainly sacrifice her health, she had already selected a spot in the infirmary where her bed would be placed when she returned, and she led the young girl to look at it.

It was not, however, Marie-Claire who died, but Isabelle-Agnes, who a few years later succumbed to the hardships and anxiety of her mission work. Marie-Claire lived on for twenty years, but she used to say that she had never known a day's health after her return from Maubuisson.

The little community bade adieu to their Abbess with many tears; they had been trying to understand the meaning of union with God, and to learn submission to His will, but they had not foreseen this early separation from their teacher and guide. Agnes, who felt it more keenly than anyone else, entered the church as soon as they had left, and threw herself at the foot of the cross, sobbing, ' Ecce nos reliquimus omnia,' and repeating the *omnia, omnia,* as if her heart was broken. There is perhaps nothing more beautiful in the story of Port Royal than the love of these Arnauld sisters and their loyalty and fidelity to Angélique.

But Anne Arnauld was unmoved; when she was reproached with coldness, she reminded her companions that she had received her veil on the previous day. ' I had too much joy yesterday to be able to weep to-day.' She is the nun who ' danced for joy' when she was alone.

For a few days Angélique and her three companions stayed at M. Arnauld's house in Paris, where they were joined by the nun who had accompanied Mdme. d'Estrées to the *Filles Penitentes,* and now wished to return to Maubuisson.

It was thought desirable to prepare the Ladies for what was in store for them, therefore M. de Citeaux sent word that he was making every effort to fulfil his promise, and hoped to induce Mdme. de Port Royal, who had passed her noviciate and taken the veil at Maubuisson, to undertake the charge of their abbey; in which case he would conduct her thither in the course of a few days.

The Ladies were filled with dismay, but they saw that the thing was done; opposition would be useless, and they must submit. A few days were allowed for preparation, and then the Abbess set out to take possession of her new domain.

When she arrived the nuns were chanting in the chapel, but so discordant were the sounds uttered, that the effect produced was that they were quarrelling. However when the service was ended they came out to receive the Abbot and Mdme. de Port Royal with due respect, though very coldly.

Angélique met them with her characteristic frankness and had a kind word for every one. She saw among them a certain Mdme. Desmarests, whom she had formerly known, and called her great friend. She recognized her immediately and kissed her, saying, ' Bonjour, ma grande amie,' as she used to do when a child. The Ladies were charmed by her cheerfulness and simplicity, and began to think that perhaps their fears were unfounded.

The Chapter was next assembled, and Angélique solemnly installed in the place of Mdme. d'Estrées, with full power to order and dispose all things spiritual and temporal as she should think desirable for the welfare of the abbey. The Abbot then left her and returned to Paris, well pleased no doubt at the conclusion of his task.

It was a difficult position for an Abbess of twenty-six, supported by one elderly nun and two girls of eighteen and nineteen years old; and in the midst of a large hostile community, all eyeing them with suspicion !

The first few days passed quietly enough ; Angélique showed a very conciliatory spirit ; she spent her time in renewing old acquaintances and forming new ones. The Sister who had formerly been her governess was now blind, and infinite tenderness to all forms of human suffering led her to show great attention and affection to the lonely woman, to whom she paid a daily visit. In the midst of this luxurious household her own dinner throughout Lent consisted of a large piece of common household bread—for that used in the refectory was too fine for her—and a few leaves of salad without oil or vinegar. She would not have it brought on a plate, a hole was made in the bread, the salad put into it, and she ate it by the side of her blind friend.

The first feeling of Maubuisson was one of unfeigned astonishment at Angélique and her companions. Their piety, humility, and modesty were strange phenomena within those walls, and the lay-sisters used to make appointments to meet where they could stand and watch them.

There were at this time twenty-two nuns in an abbey intended to receive a hundred, and thus they were able to live in great luxury, and had lay-sisters to wait on them, and numerous attendants and servants. Nearly all of the nuns had been compelled to take the veil against their will, and their subsequent life had never borne the slightest relation to the duties of their vocation. They did not even know these duties by name, were ignorant of the very elements of Christianity, and unmindful of all religious ceremonies.

A monk of St. Bernard was their confessor, and it is said that he did not bear the name in vain, for as they did not know how to confess for themselves he used to go through a list of the sins which he thought it probable they would have committed, and they answered yes or no to his questions ; upon which he gave them absolution without further inquiry. But as he often reproached them for their ignorance they resolved to remedy it, so with much labour they drew up three forms of confession, one for Saints' days, one for Sundays, and one for week-days. These they wrote in a book, which was passed from one to the other, and from which they read as they went one after the other to the confessional. They certainly did chant all the services from the first note of matins to the last of complines, but they did so at the hours most convenient to them, and so fast and out of tune that it was impossible to distinguish a single word, and difficult to believe that the horrible din was produced by human voices. In all other respects the abbey was like the country seat of a nobleman, it was always filled with guests, and there were theatrical performances in which the nuns took the chief parts, and dancing parties. Many of them had private gardens and pavilions, in which they gave choice collations to a favoured few. In the summer-time vespers and complines were chanted early in the afternoon, one after the other, and then the Prioress and nuns walked out on the Paris road towards the fish-ponds, where the monks of St. Martin le Pontoise used to meet them and dance with them. The thing was done quite openly, as if no one could disapprove of it. It is unnecessary to dwell upon the darker shades of the picture. The reader may be sure that they existed, and that Mdme. d'Estrées was no more alone in her vices than in her pleasures.

Angélique found it no easy task to induce the Ladies to renounce what they considered their 'liberty and privileges ;' but they could not resist her authority, and therefore by the advice of the elder nuns they submitted for the time being. Before long the rule of strict seclusion was established, the entrance of secular persons forbidden, parlours built and gratings interposed, and there was external propriety throughout Maubuisson.

But when after such opposition and with such difficulty as we may well imagine, the first steps had been taken, Angélique found that she could make no further progress. The habits and vices of a lifetime were ineradicable, and it was not possible to reform the Ladies of Maubuisson. Of course she could put an end to scandalous impropriety and shut them up within the cloister walls ; she could, with more or less difficulty, compel them to submit to rules which they saw she had the power to enforce, but she could not make them love virtue and holiness. They were irreligious, unreasonable, discontented, mutinous, and irreverent, and Angélique found that she had no influence whatever over them. But she did not despair ; she saw yet another chance, and took immediate advantage of it, as it offered an opportunity for carrying out one of her favourite plans. She would select and train a band of portionless novices who might pass into the ranks of the nuns, and by degrees modify or replace them.

The Abbot of Citeaux acceded to her request and authorized the reception of forty ladies, to be chosen for their piety and virtue. As soon as it was known that this wealthy house was receiving novices gratuitously a large number of candidates came forward. But the majority were influenced by the desire of securing a comfortable home, and obtaining admission to a fashionable monastery. Angélique soon discovered these motives, and out of all who presented themselves she selected no more than thirty-two.

Sister Isabelle-Agnes of Port Royal was mistress of these novices, who were separated from the nuns. They lived in a different part of the abbey, and used a different refectory. But the whole community met in church, and there the nuns chanted with their usual indifference and irreverence.

It was in vain that Angélique drilled her novices, teaching them the value of every word, every syllable, every note. In vain she tried to drown the harsh discordant voices of the nuns with the sweet, clear ringing notes of the young girls. The struggle lasted five years, and left the ancients as victors on the field. And yet Angélique used to say it was not all in vain ; certainly the elders did not improve, but the young ones learnt patience, charity, and humility.

During these five years Angélique never once alluded to the pain which the chanting of the nuns gave her. They were thin-skinned, and impatient of reproof and suggestion ; it would have been impossible to live in peace with them if she had possessed less tact and self-control. She found she could not teach them, but she could learn from them, and could practise the virtues which there was no hope of inculcating.

In addition to the time devoted to worship and the preparation for it, Angélique was always present with her novices during the hours appointed for the manual labour enjoined by the Cistercian rule. They carried wood for the kitchen fire and all other fires throughout the abbey ; swept the passages, church, dormitories, and cloisters ; scoured the kitchen utensils, hung out the clothes to dry, dug the garden, and did all as if these were the greatest pleasures life had to bestow. Angélique not only took her own share of the work, but went from one to the other with just the word of encouragement that each one needed. She would remind some of the life of our Lord Jesus Christ upon earth, which they

were permitted to imitate; some she would exhort to follow the
example of the holy Fathers; whilst there were others upon
whom she impressed the necessity for humility and self-
mortification. She knew not only the spiritual needs but the
physical powers of every novice, and the tasks were so
judiciously appointed that each one could do what was required
of her; in this manner absolute silence was maintained, and
there was no chattering and gossiping over the work.

The novices waited on the nuns, and treated them with
respect and attention. It was no easy duty. Doubtless
they needed the encouragement and frequent exhortations
which we read that the Abbess gave them, for the elders
must have made large demands upon their forbearance. The
example of Angélique was more powerful even than her pre-
cepts, and she practised greater self-denial than she preached.
No word of reproach or complaint escaped her lips. She was
cheerful and patient with the Ladies, and the worst cell in
the dormitory, the oldest dress in the house, the poorest scraps
of food left by the novices from their scanty meals she still
chose for herself. She had taken possession of a small dark
chamber, hitherto used by lay-sisters and servants; she says
it was her 'greatest consolation,' for when she was in it she
seemed to be in the small stable at Bethlehem, of which
Jesus Christ was the only light.

Thus we see on the one hand a band of young and pious
women, earnest and self-denying, trying, as best they could, to
lead a holy life; and on the other a number of women no longer
young, bound by the same vows, dwelling under the same
roof, but self-indulgent, vicious, and irreligious. No fusion of
the two was possible, and Angélique again saw that she had
failed, and that she must for the present be content with external
propriety which she could enforce, and peace which she was
able to maintain by removing all legitimate ground for complaint.

But even her brave heart was sometimes dismayed at the
difficulties with which she had to contend; and, just when she
most needed it, God sent her, as she used to say, St. Francis de
Sales as friend and counsellor. He visited Maubuisson for the
first time at Easter 1619, and for the last in the September of
the same year. When he said farewell Angélique had reached
the point of deepest depression. She had hoped that his influence
would have had some effect upon the Ladies, and that ·

prayers and exhortations would have brought them back to God and the paths of righteousness. With him she lost that hope. He was leaving, and the Ladies were unchanged. He tried to encourage her, told her that this was only the seed-time, and that some day she would look upon the harvest, a prediction which she gratefully accepted. We must recur to St. Francis in a subsequent chapter, but one incident connected with his visit has its place here.

He was once accompanied to Maubuisson by his brother, M. de Boisy, who took special notice of a nun, remarkable even at Maubuisson for vanity and affectation, the peculiarity of her dress, and her desire of attracting attention. She was called Mdme. de la Serre. M. de Boisy found that she was proud and worldly but at the same time intelligent. He thought it would be a great triumph to win her over to the side of Angélique and the novices, and therefore had several long conversations with her. No doubt she found the attempt to convert her more interesting than the quiet life she was then leading, and at first promised amendment, nay even consented to give up her fanciful dress. She did not fulfil her promise, and after trying in vain to induce her to take this first step in the right direction, M. de Boisy threatened her with God's anger if she neglected his warning. But his threat had no more effect than his exhortations, and he left her unchanged in heart and appearance.

A few days after St. Francis had said farewell to Maubuisson, Mdme. d'Estrées the imprisoned Abbess returned.

By the help of her brother-in-law, the Count de Sanzi, and some other nobles she had made her escape from the *Filles Penitentes*, and she reached the abbey with an armed escort about six o'clock in the morning. They demanded admission at the door in the courtyard near the fish-ponds, which the porter refused. They then broke open the door and threatened to throw him into the water. He called for help and was heard in the church which was near this gate; but only one person knew the meaning of the cries, this was Mdme. de la Serre, who advanced to a side door and waited for a further signal. The porter did not dare to alarm the house. Mdme. d'Estrées was in the courtyard, and he was so terrified at her threats and violence that he thought it best to escape and make his way to Paris and M. Arnauld. Mdme. d'Estrées therefore went on unopposed to the church, and was admitted by Mdme. de la Serre, who had been forewarned of the attempt, and had procured false keys, with which she opened the doors.

At the moment when the old Abbess entered the church Angélique was coming out of a confessional near the door, and the two met face to face. Mdme. d'Estrées exclaimed, in great excitement :

'Madam, you have been quite long enough in my place; I have now come back to my own house, and you must go out of it at once.'

Angélique very calmly replied : 'I am quite ready to do so, madam, when those who placed me here give me permission to leave.'

Mdme. d'Estrées angrily repeated that she should go, and go at once. But Angélique made no further answer, and quietly conducted the Abbess from the church to her own apartments in the abbey. Now these had been occupied by Angélique; which means that she had considered them as common property, and had placed in them novices who were ill and required care. There were mattrasses on the floor, and the rooms had been converted into an infirmary. Mdme. d'Estrées looked around, and then said, contemptuously :

'Take all this dirt out of my rooms. What is the meaning of this disgusting mess ?'

'Madam,' replied Angélique, coldly, 'if your rooms are not in good order the fault is pardonable; we had no reason to expect you here.'

The young Abbess left the room and went to the kitchen, where she ordered a particularly good dinner for the old one, and afterwards summoned her novices, told them what had happened and what she should expect of them.

Undoubtedly the spirits of Angélique would rise at this crisis; others were anxious and apprehensive, but she was calm.

Both Abbesses were present at the nine o'clock service, Tierces, and grand mass was solemnly chanted by the novices. Mdme. d'Estrées did not enter the choir, and Angélique, as usual, occupied the Abbess's throne.

'What presumption!' exclaimed Mdme. d'Estrées; 'my pupil actually takes my place in my presence!'

But this step produced considerable effect on the nuns.

They had seen the humility and charity of Angélique, her patience and forbearance, and had despised her for them. Now they were to see this other side of her character, which they were better able to appreciate. She and her novices partook of the Holy Communion after mass, so that they might be prepared for whatever it should please God to send them, and then they went to their household work as usual.

Meanwhile Mdme. d'Estrées visited every part of the abbey, and saw all her old friends and former companions. She paid special attention to the two nuns who had charge of the keys, and in the presence of Angélique asked to have them restored to her. She found that this demand had been forestalled; the keys had already been given up to Mdme. de Port Royal.

When dinner-time came, Angélique saw that Mdme. d'Estrées was duly served, and then joined the novices in the refectory. They were sad and heavy at heart, for all the nuns had rallied round their old Abbess, and the new comers felt that they were lonely and friendless. They seated themselves in silence at the refectory table, and then Angélique said :

'My sisters, we cannot foresee what will happen to us on this day, but all things are in the hands of God, and we can trust ourselves to Him. Perhaps we may have to leave this house. We must be prepared for whatsoever may happen, and our duty now is to eat, so that we may be strong and able to endure whatever it is the will of God that we should suffer.'

Then she took her seat : they dined, read, and chanted grace as usual, although they knew that Mdme. d'Estrées could hear them from her room, overhead, and would ridicule them.

After dinner, Dom Sabatier, the confessor who had been appointed by the Abbot of Citeaux, sent for Angélique to the parlour, and she found that he had gone over to Mdme. d'Estrées. He endeavoured to persuade her to leave the abbey quietly, and not expose herself to the violence of which the Count de Sanzi and his followers were capable ; and tried to frighten her by repeating and exaggerating their threats. But Angélique was immoveable. She must submit to force, she said, but short of that nothing should make her faithless to her trust.

When Dom Sabatier ceased speaking, Mdme. d'Estrées,

H 2

who had entered the room, again tried to induce her to leave Maubuisson. Finding that her words were of no avail, and being determined to gain her end by fraud or force, she asked Angélique to accompany her to the church.

'Certainly, madam,' answered Angélique; 'we could not be in a better place.'

Followed by the novices and her faithful nuns from Port Royal, she entered the church and knelt to implore the help of God. Mdme. d'Estrées was accompanied by the Ladies of Maubuisson, and went from one to the other, urging them to remove her rival by force. This, whether from respect or fear of the consequences, possibly an admixture of both motives, they refused to do; but they consented to remain as passive spectators of the scene that followed.

Mdme. d'Estrées advanced to Angélique, and in a loud and angry tone desired her to go out of the abbey; receiving the answer so often previously given, she seized and tried to drag her to the church door and push her out. The faithful novices and nuns, all except Anne Arnauld,[1] who knelt in prayer, gathered round her and in the struggle which ensued, Mdme. d'Estrées snatched off Angélique's veil; upon this a young and lusty novice, indignant at the outrage offered to her beloved Abbess, knocked down Mdme. d'Estrées, tore off her veil and head-dress, and threw them away. Mdme. d'Estrées screamed for help, but the nuns stood aloof; she then called out, 'Help, brother, help; they are killing me!'

This was the signal for which the nun with the false keys was waiting. She immediately opened the church-door, and the Count de Sanzi and his followers rushed in with their swords drawn; some of them even fired off pistols to produce a panic. The Count de Sanzi and Mdme. d'Estrées seized upon Angélique and dragged her towards the door; the novices held her back; the struggle went on for some time, until, thoroughly exhausted, she entreated the novices to yield, and she was carried into the courtyard and placed in a coach which was in readiness. Mdme. de la Serre tried to prevent any of her adherents from leaving the church, but this was impossible, they forced their way out, filled the coach, scrambled on the coach-box, clung to the wheels, and hung on to the imperial.

---

[1] She had joined her sisters at Maubuisson a few weeks previously.

It was of no use for the Count de Sanzi to draw his sword and
pretend that he was about to strike; they would not give way,
and he was obliged to tell the coachman to stop, or some of
them would have been killed.

There was a moment's pause, and one of the nuns said to
Angélique: 'Whither are we going, my mother?' Immediately
it flashed upon Angélique's mind that she was not safe in the
hands of these men, and did not know where they would take
her or what indignity they might be capable of inflicting. She
sprang out of the coach, and once more was surrounded by
her faithful followers. Mdme. d'Estrées, surprised and amazed,
saw that she must try other means. She placed one of her
men-servants at the outer door of the abbey, told him to allow
Angélique and the four nuns from Port Royal to go out, but
no one else, and then returned, and partly by force and partly
because Angélique was too weary to resist she led and pushed
her out of the gate.

But the novices suspected the design, and one amongst
them, who was both brave and strong, went up to the man at
the door and told him in a resolute tone that if he attempted
to prevent them from going out, they would certainly crush him
to death behind the door. A companion, in order to show
that this was no idle threat, pushed the door back and gave him
a terrible squeeze between it and the wall; she then passed
through and seized Mdme. d'Estrées who was outside, took her
round the waist and seated her on the grass; holding her there
in spite of her struggles until the Sisterhood had all joined Angélique. They hurried through the open door, behind which the
unfortunate man was tightly wedged, and by way of reminding
him to be quiet each one squeezed the door against him as she
passed.

The Count de Sanzi does not appear to have interfered
further, and probably thought his work was ended when Angélique was ejected from the church.

One novice was left behind. She was busy with her duties
in the dairy, and knew nothing of what had taken place until she
returned and found her Abbess and companions gone. She insisted on following them, and as the novices must by this time
have gained considerable reputation by their prowess, no one
was inclined to oppose her, and the doors were opened.

The unseemly contest was ended, the abbey doors closed

against them, and Angélique and her followers were alone on the high road. They knelt in prayer together, and then Angélique resolved to go to the neighbouring town of Pon- toise; the plague was there, so she stopped at an outlying village and procured cordial waters, of which they all partook.

She arranged her little procession in due order, first the postulants, then the novices and nuns, and last of all herself. But they had no veils, how were they to enter a town! Angé- lique was never at a loss, she walked up to one of the postulants and, without a word on either side, clipped her long black skirt round the waist, tore it into small veils and distributed them. They entered Pontoise, say the memoirs, 'with a modesty and piety which were truly edifying.' The inhabitants marvelled greatly at this strange procession, headed by a postulant in a black bodice and green petticoat, and walking through the streets as quietly and in as perfect order as if they had been in their cloisters. The return of Mdme. d'Estrées had already transpired, and soon the rumour ran : 'This is the good Mdme. de Port Royal; the wicked Abbess has come back and turned her out.'

The little band entered the first church they came to, and knelt in prayer, waiting to see what God would send them. The news of their arrival spread rapidly, and before long the Grand Vicar and M. Duval, a doctor, went to Angélique and offered assistance ; the Carmelite convent begged for the nuns, whilst the Ursulines asked for eleven novices, and the Hôtel Dieu said they could receive the whole party. Angélique very humbly thanked them, but thought it best to accept the vicarage, which the Grand Vicar had placed at her disposal, because they would not only be together, but would thus put themselves under the protection of the Bishop.

Before leaving the church they chanted vespers, and then walked in procession to the vicarage. The streets through which they passed were crowded with spectators, many of whom knelt as Angélique went by.

The Grand Vicar installed them in his house, had a private chapel prepared in which they might hear mass, and then left them. Charitable persons sent beds, bedding and food, and two gave money which Angélique needed, for she had brought none from Maubuisson. She says that it made her very happy to think that she was so poor as to be really in want of alms.

When the novice who had been in the dairy reached Pontoise late at night, she brought with her a gold coin which she had found on a window-sill. Angélique received it as the gift of God, and said that it 'did her good.'

The novices were so well trained that there was no difficulty in maintaining order and silence, they went about their ordinary work just as if they had been at Maubuisson. Anne Arnauld, Marie-Claire, and Isabelle-Agnes were with their sister and Abbess, and were doubtless of great service at this time. On the following day mass was said in the chapel, and when vespers were chanted in the afternoon many persons were present, and all were impressed by the sweet voices and devout demeanour of the nuns.

At Maubuisson there was a very different scene, and one which it is not pleasant to dwell upon. Dom Sabatier wrote to M. de Citeaux on behalf of the Abbess, saying that as she had succeeded in regaining possession of the abbey and had such very influential friends, it would surely be better to let bygones be bygones and come round to her side.

Now the porter who had started for Paris when Mdme. d'Estrées forced her way into the abbey, lost no time in apprizing the Arnaulds of Angélique's danger. On the following day an order was obtained to arrest and bring Mdme. d'Estrées back to Paris, and reinstate Angélique; and Maubuisson was again surrounded by archers and closely guarded. Mdme. d'Estrées had been warned of her danger, and disguised as a servant she escaped by a secret door which she had often used. The nobles who accompanied her found themselves in an awkward position, and sought safety in flight before the arrival of the archers; whilst Dom Sabatier jumped over the abbey wall. Mdme. de la Serre had not time to escape, so she took some important papers which the Abbess had been unable to carry off with her, and hid herself in a high cupboard, the entrance to which was concealed by tapestry. She got up by means of a ladder, and did not forget to take a store of provisions with her.

Archers were stationed in every room, for the officer in command thought that some of those he had orders to arrest must still be in the house. Towards morning the guards in the empty dormitory heard a noise, as of some one 'blowing her nose after she had been crying;' they examined the walls and discovered the hiding-place of Mdme. de la Serre. But she would not allow herself to be taken, and threw down ladder and man on it when they tried to reach her. There was no alternative but to order her to come down in the king's name, and threaten to shoot her if she did not comply. Whereupon she gave herself up, and together with an accomplice was removed and imprisoned.

Mdme. d'Estrées was not discovered for six months; she was then taken back to the *Filles Penitentes.* She frequently made her escape, but was recaptured, and never again reached Maubuisson. At one time she was a prisoner in the Châtelet, and Père Bernard relates how he found her there in bed with a bottle of wine and a plate of sausages by her side. She spent all her income in successive lawsuits for the recovery of her abbey, and at length died in a small house near Paris, poor, wretched, and abandoned by all her friends.

She had intended to make her youngest daughter her coadjutor and successor, and the Ladies kept the child with them for some years in the hope that her wishes might be carried out; but when it was evident that Maubuisson would never be restored to her family, the father of the child removed her and placed her elsewhere.

At ten o'clock on the night after that on which Mdme. d'Estrées had been expelled from Maubuisson, a company of soldiers arrived at Pontoise to inform Angélique that she could return whenever she pleased. 'At once then,' she replied, and told the good news to the Sisters. They needed no time for preparation, and in a few minutes the solemn, silent band were on their way back to Maubuisson. Clergy and laity crowded into the streets and accompanied them for some distance, and they were escorted by mounted soldiers who carried torches. On their arrival Angélique despatched a considerable number to the kitchen, where they passed the night in preparing food for the soldiers.

Fifty archers were stationed at Maubuisson for six months. The abbey was not considered safe whilst Mdme. d'Estrées was at large, for her friends were resolved to frighten Angélique away, and they watched the house and fired guns through the windows whenever they found an opportunity. But even this persecution ceased after a time; at Angélique's request the guard was withdrawn, and all things resumed their old aspect.

CHAPTER IX.

FRANCIS DE SALES was born at the Château de Sales, in Savoy, in 1567. He was the eldest son of good and pious parents, and before his birth his mother vowed to dedicate him to the service of God. His father was a Seigneur de Nouvelles, who, after his marriage with the heiress of the house of Boisy, was known as the Seigneur de Boisy. The family, which was one of the oldest and best in Savoy, did not at that time take any title from the estate of Sales, which was made a barony in 1613, and a marquisate in 1664. Francis received the tonsure when he was eleven years old, and was sent to the Jesuit college at Paris, where he devoted a considerable part of his time to theological studies.

The condition of France at that time was one which could scarcely fail to impress a sensitive and thoughtful boy. The country had been devastated by civil and religious wars during the reigns of Francis II. and Charles IX., and they were continued with unabated fury under Henry III. Four Catholic, opposed by four Huguenot armies had overrun the finest provinces of France; and the League, which was then in process of formation, threatened to introduce a third party, opposed to both the others. Cities were taken and retaken, pillaged, and left in ruins. Churches were destroyed, the old religion was entirely banished from one part of France, and not firmly established in the other. Discord and division reigned not only in the State, but in the family, where father was opposed to son, and brother to brother. There were as many tyrants in a province as there were nobles; the king was despised by some of his subjects, and hated by others, and the laws were openly violated. The love of God seemed to have no place in men's hearts, and in its stead there was fear ; some fear of God and still more of everlasting punishment.

Francis, who was keenly alive to all influences around him, did not escape this one, and when he was a young man, a great fear of hell fell upon him. But his nature was tender and pure, and he had too much courage to fear it as a place of mere physical torment. His terror lay in deeper and darker depths : to him. hell embodied a more awful doom, for he believed that he should be there destined to hate and blaspheme God through-out eternity. The thought weighed on him continually, and threw him into a state of profound melancholy. He felt that he was a predestined reprobate, and that nothing in this life could compensate for an eternity without God. One day he entered a church in Paris where there was a picture of the Virgin, kneeling before which, when he first came to Paris, he had made a vow of perpetual chastity. Once again he fell on his knees and, moved by a sudden impulse, implored that if he was so wretched as to be destined to hate God eternally after death, he might at least love Him with all his heart during life. In a moment his peace of mind was restored ; he rose from his knees tranquil and re-assured. The dark fear had vanished, and it returned no more.

He left Paris to study law in the University of Padua, and after taking his doctor's degree, returned to the Château de Sales, at twenty-six years old. His mother had forgotten her vow, or perhaps thought that her son's pure life and spotless reputation were the fulfilment of it. His father's plans opened out a brilliant and happy future before him. A seat in the Senate of Chambery had been already secured, and a noble and beautiful bride awaited him. He could not at once oppose the wishes of his parents, and so, with a perplexed and heavy heart, he entered upon his public duties, and began to pay his addresses to the lady. But everything within and around him reminded him of the work he was neglecting, and the service of God which ought to be his first duty and chief pleasure. Riding through a wood, he was thrown from his horse : his sword leapt from the scabbard, and sword and scabbard formed a cross. Three times the same accident happened : three times his eye fell upon the same symbol.

He had no misgiving as to his vocation; but his extreme docility, his sweet temper, and sympathetic, kindly nature, made it very hard for him to oppose his parents. And they, when they looked upon their handsome son, richly endowed, well educated, excelling in all manly exercises, with his fine voice and fine manners, could not relinquish the hope of seeing him take the place that ought to be filled by the heir to the family honours and estates.

His cousin, Louis de Sales, who was a canon of Geneva, espoused his cause, pleaded with the parents, and convinced them by getting Francis appointed Provost of the Chapter of Geneva. He was a layman when he was elected to this post of high ecclesiastical honour; but within the course of a few months the various orders of the Catholic Church were conferred on him, in spite of his earnest petition to wait the appointed time before receiving them. He was twenty-four years older than Angélique Arnauld, and just at the time when her grandfather had begun to think of providing her with an abbey, Francis de Sales had obtained a dignity which placed him at the head of the Chapter of Geneva. One appointment was as irregular as the other, and at that time as common.

The Bishop of Geneva had been compelled by the Protestants to abandon the city in 1533, and had chosen Annecy, on the southern side of the lake, as the capital of his diocese. Annecy was, therefore, the scene of the early labours of Francis. He used to preach and teach in the neighbouring villages, and wherever he went, his eloquent words stirred the hearts of his hearers and made them desire to turn to God. He says that he constantly had before him the words, 'He was a burning and a shining light.' In order that he might shine he desired to burn, burn with love to God and zeal for the salvation of souls; he, therefore, prepared for his sermons not so much by study as by fervent prayer. But his success as a preacher was due quite as much to his practical beneficence as to his eloquent words. He was infinitely generous and tender, loved to give money, sympathy, help of all kinds. Seeing how impossible it was for the clergy to cope with the destitution around them, he established a secular fraternity called the Brotherhood of the Cross, the members of which visited the poor, instructed the ignorant, assisted the needy, buried the dead, consoled prisoners, and endeavoured to adjust disputes without lawsuits.

The result of his legal studies at Padua seems to have been, that next to sin he dreaded law. The Brethren of the Cross were to act as arbitrators in disputes, and to spare no pains necessary to enable them to form a just decision on the merits of cases submitted to them, and to reconcile adversaries. They were not to forget that true piety does not exclude the virtues of a good citizen, and the observances that help to make life agreeable. Devout Christians, he said, need not be dirty, brusque, and rude. On the contrary, if they wish to win others to religion, they must teach them to love it ; and must show that gloom and despondency are not true piety. God has taught us to call Him Father, in order that we may place filial confidence in Him. And thus, by deeds and words, Francis won many hearts.

During the war between Francis I. and the Duke of Savoy, in 1535, the Swiss had seized the Duchy of Chablais, and the bailiwicks of Ternier and Gaillard, and the inhabitants had been converted to the reformed religion. Twenty-nine years later, the Duke's son and successor regained possession of many of the provinces lost by his father, and among others, of those taken by the Swiss. But in the treaty by which they were ceded, a clause was inserted to the effect that the Catholic religion should not be re-established. The terms of the treaty were respected until 1589, when the Swiss made an ineffectual attempt to regain the Chablais. The Duke thereupon said that he was no longer bound by this clause in the agreement ; and that as he could not rely upon the fidelity of Protestant subjects, he should take means to extirpate their heresy. In 1594 he requested the Bishop of Geneva to organize a mission for the conversion of the Protestants. The task was not an easy one. The reformed religion had been established for sixty years, and the inhabitants of the district were so hostile to the Catholics, that when the Bishop read the letter which he had received from the Duke to the clergy of his diocese, there were only two volunteers for the missionary work. They were Francis and his cousin Louis de Sales. In vain M. and Mdme. de Boisy implored their son not to risk his life in so hazardous an enterprize. He would not listen to their prognostications of danger and defeat, and the cousins set out upon their mission alone and on foot.

When they reached Allinges, the Governor of the Chablais

showed them the garrison under arms, and a park of artillery with which he was prepared to co-operate in the conversion of the heretics.   But Francis believed that he should have no need of assistance from the temporal power, and that his preaching was all that would be required.   In this he was mistaken ; the inhabitants would not meet him, would not listen to him, would not receive him into their houses.   But in spite of many hardships and even dangers, he persevered through a most inclement winter, walking many miles daily, arguing and pleading wherever he could obtain a hearing, and in time he made some converts.   The accounts of his mission are all derived from Catholic sources, and the dangers he incurred are no less exaggerated than the successes which he achieved.   We hear of innumerable attempts at assassination, of hundreds of Calvinists converted by a single sermon, and of Calvinist ministers who do not venture to fulfil their engagements and meet him in public.   These, doubtless, are fables ; for at the end of two years, the Duke of Savoy and the Bishop of Geneva were so little satisfied with his success, that he was summoned to Turin, to confer with the Duke on the necessity of adopting harsher measures.

The Duke's motive was exclusively political, and that of Francis was religious, but each was willing to give and take ; and it was Francis who dictated and secured the adoption of measures by which a violent political pressure was put upon the Calvinists, so that they had to choose between expatriation and apostasy.

The Duke's *ultimatum,* drawn up by Francis, set forth that Calvinist ministers were to be banished from the States of Savoy ; that all public offices and dignities should be taken from Calvinists and given to Catholics ; that the ecclesiastical revenues, which had been usurped by the heretics, should be refunded and employed in repairing churches, and providing for the maintenance of Catholic priests and missionaries ; that a Jesuit college should be forthwith established at Thonon ; and that no public worship should be allowed in the Chablais and the bailiwicks, except that of the Catholic Church.

This decree was promulgated ; the inhabitants who would not abjure their religion were expelled ; those who remained were presumed to be Catholics, and were not allowed to profess any other faith.

It is impossible and unnecessary to attempt to justify the conduct of Francis de Sales, or to call attention to the readiness with which he threw away spiritual weapons and had recourse to the temporal power, exercised in its most aggressive and overbearing manner. He did precisely what others, Catholic and Protestant, were doing at that time ; and therein lies his blame.

The Duke of Savoy was greatly impressed by his astuteness ; so much so, that he always afterwards suspected him of political intrigues, chiefly with France, and manifested his suspicions in ill-will and harsh restrictions which affected Francis and also other members of his family ; and therein lies a part of his punishment.

It was thus that the Chablais was brought back to the Catholic faith, and thus that Francis *converted* the 72,000 heretics of whom we are told in the act of canonization.

Personally, he was never intolerant or harsh. He passed through his province preaching, teaching, ministering to the sick and needy, taking no thought of his own life and health, and abounding in manifestations of love and goodwill. His friends entreated him to show some consideration to himself as well as others. ' It is not necessary that I should live,' he replied, ' but it is necessary that the Church should be served.'

A Calvinist once raised his hand, and said, ' If I smite you on the right cheek, will you turn the other also, as the Gospel commands you ? ' ' I don't know if I shall do it,' said Francis ; ' but I know that I ought to do it.' And the gentle tone and unfeigned humility of the reply convinced his opponent that he was at any rate no hypocrite, who could be startled out of his assumed character and made to show his true nature.

There can be no doubt that, as a missionary, Francis placed Catholicism in its most favourable light. He was face to face with a hostile majority, and could not have maintained his position if his life had not been pure, and his words gentle and persuasive. But when the Duke's edict reduced the majority to submission, Francis was unchanged ; or, if changed, it was only because his humility, charity, and purity burnt with a clearer, brighter flame. We cannot fail to be struck with the lofty moral impulses, the enthusiasm and sympathy, which are characteristic of him ; but, at the same time, we see that a conscience originally sensitive, and sensitive still on many points, had been seared by his early training. His Christianity was not free from a taint of worldliness. He visited the celebrated Beza, Calvin's friend and biographer, and held many conversations with him. We have no trust-worthy report of these conversations, and have reason to doubt whether Francis was as convincing and overwhelming in argu-ment with the great Calvinist theologian as Catholic biogra-phers are inclined to think. But it is certain that he did not shrink from attempting to bribe a man who was as earnest and scrupulously conscientious as he was himself. He was entrusted by Clement VIII. with a secret mission to Beza, and was empowered to offer him an honourable retreat in any place he might select, and a pension of four thousand crowns in gold, if he would return to the fold of the Roman Church. This is told by his Catholic biographers, and not by his opponents. Indeed, Francis never doubted the influence of worldly motives upon Christians. He made use of them in the so-called conver-sion of the Chablais, urging that 'many would escape banishment from Paradise because of their desire to escape banishment from their country.' He thought it possible to corrupt Beza. Throughout life he conciliated the world and attempted to link together Christian motive and worldly act. He thought ill, and had reason to think ill, of the Duke of Savoy; but he wrote lofty panegyrics, praising him as a man and a Christian. He thought ill, and had still more reason to think ill, of the Church of Rome; and he spoke well of it. He was of a gentle, peaceful, and affectionate disposition, an enemy to strife and discord, willing, in fact, to purchase peace at any price; and in order to obtain it. he made concessions unworthy of an honourable man. But it must be acknowledged that he never sought his own advantage, or was actuated by any dis-creditable personal motive. The Bishop of Geneva selected him as his coadjutor, and there can be little doubt that, although he allowed his objections to be overruled, he sincerely wished to refuse the honour forced upon him. He subse-quently declined much higher preferment, which was more than once offered to him.

As the result of a war between the King of France and the Duke of Savoy, in 1599, the bailiwick of Gex, in the diocese of Geneva, was ceded to France, and the Protestant inhabitants hoped to escape the conversion which had befallen their neighbours of the Chablais, by appealing to the provisions of the Edict of Nantes. But the Catholic clergy of the diocese resolved, if possible, to 'bring them back to the mother Church,' and sent Francis, whose efforts had hitherto been crowned with success, on a mission to the King of France. He was very favourably received by Henri IV., who offered him a pension, and a French bishopric of much greater value than that of Geneva. His Lent sermons in Paris were listened to by a fashionable crowd. We may be sure that M. Arnauld was not absent on these occasions. He appreciated the eloquence of the pulpit as much as that of the bar, and was attracted by things noble as well as by things of good report. Francis met with a brilliant social success, but his political mission was a failure : the King of France was neither able nor willing to break faith with his Protestant subjects, and informed him that he must rely on spiritual measures alone ; rather a poor prospect, as Francis well knew. And with this answer, he was on his way home, when he heard of the death of his colleague, and was greeted as Bishop of Geneva.

Perhaps the most noticeable fact connected with this visit to Paris is, that we owe to it the 'Introduction to a Devout Life,' a work of which there were no less than forty editions during the first fifty years after it was published ; which was done into English, 'painfullie, for the benefit of many soules in our poore distressed countrie,' says the translator ; and had reached a third edition in 1614, whilst in 1637, in the thirteenth year of Charles I., a royal proclamation was issued, commanding it to be called in and publicly burnt, on account of the 'divers passages tending to popery,' which the King could not tolerate, 'out of his pious and constant care to uphold and maintain the Religion professed in the Church of England in its purity, without error or corruption.' Francis is said to have been impelled to the work in consequence of a wish expressed by Henri IV., that some one would write a book to show that those who were obliged to live in the world might still lead a Christian life. It is possible that the suggestion came from the King, although it seems an unlikely one for him to have made ; certainly no one was better fitted to carry it out than Francis. He did not believe in the separation of the Church and the world, or in the necessity of privation and

austerity.   He was orthodox of the orthodox in Catholic
dogma and theory, but in practice he was inclined to depart
from many hitherto received notions.   His Brotherhood of the
Cross was a lay society, and his original plan for the Order of
the Visitation was to make it a lay society of women.   He
believed that king, courtier, soldier, and priest might all lead
a devout life : God's grace was open to all, and man's nature
inclined him to turn towards God.   It may be that the
Bishop's hostility to Calvinism induced him to take up a position which entitled him to contradict the Calvinistic statements as to *nature* and *grace*, and certainly his own tender and
sympathetic nature made him look kindly upon humanity,
tolerate weakness, and excuse faults.

The world around him furnished analogies, which he seized
eagerly, to show that God was acting in one and the selfsame
manner throughout the universe, and that the attitude of the
soul towards God ought to be that expressed in the maxim
constantly on his lips, 'Ask nothing, desire nothing, refuse
nothing.'

In his 'Introduction to a Devout Life[1]' he says, 'As
the mother pearles do live in the sea, not taking one drop
of salt water into their shells, and towards the Cheledonian
Islands there be fountains of sweet water in the midst of the
brackish sea, and a small kind of fly called Pyraustes born
and bred in hot burning ovens and furnaces flies in the
flames without scorching her wings, so a vigorous and constant
heart may live in the world, and not participate in the vaine
humours of the world, find out fresh springs of devotion
in the midst of the brinish waters of temporal affairs, and
may flie without harme among the flames of earthly occupation, and yet not burn the wings of holy desire.'   And
he tells how temporal burdens may be 'as the bundles
of cinnamon which, with sweet and recreative odour, com-
forteth those that carry them through the boiling sands of
Arabia.'   The thoughts contained in the work are addressed
to Philotheus, or a Lover of God.   The Bishop begins, 'My
dear reader : I beseeche thee to reade this preface for thy satisfaction and myne. . . . The Paynim historians report of a
mayden called Glycera, greatly delighted in making of nosegays, who could so fitly and properly varie and change the

---

[1] English edition of 1614.

dispositions and mingling of the sweet flowers in her posies, that with the selfsame flowers she would frame many divers kinds of nosegays;' and he goes on to show, that in like manner doth 'the Holy Ghost dispose and order, with ever-changeable varieties, the instructions of devotion which He gives by the tongues and pennes of His servants.'

Doubtless, the exuberant fancy of the Saint sometimes makes him appear to lack reverence, although he never does so in reality. As the Islamite treasures every scrap of paper, because the name of God may be written on it, so he every leaf, or stone, or legend. 'The maiden called Glycera' suggests to him the action of the Holy Ghost, and he does not scruple to say so. The fanciful allusive style, rich in metaphor, and with a certain suggestion of mysticism, falls short of the deeper feeling and imagination which mark the mystic. But the seventeenth century was not the age of mystics; and it was a time when men looked for and were attracted by, the graceful and poetical fancies which those who are very much in earnest are apt to resent.

Francis de Sales recoiled from the stern Calvinistic doc-trines which he had combated in the Chablais, and from the hard logical creed of Calvin and his disciple Beza. He believed that man has a natural inclination to love God, which he received in Paradise and has never entirely lost. He would not accept election and predestination in any shape or form, and held that Redemption through Christ was more than co-extensive with the fall of Adam, and that humanity re-gained in the Son of God all, and more than all, that it had lost in the first man. The doctrine which he expounded with so much eloquence and fervour was not a hard one. It was received gladly in France, and also in England where there was a strong reaction against the severity of the Puritans. Marie de Medicis sent the 'Introduction to a Devout Life' to our own James I., who was delighted with it, and always carried it about with him, finding in it an 'unction' wanting in Protestant works.

This same unction is not the most attractive part of the writings of Francis de Sales; but as works of fancy, they are perhaps unrivalled. And fancy is here used in its highest sense, to indicate the graceful, thoughtful, suggestive mind, which looks with love and interest upon every living thing, bird or beast, insect and plant, and learns from them some lesson of love to God and man.　　There is a tendency, perhaps, to overlook dark shades, to ignore evil and crime and to live in the sunlight as if there was no night, which, in Francis de Sales, is the natural tendency of a pure and happy nature, contented with the outside of things, and taking up indiscriminately fact or fable, if it served to illustrate his views.

In another celebrated work, his treatise on 'The Love of God,' he says :

'Among partridges, it often happens that certain of them steal the eggs of the others, in order to sit upon them ; and this they do, either from their anxiety to become mothers, or from stupidity, and not knowing their own eggs.　　And now follows a strange thing, and nevertheless the truth of it is well certified, for the partridge which has been hatched and fed under the breast of a stranger, when it hears the voice of the hen which laid the egg which produced it, forsakes that thieving stepmother, goes back to its true mother, and follows her, being drawn to her by ties of birth and blood.　　It is the same with our heart, O Theotimus ! for, although it may be born and nurtured, and brought up in the midst of things material, and base, and transient and, as we may say, under the wings of nature, nevertheless, at the first glance that it casts upon God, at the very first recognition of Him, the original natural instinct of love to God, which had been dormant and unperceived, is roused up and called out in a moment.'

He says elsewhere, that God has not left this natural inclination to love Him above all things in our hearts for nothing ; but that He uses it like a handle, in order that He may take hold of it, and turn us gently, and draw us close to Him ; and it is like a fine thread, which is attached to small birds to prevent their escape, and, by means of it, God can check us when it pleases His Divine mercy.

'This inclination,' he says, 'is an indication and memorial of our first Author and Creator, impelling us to love Him, and giving us a secret intimation that we belong to Him.　　It is the same thing with stags.　　Great princes sometimes put collars around their throats, with their arms upon them, and then, although they are let go, and set free in the forest, everyone who sees them, knows not only that once upon a time they belonged to the prince whose arms they bear, but also that they are still reserved for him ; and it was thus, as historians tell us, that the extreme age of a stag was once recognized, for, three hundred years after the death of Cæsar, he was found, wearing a collar, with the device of Cæsar, and these words, "Cæsar set me free." '

Although we have a natural inclination to love God, Francis urges that we are not able to love Him without His help, and he illustrates his meaning by saying :—

'Eagles have a large heart and great strength of wing, but yet their sight greatly excels their flight, and their eyes are more powerful and more rapid than their wings ; in the same way our hearts, which are filled by a sacred natural inclination towards God, have a clearer knowledge of His worthiness to be loved than strength of will to love Him. . . . In fact, O Theotimus, our sorry nature, wounded by sin, is like those palm-trees which we bring from abroad, and which certainly do make abortive attempts at producing fruit in our own land, but as to bearing dates of full size, and ripe, and well-flavoured, that is only possible in more favoured climes.'

Francis de Sales, as Bishop of Geneva, was unchanged. He retained all the simplicity of his early years, all his youthful disregard for wealth and luxury, all his first love of gentleness, meekness, and purity. He said that a prelate ought not to be distinguished from a priest merely because of his fine clothes, and he would not therefore wear silk, velvet, or lace, but retained the woollen garb he had worn hitherto. Nor would he live in a fine well-furnished house. His palace was scrupulously clean and well kept, for he said though luxury had always been a vice, dirt would never become a virtue. But there was no costly furniture ; everything in it was plain and simple ; the pictures were few in number and of no value ; they were chosen as aids to devotion, and not as works of art. He kept no carriage or vehicle of any kind, and visited his diocese on foot, unless bad weather or the state of the roads compelled him to go on horseback. He was frugal and temperate, but he did not approve of austerity or severe penance, and did not wish his piety to consist in extraordinary self-mortification, but in doing the will of God. Fasting in accordance with one's own will, he considered as a temptation of the devil. We ought to say to it, 'Get thee behind me, Satan.' On another occasion he said : 'Remember, that to eat little and work much ; to have

great anxiety of mind and to refuse sleep to the body, is like
trying to get another journey out of a horse which is knocked
up, without first giving it a feed of corn.'

His household consisted of four male servants, whom he
treated with great kindness, saying : 'A capful of wind in the
sails will drive the vessel on more quickly than a hundred
strokes given by galley slaves chained to the oars.'

It was very difficult for Francis to deal with those priests of
his diocese who had been guilty of crime and were imprisoned
at Annecy, for he could not refuse pardon when they implored
his mercy, even although he found that in many cases their
repentance was not sincere. His brother, Jean François de
Sales, who had been appointed his coadjutor, was a grave
silent man, inclined to severity. When a priest relapsed
into crime, he refused to show him any further mercy. But
Francis dwelt upon the infinite tenderness of God towards
sinners, His ears are always open to their prayers, and His
compassion can always be touched by their tears. 'What,'
said he, 'can it be wrong to follow such an example? God
has so often been moved by my tears, and shall I be insensible to those I see flowing from the eyes of my brethren?
God listens to the prayers of miserable sinners and grants
them ; and shall I, who am only a man and a miserable sinner
like themselves, be deaf and hard-hearted?'

'True,' replied his brother, 'but God sees the heart and
pardons only those whose repentance is sincere, whilst you who
have not the same advantage forgive every one indiscriminately.
Doubtless there are some whose hearts are touched by your
compassion, and they are converted and sin no more ; but
others take advantage of it, and, being certain of forgiveness,
they do evil with impunity, and become incorrigible.'

Frances yielded to these remonstrances so far as to compromise matters by leaving the criminals to his brother, and
taking a long circuit on his way to church so as to avoid
the prison.

There was once a mad priest sent to Annecy who was so
violent that he was confined in a wooden cage. Francis
visited him, and watched him with tears. He prayed for a
time in silence, and then desired that the door of the cage
might be opened as he intended to go in. Remonstrance was
in vain ; he entered alone, and taking the madman by the

hand said : 'Put your trust in God, my brother!' and laying one hand gently upon his head he stroked and smoothed his hair. The poor fellow was soothed and grew quite calm, and Francis, still holding his hand, led him to his own house, clothed him, seated him by his side at table, and sent him home in his right mind. We should hesitate to acknowledge that this incident is rightly placed among the miracles attributed to Francis ; but it is very human and beautiful.

It is almost needless to say that he was very charitable. He gave away all that he had, the clothes off his back when he had nothing else to give. The Princess of Piedmont presented him with a valuable diamond. He accepted it reluctantly, and only on condition that he might use it for the benefit of others. Whenever, therefore, he was in want of money he pawned the diamond, redeeming it again as soon as possible. A gentleman who had visited him was asked, 'Did you see the Bishop's diamond?' 'The Bishop's,' he replied; 'why it belongs to all the beggars in Annecy!'

Perhaps the most charming picture we have of Francis de Sales is that given by Père Louis de la Rivière :

'Every Sunday and during Lent on Saturdays after dinner, St. Francis used to teach the catechism to little children ; and about an hour before the time a herald, wearing a violet doublet, went round the town ringing a bell, and calling out :

'"Christian doctrine ! Christian doctrine ! Come and learn the way to Paradise."

'I have had the honour of being present at this blessed catechism, and never in my life did I see such a sight; the delectable and truly pious father used to sit on a kind of throne with four or five steps leading to it, and all around him thronged the little children, and many there were of riper age who did not disdain to come and gather spiritual food. Never was there so great a pleasure as to hear him expound the rudiments of our faith, and to see what a wealth of comparisons came crowding to his lips to explain them. He looked at his little people, and the little people fixed their eyes on him : he made himself a child in order that the perfect man in the likeness of our Lord and Saviour might grow within them.

'When you saw him in the midst of little children he seemed to be in his element. They were his felicity and his chief delight ; he caressed them and fondled them with such smiles

and so tenderly, that never was seen the like. And they for
their part would talk to him in all confidence and with great
secrecy ; seldom did he leave his house without finding himself surrounded by this flock of lambs, who saw their kindly
shepherd, and ran to ask his blessing. Sometimes his servants
would check the children, and make signs to them to run away,
fearing lest they should be troublesome. But when he saw
this he would reprove them gently, and say quite kindly, " Oh,
let them come! let them come!" and then he would fondle
the little ones and pat their cheeks, saying, " They are my little
family, my little family, all these dear little folk." And it used
to be considered almost a miracle when the babies, still at the
mother's breast, would crow and dance at the sight of him
coming along the street, and would fret and scream if they
were not taken quickly to the holy man, but after he had
greeted and blessed them they were quiet and content.'

Francis made it a rule never to see or speak to a woman
alone, and he said, 'When you write to a woman, let it be with
the tip of a penknife rather than the point of a pen, so that
you may say nothing superfluous.'

There was no woman in his household, and he habitually
guarded himself against women as the greatest danger he had
to encounter. He contrived to avoid their presence, but with
all his precautions he could not escape their influence, and
foremost among his friends we find a woman, Mdme. de
Chantal, who founded the Order of the Visitation.

CHAPTER X.

In 1619 the Cardinal of Savoy went to Paris to propose a marriage between the Prince of Piedmont and a Princess of France. On this important mission he was accompanied by the Bishop of Geneva, who left his diocese to the care of his coadjutor and brother, Jean François de Sales. It was twenty years since Francis had visited France, and during that time his fame and popularity had greatly increased. The churches in which he preached were again crowded to excess; noble penitents entreated him to direct their conscience; rich preferment lay at his feet. He was no ascetic either in word or deed, and with enjoyment which he did not attempt to conceal, he took part in gorgeous ceremonies, and received flattering attentions from all the wealth and beauty in France. His words gave a correct image of his heart, and this deceived the world, for it seemed impossible that he could really be what he seemed. There were many who imitated his gracious manner and used his honeyed words; but they lacked the true heart, the pure, simple nature, and intense reality which were characteristic of him. He was a dangerous model, because all that marked him outwardly could be so easily put on, whilst that which made him what he was could not be imitated. The school of Francis de Sales, weak, sentimental and tolerant of evil, has reflected back a discredit which he does not deserve, and against which those who know him have a right to protest indignantly.

Angélique Arnauld was at Maubuisson in 1619. One of the novices whom she received there was a daughter of the

Introducteurs des Ambassadeurs. The father of this young lady was very anxious that she should be confirmed by the Bishop of Geneva, whom Angélique also had a great desire to see. She had long been interested in Mdme. de Chantal's work, and even wished to join the Order of the Visitation.

She was therefore grateful when, on the 5th April, 1619, the father of her novice brought the Bishop with him to Maubuisson. She writes of this occasion : ' I had always had a great desire to see him ; and when I did so I had a still greater wish to place my conscience in his hands, for it was clear to me that God was working in and by this holy Bishop. I had never yet found anyone at all like him, although I had seen all those who had the greatest reputation for piety.'

We have no account of this first meeting. Marie Claire, who was with Angélique at the time, and who could have described it, died before the nuns had been commanded to write the numerous memoirs which afford material for the history of Port Royal. Angélique used to thank God that, after all, very little would be known about her, because the sister who knew her life thoroughly had taken all with her to the grave. But it is certain that, from the first meeting, she believed that her Father in heaven had sent her a spiritual father upon earth, the guide and director whom she had so long been seeking ; and that Francis de Sales recognized her noble nature and the importance of the work she had undertaken.

After the first visit she wrote to beg him to return to Maubuisson. He did so ; and went there several times before he left France, staying on the last occasion for nine days. At Angélique's entreaty he also visited Agnes at Port Royal and their father at Andilly.

M. Arnauld was delighted to welcome the Bishop to his well-ordered country house, where children and grandchildren were gathered round him ; and the whole family had good reason to be proud of the friend whom Angélique had gained for them.

It is difficult to say how many of M. Arnauld's twenty children were alive and at Andilly in 1619 ; probably ten or twelve of them. We know that his eldest son, d'Andilly was there with his own wife and several children ; their third, was a very beautiful little boy named François ; the Bishop looked at him

and said : ' What a fine child ! but there is death in his eyes.'
And so there was ; three days later he was attacked with small-
pox, which proved fatal.   This prediction need not be called
a prophecy ; but it shows the searching glance which always
sees much that is hidden from a casual observer.

M. Arnauld's second son, de Trie, was also at Andilly, and
of him the Bishop predicted that he would leave the bar and
enter the Church.   He did so not long afterwards.

Mdme. le Maître, whose married life had been most unhappy,
was separated from her husband, and had returned with her
five sons to her father's house ; she had resolved to enter a
convent as soon as their education was completed, and took the
first of the conventual vows, that of perpetual chastity, during
the visit of St. Francis.   Her eldest son Antoine le Maître,
who was eleven, made a general confession to the Bishop ;
whilst his ' little uncle,' Antoine, M. Arnauld's youngest and
twentieth child, received the holy man's blessing.   Magdalen
Arnauld, who was eleven, was a very pretty child, and the
Bishop predicted that she would be a nun, if her *mirror* did
not stand in the way.   The mirror did not stand permanently
in the way ; and again the prediction, or, as the Arnaulds
call it, the prophecy, was fulfilled.

Angélique had never relinquished her desire to give up her
abbey and follow Christ as one of the poorest and lowest of
his servants, and the visit of Francis de Sales rekindled the old
flame ; she longed to become a sister of the Order of the Visitation.   But Francis would not listen to her proposal, or allow her
to leave her own order, in which he saw that she was needed.
She thought, however, that if she could free herself from Port
Royal, Mdme. de Chantal would certainly not refuse to receive
her.   She therefore wrote to tell her father that her work at
Maubuisson would not be completed for several years, and that
it would be desirable to have another Abbess appointed,
as a convent could not long be governed by a nun like Agnes
without authority.   M. Arnauld was more than equal to the
occasion, and again he made Angélique's scruples serve his
own ends.   He wrote, after some delay, to say that he thought
her objection valid, and quite agreed with her ; and that he
would provide a remedy by making her sister Agnes coadjutrix
of Port Royal ; she would then have the requisite authority
in Angélique's absence.   He had obtained a brief from

Rome so rapidly and secretly that Angélique knew nothing
until the whole matter was arranged, and the letter which
announced his intention was accompanied by proofs of its
fulfilment.   She discovered that, instead of renouncing her
abbey, she had secured it for a second member of the family.

When the Bishop heard of the transaction, he said, 'What,
my daughter! And are you also one of those who wish to keep
benefices in their own family?'   Angélique had no difficulty in
explaining her real wish and aim, which he appreciated.   It was
a curious protest from a man whose brother was his coadjutor
in the see of Geneva.

He left Maubuisson in September 1619, and Angélique saw
him no more.

It was only a few days later that Mdme. d'Estrées escaped
from the *Filles Penitentes* at Paris; and Angélique felt that his
visit had been a preparation for that stormy scene in the church,
and the walk to Pontoise, as well as for the triumphant return
to the scene of her labours.

Three years later, in 1622, Francis de Sales died.   His
friendship for Angélique had been unbroken, and she received
numerous letters from him, a few of which have been preserved,
and are those which in his collection are addressed, 'To an
Abbess.'   Many were destroyed a few years later as a 'mortification,' and it is probable that it was very effectual.   She did
not value the letters as her own personal possessions, and
deprecates the too favourable terms in which she is mentioned
in them; but she considered them, and justly, as treasures which
Port Royal might well guard with jealous care.

In one of them he says, 'I begin where you end, my very
dear and truly well-beloved daughter; for your last letter ends,
"I think that you know me."   Yes, certainly I do know you,
and know that your heart is entirely set upon serving God; but
I know also that your very ardent and impetuous nature sometimes carries you away.   Ah, my daughter, do not, I beseech
you, imagine that the work begun in you can be so soon completed.   Cherry-trees bear fruit quickly because they produce
nothing better than a cherry, soon ripe and soon over; but the
palm, that prince of trees, is said to bear no dates until it has
been planted a hundred years.   Mediocrity may be acquired
in twelve months; but, alas! the perfection at which we aim
does not come, dear daughter, for many years.'

"Oh my daughter, cannot you prostrate yourself before God when a thing happens, and say quite simply: "Oh my God, if this is Thy will it is my will also, and if it is not Thy will then it is not my will," and then pass on from this matter to some action or exercise which shall divert your mind? But, my daughter, I will tell you what you do in such a case. When this trifling matter enters your mind you are angry and will not consider it, you are afraid that it may prove a stumbling-block to you. This fear robs you of all strength, and leaves you pale, and sad, and trembling; and then the fear itself displeases you and engenders another fear lest the first fear and the terror to which it has given rise should lead you into evil, and it is thus that you bewilder yourself. You are afraid of fear, and then you are afraid of the fear of fear. You are annoyed at an annoyance, and then you are annoyed at having been annoyed with an annoyance. Just as I have seen persons who put themselves into a passion, and then are angry at having been in a passion. It is like the circles which we see when we throw a stone into a pool of water, for there is first a little circle and then a larger and another, and then another.'

Again he says: 'We must not be too severe with ourselves, our faults, and imperfections; for although it is in accordance with the dictates of reason that we should be annoyed when we have committed a fault, yet we must be careful not to cherish bitter angry severity, for it is thus that many are bitter because they have been bitter, and angry because they have shown anger, and are vexed because they have been vexed. We must strive to feel such sorrow for our faults as shall be firm and constant, but tranquil, gentle and peaceful. For just as a judge executes justice upon offenders far better when he passes sentence in a calm mind under the sway of reason than when he passes sentence with anger and impetuosity (because if he allows himself to be influenced by anger he does not punish faults according to their magnitude, but according to his own state of mind), in the same way we punish our own faults much more effectually by a persistent and tranquil repentance than by bitter, impetuous and angry repentance, because that impulsive sorrow does not result from the nature of our sins but of our own inclinations.'

Angélique was at this time exposed to two antagonistic influences, which possibly neutralized each other. The Ladies of Maubuisson opposed and ridiculed her; whilst admiring friends, relatives and her faithful nuns, thought and said that she was perfect, and received her words as oracles. She stood in need of some one who would appreciate her work and aims, and at the same time not rest contented with what she had already achieved, but lead her onwards. She found such a friend in St. Francis, and surrounded as she was by difficulties of all kinds, his favourite saying, 'Ask nothing, desire nothing, refuse nothing,' indicated the frame of mind which she most needed to cultivate. Another of his sayings commended itself to her at once, for she, like the saint, was blessed with a sweet temper, and inclined to ways of pleasantness; it was: 'More flies are caught with one spoonful of honey than with ten barrels of vinegar.'

Francis made many inquiries as to the rules of Maubuisson and Port Royal, and after hearing them, said, 'My daughter, wouldn't it be better not to try for such large fish, and to take more of them?'

She told him of the difficulty she had experienced in finding a director of conscience, and that therefore she had been obliged to take advice and assistance from all sides, which was in reality guiding herself. He answered that 'she need not be uneasy on that point, as there is no harm in seeking from several flowers the honey which we cannot find in one.' Angélique admired the answer, but thought it would be dangerous to act upon it; and indeed it was rather a fanciful evasion than a true solution of her difficulty.

There is nothing that shows the strength or vitality of Angélique's nature more than this friendship for Francis de Sales and the lasting esteem with which she honoured his memory. She was not of those who seek first one guide and then another, quickly adopt and as easily abandon views and principles, who are led in opposite directions all unconscious of a change, and renounce a leader from caprice rather than conviction. She weighed the words and worth of St. Francis, though he was fifty-three and she was twenty-eight; she distinguished maxims that it would be dangerous to act upon; but she also recognized his loving insight and lofty aspirations, his faith in God and faith in man, and she never relinquished what she had once gained; truth and goodness, once seen, were never lost sight of by her. What Francis de Sales taught her she never forgot; his gentle words were often on her lips, still oftener we may believe in her heart.   His firm faith in the love of God to man and of man to God, lends a tender compunction to the sterner doctrine which she received from later guides; the recollection of his gentleness helped her to subdue her own impetuosity, and to overcome her impatience with the faults of others.   She maintained that he was firm as well as gentle, and contrasted him with the Jesuit fathers, saying that of all the priests she had ever known his motives were the purest and most unworldly.

'I opened my heart to him without any reserve,' she says, 'and he spoke to me with equal frankness.   I can assure you that he did not conceal from me his most secret and important thoughts on the state of the Church and of several religious orders, the spirit of which he knew and did not approve, as he thought it too intriguing, too worldly, and too politic.'

More than thirty years later she had a long conversation with her nephew le Maître, which represents her recollection of the sentiments, if not the exact words, of her early friend. Le Maître wrote down all that he could remember as soon as his aunt left the room, and although we cannot therefore look for verbal accuracy in this recollection of an old memory, it is important enough to warrant translation.   It shows what were the subjects that occupied the mind of Angélique as well as that of the Bishop; that she was not engrossed even then by the overwhelming cares of Maubuisson and Port Royal, but could look beyond them to the Church of which she was a member, and trace the disorders of the individual and the community to the immorality and irreligion of the Court of Rome which ought to have been the source of light and truth.

Le Maître says: 'On the 6th of April, 1653, I was talking to her about the Bishop of Geneva, and she said, "That holy man helped me very much, and I think I may venture to say that he honoured me with as much affection and confidence as he bestowed on Mdme. de Chantal.   I was astonished at the manner in which he told me all his deepest thoughts without any reserve, just as I always told and always had told him mine from the very first. He certainly did not receive so much credit as he deserved for his knowledge of the condition of the Church of Rome.   His pure eye could not but see the im-

---

[1] Mémoires pour servir à l'Histoire de Port Royal, vol. ii. p. 307.

morality of monks and priests, which had been brought about by relaxation of their rules ; but he concealed his thoughts, and covered them with a veil of charity and humility."

' " He was quite as much distressed as M. de Berulle, at the irregularities of the Court of Rome, and spoke to me particularly about them. Then he said, 'My daughter, these are subjects for our tears, for in the existing state of the world it would cause great scandal to speak of them, and would do no good. These sick men love their maladies, and do not desire to be cured. The Ecumenical Councils ought to reform the head as well as the members of the Church, for their authority is decidedly higher than that of the Pope. But Popes take it amiss if the Church does not yield to them on every point, although in the order established by God a really representa-tive Council, assembled in accordance with the canons of the Church, is above the Popes. I know as much about this as any one, but discretion keeps me silent, for I see no possible result from speaking. We must weep, and pray in secret, and trust that the hand of God will adjust what the hand of man dare not touch ; and we must humble ourselves beneath the ecclesiastical powers to which we have been made subject, and at the same time entreat God to humiliate and convert them by the aid of His mighty Spirit and to reform the abuses which have crept in to degrade the lives of the ministers of the Church. We must implore Him to send holy men, animated with the zeal of Saint Charles, who will purify the Church by the fire of their zeal and knowledge, and make it without spot or stain in discipline, as it is in doctrine.' He found some consolation in opening his heart to me, and I know that he did the same to Mdme. de Chantal. He had drawn us together, as closely as it was possible to do two persons who had never seen each other." '

These extracts help us to understand the attitude of Angélique towards her Church. She believed that it embodied all the great truths necessary to salvation. So far as we know, she never experienced the slightest difficulty with regard to any of its doctrines ; the attraction which she felt as a girl towards her Huguenot aunts was not the longing for a purer faith, but a desire to be set free from the vows which bound her to a conventual life. Intellectual difficulties she had none, moral difficulties many, but she attributed them to the individual and not to the system.   Priests, monks, bishops, and Popes were fallible, but the Catholic Church was infallible.   If she could have enforced strict obedience to the rules of the monastic orders, obedience, not only to the letter, but to the spirit of them, she would have realized her highest ideal of holiness upon earth.

Francis de Sales had no more desire for innovation than Angélique.   He was contented with the theory of his Church, and found all the freedom that he needed in practice.   Angélique learnt from him to attribute every evil and all the persecution she had ultimately to undergo to the individual, and not to the Church.   Moreover, she looked upon Francis as a saint ; and the recollection of his faith and piety, his gentleness and consideration for others, his faith in the good as well as the evil in human nature never failed to kindle her enthusiasm.

Angélique retained through life the affection and veneration for Mdme. de Chantal, who was nearly twenty years her senior, which she had learnt from Francis de Sales.   They saw each other at the rare intervals when Mdme. de Chantal was called to Paris by work connected with her order.   Their first meeting took place in 1620, at Maubuisson ; Mdme. de Chantal was ill, and Angélique, who had acquired considerable reputation for her surgical skill, bled her in the hand ; the nuns preserved the blood, and dried it so as to have *relics* of the saint.

These years are eventful for Angélique.   In December 1619 her father died at sixty years of age, comparatively young for an Arnauld.   During his illness he made known his determination to renounce the world if he recovered, and to change his name from Antoine to René, or Born again.   He desired that his past life should be marked by a black stone, and that which he was about to lead by a white one.   He also made a vow that any plans formed by his wife and eldest son during his illness with reference to the disposal of the property after his death, such as selling the house, or anything of that kind, should be carried out on his recovery.   Such vows were by no means uncommon at this time, but they availed nothing, and eleven days later M. Arnauld died.   He was a good husband, and an affectionate father, shrewd and worldly, and seeking in all that he did to advance the interests of his family; but withal his aspirations were towards goodness and piety, and he strove after them for himself and his children.

The bulls from Rome appointing Agnes coadjutrix of Port Royal did not arrive until 1620, after her father's death. The appointment was most distasteful to her, and she thought that Angélique, who disliked the burden of her rank, was transferring it to her upon whom it weighed no less heavily. But there was great joy throughout the community when it was made known, and Angélique came from Maubuisson for the inaugural ceremony. Among other observances at that time it is the coadjutrix, and not the Abbess, who selects the chant for the day. Agnes opened the book at this sentence from the Apocalypse: 'These are the two olive trees.' The words were understood by the community to show the future fecundity of the abbesses as spiritual mothers, and the light which they would show forth in the Church.

But Agnes read them differently. ' *Two* olive trees, sister; we shall be *two*,' she murmured to Angélique, answering thereby the heart of the elder, who was already picturing to herself that future day when she should not divide, but altogether lay aside the burden of her rank, and leave her abbey to the care of the Reverend and dear Mother Agnes.

CHAPTER XI

MAUBUISSON was offered to Angélique, but she declined it. She said that under existing circumstances the Abbess must be a woman of rank, with influential friends; and urged that as she found the small poor Abbey of Port Royal too great a burden for her, she could not accept one that was large an ' wealthy. She pointed out that she had placed the tempora¹ affairs of Maubuisson in the hands of a man of business, so that she might devote herself entirely to the spiritual well-being of its inmates; and although she had thus undertaken only one half of the duties of an abbess, the task was too difficult for her.

She suggested that Mdme. de Soissons, natural daughter of the Comte de Soissons, and half-sister of Mdme. de Longueville, had all the qualifications necessary for so important a post. Her high birth (for illegitimacy was not considered a stain upon it) would be a security against any danger from Mdme. d'Estreés, and would be appreciated by the Ladies. She was a nun at Fontevrault, and had a reputation for piety and conformity to the rules of the Order which led Angélique to hope that she would undertake the reformation of Maubuisson. The abbey was offered to her and accepted. She went to it at once; but Angélique ruled the house for thirteen months longer, until Bulls could be obtained from Rome and the new Abbess formally installed.

When Mdme. de Soissons was expected the whole convent insisted that Angélique should have a new gown. She yielded to their wishes, especially as they urged the necessity of showing respect to the Abbess-designate. After she had put it on she was in conference with her novices, and could not refrain from looking at her dress and exclaiming, ' What a gown ! Is it possible that I am obliged to wear such a gown as this!' And then, in her love of sacred poverty, she forgot the subject on which she had been speaking, and talked to her pupils of the poor in spirit and the poor in this world's goods, who had nothing and hoped for nothing, until they were moved to tears. A few days later she exchanged the new gown for a shabby white one worn by one of the postulants, of which she grew so fond that she wore, and darned, and patched it, until no scrap of the original material remained.

She was disappointed in Mdme. de Soissons, whose friends had given an exaggerated account of her piety in order to enlist Angélique's sympathy in her favour. The new Abbess was luxurious and self-indulgent. The Capuchin monks and Jesuit priests defended her habits, and told Angélique she ought to make allowance for a Princess, who had made far greater sacrifices to become a nun than she had done, and who had no love of poverty and asceticism. Angélique replied that she no longer considered her as a Princess but as a nun, and that she ought to live like one, and not like a Princess. The new Abbess had no intention of reforming Maubuisson, no interest in Angélique's aims. They treated each other with respect; but that was all, and Mdme. de Soissons' coldness gradually changed to angry intolerance and culminated in bitter reproaches against Angélique for having ' filled the house with beggars.'

'Madam,' said Angélique, 'if you think that your monastery, which has thirty thousand francs a year, is overburdened by those whom I have admitted, we shall not think so at Port Royal, where we have only six thousand.'

She wrote immediately to her own community, and asked if they had faith and courage to share their *poverty* with the Maubuisson novices. A letter signed by the whole sisterhood of Port Royal told her that they would be received joyfully.

Nineteen of the thirty-two novices had now taken the veil, ten as nuns of Port Royal, and with the understanding that they were to accompany Angélique thither; and nine as nuns of Maubuisson. As the removal of these nine would reflect unfavourably on the Abbess and the monastery, it was certain to be strongly opposed by Mdme. de Soissons; she would

rather keep the 'beggars' than have it said that they would
not stay with her.   But when they found that Angélique and
all their companions were about to leave, they implored her
to take them also.   She could not refuse their entreaty, and
thought that it would be a failure of duty to abandon them.
They drew up a petition, which was forwarded to the General
of the Cistercian order, together with the letter already referred
to from Port Royal. Considerable influence was used to induce
the Abbot of Citeaux to grant their request, and the matter
was kept so secret that Mdme. de Soissons and the Ladies had
no suspicion of what was going on.   When the Abbot sent
permission for the removal of *all* those whom Mdme. de Port
Royal had received there was great rejoicing ; but Mdme. de
Soissons was surprised and angry, and never forgave Angélique
for her share in the transaction.

Angélique wrote to her mother, who now was a widow,
asking if she would send carriages to Maubuisson to convey
them to Port Royal ; but she added that her mother was not to
do so unless God inclined her heart to bestow this alms freely.
Mdme. Arnauld sent the carriages required, and female attendants to escort the travellers.   Angélique spent a few days in
Paris at Mdme. de Chantal's monastery of the Visitation, and
with her mother ; her companions went direct to Port Royal.

She feared that the excitement caused by their arrival would
lead to a great relaxation of discipline, therefore when they
left her she imposed a rule of absolute silence until they
should meet again.   When they were near the end of their
journey, and had reached the summit of the hill, from which,
looking down into the valley beneath, they could see the top of
the steeple of Port Royal, they were to recite together :
'Set a watch, O Lord, before my mouth ; and keep the door
of my lips,' and from that moment their lips were to be sealed
until she rejoined them.   As, however, it was necessary to
provide means for their identification, she wrote their names
upon tickets which were sewn to their sleeves.

They arrived at Port Royal on the 3rd of March, 1623.   It
was a fête-day for the monastery, and all the Sisters went out in
procession to meet them, chanting *Te Deum*, with hearts full
of gratitude to God for this great and good gift, and of love
towards those who were bringing 'sacred poverty' to the
monastery. They drew near to welcome the guests, and lo, they

were all dumb, and the answer of each one was to point to her
sleeve. It cannot be doubted that Port Royal had had pleasant anticipations of long stories about Maubuisson, Mdme.
d'Estrées, and the Ladies, and that they felt a momentary
disappointment at finding these were not to be realized. But
their own discipline was scarcely inferior to that of Angélique's
thirty-two, and their fervour and piety received a fresh impulse
from the accession of this silent devout band.

Angélique returned on the 11th or 12th of March, and was
received with great joy. She removed the seal of silence from
the Sisters, who had been dumb for nine days ; but it was only
to greet them tenderly, and ask after their welfare ; each one
then returned in silence to her accustomed work.

There were now more than sixty persons in a monastery
which had thirteen cells in the dormitory. Angélique says :—

' I built some new ones of lath and plaster, very poor. The
splendour of the house I had just left, and its wealth, had shown
me how these unfortunate tares choke the good seed. I had
seen so much of the accursed evil and detestable monuments
of vice in that house, and how completely they had destroyed
the work of the holy queen who had founded it,[1] that I was
more than ever in love with sacred poverty; and as far as
possible I had taught those who accompanied me to love it,
and they had a great affection for it, and were delighted to
find themselves in a house so poor and peaceful as Port Royal.'

Angélique's sisters Agnes and Marie-Claire, together with
Sister Isabelle-Agnes, possessed great influence, and their zeal
made them eager to discover new methods of serving God
and sacrificing themselves. They submitted all their plans
to Angélique, who modified some and rejected others, being
guided by that excellent common sense which made her avoid
extremes. There was at that time a violent recoil from Maubuisson. The example of the idle, gossiping Ladies, with their
scandal and mischief-making, had given rise to an exaggerated
notion of the sanctity of silence ; and the faith of the community
in this *virtue* was so great that they resolved to abolish conferences which were not in accordance with the rule of St.
Benedict.

All the nuns worked by turns in the kitchen, and Sister
Isabelle-Agnes was there for six weeks in Lent. During that

---

[1] Blanche of Castille, mother of St. Louis.

time she never spoke one word, either superfluous or necessary, but made herself understood by signs.   It was owing to
her influence and example that a wave of silence swept over
the monastery, and the enthusiasm which had been kindled, and
for which there was no adequate outlet, was employed in
checking itself.

During this period a young nun was sent to a cell which had
been assigned to her and was supposed to be duly furnished.
Upon entering it she found that it was full of bundles of firewood; she wrapped her cloak round her and lay down quietly
in a corner; made no remark on the following day, and
continued to occupy it in uncomplaining silence.   One day she
was wanted, and the sister who was sent to fetch her opened
the door and found nothing, as she thought, but a store-closet
full of firewood; so she returned, saying there must be some
mistake, as the cell was not occupied.   The young nun was
sent for and asked where she slept?   In that place, she answered,
and it did very well for her.

This was nothing extraordinary at a time when poverty and
mortification of every sense were sought for and received with
gratitude at Port Royal.   The slothful, selfish lives of the
Maubuisson Ladies, their wealth and love of pleasure, had
made an indelible impression on young and ardent natures.
They were willing to suffer any privation and hardship, rather
than desecrate their high vocation and bring into disrepute
the holy name of nun.   As the drunken Helot to a Spartan
youth, so was Maubuisson to Port Royal.   It was associated
in Angélique's mind with a sense of failure and of her own
insufficiency; but to the world, the matter bore a very different
appearance.   Maubuisson was a splendid success; the Abbess
had been removed, the nuns were reformed, religious observances re-established, and the rules of the Order were now
observed.   The young Abbess of Port Royal had effected
these marvellous changes, she and a band of holy maidens
who were devoted to her, and who followed in her steps.
They had now returned to a home which was the abode of
piety and good works.   The holy lives and good deeds of the
Sisters were talked of far and near.   Before long nuns from
other convents began to ask permission to join Port Royal,
and Angélique would not refuse any who were really in earnest,
and were drawn to her by motives which she respected.

Her youngest sister, Madeleine, born in 1607, entered upon her noviciate in 1624. 'When I passed through Paris in 1818 on my way to Maubuisson I stayed at my father's house, and there I found my little sister Madeleine, who was very pretty and knew it, and was also very worldly. When I saw this I was quite grieved, and said : "How is this, little Madeleine ; won't you be a nun and come and live with us?" To which she replied quite pertly : "No, sister, I have not the slightest desire to do so." "Why, my child, then what do you want?" "Well, sister, I want to be married." Upon which I asked, "And pray why do you want to be married?" "Because I am so fond of babies," she replied. "I love them with all my heart. I am never tired of kissing and nursing my little nephews, and that makes me wish to have babies of my own." This simplicity of a child of ten years old who did not know what marriage meant, and only looked upon it as the means of procuring little children to play with, made me laugh at first, but afterwards I was very sorry to see her so frivolous and with no thought of serving God.'

Doubtless the visit of her Abbess-sister produced a great impression upon little Madeleine, and the result of it may be seen in a dream which she never forgot. One night, when she was eleven years old, she was sleeping in the room of her sister Mdme. le Maître. She dreamt, or, as she thought, had a vision of St. Madeleine, her patron saint, standing in a thorny desert, and stretching out a white and beautiful hand, with which she beckoned to her to draw near. She did so, and the saint pointed to a nun's white dress, and gave her some butter—a symbol, as she thought, of the food of those who abstain from meat. The child aroused Mdme. le Maître, recounted her dream, and said that she intended to be a nun. Her sister laughed, told her that she and her intentions were very young, and she had better go to sleep again. She replied, 'Well, you will see what comes of it. It is quite true that my resolution is very new just now, but soon it will be hours old, and then days, and weeks, and months ; and at last years will show you that I am in earnest.' On the morrow she told her parents and friends of her intention, and they also laughed at her. She was very pretty, very lively, admired and beloved by all who knew her, and she was her father's darling ; but her resolution never faltered. In 1624, when she was fifteen years old, she forsook her *mirror*, entered upon her noviciate, and in 1625 fulfilled the prediction uttered by St. Francis, and became a nun.

Very soon after she had taken the veil her ardour began to relax. Like all the Arnaulds, she was high-spirited, gay, and light of heart. The solitude of the monastery was irksome, the implicit obedience required of her very difficult. Instead of submitting, she contradicted and argued. Angélique's tenderness and patience never failed her at such a time, but when she found that instead of producing a good effect they tended to increase the self-sufficiency and vainglory of the young nun, she resolved to 'drive out the demon of pride by confusion.' So one day, when Madeleine had disputed instead of obeying, she seriously reprimanded her, and then boxed her ears soundly. 'The proud devil left her from that day,' we are told, 'and until her death she was remarkable for her simple, unaffected piety, her humility and submission.'

After an example of Angélique's severity it is only right to give one of her tenderness. During her absence at Maubuisson Sister Marguerite, who had at first been received as lay-sister and had taken the veil after some years' residence at Port Royal, was rather troublesome. When Angélique returned she removed her from the office of cook in order to give her rest, which she seemed to need. But Sister Marguerite resented the interference of her Abbess, and her temper was so violent that at one of the high festivals of the Church, Angélique would not allow her to partake of the Holy Communion. Sister Marguerite resolved to run away, and spoke of her intention to the Confessor, who did not however tell the Abbess. When night came she went to a room where the secular dresses, discarded by the novices, were kept, and changed her own for one of them; and she stole some relics which were kept in a cross above the altar. The convent walls were so low that with the help of a ladder she easily got over them, and was soon in the open field. And then a great fear of wolves fell upon her, for at that time there were many in the country. She had often heard them howling around Port Royal, and knew what havoc they committed among the flocks. But anything was better than being devoured by them. She knocked at the door of a poor woman who lived in a cottage near the abbey and entreated her to let her sit by her fire till morning. But

the woman said, 'I don't know who you are, I don't know anything about you; why do you come to me? Go about your
business.' And then the nun entreated so piteously that the
woman relented, and allowed her to come in and sit by the
fire. As soon as it was daylight the unwilling hostess told her
to go, and she went out and made her way to Paris, where
she had a sister in service. At the sight of her the sister said,
'Oh, you wretched woman! what have you done?' for she
thought she must have committed some crime, and had run
away to escape punishment. 'I am lost!' was the only
answer of the nun. As her sister could get no information
from her she took her to the confessional of the monks of
St. Bernard, where she was told that the Fathers would not
confess secular persons. 'I am a nun,' she said, 'and I have
run away from Port Royal.' She was sent to a place of safety
and a messenger was despatched to her Abbess. Meanwhile
on the following morning the priest of Port Royal was in the
confessional, when a man asked for him and said, 'My father,
somebody has tried to rob you in the night, for there is a ladder
against the convent walls.' The priest immediately suspected
what had happened, and search was made for Sister Marguerite
throughout the house and in the neighbourhood, but all in
vain; the priest set out on horseback, but could obtain no
tidings of her. Angélique and the sisterhood fasted and
prayed, and implored God with many tears to have mercy on
her and restore her to them. At length news came that she
was in Paris, and would be kept there until Angélique could
send for her. She did so on the following day, and Sister
Marguerite reached Port Royal at night. When the carriage
wheels were heard Angélique had all the lights put out so that
no one might see the return of the poor penitent, and she
stood alone at the open door, and took the wanderer in her
arms and kissed her, with no other words than 'Oh my dear
child!' Then she led her into the convent and took off the
secular dress and gave her the garb she had discarded, and
appointed a nun who was her special favourite to be her constant companion. But it was in vain; Sister Marguerite was
one of those who was repelled by the purity of heart and life
which she saw around her. She ran away a second time, and
Angélique, seeing that nothing could be done for her at Port
Royal, allowed her to be sent to another convent, reproaching

herself for not having done enough or done it in the right way.

Shortly after her return from Maubuisson, Angélique was asked to send two nuns to the Abbey of Lys, one to act as Prioress, the other as mistress of novices. She selected for the first post Sister Anne Arnauld, and for the last Sister Marie des Anges. They laboured at Lys very much as Angélique had done at Maubuisson, but in the end they were successful, and Lys was reformed.

The Abbess of Lys had promised the Princess de Tremouille to select her cousin, Mdme. de Tremouille, as coadjutrix; but she broke her word, and conferred this favour upon Mdme. de Rissé. The Princess was deeply offended, and there was a strong party in her favour among the nuns, who were resolved not to alienate such an influential patron. They therefore consented to the proposal made by her, that Mdme. de Rissé should be forcibly ejected from the abbey, and Mdme. de Tremouille installed in her place. This was done.

The Abbess had been suspended by the Superior of the Order for many and great faults, but she would not submit to the sentence which deprived her of all authority; and would not allow Mdme. de Tremouille to take her place and usurp the post of coadjutrix.

We may take this as a fair example of many of the difficulties which Angélique was now called upon to solve. In 1625 she joined the two Port Royal Sisters. The Abbess was tormenting Mdme. de Tremouille in every possible way, and was determined not to resign her functions, although she had been formally suspended. When the bell rang for divine service, she used to hurry to the church, obtain possession of the throne of the Abbess, direct the choir, and chant the benediction; thus giving rise to great confusion and disturbance. Mdme. de Tremouille wished to stay away altogether, because, for example, at vespers, when she began to chant *Paternoster*, the Abbess would shout as loud as she could, so as to drown her voice, and the nuns were not only scandalized, but were beginning to be divided in their allegiance.

Mdme. de Tremouille would go to Angélique and throw herself weeping at her feet, saying that she could endure it no longer, and must remain in her own room. But Angélique replied that this was ordained by God as a punishment for

having obtained the office of coadjutrix illegally; she must
not only submit to this decree, but accept it willingly; when
the Abbess took the high seat, she must take the low; but she
must not refrain from attending divine service, for those who
had placed her in authority intended her to exercise it.   She
must not shrink because of difficulty, but must endure, and show
great forbearance; when she had anything to do which she disliked exceedingly, she must first of all ask God to help her,
and must offer at His throne the sacrifice which she was
about to make.

Still, whenever she was alone with the nun who accompanied
her, she used to throw herself on her knees, and say, ' Now let
us pray God to help Madame.'   No doubt in those days she
lived over again the sorrows and humiliations of Maubuisson;
but she never faltered in her duty, and it was the strength of
her nature which made its tender sympathy so precious.

She found that her presence irritated the Abbess so much
that she did not attempt to see her; but in order to show due
respect, sent her companion, Sister Angélique de St. Agnes de
Marle de la Falaire, to pay a ceremonious visit every morning in
her stead.   The Abbess used to take no notice of this nun with
the long name, but would turn to the little birds which filled her
room, and of which she was very fond, and tell them that they
had much more sense than human beings, and she found them
much more amusing.   The nun entreated Angélique not to send
her, for she disliked her mission and was afraid of being alone
with the Abbess, who lived in a house which was quite apart
from the rest of the building.   Angélique replied that she
would not send her if she thought there was any personal risk;
but this she did not believe, and it was easy to see that the
Abbess really had some shade of preference for her, so that
they must persevere, and try to soften her heart.

Angélique's wisdom, her strong sense of right, and also her
influence, enabled her ultimately to make satisfactory arrangements for the community at Lys.

Her uncle on the mother's side, M. de Druy, was President
of the *Grand Conseil;* he was induced to take up the matter
and dispose of the chief difficulty by procuring the deposition
of the guilty Abbess, and giving Mdme. de Tremouille permission to exercise her full rights.   Angélique, however, told
her and the community that they must pause until justice

had been done to Mdme. de Rissé; whether they liked it or
not, she was now legally their Abbess, as she had been appointed
coadjutrix by the Abbess who had been deposed.   She persuaded them to wait until Mdme. de Rissé had been nominated
to another abbey, and then to write to the king, and ask for
Lys for Mdme. de Tremouille.   Through her influence and
exertion, both matters were satisfactorily arranged.

When the Abbess heard that she was deposed, she gave way
to an uncontrollable fit of fury, and after displaying the most
outrageous violence, announced her intention of partaking of
the Holy Communion with the rest of the community.   Angélique was horrified, and insisted that such a desecration must
not be allowed.   She spoke so strongly to the Confessor
on the subject, that when, in spite of all attempts to dissuade
her, the Abbess came forward to the communion-table, he said,
that as her crimes had been public, so he must publicly refuse
to administer to her.

We can imagine the lengthy conferences at which Angélique
had to preside, and the arguments and persuasions necessary
to bring the nuns of Lys to a right mind.   She often sat up
talking until 11 o'clock at night,—a very late hour for one
who began the day at 2 A.M.   When the conversation was
ended, she would say that she felt exceedingly tired, and yet
would do the same thing on the morrow; or if she met a nun
whom she was trying to convince and win to the service of
God, she would stand talking to her for an hour or two, with
no thought of fatigue.   The Sister who accompanied her on
her journeys said years afterwards, that she could still hear
the 'True, Madam; quite true, Madam,' which formed the
invariable answer of those whom she was addressing.   They
were not always conquered by the truth, but they always said,
'When she speaks, all that she asks you to do seems so right
and reasonable that you can't refuse her.'

Among other things whilst she was at Lys, she persuaded a
vain nun to cut off her long and beautiful hair, which was a
great 'snare' to her, as it required much time and skill
to arrange her head-dress so as to show it all off to advantage.

After Angélique's return from Lys, she heard that the new
Abbess of Maubuisson was dangerously ill, and Mdme. de
Longueville applied to her for a nun from Port Royal fitted to

be her coadjutrix and successor. She refused the request, for she knew that the Duke de Longueville had an illegitimate daughter of nine years old, who was a pupil at Maubuisson, and she suspected that, as usual, a nun who could easily be removed was to be put in to fill the position of Abbess until the child was of an age to receive it. But whatever the Duchess may have desired, she protested that she had no such scheme, and that her only aim was to reform the monastery. Angélique therefore yielded, and promised to send Sister Marie des Anges, who had been three years at Lys, and was now about to return to Port Royal. To this excellent nun so high an office offered no attractions. She wept bitterly when Angélique told her of the proposal, and asked if her vow of obedience compelled her to accept it. Angélique answered that she thought not, and yet it might be that God required this sacrifice at her hands. At the word *sacrifice* Sister Marie des Anges yielded ; she took up the dignity of Abbess as a burden which she was to endure for the love of God, and in obedience to His will.

Mdme. de Soissons died in December 1626, and at the request of Mdme. de Longueville, the king at once gave the abbey to Sister Marie des Anges, or, as she is henceforward called, la Mère des Anges. She was accompanied to Maubuisson by eight of the nuns whose removal had caused such estrangement between the two monasteries, and by Agnes Arnauld, who was a powerful auxiliary ; her mystic talk, saintly fervour and ascetic life made a powerful appeal to the imagination, whilst her unobtrusiveness as a simple nun excited none of the jealousy which both Angélique and the Mère des Anges called forth.

Angélique wrote out four rules for the new Abbess, which bear testimony to her practical wisdom and piety, and to the evenly balanced mind which enabled her to discern the path of duty, either for herself or others.

The rules were :—

1. To be very charitable to the poor, and give them large alms, because the great wealth of the abbey had really been intended by the Founders for their service.

2. To receive portionless girls, and never to refuse any who had a genuine vocation.

3. To have nothing whatsoever to do with the monks of

Pontoise, whether Jesuit or Capuchin, and never on any
pretence to allow them to talk to the nuns.

4. To kneel at least three times a day before the Holy Altar
and offer her life and all that she had to Christ, asking Him
for grace and strength to fulfil the duties of her position and
to labour faithfully for the welfare of the souls committed to
her charge.

Marie des Anges was twenty-two years at Maubuisson, and
her compliance with the instructions in the first part of Rule 3
brought upon her the relentless and persevering enmity of
the monks during the whole of that time.   They alienated the
nuns, whom they still saw in the parlours and talked to through
the gratings; and induced them to insist on the return to
Port Royal of Anne Arnauld, who had taken the place of
Agnes.   They could not forgive the Abbess for taking into her
own hands the management of the large revenues of the abbey.
They said this was not the province of a woman; she ought
not to interfere in business matters, to attempt to give spiritual
advice, or exercise any control over the conscience and conduct
of her nuns: this was the province of the priests and monks
and confessors, and any interference was an act of injustice to
them which imperilled the souls of the nuns.

It was in vain that the Abbess gave help to every monk who
needed it.   There were always ten or twelve of them in the
abbey, who were sumptuously regaled.   They had money for
their doctors' degrees, for clothes, church ornaments, vestments,
journeys,—in fact, for everything that they demanded.   But it
was not enough.   They wanted the absolute disposal of all
the funds.   When this was refused, they tried to induce the
Abbess to erect fine buildings, or put up a magnificent altar, as
they knew that the supervision of the works must be entrusted
to them.   But she replied that Maubuisson was already too
magnificent, and that in time of war, when there was so much
destitution and poverty, it behoved her to give large alms.
She could not convince them, and they could not influence her.
Her charity was so unostentatious and unobtrusive that they
could not obtain details which they would have had no hesitation in misrepresenting, but they knew the poor said that the
good Abbess was a mother to them.

English and Irish, as well as Frenchmen, who had been
reduced to extreme poverty by the disturbances of those un-

settled times, were helped by her; she gave portions to destitute maidens who wished to enter a convent; apprenticed many young children to different trades; gave small pensions to unmarried ladies who had been reduced to poverty; and finding that the abbey was deeply indebted, she paid off all its liabilities, restored it to wealth, and made it a place of refuge for the poor and needy.

The monks lodged complaints with the General of the Cistercian Order, and asked him to inquire into the charges they brought against her. He did so, and she rendered him a faithful account of her stewardship. As a result of the visitation, he said he thought she was the most virtuous Abbess in the Order.

But the nuns, encouraged by the monks, opposed all her plans for the spiritual welfare of the monastery, and she found that she must be content with promoting the temporal well-being of the poor, and must abandon the hope of making her abbey 'rich in deeds of grace.'

She laboured at her post for twenty-two years, and then Angélique thought it was time she should be released, and proposed that she should be allowed to resign. Her request was granted. Marie des Anges most thankfully returned to Port Royal, where she asked to be allowed to take her place with the novices, in order that she might again learn the obedience which she feared that she had forgotten in these twenty-two years of command.

CHAPTER XII.

ANGÉLIQUE writes of the period which followed her return from Maubuisson with a fervour of happiness. The revenue of Port Royal was not increased, the house was not enlarged, and yet, for three years, eighty nuns were fed and lodged where formerly there were only sixteen. God had granted poverty in answer to their prayers, and they received it joyfully; one greater gift was still in store for them. This world was only a stepping-stone to the next; life chiefly valuable as a preparation for death; death would crown all their efforts with victory, and open to them the gates of the kingdom of heaven.

Their ignorance of the laws which govern physical well-being, and the contempt which their creed had taught them for this world and the human body, soon brought about the realization of their highest hopes. Sickness and death reigned at Port Royal. Angélique writes :

'God, of His great mercy, now began to take these precious souls out of the world and to call them home to Himself.'

Fifteen nuns died in the first and second years after their return from Maubuisson, and twelve in the third. The infirmary was always full; the overcrowded cells were beginning to look empty. 'It was a great sign of grace and a special manifestation of the love of God,' they said ; but friends could not be brought to look upon the mortality in this light, and asserted that the locality was unhealthy and likely to promote disease.

The drainage of the high lands surrounding Port Royal had been long neglected, and the stagnant water had gathered into pools and formed marshes on all sides of it. It was suggested that the community should leave the abbey, and we have now to consider the motives which led to the adoption of this scheme.

Madame Arnauld had five daughters in Port Royal: Angélique, Agnes, Anne, Marie-Claire, and Madeleine. Mdme. le Maître had expressed her intention of taking the veil as soon as the education of her sons was completed, and had urged her mother also to join the community. Mdme. Arnauld laughed, and replied :

'How can I begin to learn obedience at fifty, when I have been exercising authority ever since I was twelve !'

Nevertheless her heart was with her five daughters, and her chief desire was to be near them. She took refuge at Port Royal in 1623, when the plague was raging in Paris, and discovered that the sanitary conditions of the abbey were no better than those of the city, if so good. This was one reason for desiring the removal to Paris. Another was that she could not leave her eldest daughter, Mdme. le Maître, alone in Paris with so great an anxiety and responsibility as the charge of her five sons. These two circumstances induced her to urge the translation of Port Royal to Paris, and two years later she offered to defray the expense of the removal, to provide means for the purchase of a suitable residence, and also, if her request was granted, to take the veil and end her days under the same roof as her dear daughters. Tempting as this offer was, Angélique would not have accepted it unless she had been drawn by other motives which appealed to her even more strongly.

When she at first undertook the task of reforming her monastery she had met with constant opposition from the Cistercian monks who were sent to her as confessors. There can be no doubt that they would have succeeded in stifling her efforts, if, through her father's influence, the Abbot of Cîteaux had not supported, and to some extent encouraged her. The Abbot of Clairvaux was also friendly, and so was the Abbot de la Charmoye, her Superior. But the two first Abbots died, one in 1624, and the other in 1625 ; and the men spoken of as their successors had already intimated their intention of bringing back Port Royal to the 'customs of the Order,' that is to say, they proposed to interdict what they called the 'peculiarities' introduced by Angélique, and to withhold the permission granted by their predecessors for those changes which were in reality a return to the old rules.

When this was known at Port Royal, it was resolved that each nun should spend a portion of every day before the altar in prayer to God for help. They knelt there by turns throughout the whole day from the time when danger first threatened them ; and when the friendly Abbots died, prayers throughout the night were added to those of the day.

Angélique began to think that perhaps God did not intend her to find help in her own Order, but to look for it elsewhere than among the Cistercians ; and thus she was led to contemplate a removal from Port Royal as the means indicated for her deliverance.

This view was fostered by the noble friends and patrons who were beginning to look upon monastic reform as a pleasant variety of religious duty.   M. Arnauld, Francis de Sales, Mdme. d'Estrées, and the Duchesse de Longueville had made Port Royal the talk of the day; a brother of Louis XIII. had visited the abbey to see the community, and asked particularly which of them was *The Saint;*—for Genevieve le Tardif, one of the Maubuisson novices, had already acquired a reputation for sanctity which had reached Paris and the court. But Angélique 'did not expose her relics, for fear of losing them.'   She would not run the risk of sacrificing that humility and poverty of spirit which were the most precious possessions of a nun, in order to gratify idle curiosity.   If she could have foreseen the result of a removal to Paris she would not have consented to make a show of her community in order to please the court and the bishops, and to try to restore that odour of sanctity which the Church had lost.   She did not anticipate this danger, and no longer had her father to appeal to for the advice which his knowledge of the world and shrewd practical wisdom made so valuable.   She accepted in all simplicity the assurance of her friends that Paris would give her additional opportunities of devoting herself and her nuns to the service of others who were still in spiritual darkness.

Thus the mortality at Port Royal, the entreaties of Mdme. Arnauld, the hostility of ecclesiastical superiors, and the influence of certain churchmen and friends of high birth whom she always treated with very great deference and respect,

all drew Angélique to Paris ; and soon after her return from
Lys she went there for the express purpose of finding a house
to which the whole convent might be removed with as little
delay as possible.   She stayed on the way for eight or ten
days in the convent of Poissy, at the request of the Abbess, to
encourage and direct the good work which she had begun ; and
the numerous inquiries and demands for advice and assistance
which she now received showed her that Paris would be a convenient centre and starting-point for missionary labour.   But
there were many difficulties to be overcome.   The Archbishop
of Paris and the Abbot of Citeaux must be induced to sanction the change of residence ; a house must be found, and it
was obvious that an increase of income would be required
to support so large an establishment in a city like Paris; but
Angélique rejoiced to think that they would be really poor,
nay, possibly brought to depend on God for their *daily* bread,
and she transposed this item to the credit side of the
account.

Mdme. Arnauld disposed of one difficulty by purchasing
the Hôtel de Clugni in the Faubourg St. Jacques, which was at
that time almost in the country ; and, with the consent of the
Superiors, Angélique, and a few of the sisters and scholars,
took possession of it in December 1625.   The remainder were
to follow as soon as possible, for twelve nuns had died in the
course of this year, and a great many more were so ill that it
was necessary to remove them at once.

The Queen-Mother, Marie de Medicis, consented to become
the Founder of the new house, Port Royal de Paris, as it was
called.   The letters-patent from the king, authorizing the
removal of the nuns, are dated December 1625.   They are
curious documents, and characteristic of the abject servility of
the age.

' Louis, by the grace of God King of France and of
Navarre, to all present and to come, greeting.

' Every act which tends to promote the glory of God and to
increase His worship is greatly to be esteemed, but those which
emanate from Illustrious Persons are so much the more com-
mendable as their authors are of higher eminence than others.
And when those whom God has raised to sovereign dignity
employ themselves in good works, the Divine Majesty is much

more glorified and the edification of the people is very much greater than at any other time; the gratitude of those who are at the height of worldly prosperity, and the fact that they offer at His feet the good gifts which they have received from Him does extraordinary honour to God, and calls down blessings upon their reign. Moreover, the force of their example exercises a gentle compulsion over their subjects, who cannot refrain from imitating the piety which shines with so bright a lustre in their princes.

'As therefore the Queen, our very honoured Lady and Mother, has represented to us that, as some acknowledgment of the grace and favour of God, she wishes to promote the re-establishment of discipline and the return to the ancient piety of all religious Orders, and especially that of St. Bernard, to which she is more particularly devoted, and more particularly those convents for nuns in the Order in which reform is beginning to make such progress that we may look for great results if it pleases us to support and protect its zealous promoters; and seeing that no one has worked more worthily or with greater success to secure the strict observance of the rules of the said Order than our very dear and well-beloved sister Angélique Arnauld, therefore——'

And so on through an inflated page of self-glorification to give permission, with the consent of the Archbishop of Paris, for their removal from an unhealthy locality in which they were dying fast, where they were far removed from other towns and villages, could not obtain help in time of need, were exposed 'to all the privations of the desert,' and even to the lawless excesses of men-at-arms, and to authorize their establishment in Paris.

Angélique wished to leave a certain number of nuns at Port Royal *des Champs*, as it is henceforth called, and to keep up both houses. But the Archbishop insisted on the removal of the whole community. A chaplain was, however, left at Port Royal; there was daily service in the church, and the manorial and feudal rights of the abbey were maintained.

Angélique paid her workmen at Port Royal for the last time from a bag which contained every coin at her disposal. When she had paid all away, a poor man came forward and asked for alms; she said that she had no more, and stood for a moment in sad silence; then she stooped, took off her shoes and gave them to him.

The Paris house was not large enough to accommodate them all, so that a gallery was added, and the garrets converted into dormitories; by this means at the end of the year they were all lodged, though they were even more crowded than they had been at Port Royal *des Champs.* The choir was so small that only one-fourth of the nuns could enter at a time, and they dined in relays in the little refectory. Still in spite of the inconveniences they were quite contented, and went about their ordinary work in silence and with devout humility.

But it was not an easy time for Angélique. She saw that extensive additions were absolutely necessary for the permanent accommodation of a large community, and that she must either diminish her numbers or build. The latter was difficult; the former impossible. Any other Abbess would at once have looked out for two or three wealthy girls, persuaded the parents to place them with her, and their portions would have supplied the requisite funds. Angélique not only did not do this; at this very time she refused to receive three girls whose parents offered 39,000 francs as their portion, because she found that they had no desire to enter a monastery, and no *genuine vocation*, but were merely being put out of the way in order that their sisters might make better marriages. In later years she thought that she had done wrong in not giving them a trial at Port Royal, for, as it happened, they made good nuns in the monastery to which they were sent. But in 1626 she could not have relaxed her rule without seeming to abandon her principle, since her experience and knowledge were not then sufficiently large to guide her in applying it. Moreover she had discovered that wealthy nuns had influential friends with will and power to interfere with the plans and arrangements of an Abbess; and she had also found that her penniless nuns with a *genuine vocation* had no one to intrigue on their behalf.

All her life she had entertained the greatest horror of debt, and yet she now chose it as the least of the evils before her, and resolved to build with borrowed money, and to pay interest from her income, already sadly too small for the expenses of Paris life.

Undoubtedly if Angélique's father had been alive, none of these things would have happened. He would have pointed out to her that to drain and enlarge Port Royal would have been not only prudent but comparatively easy ; whereas, to remove nearly a hundred persons to Paris, procure suitable accommodation, and maintain them there, was a very arduous undertaking, and must end in the acceptance of offers of help, and the loss of that independence which had hitherto given her so much power. But M. Arnauld was dead, Francis de Sales was dead, so was the friendly Abbot of Citeaux; and Angélique was at this time under the influence of the Bishop of Langres.

Sebastien Zamet, Bishop of Langres, was son of the Italian of the same name, who came into France with the Medicis, and whose name is associated with the business transactions, pleasures, and intrigues of Henri IV. It was at the house of M. Zamet, the financier, that Gabrielle d'Estrées was seized with the sudden illness of which she died in a few hours. He had amassed an enormous fortune, and his influence secured the rapid advancement of his two sons, one in the army and the other in the church. The soldier was renowned for his courage, and was known and dreaded by the Huguenots as ' the great Mahomet.' The priest was a worldly, wicked man, with no aim beyond his own advancement. He was at first Almoner to the Queen, Marie de Medicis, and was subsequently promoted to the bishopric of Langres. He lived as a courtier in great pomp and splendour, and was remarkable for the magnificence of his dress, equipage, and household. In 1622 his brother the Major-General was wounded at the siege of Montpelier, and died in the arms of Angélique's brother, d'Andilly, and in the following year the Bishop was attacked by severe illness and lay at the point of death. He was overwhelmed with horror and contrition when he thought of the past, and resolved if he was spared to lead a new life. He recovered, and immediately renounced the world and devoted himself to the duties of his diocese. He determined to emulate the zeal and penitence of St. Charles Borromeo ; and Cardinal de Berulle, whom he knew, sent one of the Fathers of the Oratory to him as a spiritual director. The court of France was astonished and edified at his conversion, and his asceticism created a greater sensation than his excesses. He spent whole days and nights in prayer and weeping ; made his visitations as Bishop on foot ; and spoke of spiritual things in such an ' elevated manner ' that 'those who listened were quite detached from the earth.' Among those who listened was the Abbess of Tard at Dijon, who forthwith reformed her monastery in accordance with his suggestions. Mdme. de Chantal heard of his zeal and piety, and visited him on her way back to Savoy, after she had established a convent of the Order of the Visitation in Paris. She told him of Angélique and her work, and found that he had visited Port Royal during the absence of Angélique at Maubuisson.

He was summoned to Paris in 1625 on ecclesiastical affairs; and whilst he was still in the first fervour of his conversion Angélique became personally acquainted with him. She thought that God had sent him to her, and, in accordance with the doctrines of the Romish Church, believed it to be her duty to submit her own will and judgment without reserve to a spiritual director and guide. On one point she felt special need of help; from the time of her conversion at sixteen she had been persistently uneasy at keeping possession of Port Royal and remaining in the Cistercian Order. She had renewed her vows more than once, but always with considerable mental reserve; and since she had become acquainted with Mdme. de Chantal she had cherished the hope of some day joining the Order of the Visitation. She now opened her heart to the Bishop of Langres, told him her doubts, fears, and hopes, and confessed that the prospect of a change which distressed her mother and sisters, also unsettled her own mind. He insisted on an absolute renunciation of this desire and intention, and said that when next she received the Holy Sacrament in the chapel of Port Royal she must renew her vows without any reserve whatsoever, so that she might have no pretext in future for leaving her own Order. She obeyed him, but says that the effect of sacrificing her own will and giving up long-cherished hopes was 'as if she had been compelled to become a nun against her will;' however, from that time forth her conscience was at peace, and she lost the desire for change.

This was the only service which Angélique received at the Bishop's hands; and in the period now before us we shall see how gravely her work was compromised by the influence of a vain and worldly man, whose conversion was transient and superficial.

The Abbot de la Charmoye, Superior and Visitor of Port Royal, had always been kind and considerate to the daughter of his friend M. Arnauld, and had not offered any opposition to Angélique's plans.   He was now removed from his office by the new Abbot of Citeaux, who had determined to put down the Abbess of Port Royal and her reform.   But when Angélique saw what she had to expect, she resolved to follow the advice of the Bishop, withdraw from the jurisdiction of the Abbot of Citeaux, and place herself under that of the Archbishop of Paris. This change offered many advantages ; it would set her free from the intrigues and interference of the Cistercian monks, and release her from their presence in the monastery.   She had unwillingly endured them for many years, and spoke and wrote with contempt of their selfish, indolent lives.   They were servile or imperious, the slaves or the masters of an Abbess, must be constantly watched and guarded against, and the only remedy was to change them frequently, so that they should not acquire much power for evil amongst the nuns.   To be free from dependence on the Cistercian Order implied deliverance from the monks as well as from the Superior who had threatened to treat her as recalcitrant, and drag her back into the evil courses of her predecessors.   We need not wonder that she listened to the Bishop and the Fathers of the Oratory whom he had introduced, for she had no reason to suspect them of interested motives, and believed that they were sincerely anxious to promote the welfare of Port Royal.

The Bishop had formed a project in which the Duchess de Longueville was greatly interested.   He wished to found a new Order of nuns specially consecrated to the adoration of the mystery of the Holy Eucharist.   Their constant presence before the altar was to atone for the outrages offered by the ' blasphemy of the Protestants,' and the 'sacrilegious communion of unworthy Christians.'   Angélique entered warmly into this plan, which was in reality a development of the practice already established at Port Royal, and she entreated the Bishop to procure the consent of the Court of Rome for the establishment of such an Order.   But the Port Royal Sisters begged to be allowed to add perpetual adoration to the other pious practices of their rule, and to unite the glorious title of Sisters of the Holy Eucharist to that of Sisters of St. Bernard.   Mdme. de Longueville approved of the suggestion, and seconded it ; but the Bishop would not consent to any modification of his plans, and intended the new Order to follow the rule of St. Augustine and not that of St. Bernard. A petition was presented to the Pope in the name of Mdme. de Longueville, asking leave for the establishment of an Order of the Holy Eucharist, of which the Duchess was to be the Founder, and the Archbishops of Paris and of Sens together with the Bishop of Langres, the Superiors. A bull to this effect was granted, and also another, for which Mdme. de Longueville asked at the same time, permitting Port Royal to withdraw from the jurisdiction of the Abbot of Citeaux and place itself under that of the Archbishop of Paris, retaining all the advantages and privileges which the Cistercian Order enjoyed or might enjoy.

By Angélique's advice the Abbess of Lys also obtained permission to withdraw from the jurisdiction of the Cistercians, and place herself under that of the Archbishop of Sens, in whose diocese she resided.

By the advice of the Bishop of Langres, the Abbess of Tard de Dijon withdrew at the same time from the jurisdiction of the Cistercian Order, and the examples of Port Royal, Lys, and Tard were followed in many other abbeys, so that we need not be surprised to find Angélique beginning to incur the bitter hostility of the Cistercians. The new Abbot of Citeaux was avowedly hostile, but she had many friends in the Order who were proud of her achievements, called her a St. Theresa, and were ready to defend and support her. All these she now alienated. Meanwhile her reputation had been increased by the removal to Paris. She was visited by the Queen-Mother and the court, and influenced the world as well as the Church. Abbesses entreated that one or two of the saintly Sisters of Port Royal might be sent to instruct and guide them, and penitent abbots asked for shirts of the coarsest serge, which they did not always wear.

Some of the missionary expeditions of that time were without apparent result, and others were not free from attendant evils. When Agnes returned from Maubuisson in 1627, she was sent to Gomerfontaine at the request of the Abbess, and found the spiritual and temporal condition of the abbey so deplorable, that, in a letter to Angélique, she said she thought God must have sent her to this spot in order that she might understand the full force of the passage, ' He descended into hell,' and that this was the only result she expected from her visit.

In 1628 the Prioress of the Cistercian monastery of St. Aubin was received at Port Royal with four of her nuns, and in the following summer Angélique returned with them to inaugurate the good work of reform in their own monastery. She took with her Sister Suzanne de St. Esprit, a nun of great promise, whose piety, humility, gentleness, and submission were most edifying to the community. After their labours at St. Aubin were ended they went to Gif, intending, at the request of the Abbess, to make a stay of some duration; but Angélique was compelled to return to Paris by ill-health. Suzanne de St. Esprit was a valuable servant, and whilst under Angélique's control, a shining example of what a nun ought to be, but she was vain and ambitious, and these qualities had not been eradicated by her training, they had merely taken a new direction. It was from vanity, not from piety, that her conduct during her noviciate had been that of an angel, and the appellation of *Saint* was a title of honour she made every effort to acquire. Under the eye of her Abbess her conduct had been as edifying at Gif as it had been at St. Aubin, and it was decided that she should remain when Angélique returned to Paris. She made a long stay at Gif, and underwent the gradual deterioration which is the certain result of flattery and gratified vanity.

It is unnecessary to dwell upon or even to enumerate the missionary efforts of Angélique and her nuns, and we must be contented with a single example of the hardships which often attended their journeys. The Bishop of Langres had requested that Sister Marie-Claire Arnauld and another nun should be sent to Dijon in autumn, although the weather was so bad and the roads so impassable that they do not seem to exaggerate when they say that they undertook the journey at the risk of their lives. It cost Angélique a great struggle to obey the Bishop, and allow them to set out in November; for Sister Marie-Claire and her companion were very delicate. The latter was the same nun who had accompanied Angélique to Lys. She says that when the morning came on which they were to start, the Abbess entered her sister's room, saying that she had been so anxious she could not sleep, and could not make up her mind to send them, for she feared the Sister with the long name would die on the road. But her *obedience* triumphed, and the young nuns were despatched in charge of an older secular lady. They had to encounter sickness, bad weather, and great hardships; and their only consolation through it all was that their Good Mother was thinking of them and praying for them, and that she had foreseen all their difficulties. The floods were out, and one day a great rush of water overflowed the door of the carriage, and nearly swept away Sister Marie-Claire, who with difficulty was caught and held back by her companions. At another time the carriage stuck in the mud, and ultimately broke down in the middle of the fields; it was late at night, and they had to grope their way for six miles on foot. Marie-Claire and the attendant lady kept together, but the poor Sister with the long name strayed away; she was, however, overtaken by a gentleman on horseback, who dismounted and led her by the hand. They shouted as loud as they could to let her companions know where they were, and the direction in which they must go, and at length they all reached the hostelry in safety, though 'wet to the waist' and almost worn out with cold and terror. The cavalier then took leave of them. They always spoke of him afterwards as 'The good angel;' and the adventure was possibly the romance of their lives. The nun ends her narrative with 'Only picture to yourselves a nun walking for six miles alone with a man!' After all, they were compelled to return to Paris and wait until the following March before attempting the formidable journey to Dijon.

The missionary nuns left their monastery with the reputation of saints, but unless their love of God was unalloyed by vanity and love of self, they fell away from the high standard which Angélique had taught them to strive to attain, and began to desire the notice and notoriety which she had enjoined them to shun. But she herself remained unspoilt, and for some time her very purity of aim and conduct blinded her to the change that was going on around her.

Port Royal was becoming a place of fashionable resort. The devotion of the nuns to the Holy Eucharist was talked of by the Bishop of Langres. The Fathers of the Oratory paid them frequent visits, talked to them in the parlours, and reported their words; whilst their little chapel was frequented by court ladies. It was asserted that a lame girl had been enabled to walk by means of prayer and at the command of Angélique. The Abbess, however, at the close of her long life said that she did not believe in any of the miracles attributed either to her or her contemporaries. Her protests and warnings are clear and emphatic, and there can be no doubt that she looked back upon the miracles of that period as delusions which were sometimes conscious, sometimes unconscious, and always to be avoided.

Not so the Bishop of Langres. He had secured the interest of the court and the world of fashion, and he now felt that Heaven ought also to declare for him by some special sign. A new Order of nuns was about to be established, a fresh impulse given to the Catholic Church, and there must be miracles and visions, whether Angélique liked them or not. So the Fathers of the Oratory listened and made notes, wrote down dreams and concocted wonderful versions of so-called visions, incited those nuns who had a reputation for sanctity to pray and fast, and remain in solitude until 'God should reveal Himself to them.' When the exhausted body allowed the mind to wander uncontrolled by sense, and the long-desired words or signs seemed to have been vouchsafed, the Fathers were at hand to question and examine, and extract something more marvellous than even the excited and ill-regulated fancy of a weak woman deprived of food and sleep had ventured to imagine.

The nuns were so completely deceived, and acquired such certainty as to the power granted them by God, that the most zealous resolved to try their hands at a miracle. Now thirty years previously, when the child Angélique went to Port Royal, there had been a certain neglected deaf and dumb Sister whom she pitied and tried to cheer and comfort. When as a girl of sixteen she began the reform of her abbey, this same Sister understood by signs what was going forward, and brought her little private stores and laid them at Angélique's feet. Now, an old and feeble woman, she was unable to comprehend the strange scenes around her, and was therefore selected as the first subject upon whom the nuns would operate. They pictured to themselves her delight and surprise when her ears should be opened and her tongue unloosed, the gift of speech miraculously bestowed upon her, and she raised as from the dead to praise and glorify the Lord. They placed her on a chair in the middle of the choir with sixteen wax-lights round her, emblems of the sixteen centuries which had elapsed since the birth of Christ, and of sixteen corresponding attributes of His divine character. They passed the night in the choir in prayer and watching, and vain efforts to cure the deaf and dumb Sister. From time to time they went up to her to see how the miracle was getting on, spoke to her and tried to make her answer, but they got ' no more answer than Gehazi,' writes one of the Sisters ; when he laid the staff upon the dead child's face, and there was ' neither voice nor hearing.' Clearly the miracle was a failure, and when the morning came the sixteen wax-lights were extinguished, and the poor bewildered old woman was released.

It was also about this time, 1628, that Agnes wrote the *Secret Chaplet* which ultimately had disastrous results for her monastery, and caused a complete division among the promoters of the new Order. One day a nun was reciting a little Chaplet of three words, pausing and meditating after each one that she uttered; they were *Jesus, Love, Pardon*, and it came into her head to substitute for them *Adoration to Christ Jesus in the most holy Sacrament ; Honour to Christ Jesus in the most holy Sacrament ; Glory to Christ Jesus in the most holy Sacrament.* She told this to Agnes, who liked the idea, and for some time recited the new Chaplet as she knelt before the altar, dwelling upon each of the terms and meditating upon the Adoration, Honour, and Glory of Christ. After a time it occurred to her to increase the number of the attributes to sixteen, in honour of the sixteen centuries during which the Holy Sacrament had been instituted ; and to enumerate the Holiness, Truth, Plenitude, Sufficiency, Dominion, Illimitability and other mystical and incomprehensible attributes of Christ ; closing her meditations by a prayer. This Chaplet was shown to Father Condren, one of the Fathers of the Oratory, who approved of it so much that the Bishop of Langres had it printed, and we are told that it was greatly admired. Father Condren asked Agnes how she understood these terms, and if she had no further thoughts about them. Agnes replied that she had, but that it would be easier to write than to explain them. So she wrote them ' without reflection,' as Angélique says, trying to discover and exhaust the mystic meaning of the attributes, and becoming quite unintelligible in the endeavour. She sent a copy of this longer chaplet to the Bishop of Langres, who told her that she must revere these thoughts as not her own, but the thoughts of Christ Jesus in her, and it was shown to the Archbishop of Sens, who also approved of it.   Copies were given to a Carmelite Abbess, Marie de Jesus, who was a very intimate friend of Angélique, and to the Abbess of Lys, but with these exceptions the Chaplet was preserved as a sacred possession, known to very few of the nuns of Port Royal, and used by none of them.

The Bishop and the Fathers urged Sister Genevieve, *the Saint*, to write her thoughts concerning the new Order, and encouraged her in the belief that her utterances were inspired. Some years later her voluminous writings were inspected by a niece of Angélique's, who said she had learnt from them that everything has its proper place, and that a nun's place is the silence and solitude of the convent.

Shortly after the removal to Paris, a certain Mdme. de Pontcarré, who was separated from her husband, desired to live in the retirement of a convent, without taking religious vows.   She was a friend of Angélique's sister Mdme. le Maître, who believed that her piety was genuine, and urged Angélique to receive her at Port Royal, where the money she proposed to pay would be most useful.   Angélique listened to the advice of friends, and against her own judgment consented to the arrangement.   She acted without the knowledge or advice of the Bishop, who had left Paris for a time and was visiting his diocese.   He found on his return that Port Royal had acquired 80,000 francs, and an agreeable inmate, and resolved that, in addition to the enlargements already made, new cloisters and dormitories should be built with Mdme. de Pontcarré's money. The benefactress laid the first stone in the following year, but her money barely sufficed to raise the walls of the new buildings. In order to complete them Angélique was compelled to borrow, and then to borrow again in order to pay interest.   The Bishop wished no expense to be spared, and the debt ultimately amounted to 130,000 francs.

Mdme. de Pontcarré entered Port Royal in 1626 when, like the Bishop, she was in the first fervour of her conversion.   Her husband was then living, but he died shortly afterwards.   An agreement had been drawn up in which she offered 80,000 francs to the abbey on condition that the money should be

restored if she was sent away by the community ; but retained
if she left of her own free will.   In consideration of this sum
she asked for a place on which to stand her bed, a space of
four feet around it, and a lay-sister to wait upon her.   In fact
she asked so little, and that little with such humility, that
Angélique and the Sisters thought she really intended to ' seek
salvation,' and gladly signed the agreement.   Angélique never
forgot a benefit, and always gave more than she had promised.
Instead of the four feet around her bed, she assigned to Mdme.
de Pontcarré a whole room, and that one of the best in the
house, and appointed two lay-sisters instead of one to wait
upon her.   Mdme. le Maître was at first her constant companion,
Angélique paid her frequent visits, and the whole community
was commanded to show every attention to her wishes and to
see that she was well served in every respect.   She is described as vain-glorious, imperious, and wanting in stability
of purpose, but Angélique says she really loved that which was
good, and had such a strong leaning towards virtue, that, under
proper guidance, something might have been made of her.
She was conscious of her own defects, and had attempted
to guard against one of them by the offer to sacrifice her money
if she left Port Royal by her own wish.   She hoped her love
of money would outweigh her love of change.

At first her conduct in the abbey was all that could be
desired.   She found herself occupation within the convent
walls, and was cheerful and contented.   She played remarkably
well upon the lute, and when the Bishop returned to Paris she
was desired to take her lute into the parlour and play to him.
After listening to her, he said that she ought to offer this accomplishment as a sacrifice to God.   She obeyed without a murmur,
gave away all her lutes and music-books, and never again
alluded to them.

The Bishop visited her frequently, seeing her in the parlour
and through the wicket, according to the rules of the convent.
They had long conversations which referred to spiritual matters
and the state of her soul, and were very edifying.   But before
long he began to take the control of the temporal as well as
the spiritual affairs of the monastery, and then it was natural
that he should also discuss the temporal affairs of the individual.

When the dormitory and cloisters were completed, a gallery

above the parlours and on the same floor as Mdme. de Pontcarré's bedroom, was placed at her disposal. She divided it
into sitting-room, study, and an oratory, the latter 'inlaid
with precious stones,' and built a tower adjoining her apartments with a private staircase and an outer door. Moreover, she threw out a broad balcony before the windows, in
which there were a number of orange-trees in tubs. The
Sisters carried eighteen or twenty buckets of water for them
daily. She next engaged an agent, who lived outside the
monastery, attended to all matters of business, and made
arrangements for her comfort and pleasure, so that she was
quite as free and independent as when she was 'in the
world.'

The Bishop now visited her in her own apartments, and
before long the nature of their conversations was changed.
He was seeking his own amusement, not her edification ;
as years passed on his religious impressions began to grow
faint, he was intolerably weary of the life he had chosen,
would not speak of religion or conscience, and cared for
nothing but to try to amuse himself in Mdme. de Pontcarré's
society. He spent day after day in her parlour and dined with
her ; or she went out to dine with him, going and returning by
the private staircase in the tower. She entered readily into
all his views and aims, and as his prestige and influence in the
monastery included her own, she took great pains to keep up
his reputation as saint and ascetic, and to foster the outbursts
of religious excitement which he sought to substitute for the
unassuming piety and self-denial which had hitherto been characteristic of Port Royal. The nuns were taught that they
had been made stupid under the old system, and that if the
rules of the Order were now to some extent relaxed, it was not
to encourage self-indulgence, but to make them more spiritually
minded and enable them to win more souls to God. Sharp
and excessive penance took the place of the steady discipline
of the good old times ; matins at two in the morning were
discontinued, but the nuns were encouraged to spend whole
nights before the altar in prayer, accompanied by flagellation
and other mortifications of the flesh, which were afterwards
discussed and quoted as signs of special grace.

The Bishop desired to attract the court and turn the eyes
of the world upon himself and his disciples. For a time he

seemed likely to succeed. Angélique was often sent on mis-
sions, and in her absence her influence was undermined and
the spirit of Port Royal gradually changed; whilst she, with
her noble earnest nature, did not suspect the danger to which
she was exposed until it was too late and the evil was
accomplished.

CHAPTER XIII.

ANGÉLIQUE'S FALL.

THE Queen-Mother, Marie de Medicis, visited Port Royal in 1628, whilst her son Louis XIII. was besieging La Rochelle.

'Have you no favour to solicit?' she said to Angélique, as she was leaving, 'for when I visit an abbey for the first time I grant whatever is asked.'

Angélique answered by humbly entreating that when the King had taken La Rochelle he would permit her to resign her office, and allow Port Royal to be governed by an Abbess elected every three years by the whole sisterhood.

The Marquise de Magnelai (Marguerite de Condi), who accompanied the Queen, supported Angélique's prayer, saying that there was no fear of its serving as an example or being used as a precedent, for there were certainly not many abbesses in France, with sisters and nieces, who would think of renouncing their rights and power in order to establish triennial election.

M. d'Andilly, Angélique's eldest brother, also solicited this favour at court on his sister's behalf, and was laughed at and told that he was taking as much pains to injure his family and get rid of an abbey as others did to serve theirs and procure one. However, the request was granted, and letters-patent were issued which sanctioned Angélique's resignation and the triennial election of an abbess by the sisterhood. Angélique was influenced by the advice of the Bishop of Langres and the example of the Abbess of Tard. The Bishop had succeeded in withdrawing Tard from the Cistercians and placing it under his own jurisdiction.   At Tard all his views were accepted, his plans carried out, and he could rely on the nuns and the Abbess; but he was beginning to find Angélique troublesome, untractable, and too much in earnest.   She wanted realities, and he wanted show.   Moreover the Arnaulds together were like the bundle of sticks in the fable, and he saw that they must be separated.   He told Angélique how much he longed to unite the two abbeys and to see the same spirit and the same practices in both, and proposed that Agnes Arnauld the coadjutrix and Sister Genevieve (the *Saint*) should be sent to Tard, and that as soon as possible the holy Abbess of Tard, Jeanne de Pourlans, who had renounced her title and established triennial election, should visit Port Royal accompanied by one of her nuns, and instruct them in the purer and more austere rules of her abbey.

Angélique gladly consented, for she believed that piety and zeal for religion were the motives that led him to desire to modify the customs of Port Royal.   In September 1629, Agnes and Sister Genevieve were sent to Tard, or rather to Dijon, whither the community of Tard had been removed on account of the unsettled state of the country and the dangers to which they were exposed in that time of civil war.   It is quite possible that the removal of the Monastery of Tard to Dijon in 1623 was an example urged upon Angélique and which influenced her, when Port Royal was transplanted to Paris; just as the resignation of the Abbess and the strict discipline of the monastery were now set before her as a pattern for imitation.

The selection made by the Bishop was a judicious one. From his point of view he did well to separate the sisters.   He had encouraged the mystic and ascetic tendencies of Agnes, her belief in dreams and visions and revelations.   He had urged her forward, instead of holding her back as Angélique had hitherto done, and she had not yet discovered that what he called sanctity was a hollow show, and the man himself false and superficial.   Her companion, Sister Genevieve, had already obtained the reputation of a Saint, and under the manipulation of the Bishop and the Fathers of the Oratory had learnt to consider prayer and fasting as the only interests and highest labours of life.

After Angélique had parted with her sister, she took counsel with the Prioress and Sub-prioress quite simply and cheerfully, and as if they could supply all that she had lost in Agnes. When letters reached her from Dijon in which Agnes described in the most glowing terms the strict discipline of Tard and the austerities practised by the nuns, Angélique read them with enthusiastic delight. She would take aside her sister Marie-Claire, and another nun, that they might listen to these 'beautiful letters;' and when they suggested that the discipline of Tard must be very severe, she would interrupt them with great warmth, saying :

'Oh, my children, do not say so! Surely, we are only too happy; we have found the way of truth at last. As for me, I am enchanted. M. de Langres is a true man of God. Whatsoever he does is well done, and it is impossible to find any fault in it.' And then she would embrace them saying, 'Courage, courage, dear children. You do not know the joy that fills my heart.'

New letters produced fresh transports and eager resolves to follow the example of Tard, and at the end of five months she was wrought up to such a pitch of enthusiasm, that she could talk of nothing else, and thought Port Royal was not to be compared with Tard in virtue and godliness, and that she herself was the most imperfect member of the community. A few months later, Sister Marie-Claire and the nun with the long name undertook the perilous journey to Tard, previously described. They were despatched by the orders of the Bishop, who, says the narrator, 'took pleasure in stripping la Mère Angélique of all whom she loved best, and who were of most value, in order that he might be better able to change the arrangements of Port Royal.'

In 1630, at the first triennial election held at Tard de Dijon, Agnes Arnauld was chosen Abbess; and Jeanne de Pourlans, the Abbess who had resigned, went to Port Royal. Angélique treated her as a guide who was to instruct her in the paths of holiness, and as an ecclesiastical superior in whose presence she was to maintain a humble silence. Jeanne de Pourlans held no office, but she had supreme power, and reported to the Bishop whatever did not meet with her approval. For example, some labourers had been allowed to pass unattended to their work in the monastery. This was an accidental occurrence, but Jeanne de Pourlans reported it as if it had been habitual, and Angélique in consequence received a sharp rebuke. The nuns were annoyed at this, but she said : 'Do not be angry on my account, for truly I am delighted to have some one to watch over my conduct and actions, and tell me of my faults.' Whenever la Mère Jeanne found fault with anything, Angélique begged her to suggest a remedy, and in every way she placed the authority of this stranger above her own.

Some of the changes seemed injudicious, if not injurious, but she said : 'God allows this in order that I may die to self. It is of very little importance whether mere matters of detail are arranged in one manner or another, but it is of great importance that I should learn to renounce self and my own will.' And then she would quote Tauler to her companion, saying : 'God blinds the eyes of many of the just in order to humble their souls according to His will.' She also said : 'God takes more notice of the evil in us that is the cause of our faults than of the faults themselves. That is why we must struggle daily against the sin which has most hold over us, and daily get the better of it in something.'

When others spoke with disapproval of the new arrangements, she would not listen to their misgivings, or acknowledge that there were any grounds for them.

Gradually, her influence in Port Royal was undermined, her failings were magnified into faults, her indifference to petty details was looked upon as culpable irregularity, her generous warmth of feeling as evidence of an undisciplined nature, and her objections to form and ceremony and pomp and show, as proof of the absence of true piety. The Bishop, Mdme. de Pontcarré, the Abbess from Tard and the nuns who accompanied her, led away all the young and ardent Sisters ; whilst the discipline of the elders was so perfect that they took no notice of anything around them. They remained silent and submissive, and were not enlightened as to the changes which were gradually transforming Port Royal. The two sisters, Agnes and Marie-Claire Arnauld, who comprehended the nobility of Angélique's nature and aims, and had the power of making others understand them, had been sent to Tard ; Anne was still at Maubuisson. There remained Madeleine, a young girl, with remarkably little character and intellect for an Arnauld, and Mdme. Arnauld, who had taken the veil in 1629 at fifty-six years old, and was so much occupied with the duties

of her new vocation and learning her psalter, an occupation
which cost her sight, that she was scarcely conscious of external
events.

As the time drew near for carrying out the provisions of the
letters-patent and electing an Abbess, it was understood and
desired by all, with the exception of a minority of the older
nuns, and Angélique, who did not understand the real nature
of the changes she was so anxious to promote, that there would
be a new ruler and a new rule in Port Royal. Angélique gave
in her resignation; Agnes, the coadjutrix, sent hers from Tard;
and in July 1630 Genevieve the Saint, who had returned to
Paris, was chosen Abbess, whilst Jeanne de Pourlans, former
Abbess of Tard, was appointed Prioress.

Angélique Arnauld, Abbess of Port Royal for twenty-eight
years, is now for the first time in her life a simple nun. The
only emotion which she showed at her resignation was 'great
joy.' Many of the nuns wept around her, but she spoke to
them with 'much joy.' Sister Garnier,[1] a nun who had been
one of her oldest and most faithful friends, who was a pupil
at Port Royal in 1602 and her first novice, threw herself at her
feet weeping when the resignation was announced. 'Why are
you so unhappy, my child?' she said. 'Do you not see that
I am greatly relieved, and I shall never forsake you.'

There was an angry scene afterwards between Angélique and
Father Gondi, brother of the Archbishop of Paris, or rather
there was anger on his side, for Angélique had not informed
him of the proposed change. He did not approve of it, nor of
the election of Genevieve, which ensured the supremacy of the
Bishop of Langres in an abbey which ought to have been
guided by the Archbishop of Paris. When next he visited
Angélique in the parlour, the wicket was not opened nor the
curtain before it withdrawn, and he found he was shut out from
Port Royal.

Angélique was alone. For some time the Abbess allowed
the nuns to speak to her, but not for long; she dropped out of
her place, and it was closed against her.

The chief characteristics of Port Royal under her guidance
had been the simplicity and humility of the Sisters. They were
poor in spirit as well as poor in this world's wealth; they thought
nothing common or unclean, and performed the humblest

[1] See page 64.

duties and ate the humblest fare contented and cheerful. But the new Abbess Genevieve and the Prioress soon changed the spirit of the house; or rather the Abbess submitted in all things to her Prioress, not at first recognizing the great change that would thereby be introduced. She was merely a pious nun engrossed by her devotions, following in all respects the advice given her by those whom she thought herself bound to honour and obey. The Prioress said that their extreme docility had made the Sisters very stupid, and they must really sharpen their wits a little. Many of them could not write when they entered Port Royal,[1] and if Angélique found that they were women of moderate intelligence whom she could never employ in duties that necessitated writing, she had thought it unnecessary to have them taught. In this matter we must judge her by the standard of her own age, and not by that of ours, and must remember that she did not make these ladies ignorant, but found them so. However, ignorance was to be abolished, all the nuns were to be taught everything, and whereas in former times no writing-desks were to be found except in the cells of those who had accounts to keep or letters to write on behalf of the community, there were now writing-desks in every cell.

Many of the nuns spent the whole day in the parlours talking to the Fathers of the Oratory, and then afterwards they wrote accounts of these conversations to 'form their minds;' others were sent to the sacristy, not because they had any special aptitude for the work, but to give them pleasure. No pupils were to be received in future of lower rank than the daughters of an earl or marquis.

The new rulers would no longer tolerate coarse, meagre fare; there must be different soups every day, and omelettes and spices, and good things hitherto unknown; and then for penance they would eat caterpillars, and 'similar filth.' Their gowns were not to be mended or patched. They were to have four new ones a year, and their mantles were to be frequently cleaned and renewed. They had forks, which had not hitherto been used, and the cells were tastefully decorated, in order, so they said, that noble ladies who were now admitted within

---

[1] Claire Martine, spoken of by Anne Arnauld at p. 81, was one of these ignorant nuns; entire absence of education was not an uncommon thing in the seventeenth century.

the monastic precincts might not be disgusted with religion. In the church there were perfumes and fine linen and flowers; all the ecclesiastics of note were asked to say mass or preach, and there were new faces every day.   At the same time, extravagant austerities were encouraged which Angélique had never sanctioned; prolonged fasts, terrible scourgings, the most humiliating penances that could be devised, so that one day when she saw a nun whom she had looked upon as undisciplined, submitting to extreme punishment she was amazed, and thought this was indeed a miracle; but when the time of recreation came, the same nun was joking and laughing as much as she had wept in the morning, and Angélique said to herself, 'Surely, they make fun of everything.'

'What is the use of all this?' she could not help asking herself, and the answer of her own heart was, 'To destroy self, and my own will, and the *I* and *my*.'

But one trial came that was too great even for Angélique: the new rulers asked whence she had taken three of the novices, saying that they intended to send them back wherever it might be, as they were a burden to the house. Now Angélique had taken them out of charity, and to save them from some great but unspecified danger. God had given them into her hands, how could she forsake them; and yet she must not resist authority, she must not even complain. She wept day and night before the altar, praying God to help her, and the hollow eyes and worn cheeks showed what she suffered, and moved those around her to pity, or showed them that they were going too far. They said that they would not hurry her, and gave her time to find another home for the poor portionless girls.

It was not an easy thing to unlearn the habit of a lifetime and to forget that she had once ruled Port Royal; but she did her best to make herself the lowest and least of the community. One day she met a little convent pupil wearing ragged shoes, and asked why they did not give her better shoes than that, and then checked herself, saying, 'Ah, mon Dieu, what a pity it is that I must always interfere in things that don't concern me!'

We learn from others something of the humiliations to which she was exposed at this time, though no word on the subject escaped her own lips. She entered her noviciate again, and was condemned to humiliations that the other novices did not endure; she bore them so patiently that the hearts of many were touched. Shortly after her resignation she was sentenced to perform penance before the sisterhood assembled in the Chapter-house; she was bareheaded and barefooted, and as the pavement of the newly completed building was very damp, she suffered severely in consequence. Among other things she was told at this meeting not to imagine that she had done anything remarkable in resigning her abbey; she had done no more than her duty. Sister Garnier, the nun who loved her, had her eyes fixed upon her, and says that she seemed 'incredibly composed.' The Sisters were after this forbidden to address her on any subject; she was condemned to absolute silence; and many of the nuns seemed to take delight in depreciating her and expressing their love and esteem for the new Abbess and Prioress in her presence.

Three or four months after the election she was sent to the schoolroom as mistress of the convent pupils, and she also swept their rooms, and performed all kinds of menial duties under the direction of the new Prioress. She was very fond of children, and easily gained their affection. Each child thought that the good Sister loved her the best of all; and although they tried to find out her favourites, they could not do so; neither did they discover that she really greatly disliked a little troublesome discontented child, with no signs of 'grace,' to whom she was so kind that this little one was supposed to be her special pet. She treated the Abbess Geneviève with profound respect, speaking to her on her knees, and kneeling whenever she met her, and she taught the children to render her implicit obedience. Some childish fault of her pupils was once reported to the Abbess and visited with severe and unmerited punishment. Angélique addressed the children on the subject; she was too honest to magnify the fault, which she said was not so great as the Abbess thought, but she upheld the authority of her Superior, and told them that they must submit to the punishment which the Reverend Mother had inflicted.

It was considered necessary to humiliate Angélique still further, and we cannot but marvel at the malignity and petty spite of the penances devised. Several times in the refectory a so-called history of her life was read aloud before the Sisters, which was a tissue of insult and untruth. She was accused of going to church 'as dirty as a pig,' and was told in conclusion that if she was appointed Abbess of the Monastery of the Holy Eucharist, of which there was already some talk, she would make it ' a dirty, disorderly house, like Port Royal.' The humility of the nun had not quite extinguished the pride of the Arnaulds or the truth and integrity of her nature ; and she continued to eat her dinner unmoved. After dinner the Prioress asked why she had gone on eating during the reading, and she answered that 'she was not thinking about it.' In addition to the silence within the convent to which she had been condemned, she was not allowed to correspond with Agnes, or to communicate with her friends at the parlour-wicket. The letters from St. Francis de Sales, which she had looked upon not as a private treasure but as a valuable possession of the monastery, were torn up, and used to cover jars of preserves. She bore all in silence and without a murmur, but after two years of this treatment still further humiliations were devised, and she was subjected to innumerable petty indignities. Once, when all the sisters and pupils were in the refectory, she was told to rise from the table, and a basket full of the most disgusting filth was put round her neck. She was led in succession to all the refectory tables by a nun who said, 'Look, my sisters, at this wretched creature, whose mind is more full of perverse notions than this basket is of filth.' Angélique gravely thanked the sister who had devised this *mortification* for her, but she said afterwards she thought she should have heaved her heart up at the horrible stench.

Another time she entered the refectory wearing a large paper mask, on which was written, ' My sisters, pray to God for this hypocrite. Pray to God, and ask Him to make her conversion a real and not a pretended one ! '

Meanwhile, what thoughts were passing through her mind, and what did her own experience as a nun teach her ? She says that at first she scarcely noticed many things that would have pained her, because she was so glad to be free from responsibility, and to realize the longing of so many years, and live for God alone, with no duty except duty to God. She had always desired to learn absolute obedience and submission, and to have her own will and judgment trampled down. Now that her longing was fulfilled, she took up her cross cheerfully, endured insult and reproach in silence ; but she could not stifle

the voice of conscience, or shut her eyes to the actual tendency
of all that she witnessed. She learnt other lessons than
humility and obedience, and found that it was possible to obey
man and disobey God, to conform to the will of the priest and
not to do the will of God. She was the same Angélique whose
earnest nature and still sad face, speaking of struggle and
victory, had touched the hearts of worldly nuns in olden times ;
and her steadfast endurance, her gentleness and humility, and
the new light shining into her own soul, were filling with
doubt the hearts of those who had been alienated from her, and
teaching them to ask themselves whether hers was not the true
piety and true devotion, and not that other which had usurped
its place. They had been led away by novelty, love of change,
and the flattery of the Fathers ; had expected to see their late
Abbess converted by her penance into a fasting, praying saint,
a seer of visions and worker of miracles. When it became
obvious that she submitted to the new rule from obedience and
not from conviction, and would become none of these things,
their own faith wavered. She was shut out from the nuns
by a wall of silence; from her friends by the closing of the
parlour wicket ; and from her sisters by the refusal to allow her
to write or receive letters ; and even then her influence was felt
in Port Royal, and the Bishop began to grow uneasy, and to
feel that, after all his efforts, this silent nun might make his
labours vain.

One day he said to her, ' You are an obstacle in my way !'

'How can that be,' she answered, 'when I never even
speak to any one ?'

'Your very shadow is an obstruction,' he replied.

'Send me wherever you please,' said Angélique, 'I will go.

There is more than submission in these words : they tell of
sorrow, almost of despair. Henceforth the reform she had
laboured to establish, Port Royal that she had loved so dearly,
were to be as nothing to her. She was to go forth alone and
unheeded to end her life, and she had seen her life-work perish
before her eyes. We must look back and try to understand
the successive steps which had led her to this point.

At the time of her conversion she desired, in accordance
with her duty as a nun and a Roman Catholic, to submit to
the authority of her Church, to find a Director of conscience to
whom she could render implicit obedience. Priest after priest

had been sent to Port Royal, but she always saw *through* them, found that they were shallow, selfish, and worldly, and discarded one after the other. She followed their advice to a certain extent, obtained information from them as to the rules of the olden times which she longed to restore, but never placed herself unreservedly under their guidance, not even under that of the good old Fathers Pacifique and Archangel, whose advice was so valuable to her when she reformed her convent.

There seems little doubt that we must attribute an independence of thought and action which was opposed to the theory of a nun's condition to her father's influence. He was a good Catholic, but as a man of the world he knew too much of priests and priestly influence to allow his child to follow them blindly; and there can be little doubt that Angélique's insight into the character of the Cistercian monks was mainly owing to his shrewd remarks. During his lifetime she was never a nun shut up within her convent walls, but had an outlet for wide sympathies, and was free to mould her life and actions according to her own needs and those of her community. Neither did her Church put in that claim to obedience which was asserted after her father's death. M. Arnauld was consulted about the mission to Maubuisson, and his consent obtained before it was proposed to her. The temporal affairs of the monastery were placed under his charge, and the Cistercian monks could not find fault with his disposal of them, for old dilapidated buildings had been gradually improved or rebuilt, the revenue increased, and its expenditure so wisely directed that, although monks and confessors were not deprived of their due, there was enough to support a large number of nuns, and something to spare for the poor and needy.

At Maubuisson Angélique's desire to place herself under the authority of a spiritual guide to whom she could render implicit obedience was as strong as it had been when she was a girl at Port Royal, and she found in Francis de Sales all that she had hitherto sought in vain. But it is not impossible that his honeyed words prepared her to receive that homage and adulation from which she had hitherto shrunk instinctively, and which is one of the greatest dangers to which a devout Catholic is exposed.

Angélique believed the Bishop of Langres to be a fitting

successor to Francis de Sales, and thought she had found in him her long-sought guide. She submitted her own will and judgment to his, and considered it her highest wisdom as well as her chief duty to render him unquestioning obedience. When he demanded control of the temporal as well as the spiritual affairs of the convent she placed them also in his hands. She had to learn for herself and from her own experience that this is an error which must lead to disastrous results, and that we cannot get rid of the duties and responsibilities which belong to our own individual existence without sinning against others and against our own souls.

She had attributed the degradation of the nuns of that period and all her early difficulties at Port Royal to the Cistercian monks, and had expected to be free from further trouble when she was no longer under their jurisdiction. She discovered that worldly bishops and priests are not only as bad as the monks, but worse. The Fathers of the Oratory, with the Bishop at their head, listening to idle dreams which they declared to be revelations and rhapsodical nonsense which they said was inspired, professed themselves the humble servants of these holy nuns ; but they were in reality exercising a stern tyranny over them, leading them whithersoever they would, downward into a path of corruption, deception, and lies. What had she brought upon herself and her nuns ! What must she have felt as she saw Mdme. de Pontcarré, and her orange-trees, and the nuns toiling up the staircase with the heavy vessels of water ; and thought of the choice little dinners with the Bishop, and the comings and goings by that private entrance ! These were the things she had protested against so strongly and had tried to *reform* at Maubuisson, and now they had fallen upon her, nay, rather, had she not brought them upon herself !

'Send me wherever you please ; I will go.'

CHAPTER XIV.

POPE URBAIN VIII. had given his consent to the establishment of the Order of the Holy Eucharist in 1627, but the sanction of the King of France and the Archbishop of Paris was also necessary, and this had hitherto been refused.

The Archbishop was very angry when he discovered that the Archbishop of Sens and the Bishop of Langres were associated with him as Superiors of the new Order; and there can be little doubt that through his adverse influence the King withheld his consent for three years. He would have withheld it longer, but in 1630 he was seriously ill at Lyons, the physicians thought his case hopeless, and the Viaticum, or Sacrament for the Dying, was administered to him. After receiving it he recovered, as it seemed, miraculously; and he made a vow to show his gratitude for this great mercy in such a manner as to do special honour to the Holy Eucharist. Mdme. de Longueville entreated him to grant permission, so long withheld, for the establishment of an Order, devoted to perpetual adoration of this sacred mystery, and he complied with her request. But the Archbishop of Paris was still inexorable. His consent would have given the Archbishop of Sens and the Bishop of Langres a right of jurisdiction in his diocese, which he was resolved they should not exercise. The Bishop of Langres made every effort to overcome his objections, and was at length so far successful that in 1633 he yielded on condition that a fresh bull should be obtained within twelve months granting him exceptional privileges and prerogatives.

There was, however, another difficulty in the way. The Pope had nominated Angélique Arnauld as Mother Superior of the new Order, and in 1627 M. de Langres had approved of the nomination. He did not do so in 1633.

When he had first discovered that Angélique would never carry out his plans, he had cast his eyes upon her sister Agnes, and in sending her to Tard had expected to prepare her for future work, as well as to separate her from Angélique. Before long, however, he found out that the Arnaulds were not the material out of which men fashion a useful tool. But the Abbess who had resigned Tard de Dijon was exactly fitted for his purpose; and with the nuns who had accompanied her to Paris, the Mères de Dijon as they were called, would have moulded the new Order according to his will, and have secured his ascendancy within the convent walls. He therefore obtained the consent of Rome to the substitution of the Abbess Jeanne, late of Tard, for Angélique, and hoped that the change would also be sanctioned by the Archbishop. But on this point M. de Gondi was immovable. He did not propose to carry out the plans of the Bishop; he knew what influence that prelate had obtained at Port Royal, how Angélique and her work had been superseded, and the Mères de Dijon reigned in her stead. His brother, Père Gondi, would have much to tell him on this head. At length he grew tired of the Bishop's importunity, the names of the Mères de Dijon, and the intrigues which had lasted for six years; he commanded the nuns of Tard and those of Port Royal to return to their respective monasteries, and Angélique to assume her post and undertake her duties at the new institution. The Bishop urged one final objection, Port Royal was too poor to bear the expense of the journeys; the Archbishop said he would pay them. In a moment everything was changed. The Bishop found that the Archbishop was too strong for him and had vanquished him at every point; and that too when he thought he had secured all that he desired; supreme power at Port Royal, Tard de Dijon, and the Holy Eucharist, and the suppression of Angélique, whom he could set on one side, or banish to a remote convent, where she would no longer interfere with his plans. 'Send me wherever you please,' she had said, 'I will go.'

These words were engraved on her mind, so that after many

years she repeated them to her nephew M. le Maître. They had cost her a great effort, and in uttering them she made the crowning sacrifice of her own will. She had taken pleasure in resigning her post as Abbess, but now she was called upon to make a far greater sacrifice, to give up her life and work as a nun of Port Royal, and consent to banishment. Suddenly the dark clouds rolled away and morning dawned. She was desired to select certain companions, and go to the Convent of the Holy Eucharist, there to resume her old rank as Mother Superior.

The conditions of the new life were hard and distasteful to her, for they had been laid down by the Bishop of Langres. He had decided that the convent should be in the heart of the city, and within easy reach of the great ladies of the court. The church attached to it was to be more magnificent than any other in Paris. Every nun who joined the Order was to bring with her at least ten thousand francs, belong to a good family, and have fine manners and a cultivated mind, so that she could receive 'princesses.' The dress was to be of the choicest materials, white and scarlet, and to be made in a becoming manner, so that, as the Bishop said, it might be 'supremely august.' The nuns were, moreover, to be devout women, constant in prayer and fervent, able to speak upon spiritual matters with luminous piety; in fact they were to be pre-eminently fitted to serve two masters, God and mammon.

In the old days Angélique would not have consented to accept any work that was burdened by similar conditions; but the discipline of the last three years had taught her submission, and her sufferings had made her long to escape from the snares in which she had been taken. With the proceeds of a legacy left for the purpose by a certain Mdme. Bardeau, she purchased a house near the Louvre, and in 1633, accompanied by three nuns and three postulants whom she had selected, and one postulant appointed by the Bishop, she took immediate possession of it.

This postulant, Mdlle. de Chamesson, was a special favourite with the Bishop. She was young, attractive, intelligent, well-born, and well-bred. She had scarcely said farewell to the world although she was about to bind herself by the vows of the convent; she understood society, and was popular; but most of all she believed in the Bishop and obeyed him.

It was not unnatural that he should look upon her as a very
fitting person for any office of trust in the Holy Eucharist.
He therefore selected her to accompany Angélique, and be her
constant companion ; to be with her in the parlour where
visitors were received, and to be consulted on every subject.
Angélique the Abbess was to do nothing without first asking
the advice of Mdlle. de Chamesson the postulant. She sub-
mited cheerfully, and tried to give all and more than all that
Mdlle. de Chamesson expected and the Bishop required.
The young lady was to be the future Abbess of the Holy
Eucharist ; Angélique saw this, and very gladly promoted the
plan. Of the nuns who accompanied her, one was her first
cousin, Anne de St. Paul Arnauld, and one of the postulants
was her niece, Catherine de St. Agnes Arnauld.

M. Arnauld d'Andilly, Angélique's eldest brother, had fifteen
children, of whom five died in infancy ; six of the remaining
ten were girls, and all six became nuns in Port Royal. Catherine
de St. Agnes, born in 1615, was the eldest of the six sisters.
She had been sent to Port Royal at eleven years old, and now,
at seventeen, was preparing to take the veil. With the exception of Mdlle. de Chamesson, Angélique was surrounded
by faithful friends and relatives, and once more her marvellous
power of organizing a religious community, of exercising due
influence and control over every member, ascertaining the
capacity and wisely allotting the task of each one, was called
forth. Moreover, she never failed to recognize the individual
merit and capacity of every human being with whom she came
into contact, and in this, perhaps, lay the secret of her power.
She could always do something with everybody, though,
perhaps, it was not exactly what they or others expected.
The Bishop must have looked with some apprehension at
Angélique and her companions, who were to be the nucleus
of his august assembly of holy women in stately robes. You
might do what you liked with Angélique, she would be shabby
in spite of every precaution, and she would contrive to inspire
such respect and affection for the 'sacred poverty,' which it
was a nun's privilege to share, that it was in vain to try to
diminish or oppose her influence. It was doubtless a relief to
the Bishop when the Archbishop of Paris prohibited the reception of any new members into the community until all his
demands were complied with. During the time that must

elapse, Angélique might be superseded, and all his efforts
were directed to obtain this result.

There was at this time a certain nun of whom he thought
very highly. She was Subprioress of the Carmelite Convent
at Paris, and he endeavoured to induce her to leave her own
Order so that he might obtain her services for the Holy
Eucharist. She had no strong attachment to the Carmelites,
and was willing to be guided by the Bishop; her charity was
universal, and she was so disinterested that when a lady told
her she intended to give eighteen thousand francs to the Carmelites, she said that they did not want it, and it would be
much better to give this sum to the Convent of the Holy
Eucharist.

Now when the Carmelites heard of this they were not
pleased; and thought they had not done well to listen to the
Bishop and allow the Subprioress to receive visits from noble-
men and court ladies on the plea that she had a marvellous
gift for gaining souls to God. They consulted their ecclesiastical superior, Cardinal de Berulle, and on his next visit to
the convent he put an absolute prohibition upon all visits to
the parlour, deposed the Subprioress from her charge, and
condemned her to strict and solitary confinement, which she
endured for ten months with exemplary patience and humility,
and then died.

The Bishop was angry; he reproached the Carmelites with
having ill-used the Subprioress and caused her death, and
said that she was a Saint. But they replied that her death
lay at his door, for he had done her great harm by his
praise and flattery. Her sister was Prioress in the same
convent, and one day she told the Bishop that he was ruining
the nuns, and she begged he would never enter the house
again. He obeyed, but he had already inspired the Carmelites,
who also called themselves Sisters of the Holy Eucharist,
with a jealous fear of the new Order. The Fathers of the
Oratory fanned this flame of jealousy by proclaiming far and
wide the merits of the Order founded by the Bishop of Langres,
and implying that it was superior to any already existing.
There can be little doubt that the Bishop intended to play
them off against each other, and to obtain a hold over both
by calling out an evil spirit of rivalry. Angélique writes:
'There was a time when I was tempted to be jealous of some

nuns in the Faubourg St. Germain, who had usurped as it seemed to me the name of the Holy Eucharist. But by God's grace I did not yield to this temptation, although if it had not been for His help, I was weak enough and worldly enough to have given way to it.'

The new Order was a failure. The three Superiors were each resolved to occupy the chief place and to exclude the other two, and the world began to laugh at them. Cardinal de Berulle told the Bishop of Langres that Founders ought to be Saints, separate from the world, pre-eminent in good works, filled with piety and every virtue, and that he thought neither the Bishop nor his coadjutors had the necessary qualifications for the work.

It was quite true, and after numerous intrigues too mean and uninteresting to follow, the two Archbishops resolved to suppress the Order, rather than allow it to be associated with the name of the Bishop. The Archbishop of Paris would not allow any new members to join the community, nor the postulants to take the veil; so that it must soon have been starved out, consisting as it did only of Angélique and her three nuns. The Archbishop of Sens resolved upon employing more active means, and at the instigation of the Carmelites called in question the orthodoxy of the community.

The means were ready to his hands. He obtained possession of a copy of the mystical *Secret Chaplet* written by Agnes Arnauld, which he had formerly seen and praised. He placed it in the hands of certain learned Doctors of the Sorbonne without telling them that the author was a nun; and they passed a grave censure upon the work, saying that it was full of error, false doctrine, and extravagance, and was irreverent if not impious. This verdict was soon noised abroad, and all the faults charged upon the book were attributed to the Sisters. They were looked upon as heretics, and the defence they had to offer, namely, that they knew nothing about the *Secret Chaplet*, and that there was not a copy of it in the house, was considered too contemptible to deserve notice.

The Bishop was even more severely handled than the Sisters; his adversaries accused him of being the author of the *Chaplet*, and of disseminating false doctrine. He was deeply grieved at his sudden unpopularity, and sorely puzzled how to act. If he joined the dominant party and condemned the

Chaplet he would imply condemnation of himself; for he had approved of it, and told Agnes to revere these mystic words and to look upon them as inspired, and herself as an instrument which the Deity had deigned to use.

In his perplexity he turned to a man with whom he had recently become acquainted, and who was equally renowned for his learning and piety. This was the Abbot of St. Cyran, a special friend of d'Andilly's, who was certain not to judge the work of his friend's sister harshly or uncharitably, although he was predisposed to condemn it as a cause of contention, which he dreaded above all things. He studied the *Chaplet* carefully, and wrote to the Bishop saying that it was undoubtedly a *good* work and contained truths which could not be gainsaid without equal injury to faith and grace. He proposed, however, that it should be submitted to a Doctor of the University of Louvain and the Bishop of Ypres, and that they should be asked to express an opinion on its merits. This was done; and, taking into consideration that it was written by a nun for her own use, that she was not uttering dogmas or attempting to lay down articles of faith, but merely trying to explain certain religious sentiments which she valued only so long as it might please God to allow her to feel them, and was willing to part with whenever it might please God, they approved of the work.

Paris was quite agitated by the discussion; and the Sisters of the Holy Eucharist and their heresy or orthodoxy were warmly discussed. The Sorbonne Professors were angry with the Archbishop of Sens, because he had led them to suppose that the author of the *Secret Chaplet* was a theologian, and they found that they had brought very heavy artillery to bear against so slight an object as a nun. They were disposed to modify if not retract their censure, and as this did not please the Archbishop he appealed to Rome. The Pope neither censured nor approved of the *Chaplet*. He said that it did not deserve to be placed in the Index Expurgatorius, or to be censured; nevertheless he decreed that it should be suppressed and remain, as it had hitherto been, a *Secret* Chaplet, lest it should become a cause of offence to simple and ignorant persons.

But the papal decree did not extinguish the controversy: pamphlets were written on both sides; *Apologies* and *Replies* made their appearance, and the Jesuits discussed the Apologies

so unfavourably that the Abbot again came forward in defence
of the Holy Eucharist and Port Royal. After his reply the
matter died out, and he was looked upon as the victorious
champion of the nuns. The Bishop was delighted with his
new friend, and spoke of him in both convents as a man to
whom the nuns were greatly indebted, and whose wisdom
and piety made him a fitting guide for them. The Rules
of the Order were submitted to him, with a request that
he would correct and modify them. But the Abbot was
very unwilling to have anything to do with the Rules, he
had no particular esteem for the Order, and 'did not think
that it owed its origin to an impulse given by the Spirit of
God.' Being urged by the Bishop to express an opinion, he
did so, and as it showed a complete want of appreciation of the
prelate's design he was pressed no further on that point. But
the Bishop still thought that his influence would be valuable
within the convent walls, and after much persuasion induced
him to undertake the religious instruction of the nuns.

Angélique did not welcome his advent, for she was afraid
of him. She had heard of him for many years past from her
brother, who extolled alike his learning and his piety; he had
even visited Port Royal, and she had received several letters
from him.

He happened to be calling on Mdme. Arnauld on that day
fourteen years previously when she received the letter in which
Angélique asked her to send carriages to Maubuisson for the
transport of the nuns and novices to Port Royal. Mdme.
Arnauld told him why they were leaving Maubuisson, and
he admired Angélique's conduct in offering them the *poverty*
of Port Royal. He wrote to thank her for it; not as St.
Francis would have done, with warm appreciation of her
motives and graceful recognition of her good deeds, but a
letter in which the approval is accompanied by admonition,
almost reproof. Even at that time it had been suggested, or
had occurred to him, that Port Royal was a great field for
labour; and he speaks of his regret at not being influential
enough, or worthy enough, to serve as an instrument in the
work which God was accomplishing there. He praises Angélique's 'holy courage' in daring to meet what seemed like loss
of property for the love of God, and continues :—

'The goodness of God is high above our thoughts and
our faith, and we serve Him very ignobly if we are not willing

to run some risk in the exercise of charity. We ought to
remember that in the early ages of the Church the only manner
in which Christians could show their love was by dying for God.
We cannot become martyrs or sacrifice our lives, and therefore
the least we can do is to accept with joy any opportunity that
He gives us of showing our love to Him, and manifesting the
zeal of our charity by extending it to those who are devoted to
His service, sharing with them our wealth and worldly goods.
Perhaps in the day of judgment He may forgive us for not
having sought every opportunity of employing the means He has
committed to our care in doing good deeds. He may possibly
excuse us for having given ourselves no trouble to rescue the
poor wretches who drag out their lives in caves and forests, and
live like the wild beasts, abandoned or neglected. This He
may forgive, but assuredly He will reproach us for having
disregarded the needs of those whom He leads, as it were, into
our presence; more especially when we see that if we neglect
the body we risk the still greater loss of the soul. Nothing
shows so clearly that our faith is darkened and charity dead.'

After writing this letter the Abbot visited Port Royal.
There, amongst other things, he made one remark which Angélique never forgot. He said that he knew many abbesses
who had reformed their convents, but very few who had
reformed themselves. She felt that she belonged to the many,
and yet that 'by God's grace' she 'desired greatly to join the
few.' She respected the man who had spoken so frankly to
her, appreciated the passionate sympathy with which he spoke
of the 'poor wretches who drag out their lives in caves and
forests,' knew that he was very learned and pious, but his
holiness was not of a kind which she could then appreciate.
Francis de Sales was at that time her ideal. He had taught her
that she was a child of God and must respect in others and
in herself the Divine image; must be tender over her own
faults as well as the faults of others, and raise up her heart
gently, when she had erred or was discouraged. The Abbot of
St. Cyran's doctrines were much more severe, or, at least, so
they seemed to her at that time; but twelve years later she was
not so incredulous of the fact that the whole world is 'lying in
wickedness.'

The Bishop of Langres is an exaggerated and distorted image
of Francis de Sales; in whom large charity has degenerated
into the toleration of indifference; and love of that humanity

for which Christ died into love of the world and desire to obtain its approbation and applause. Angélique never wavered in her fidelity to her early guide, Francis de Sales; she would not acknowledge that he was over-indulgent as a director of conscience; but she had suffered so much, her sense of truth, right, and honesty had been so outraged by his followers tha we need not be surprised at the reaction which carried her t so stern a guide as St. Cyran.

Perhaps the contrast between the two men cannot be bettei illustrated than by the manner in which they looked upon children. Recall the picture of Francis de Sales in the streets of Geneva with the little children clustering round him, whilst he looks down smiling upon them : 'This is my little family, my dear little family,' he says of the children who were dear to him and dear to God.

But St. Cyran held very different views. Children were the seed of the devil, from whom they could be snatched away only with difficulty, and as brands from the burning. He believed in the damnation of stillborn babes, and of infants who died unbaptized. In 1622 he had received a letter on this subject from his friend Jansen, in which he was informed that some of the students of a college at Louvain had asked to have the treatise *De Statu Parvulorum*[1] read aloud to them whilst they dined in the refectory. St. Cyran's answers to these letters have not been preserved; but we know that he would rejoice to learn that the bodies and souls of the students had, as he believed, received due nourishment.

Such a guide, truthful and upright, stern, and uncompromising in doctrine, with a hard logical head, and a nature that did not shrink from the terrors developed by his views, was standing at the doors of Port Royal and the Holy Eucharist. He was loth to undertake the control of the two convents, for he knew the history of the last few years : but he was a man who having once begun a work never turned back from it. When he found that Angélique was prepared to receive him, he consented to lead her along the narrow and thorny path which she must follow, and was as little detened by difficulty or opposition as she herself had ever been.

---

[1] A Treatise written by Conrius, Archbishop of Tuam, formerly of Louvain, on 'The Condition of those Babes who die Unbaptized,' in which he proves, on the authority of St. Augustine, that they cannot escape eternal punishment.

CHAPTER XV.

JEAN DU VERGIER DE HAURANNE, afterwards Abbot of St. Cyran, was born at Bayonne in 1581. He was remarkable as a child for his intelligence, and for the energy and perseverance with which he followed his childish pursuits and youthful studies. He had none of the graceful vivacity of the south, and was at all times grave and earnest, seeking relaxation in intellectual puzzles and paradoxes — 'a fertile soil,' says his friend and biographer Nicole, 'but specially productive in briars and thorns.'

After having completed his *Humanity* in his native place, he went to Paris, to study theology in the Sorbonne. He lodged in the same house with a fellow-student named Petau, afterwards a celebrated Jesuit priest, who when he was questioned as to the nature and character of du Vergier in his youth, answered that he had a restless intellect, was presumptuous, vain, stern, reserved, and of unimpeachable morality. This account is given by an enemy, and contains everything unfavourable that could be said of him, but it is manifestly founded upon a true knowledge and appreciation of his character; we shall see that purity in life and aims are characteristic of him throughout life, as well as that independence of mind which often gives rise to the charge of vanity and presumption.

By the advice of the Bishop of Bayonne, he left Paris for the University of Louvain, at that time a celebrated school of Theology, and renowned for the controversy on grace carried on by Michael de Bay, or Baius, and the Dutch Jesuit Lessius.

Du Vergier entered the Jesuit College at Louvain, where he remained four years. At the end of his course of study he wrote, according to custom, a thesis in defence of Scholastic Theology, which was considered remarkably good, and obtained high praise from Lipsius, who was one of the examiners. Among the letters of Lipsius there are several addressed to du Vergier, which show the interest felt for him by the great scholar. In 1604 du Vergier went from Louvain to Paris, and although we know that he was pursuing his studies there with his usual zeal and diligence we have no mention of his name until 1609.

One day in that year the King, Henri IV., was talking over old times with some of his nobles, and wondering what would have happened after the assassination of Henri III. if he had lost that battle of Arques which had secured him the throne of France. Suppose, he said, he had been defeated, and in order to save his life had been compelled to put to sea in a vessel without provisions, and had been driven away from land by a storm, what then would have been the result? One of the courtiers said that rather than see his king die of hunger he would have killed himself, and furnished with his own body food for his royal master. Thereupon arose a great debate; for the king propounded the question whether such a suicide would be criminal; and on this point opinions were divided. One of the nobles present, the Count de Cramail, was du Vergier's friend and companion, and when he repeated the conversation to the young student, fresh from the schools with their questions of casuistry, and always interested in an intellectual or moral puzzle, he at once began to urge reasons in favour of the suicide. The Count was delighted, and begged him to write them down. Du Vergier did so, and they were put forward in a pamphlet which was published without his name, called: *A Royal Question; showing in what extremity, chiefly in time of peace, a subject may be forced to preserve the life of his Prince at the expense of his own;* and in this pamphlet he enumerates *thirty-four* cases of justifiable suicide. There can be no doubt that in his youth du Vergier took his pastime in intellectual gymnastics, and the accomplishment of a difficult feat irrespective of anything

beyond the pleasure of overcoming a difficulty. The pamphlet
met with great applause, and the King's Confessor, Father
Cotton, went so far as to say that the author deserved a
bishopric; but the author who had merely amused himself with
ingenious solutions of a difficult problem, most probably gave
no second thought to this *jeu d'esprit*, and it was forgotten by
him and his friends. In later years the Jesuits discovered and
republished it, expressing their horror at finding that in his
youth the Abbot of St. Cyran had advocated suicide.

There is another rather perverse pamphlet which was written
by him in 1617. The Bishop of Poitiers had taken an active
part in the struggle between Catholics and Huguenots, and
at the head of a troop of cavalry had defeated the Huguenots
in the streets of Poitiers. In the seventeenth century such conduct was called in question, and du Vergier, who was then at
Poitiers, undertook the Bishop's defence. He published a work
called : *Apology for Henri Louis Chateignier de la Rocheposai,
Bishop of Poitiers, in reply to those who say that Ecclesiastics
are not permitted to have recourse to arms in case of necessity.*
He gives a long and imposing list of cardinals, bishops, and
archbishops who have borne arms, and cites the examples of
the Maccabees, and of Samuel and Abraham. He had undertaken the Bishop's defence, and urges all that can be said in
his favour just as he had done when he wrote the *Royal
Question.* The prelate was so well pleased with this defence
of his military zeal that the pamphlet was ironically called
the *Koran of the Bishop of Poitiers.*

When du Vergier was at the University of Louvain
Cornelius Jansen was his fellow-student, and doubtless they
were acquainted at that time, but we hear of their friendship
for the first time in 1605, when Jansen, a year later than du
Vergier, came to Paris. Jansen was born in 1585; he was
a native of Accoy, a village near Leerdam, in Holland, and of
very humble origin. His father was a peasant, called Jan
Ottosen, or Jan the son of Otto, and as the family was too
insignificant to be distinguished at that time by surname he was
known as Cornelius Jansen, or Cornelius the son of Jan. It
was not a difficult thing for a clever boy to obtain education in
the Catholic Church; and when he was seventeen we hear of
Jansen as the first student of his year at Louvain. This would
be in 1602, when du Vergier, who was four years older than

his friend, had already been two years at the university. The
two young men cannot fail to have been attracted towards each
other, and when Jansen's health broke down in 1605. and he
was recommended to go to Paris, we need not be surprised to
find that a warm friendship sprang up between them. Du
Vergier was wealthy and well-born, and Jansen was the son
of a poor peasant, but neither of them attached any importance
to the external and accidental circumstances of their position :
they were equals in intellect and culture, and were equally
animated by love of study and love of right and truth.
Through du Vergier's influence Jansen, who had to work for
his living, obtained employment as tutor in a wealthy family in
Paris ; all the time that he could spare from his work was
devoted to the study of Theology.

The two friends found that theology in Paris meant the study
of the Schoolmen and not of the Fathers of the Church ; and
after six years of patient labour they were convinced that true
doctrine was extinct or overlaid with subtle casuistry, and that
it could only be restored by going back to sources which were
neglected. If it had occurred to them to study the Bible they
would probably have become champions of the Protestant faith,
but they resolved to devote themselves to the Fathers, and to
silence the endless disputes between the Sorbonne and the
Jesuits by introducing a true and pure form of Christian belief,
and re-establishing the lost faith of early ages. They found
that St. Augustine, Bishop of Hippo, was referred to as an
ultimate authority by all the Schoolmen, and they hoped to
discover in his works, the truth and light which they were
seeking.

When du Vergier's father died, his mother urged his
return to Bayonne. He complied with her wish, and in or
about the year 1611 the two friends left Paris, and established
themselves at Champré or Campiprat, by the sea, near Bayonne,
a place belonging to the du Vergiers. For five years the
two men, who were respectively twenty-six and thirty years
old, worked day and night at the pages of St. Augustine.
Jansen especially was indefatigable, and Lancelot, a pupil and
friend of St. Cyran, speaks of an old arm-chair which he had
seen with a reading desk fixed to it, in which Jansen used
literally to live, for he would seldom leave it, and preferred
sleeping in it to going to bed. He was still far from strong,

and Mdme. du Vergier used to tell her son that if he made
that good Fleming work so hard, he would certainly kill him.

Their only recreation was battledore and shuttlecock, at
which they became such adepts that when they played a game,
as they did between the chapters of St. Augustine, they would
score three or four thousand without allowing the shuttlecock
to fall.

In 1616 the Bishop of Bayonne appointed du Vergier to
a Canonry in the Cathedral, and selected Jansen as the principal of a College he was about to found. But in the same year
the Bishop was elevated to the Archbishopric of Tours, so that
his plans were not carried out. He took the two friends with
him to Paris, where after a time they separated. Du Vergier
went to Poitiers, and the Bishop, whom he defended in the
Apology, made him first a Canon of Poitiers, then Prior of
Bonneville, and finally, in 1620, Abbot of St. Cyran. He never
accepted any other preferment, and henceforward he is no
longer du Vergier, but M. de St. Cyran.

In 1617 Jansen returned to Louvain, and was almost immediately appointed principal of a new college. The two
friends had found each his appointed path and work, and they
were in opposite directions, but this did not separate them.
They carried on an active correspondence through life, of which
we can form a tolerably fair estimate as the letters of Jansen
are still extant. Jansen or, according to the Latinized form of
his name, which in common with other learned men of that
period he adopted, *Jansenius*, was more and more engrossed by
the study of St. Augustine, so that his college work was distasteful, and the prospect of a chair in the university offered
no attraction. He read his favourite author again and again,
and says that he seemed to read him without eyes and hear
him without ears. In 1621 he wrote to his friend : ' I cannot
tell you how completely my former judgment and opinion
respecting St. Augustine and others are now changed. Day by
day I am more astonished at the extent and profundity of his
intellect, and marvel that his doctrines are so little known by
learned men now, and have been so much neglected for many
previous centuries. For to speak frankly, I am firmly convinced
that next to the heretics no people in the world have done
more to corrupt and degrade theology than those brawling
Schoolmen whom we both know. So that if we could show

what it used to be in former times, and what it ought to be now, it would not even be recognized as theology. . . . I should like to confer with you fully on this point, but we should require weeks, if not months, to talk it over.　Still I may venture to say that I have discovered by incontrovertible principles that if the two schools of Jesuits and Jacobins dispute till the Day of Judgment they will only get further and further from the truth, unless they take a different course from that which they are now pursuing, for one is just as much in the wrong as the other. There is not a single person to whom I can venture to say what I think (and my judgment is formed in accordance with the principles established by St. Augustine) of the opinions held at the present time on most points, and especially on Grace and Predestination; for I am afraid lest at Rome they should treat me as they have done others, and that too before the time is accomplished, and my work completed.　And even if it is never granted me to make known the truth I have discovered, still I am marvellously content to have escaped out of the bewildering labyrinth which those garrulous Schoolmen have constructed. Any ambition I may have cherished as to obtaining a chair in the University is quite done away with by my present studies, for I see that I must either be silent, or run great risk in speaking, for my conscience would not permit me to be a traitor to the truth I know.　But God will quickly change the whole aspect of affairs if He sees fit.　Until now I have told you nothing of all this, because I myself have been nearly always in suspense, and have had to wait until I was confirmed and strengthened in the knowledge which I am only acquiring by degrees, lest I should rashly hurry into extremes.'

The doctrine which Jansen was thus carefully elaborating from the pages of St. Augustine and confirming by the authority of other Fathers of the Church, was one which offers enormous difficulties to the intellect and the moral sense.　It attracted and repelled him.　Many years of patient study were necessary before he comprehended and received it.　Ten times he read over every word of the works of St. Augustine, thirty times all those parts which relate to the Pelagian[1] controversy.　He used to say that he could pass his life happily on a desert island

---

[1] Pelagius rejected the doctrine of original sin, asserted the entire freedom of the will, and denied or accepted with limitation the influence of divine grace.

with St Augustine. He wished he had lived in the time of Joshua when the sun 'stood still in the midst of heaven,' or that he could follow the cranes in their northward flight, and find places where the day should be nineteen or twenty hours long. He used to say that he was in search of truth. When he was asked which of God's attributes seemed to him the highest, he answered Truth. On the rare occasions when he walked in his garden he was often heard to say, or rather to sigh, as he raised his eyes towards heaven : 'Oh, Truth, Truth!' He foresaw many difficulties which he did not live to experience, and he therefore desired to avoid the notice of the world and the Church until his work was finished. He consulted his friend on his great work, submitted it to him, and trusted him to promulgate its doctrines and find a *body* fitted to hold this *spirit*. After the year 1621 the two men corresponded in cipher, or secret writing, and speak no longer of theology and new principles, but of *roots* from which *trees* will grow that will help to build a certain *house*.

The friendship of St. Cyran and Jansen had been uninterrupted through life. They had a very tender love for each other. When Jansen received his first letter from St. Cyran after their separation in 1617, he says that he was not alone, and therefore he was obliged to imitate the patriarch Joseph and *go out and seek where to weep.* They met again in that year, and his first letter after the interview alludes to the tears they had shed at parting, and reminds St. Cyran that he was the first to weep.

In 1623 they were together at Péronne. Jansen arrived on Saturday, the 29th April, 'in order,' he says, 'to enter France with the month of May.' And these few words tell of the gladness with which he journeyed towards his friend.

In 1624 and 1626 they met in Paris, Jansen was on his way to Madrid, in order to oppose the claims of the Jesuits to certain privileges that belonged to the University of Louvain.

In 1635, on the declaration of war by France, he wrote a pamphlet entitled *Mars Gallicus*, in which he attacked the policy of the *Most Christian Kings* of France, and made a fierce onslaught upon Richelieu for allying himself with Lutherans and Calvinists, pointing out the disasters which he was thereby preparing for Catholic Germany. As a reward for this, he was elevated by the Court of Spain to the See of

Ypres, and three years later, in 1638, he died of the plague just as his *Augustinus* was completed.   Shortly before his death, he made a will, submitting his great work to the judgment of the Church in which he had lived and was about to die.   He addressed a letter to Pope Urban VIII., in which he lays the fruits of his studies at the feet of His Holiness, ·approving, condemning, advancing, or retracting, as should be prescribed by the thunders of the apostolic see.'   The will and letter were, however, suppressed, and two years after the death of Jansen the *Augustinus* was in print.

St. Cyran left Poitiers in 1621, and thenceforward lived chiefly in Paris, where he pursued his studies, and began to obtain remarkable influence as *Director of consciences.*

In 1626, he published a work, as usual without name, in which he exposed the errors of a Jesuit priest, Father Garasse, which is noticeable as showing the beginning of the differences between him and the Jesuits.

At Poitiers he had known Richelieu, who was then Bishop of Luçon, and who saw at once that this was a man whose genius and power would be useful to him.   It is said that St. Cyran knew certain disreputable secrets connected with the life of Richelieu, and that the crafty prelate wished to pledge him to silence respecting them.   In 1625 he offered him the place of first almoner to Henrietta of England ; and subsequently eight bishoprics, among them Clermont and Bayonne, as well as a choice of numerous abbacies, were successively offered and refused.   After each of these occasions St. Cyran attended the levée of the Cardinal and thanked him for his kind intentions.   One day the Cardinal laid his hand upon his shoulder and, turning to the courtiers who were standing near him, said: 'Gentlemen, you see before you the most learned man in Europe.'

It may be true that Richelieu's fears made him desire to silence St. Cyran by bestowing patronage upon him, but there were other reasons for his attention, and the Abbot had done good service in a matter which the Cardinal had at heart.

Pope Urban VIII. had sent Richard Smith to England as Vicar Apostolical of the Church of Rome.   The time seemed favourable on account of the good will of the Stuarts to the Roman Catholic faith, and the approaching marriage of Charles I. with a Catholic princess, Henrietta of France,

daughter of Henry IV.   Richard Smith was received by the
English Catholics with every mark of affection and respect,
and might possibly have fulfilled some of the expectations
which the Pope entertained in sending him to England, but he
was imprudent enough to split up his small party by entering
into a controversy with the Jesuits on the subject of Episcopal
Rights.   His vehement assertion of these rights was very im
politic, considering the time at which it was brought forward,
and the state of feeling on the subject in England.   The
Jesuits refused to acknowledge his claims, and he attempted
to debar them from administering the sacraments.   Each party
sought to justify itself, and each attacked the other.   Richard
Smith appealed to the Assembly of the Clergy in France, and
Richelieu, who had been his pupil, supported him warmly and
was instrumental in inducing the Sorbonne to censure the conduct and writings of the English Jesuits.   In 1632, when the
theological world was greatly excited by this controversy, a
book entitled *Petrus Aurelius* appeared.   It was of course
written in Latin, was very learned and weighty, and at the
same time full of fire and vehemence.   The object of this
work was to assert and maintain the episcopal rights, and this
was done in such a masterly manner that all the dignitaries
of the Church were on the side of the anonymous author, who
was no other than St. Cyran.   It is as difficult to discover a
motive for *Petrus Aurelius*, as for either of his previous works,
or to understand how he could stand up as the champion of
the Church and at the same time say :

'I confess that God has shown and is showing me many
things.   He has shown me that there is no longer any Church.
No, there is no Church, and there has been no Church for
five or six hundred years.   Formerly the Church was like a
mighty stream of pure water flowing through the land, but now
that which looks like water is nothing but mud ; the bed of the
beautiful river is the same, but not the stream that flows
through it.'   The Council of Trent he considered as 'first of
all a political assembly ;' and of the Schoolmen he said, ' it
is they, the Schoolmen, and even St. Thomas himself, who
have destroyed true theology.'

Sainte-Beuve in his history of Port Royal suggests that as St.
Cyran intended to attack the vices of the Church of Rome and
his clergy, he thought it well to secure influential allies, and at

any rate to weaken the forces of his enemies the Jesuits, who had many powerful friends among the clergy in France. This may be so ; but he might have foreseen, and probably did foresee, that allies would also become enemies as soon as he took up arms against them. The true explanation seems to be that like St. Francis he inveighed against the corrupt practices of the Church of Rome, but approved of her theory, and the *Petrus Aurelius* was a defence of his ideal of ecclesiastical government and of episcopal rights in the abstract.   Just because he considered this government Divine and the rights sacred he could not tolerate the manifold abuses which he was compelled to witness. Richelieu and the clergy found in him an ally who could attack with as much ability as he defended, and who was perhaps more dangerous as a friend than as an enemy.

St. Cyran did not acknowledge the *Petrus Aurelius*, and it is believed to have been dictated to his nephew de Barcos, as he used to assert with much emphasis that he did not *write* it. He declined all offers of promotion, and neither flattery nor bribes could tempt a man for whom the world and worldly success had no charms. Richelieu, foiled in all his attempts, began to suspect that St. Cyran was a secret enemy, and in 1636 the Abbot was imprisoned in the fortress of Vincennes, from whence he was not released until after the Cardinal's death.

CHAPTER XVI

THE LITTLE COMMUNITY.

ONE of the postulants who accompanied Angélique to the
convent of the Holy Eucharist, Magdalen de St. Agnes de
Ligni, has left a picture of the internal life of the little community established there; and it is interesting to notice how,
when the hostile pressure of Port Royal is removed, our Abbess
resumes her old place, like a strong steel rod which has been
bent and springs back to its original direction.

Her theory of government is that an abbess must be first
officer of the household, responsible for everything, acquainted
with everything, finding nothing too trivial, and no work too
hard for her. She understands literally the words of Christ,
'He that is greatest among you shall be your servant.' She
ministered to every want of those around her, was both friend
and servant, and laboured constantly to bring them back to
the simple piety of early days. This was not an easy task, for
their residence in Paris had destroyed their humility, and
replaced it by spiritual pride and impatience of reproof; so
that, although all, except Mdlle. de Chamesson, were warmly
attached to Angélique, she found it no easy task to rule them.

With unconquerable energy and resolution she began again
at forty-four the struggle she had gone through at sixteen, and
which had ended, after thirty years of labour, by leaving her
to be gazed at in her paper mask by the Sisters, 'Pray to
God for this hypocrite!' But she did not hesitate or lose
patience. The old objections to coarse raiment and hard
fare and poor lodging are raised again, and she meets them

with the old replies; urges the obligation of their vows and of their rule, that they are to seek poverty and to love it, and to choose that which is vile and mean; to place others before self in great things and in small, and therefore to take the lowest place as individuals and as a community.

She relied, as she had done before, on counteracting selfishness by generous charity. The poor soon followed her, and she gave money, clothing, food, all that she and the Sisters could by any possibility do without, rarely appealing to others for help, as she retained her old dislike to begging, and felt that charity does not consist in distributing the money of others. She would not go to the Parlour unless it was absolutely indispensable, saying that nuns lost their time behind the grating, and the secular persons on the other side of it gained nothing. This is the only reference she makes to the long conferences between nuns and their visitors at Port Royal de Paris, but it is enough. She put an end to the thing for herself and others; and although she sometimes relaxed her rule in favour of the poor and needy, she never did so for the world or the church. She approved of renunciation, but not of privation; and therefore, although she urged the nuns to give up, she took nothing from them; on the contrary, she did all in her power to secure their comfort. She would light a fire after matins, and fetch anyone who stayed away and insist on her warming herself. She often visited the kitchen and tasted the food that was being prepared, giving directions if she thought it not palatable; but she expected the Sisters to make no complaint if by any accident their food was spoiled, and to eat cheerfully whatever was set before them, good or bad. The cook was a lay-sister from Tard, and followed the Benedictine rule, eating no meat; whilst at the Holy Eucharist they had adopted the rule of St. Augustine, and ate meat four times a week. The cook did not prepare anything specially for herself, but reserved and consumed the scraps left by the Sisters on fast-days. Angélique heard of this and followed her to the refectory one day, where she saw that a poor and scanty meal awaited her. The Abbess made no remark, but fetched some eggs, beat them up, made an omelette, and set it before the lay-sister, saying that whenever she neglected to provide a dinner for herself she should do the same thing again. The cook was ashamed of being waited upon by her Abbess and yet could not help laughing as she told the Sisters it was the most delicious omelette she had ever tasted.

The *august robes* which the Bishop was anxious to introduce in the convent had been much discussed and warmly approved by Angélique's companions; she had therefore special reasons for purchasing and herself preparing the dresses and under-clothing of the Sisters. She was anxious to give them no cause for complaint, often asked if they had all that they required, and took no rest until she had satisfied their wants; but obviously at that time she could not trust another to purchase coarse material and to make such simple dresses as she thought suitable for nuns. They urged that finer material would last longer; she answered, 'with vehemence,' that they had better have new gowns than break their vows; and used to tell them that if, after she was dead, they tried to make their costume *becoming*, she would certainly come back from her grave and protest against it.

Six months after the establishment of the new convent her cousin, Anne de St. Paul, was attacked by confluent small-pox, and before long was in imminent danger. Angélique shut herself up in the sick room, allowed no one to enter except those whose aid was indispensable, and took every precaution to prevent the disease from spreading throughout the house. She was tenderly attached to her cousin, and would not leave her night or day, in spite of the commands of the physician and the entreaties of the nuns. Bleeding was a remedy still in vogue, and she bled her cousin frequently. It was in Angélique's arms that Anne de St. Paul died, and Angélique prepared her for the grave and buried her. Anne de St. Paul bore her sufferings cheerfully, nay joyfully. When she knew that there was no hope of recovery she made a general confes-sion, and asked for the last Sacraments, which she received with great humility and piety. She demanded pardon from all the Sisters, although there was not one whom she had ever offended or grieved by word or deed. One of those present said:

'Alas! dear Sister, how much you suffer!'

She answered: 'It is nothing, my Sister. We must remem-ber what St. Paul says, that 'The sufferings of this present time are not worthy to be compared with the glory which shall be revealed in us.' I am now a poor leper lying at the door of Christ our Lord, who was Himself willing to be compared to a leper for the love of us.'

'But, dear Sister, you are going to leave us, and we are all in great sorrow.'

'Ah no, my Sister, I am not going to leave you. Those whom God has united can never be separated; and if God gives me grace, as I trust He will do, I shall always remember our little community when I am before His throne.'

This was the only death that occurred amongst them, although there was a Sister who had the plague, so the doctor said, whom Angélique nursed and who recovered. But there was much sickness; the house was small and inconvenient, the dormitory was under the roof, very hot in summer and cold and wet in winter; neither wind nor rain were excluded, and the Sisters often had to take their bedclothes to the fire at night in order first to thaw and then to dry them.

Angélique's health was beginning to fail; but now, and during the remainder of her life, she made light of her sufferings and, as far as was possible, concealed them.

Those words, ' I shall always remember our little community,' imply not only the love of the dying nun for her home on earth, but her satisfaction with it. Standing before the throne of God she hoped to look back upon it, and we do find that it was an abode of peace and good-will and well-doing. Angélique urged the Sisters to imitate the early Christians in Jerusalem, and specially to try and resemble them in three points.

1. The docility with which they received the word of God.
2. Their separation from the world.
3. Their union with each other.

Before long there was but one heart and one soul among them. Nothing could have exceeded their tender love for each other and interest in all that concerned each other's welfare. They were very compassionate to any who were sick, bearing each other's burdens and striving to lighten them, so that every individual felt that no pain was her own, it was that of the community, who all rejoiced when it was relieved. Instead of the old efforts at humiliation, the baskets of filth, the paper masks, and the false biographies, they treated each other with respect and deference, and strove to correct each one her own fault lest they should cause another to offend.

Angélique had often on her lips at this time, and always in her heart, a saying of St. Francis de Sales, that 'in order to attain perfection it is not necessary to do singular things, but it is necessary to do common things singularly well.' She exhorted her nuns not to be negligent in small things, telling them that they could attain perfection by the performance of small duties as well as great, provided they served God with their whole heart, at all times and in all circumstances. True humility would teach them even to shut a door gently so as not to disturb those who were in the room. They were to be punctual. At the first stroke of the chapel-bell each one was to say, in her heart, *Hoc signum magni regis est, eamus !* 'It is the signal of the great King; let us go !' And they were to be as punctual in the refectory as in the chapel, and not to think that they went there to satisfy a material want, and therefore were free to stay away or enter late. Every action was to be governed by higher rules than their own gratification, and the care of body as well as soul was to be lifted into the region of duty. A story told of Angélique at this time helps us to understand the sweetness as well as the strength of her nature, and the sympathy which made her intelligible to all.

She was ill, and in the room with a nun also ill and unable to leave her bed. This Sister saw that her Abbess needed help, and said that she ought not to be left in that manner with no one to wait on her. Angélique answered cheerfully, that they must remember how many persons there were of very different condition to their own who were reduced by misfortune and had no one to wait on them ; and that if they had remained in the world it might so have happened that they had only one little maid-servant, and whilst she went to market to buy provisions for the day, they would have been left alone.

'Therefore, my daughter,' she continued, 'when there is no one in the room and we want something, we must think that the little servant has gone to market, and we must wait patiently till she comes back.'

The sick Sister did not forget this, and was never heard to complain again. When they were alone she would say, with a smile, ' My Mother, the little servant has gone to market.'

The nuns of the Holy Eucharist led a busy life. In addition to the usual services of the Romish Church at the canonical hours, there were sometimes as many as seventeen or eighteen masses said in a day. They were present at every service if possible. At first they used to be disturbed at their devotions by the noises in the street, and the absurd jokes and conversation which they overheard. After the 'sharpening of their wits' at Port Royal, they could not listen to them without laughing, and there was a perpetual giggling, which Angélique found must be repressed. She told them it was not a crime to laugh at anything ridiculous, but they were not *absorbed* in prayer, as devout nuns should be, if they were conscious of trifling matters around them. This was enough. Before long, a nun who laughed saw no answering smiles on the faces around her, was filled with compunction for her fault, and went to her Abbess as soon as service was over to confess it. Never, says Angélique, was an epidemic so quickly stamped out.

The nuns washed and kept in order all the linen needed by the priests in their ministrations, and several Bishops and other ecclesiastics sent all that was used in their churches to be washed by them. They had also the work of the house and as much work for the poor as they could find time for. Their coarse common clothing was soon worn out, and required constant mending. 'Patches,' said Angélique, 'are a nun's jewels,' and she had a large yellow patch on her own sleeve, the contemplation of which gave her great satisfaction. She had not lost her early objections to ornaments in the church; and as soon as she recovered her freedom by the absence of the Bishop of Langres, she banished flowers and embroidery from the altar, and entreated that there might be no vestments embroidered with gold or silver in her chapel. Mdme. de Longueville once sent jewels for decoration during the Octave of the Holy Eucharist, and Angélique was told by a nun that women brought their children and placed them on the altar to look at the precious stones. She was so shocked to hear this, that she went immediately to the chapel and prostrated herself before the altar with tears, remaining in prayer for a long time. She thought it a horrible profanation that a church should be made attractive, or that it should be visited for any other purpose than that of prayer and praise.

Mdlle. de Chamesson, the postulant who had been appointed as Angélique's companion, began to find that she had a difficult task. Before many months had passed away, Angélique had acquired the ascendancy to which her intellect, her noble nature, and many virtues entitled her. The affection and respect of her companions were unbounded; they said that she was love and peace embodied. Almost without an effort she had won them back to their allegiance. Silence, piety, self-denial, and grave simplicity of life, were once more characteristic of the community; of all but the young postulant who stood aloof.

Mdlle. de Chamesson tried to keep the post of observation assigned to her by the Bishop, but Angélique had moved into another region, whither she could not follow. The young lady, however, did what she could, even asked the Abbess one day why she had bought a jug without consulting her. Angélique answered gently that she had not thought it necessary to do so. In the silence of the convent Mdlle. de Chamesson's voice was often heard speaking angrily to their beloved Mother; and on one occasion the Sacristan went to them and was about to interfere, but Angélique signed to her to be silent.

' My daughter,' she said afterwards, ' it is a cross which God has sent me: shall I not bear it?'

' But, my Mother, she disgraces us all!'

' Do not say so, daughter; we must have compassion on her, and pray to God to have mercy upon her soul. We are twelve, the number of the Apostles, amongst whom Christ suffered one Judas. Shall we not therefore bear with this poor girl, who ought to make us sorry and not angry? She is really and truly blind, and we must be very charitable to her. Do not be uneasy. She will not remain here, but I cannot send her away.'

The Bishop of Langres was absent from Paris, and before leaving he had commended St. Cyran to the two convents as a man to whom the nuns were greatly indebted. The Abbot soon discovered that Angélique would be a valuable disciple. He visited her frequently, and wrote daily instructions for the spiritual guidance of the nuns; and when he understood the heavy pecuniary difficulties of Angélique's position—for she was living in an expensive house, which the royal and noble founders had not endowed with a single penny—he found means of obtaining money for the supply of the most pressing wants of the community. A year later he consented, with the approval of the Bishop, to receive the confessions of the Sisters; and they prepared for a general

confession, such as the Church of Rome requires only upon rare and important occasions. But Angélique drew back. It was a serious thing to accept St. Cyran as director of conscience. She says : 'I had already seen the necessity of submission and of contempt for the flesh and the gratification of the senses ; I knew the excellence of true poverty. God had given me so much love for these virtues, that my one desire was to find means of practising them. But my sinful nature, my levity, my inability to strengthen the first movements of grace (although my will had always remained unmoved), had caused me to commit great faults and to be unfaithful to my convictions, in consequence of which I often suffered remorse that caused me anguish too great almost to be endured. I would then begin again, but I soon fell back into the old supineness. And therefore I feared that which I really loved and desired, namely, the strong, holy, upright, and enlightened guidance of this servant of God. . . . . He was so wise, that I was afraid to show him all my folly, and so holy, that I shrank from telling him all my sins.'

Her submission however was a mere question of time, for undoubtedly she had at last found the ideal guide whom she had been seeking all her life.

There was much in the past which she had good cause to regret. She did not conceal from herself that she was responsible for the degeneracy of Port Royal, in Paris, and had encouraged tendencies which she ought to have repressed ; she acknowledged that no punishment was too severe for her faults. Once more we hear of the flagellation and privations which are sanctioned and inculcated by her Church. But her repentance was not of the kind that would allow her to dwell long in the dark chambers of remorse. She must be up and doing, striving to repair her faults and to help those whom she had hindered. She used to say that our faults ought to make us humble and strong—to teach us to distrust ourselves and place our whole confidence in God. We must not therefore fall from one fault into a second, namely, despair, but rise quickly and go humbly to God for help and pardon.

Angélique prepared for her general confession by repentance, humility, and *gratitude*. Her heart was filled with gratitude, because once again she was called by God. Every moment that she could spare she passed on her knees before the altar.

The Sisters were sometimes compelled to disturb her for some matter of importance, and she would turn to them with such a light upon her countenance that they shrank back and could not speak, and she had to ask what was wanted. She found that they hesitated to disturb her, and said that if this was the case she should no longer be free to spend every spare moment in the chapel, for it was of far more importance that she should do her duty to others than seek her own gratification in Divine worship, and they must help and not hinder her. When the Sisters saw her as in the course of her daily duties she passed from room to room in the convent, there was the same rapt look upon her face and the same light in her eyes, so that the sight of her filled them with holy aspirations, and made them long for the joy and peace which she had found.

In August 1635, the little community formally placed itself under the guidance of M. de St. Cyran.

Even Mdlle. de Chamesson did not escape the prevailing influence; she also submitted, and, confessing that the post assigned to her by the Bishop was too exalted, she prayed to be removed from it. The Abbot granted her request, and at once reduced her to the rank of an ordinary postulant. This by no means met with her approval, for she was unchanged in heart. She expected to have been treated as a penitent of distinction, and was not prepared for what she considered indifference and neglect. Meanwhile, in the absence of the Bishop of Langres, the Abbess Jeanne and the nuns from Tard de Dijon, Port Royal was also a changed house. The Abbess Genevieve and many of her nuns had returned to their old allegiance. Once more they looked to Angélique for guidance; once more they saw that the old way was the best. They also were guided by M. de St. Cyran; and when the Bishop returned he found only Mdme. de Pontcarré and a few nuns in one convent, and Mdlle. de Chamesson in the other who were still faithful to him. Therefore when, in November 1635, Angélique solicited the return to Paris of her sister Agnes, Abbess of Tard de Dijon, and the five nuns who had accompanied her, he willingly granted her request, for they were still his staunch allies. Between himself and Angélique there had arisen, as might have been expected, great coldness; and he was on the verge of an open rupture with St. Cyran.

Agnes had received the most exaggerated reports of all that

had transpired from Mdme. de Pontcarré, who wrote to her regularly, whilst all correspondence between herself and Angélique had been suspended for many years. She was informed that the Prioress of Port Royal was in favour of the Cistercian monks, and that an attempt was being made to replace the convent under their supervision; that numerous changes in that direction had already been made which were sanctioned by the Abbess, and probably suggested by Angélique. The widow sent lively sarcastic letters, turning everything and every person to ridicule, except the Bishop; and Agnes and her nuns still believed that he was not only the benefactor of the convent, but a saint who had been treated with the cruelest ingratitude. When Agnes arrived in Paris she visited Angélique before going to Port Royal; and Angélique, who was unchanged, found that her sister's heart was gone from her. Agnes listened coldly to all explanations, and was obviously unconvinced by the statements made to her. The nuns who accompanied her were much more unrestrained, and their angry reproaches and undisguised hostility induced Angélique to send a message to the Abbess Genevieve warning her of the danger of a probable division in the convent. She knew Agnes, however, too well to doubt her, and when they parted said that she gave her six months to see things for herself, and then she would be in another mind.

As soon as Agnes and her nuns reached Port Royal, the Bishop, who was in Paris, paid them a visit, and there were many pretty speeches on his side and many tears on theirs, because they had been removed from his diocese.

At Angélique's request, St. Cyran went to see her sister, and a single conversation with him dispelled her prejudices. She could not listen unmoved to his calm, clear narrative of the events of the past few years. Inquiry and observation confirmed all that he said. He had exaggerated nothing as to facts, notably those connected with Mdme. de Pontcarré. Agnes wrote to Angelique that she did not want six months, six days had opened her eyes. Angélique says:

'It was a great consolation to receive this letter and to find my sister in a different mind. I saw that God in His great goodness had now repaired the fault which I committed in sending her to Tard at the desire of him to whom I had so rashly submitted my own judgment. Our convent suffered

greatly in consequence of her absence, and would have been
entirely ruined if God in His mercy, for which I can never be
grateful enough, had not brought good out of evil.'

Angélique does not at all exaggerate the influence of Agnes
when she says that her absence was the greatest calamity which
could have befallen the convent. Angélique was always impulsive, often rash ; conviction and action followed close upon
each other, and she was incapable of deliberation. Where
truth, right, justice, self-denial, humility were concerned, she
never hesitated for one moment. She placed herself on the side
of right and accepted the consequences, whether good or evil.
She was equally rapid in detecting wrong, injustice, and false-
hood, and she could not spare them. In childhood she had
turned for help to the grave young sister, so like and yet so
unlike herself; and in every important event of her life Agnes
had been by her side. Agnes possessed the patience and
foresight which our Abbess often needed ; she saw the tendency
of events, and was not, like Angélique, engrossed by the immediate present, its hopes and fears. Less resolute, she was
also less liable to the errors of judgment which Angélique had
such good reason to lament. 'I had not consulted my sister
Agnes,' 'I resolved upon this course in the absence of my sister
Agnes,' she says repeatedly in alluding to mistakes which she
did not discover until it was too late to rectify them. Nothing
shows her unbounded confidence in her sister so much as this
desire that she should return to Paris. She knew that for many
years Agnes had only heard of her from those whom we are
justified in speaking of as her enemies, although she did not
call them so ; that they had taken different sides on an important question, one condemning and the other upholding the
conduct of the Bishop of Langres ; and that if Agnes should
remain in opposition, her life's work would be undone. She
knew that every effort would be made to convince Agnes that
the Bishop was right and she herself wrong. And yet she
desired her return, was confident that she could not be
deceived, that her judgment would be just and wise, and that
she would remedy all that had gone amiss.

But there was grief in store for both of them. Marie-Claire,
who had been sent to Port Royal at seven years old, and whom
the sisters looked upon as their child, returned with Agnes from
Tard de Dijon. She was warmly attached to the Bishop, and

would not recognize the possibility of that change in him which she was assured had taken place. At first she confesses that the accusation filled her with apprehension, and she used to pray to God, 'Thou wilt not suffer thy Holy One to see corruption.' But when they reached Paris, and Agnes as well as Angélique was, as she thought, disloyal, the generous warmth of her nature led her to resolve that she would not forsake her friend and guide, or listen to unfavourable accounts of his conduct. She therefore allied herself with Mdme. de Pontcarré, and her sisters had the pain of finding that she was the leader of their opponents.

'One of these nuns,' says Angélique, 'was my very own sister, Marie-Claire, and there was no one who believed so earnestly as she did that the Bishop was the most saintly man in the world, and that we were indeed guilty for having renounced his guidance. She used to pray for us night and day with many tears, entreating God to open our eyes. Her piety procured her the esteem of the whole convent, and her love to all around her, especially the sick, was so great that she was always ready to do anything in the world for them ; and on this account many were attracted to her side.

In Mdme. de Pontcarré's rooms the nuns received visits from the Bishop and the Fathers of the Oratory, and their grievances were discussed. There was no open breach in Port Royal, but the schism was spreading, and if it had not been for the forbearance and gentleness of Agnes there would have been an unseemly quarrel. Angélique saw this, and her heart was with her mother and sisters and the companions of her youth. Before long she found a way to join them. The new institution was paralysed by the opposition of the Archbishop of Paris, and she could not carry out his wishes because she was pledged by her promise given at Port Royal to the Bishop of Langres. She therefore proposed to the Archbishop that the Abbess Genevieve, who was under no promise, should be allowed to take her place at the Holy Eucharist, and that she should return to Port Royal. He consented, and the matter was kept so secret that very few in the new convent and still fewer in the old knew anything of it until Genevieve was installed as Mother Superior of the Holy Eucharist, and Angélique was at home again.

CHAPTER XVII

MARIE-CLAIRE AND THE ABBOT.

AGNES took the place of Mother Superior of Port Royal, and Angélique replaced her as Prioress. The two sisters laboured for seven months to restore the work which had been destroyed, and to win back hearts alienated from them. They succeeded ; and in September 1636, at the third triennial election, Agnes was chosen by a large majority of the nuns. The Bishop, the Grand Vicar, Mdme. de Pontcarré, Marie-Claire and her companions had striven in vain to influence the election. The Grand Vicar presided over the meeting, and he was exceedingly angry when he had to announce that Agnes was duly elected Abbess of Port Royal.

But the nuns and novices were full of joy, for Agnes was beloved by all, and at last Angélique found that the desire of her heart was one that could be granted. There was work for her in Port Royal, and she was free from the responsibility which she disliked.

The first important step taken by the new Abbess was to entreat the Bishop with all due humility not to visit Port Royal again. As this was equivalent to a command, and implied the closing of the parlour wickets, he obeyed ; at the same time she forbad the nuns to write to him, or to hold any intercourse with Mdme. de Pontcarré. In six months, all except Marie-Claire had yielded, but she still held out, though the struggle was literally breaking her heart. She was torn by conflicting duties and affection. She implored God to give her grace to submit to Him and to those who were set in authority over her, and at the same time she never wavered in her allegiance to the Bishop. She loved Angélique more than anyone in the world, although at the desire of the Bishop she had neither written nor spoken to her for many years lest the earthly love should draw her heart from Heaven. And now Angélique presumed to judge her saintly guide, and to pronounce him unworthy even of admission to the convent. Marie-Claire's grief was greater than she could endure, and mother and sisters tried in vain to open her eyes to the true character of the Bishop, and show her the necessity of the step that had been taken. The whole community prayed for her, but in vain. The loyalty and generosity of her nature made her faithful to the man whom she believed to be persecuted and forsaken.

Her eldest brother, d'Andilly, was now the head of the family; he had children of his own in the convent school and among the novices, and was grieved at this division in the family, and the pain it brought to all. He tried by argument to convince Marie-Claire that she was wrong, and failed as others had done ; but a week later he went to her, and said, ' My sister, let us kneel and pray to God to speak to your heart, and show you the truth.' They knelt and prayed in silence. Marie-Claire did not ask to be confirmed, but to be guided and taught. She rose from her knees a new creature, regretting the past, and earnestly desiring to be restored to the paths of obedience and duty. Angélique and Agnes were summoned, she threw herself at their feet, asked pardon for her faults, and promised in future to submit to them in all things. She saw that she had failed in her duty as a nun ; but her opinion of the Bishop was unchanged, and it was not easy to convince her that, on this point, she was wrong also. She could not, however, resist the proofs which, now that she consented to examine them, were brought before her. They were overwhelming, and she at length acknowledged that she had been deceived. Her repentance was deep and sincere. She humbled herself to the dust before God and her fellow-workers, and entreated that she might be made a lay-sister for life. She wrote a penitent letter to St. Cyran, imploring him to see her, but he would not grant her request. His refusal did not altogether arise from doubt of her sincerity, though that may have had something to do with it ; but he knew that in confession she must refer to her dislike of him and disapproval of his conduct, and he thought it would be an unnecessary humiliation to make her speak of this to him-self.   Moreover, she could not speak so frankly to him, on matters relating to himself, as she would do to another, and he wished her to open her heart freely, so that her misgivings might be examined and removed.

Six months later, he granted her request for an interview, and after that, for a few months, he saw her from time to time. She made notes of what he had said during these interviews, and submitted them to him.   He returned them with the fol-lowing letter :

' MY VERY DEAR SISTER,

' I return your notes of the thoughts which you tell me you gathered from the conversations I had with you during the time of your contrition.   Since you think they have been useful to you, I see no harm in your keeping them.   But you must never lose sight of that which St. Paul takes such pains to impress upon our minds, namely, that we must not put our trust in men, who do nothing more than plant and water, but in God who gives the increase.'

We may conclude from this that, although we have not the exact words of St. Cyran in Marie-Claire's notes, but only the effect those words produced on her mind, they are utterances that he accepts and acknowledges.   They enable us to follow his method of dealing with penitents, and show something of the kind of influence he exercised over them.

When he sent for Marie-Claire, he said abruptly :

' I had no wish to see you, or intention of doing so to-day. I came here with quite another object, but I went into the church, and then obeyed an impulse, which told me to ask for you.   This is the day of Saint Ignatius, the Martyr :—a very remarkable Saint.   Well, what do you want ?   I am here to cure you.   What is your disease ? '

She told him what her condition had been, and he seems to have suspected that her statement was over-coloured, for he replied :

' We must find out whether you exaggerate your faults, and whether in the sight of God they are as great as you think them.   Sometimes, a spirit of exaggeration impels us to say things we do not believe, and we are thus led into an evil course; so that we must inquire carefully into this matter.

'The outward and visible signs of repentance must proceed from an inward and spiritual feeling of it; the two must be closely connected, and we must be very careful not to show more than we really feel.'

A few days later she made a general confession to him, and he again exhorted her to restrain herself, and not give way to her grief:

'God is a Spirit,' he said, 'and spiritual sins offend Him more than any others. . . . Beware of exaggeration; the confession that shows most humility is that which is simple and spontaneous. We do not want any close scrutiny to remind us of our great sins; the impression which they leave is indelible, for it belongs to the immortality of the Soul. Kneel before God without words, without anxious self-scrutiny, He will understand you.'

'You cannot repent whilst you are dead in your sins. You must be *alive* to repent. That is why I have left you so long : I waited until you were *alive*, and now for five months you have lived a spiritual life.'

'When the dawn first breaks we say it is day, although the shades of night are not all dispersed. And in the same manner we ought to call the first gleam of light that God sends into a human heart *Grace*, although that heart is still darkened by the clouds of sin.'

'It is a great mistake to guide all souls alike. Each soul must have its own rules. Many things may be done without danger by the innocent, which would be most dangerous for those who are wounded by sin; for although they may be healed by repentance, they are not exempt from the weakness which their wounds have left. A soldier who has received a grievous wound, feels every change of weather all the rest of his life, even although the wound is healed; and if he values health, he does not expose himself to wet and cold, as others may do with impunity. . . . In short, the first rule of repentance is that he who has sinned in doing things that are unlawful, must abstain even from those that are lawful.'

'Beware of your tears ! I do not want grimaces and signs and gestures, but a silence of the heart and spirit that shall control every movement of the body.'

On another occasion he said to her :

'You must forget the past. If we were always obliged to think of our past sins no one could be happy. I am not satisfied with a hope that only goes far enough to hinder despair. We must have a firm and constant faith in God, who is infinitely tender to those who are in the right way, and infinitely terrible and severe to those who are in the wrong. He who has commanded us not to look back when we have put our hand to the plough, knows what is for our good ; He will not look back upon the past sins of one who is seeking His kingdom.'

Marie-Claire begged permission to remain a lay-sister for life, so that there might be no change and no risk of a subsequent fall. He replied :

'You wish the future to be settled for you. I do not like that request. Those who belong to God ought to have nothing absolutely settled and decided. They ought to act by faith, which has neither clear vision nor assurance as to the result of good works. They must look to God and follow Him always and under all circumstances. For myself, I do not want to know what I shall do when I leave this place. We are told to ask God for our bread, that is for His grace, day by day ; but I should like to ask for it hour by hour. The Christian soul should be absolutely free and unfettered. It ought to be able to pass from rest to labour, and from labour to rest ; from prayer to action, and from action to prayer ; desiring nothing, cleaving to nothing, willing to do everything and equally willing to do nothing, and to remain useless if sickness or duty should require it. There is a great advantage in a pause, for often when we are at work we are really doing nothing in the sight of God.'

He consented to her joining the lay-sisters for a time, saying : 'We will make you a lay-sister this Lent. Such changes were common in ancient times when Lent was a period of excessive penitence in order to dispose Catechumens to Baptism. You shall labour ; but in moderation, so that you may persevere. It is contrary to the spirit of true humility to seek to do extraordinary things. We are not saints because we do the same things that the saints have done. We must be contented to remain insignificant and unnoticed, and to live as it were in disguise, so that nothing out of the common shall be seen in us. You will make yourself equal to the lay-sisters in every respect, only you will try to be the most humble of them all.'

St. Cyran urges humility upon all penitents ; but it is the humility which teaches us that we are incapable of any good or great work without the help of God's grace, and not that which oppresses us with a sense of our utter inability to do any work whatsoever. Humility is to be shown in accepting our life, and trying to make the best of it. He says :

'There is no greater pride than to seek to go beyond the will of God, and to do some great work for Him by a hasty impulse of our own will ; and there is no truer humility than to accept the limits He has prescribed, and make our works within those limits great works.' He adds to this the injunction, ' When a thing is done, forget it in God.'

In all things Marie-Claire strove to follow his advice, and although the guilt of her defection was in her eyes so great that she always looked upon herself as a criminal, yet she did not seek for the extraordinary penances which her Church sanctions, and such guides as the Bishop approve. She was content to be the lowest and last in the community, the servant of all, especially of the sick. She was always ready to help them night or day, and slept so little that it was natural for the Sisters to go first to Marie-Claire upon any emergency. She was grieved if she had not an opportunity of trying to relieve pain, and as she was very skilful in preparing remedies and applying them, everyone who was ill wanted Sister Marie-Claire, ' it did them good to see what a kind heart she had, and how she suffered when they were in pain, and what delight she took in trying to find something that would give them ease.' She obtained permission to sleep in a little dark cell, or cupboard, under the staircase, so that she might be called up at any hour of the night without disturbing the Sisters in the dormitory.

All the Arnaulds have this tender sympathy with suffering, all have the same affectionate nature, so that we can scarcely say that Marie-Claire stands apart from them in this respect, but she had not the strength or vigour of the four elder sisters ; she had the heart of the Arnaulds, but not the intellect or the elasticity of their nature. Angélique, Agnes, Anne, Mdme. le Maître could not be crushed by misfortune or utterly humiliated by faults. They could not help rising and going on their way. But Marie-Claire remains as it were upon her knees; praying, waiting, weeping for three years, and then the Sisters whom she has nursed are standing by her own bedside. Her illness did not at first alarm them, but one night the nun watching by her side saw a great change, and said:

'Oh, my Sister, what is this?'

'It is Death, Sister,' replied Marie-Claire. 'I must leave you. I am going to throw myself at the feet of God, for I have no hope except in His mercy.'

And even this hope was to fail her for a time as she passed through the dark shadow. When the priest came to administer the last sacrament for the dying, she asked him anxiously, 'Oh, Father, shall I be saved?' He tried to give her confidence, but she had a great dread of death. She had been afraid to go direct to God even in prayer since her fall, and had trusted to the intercession of the Virgin; standing before her as she had done when she was a child. In her supreme hour the thought of the Virgin seemed to have faded from her mind, and a great fear of God fell upon her. But before she died she held up the cross which they had placed in her hands, and her last words were, 'Victory! Victory!'

She had not the consolation of seeing St. Cyran before her death, as he was then in prison, but she occupied every spare moment in copying letters and manuscripts which were received from him. They were written in pencil, and were often almost illegible, and always difficult to decipher. But to Marie-Claire it was a labour of love. If she had only time to write a single line, she took her pen and wrote it. The nuns were amused at this assiduity, but she would tell them gaily that certainly she had only written a few words, and yet when she next looked at the page she should be glad to see them there; for if many minutes make an hour, so also many lines make a page.

There were others in the convent who have also left us an account of the kind of influence that St. Cyran exercised over the nuns who had been flattered and debased by the priests around them. One of these is Anne Arnauld. She returned from Maubuisson in 1631, and the Sisters who were very fond of her, praised her to the Prioress Jeanne; but the nuns from Tard ridiculed all that they were told of

Anne's virtue and ability. They found her silent, humble, and submissive, and ignored her, as they did others.

When Agnes returned in 1633, Anne and her mother, Mdme. Arnauld, were both at Port Royal, but they were absorbed in their devotions, and had taken no part in all that had gone on around them. Anne saw that there was a great change, but she must also have seen that a reaction against it was already setting in, and she may have therefore waited until the return of Agnes made her way clear. Still the silence of Anne is rather puzzling, and does not accord with what we know of her at other times. She was impulsive, zealous, very quick to detect the faults of others, and not unready to point them out ; and she was haughty and could ill brook reproof or opposition. Possibly her failure at Maubuisson may have inclined her to be silent at Port Royal. With the return of her sisters, however, she resumes a post of importance in the convent, and we have from her pen some record of the influence of St. Cyran over herself and others.

The old temptation to report and exaggerate the failings and shortcomings of others returned, and she consulted St. Cyran. She had noticed these wrong things, was she to speak of them? 'Be silent for three months,' he replied. At the end of that time she told him three months had elapsed, might she now tell? 'No,' he answered, 'be silent for the rest of your life.'

There were others in the community who needed a similar lesson. The process of 'sharpening the wits,' advocated by the Bishop, had not always been compatible with keeping the temper; and jokes intended to make the nuns merry, and teach them to endure ridicule without vexation, had not always been successful. *Recreation* twice a day had taken the place of the old solemn and often silent *Conference*, and the nuns passed much time in discussing each other's faults and the penances of the refectory. These were often so absurd—when they were not disgusting, like Angélique's basket of filth—that they laughed at them first in the refectory, and then again at Recreation. To accuse a nun of a trivial fault, and devise a still more trivial punishment, had become a pastime. *Recreation* ceased when Agnes and Angélique returned, and *Conferences* were resumed ; but it was not easy to check the evil habits into which the community had fallen. Silence was the only possible remedy for them, and St. Cyran advocated silence as earnestly as Angélique did.   He urged the community to be silent and tolerant.   Those who were called upon to exercise supervision were to bear everything that could be borne.   When a fault was committed which could not be excused, they were to wait until it had been repeated three times, and were then to reprove it in a single word.   They soon found the value of this advice, for since all were trying to do right, a fault was very seldom repeated three times, and there was therefore no need to speak of it.   St. Cyran taught them that the Lord's Prayer was a daily confession of daily faults and a daily remedy for them, and that they need seek no other.

After Anne's first confession to him in 1636, she asked for penance ; he replied :

'You ask for penance, but you have got it already ; you are a nun.   If I were to tell you to abstain from meat for the rest of your life, to fast, to rise at two o'clock every morning, never to leave the house, and never to speak to anyone except through a grating, I should have inflicted a very severe penance upon you.   Well, that is what you do already.   Keep your rule, therefore, you need add nothing to it.'

He then asked what her duty was in the house, and she answered, 'the care of the children in the convent school.' He continued :

'Then you are placed in a very favourable position, for if you forgive them, God will forgive you.   If you show them mercy, God will be merciful to you.   If you take pity on them, God will have pity on you.'

She was surprised to hear work, which she disliked so much, spoken of in this manner.   She thought that she had no love for children, and had shut up her heart against them.   She had been the strict ruler and nothing more, being 'driven as at the edge of the sword' when she went to the school-room.   Now, for the first time, she recognizes that the love which rules in heaven is to rule upon earth ; that the will of God for our well-being is to be our will for each other ; and that obedience is not merely submission, but love of the will of Him who guides us.   The tenderness which had been sup-pressed comes out in a very beautiful manner, and the schoolroom, instead of being her cross, is her crown.   It was impossible that she should overcome her scruples completely, because many of them arose from the human error, mixed with the divine truth, of her belief. The faults of the children caused her as much pain as her own ; but she remembered St. Cyran's injunction to speak little, endure much, and pray more. She bore the burden of the children's faults and did penance for them herself, for she could neither pass them over nor forget them. She no longer visited childish faults with severe punishment as she had formerly done, or exacted repentance and contrition which the children were unable to feel ; but she had not learnt that the tenderness of their Father in heaven was as great as her own, and thought that she must appease Him by her own sufferings.

Her niece, Marie-Charlotte, one of d'Andilly's six daughters, was in the convent school at this time, and gives a charming account of her. We see what a struggle she had to keep back her love, and to temper it with as much severity as she thought absolutely necessary for the children's welfare, so that she might not encourage the evil which it was her duty to check. It was so pleasant to her to gratify them that she could not help giving them sweetmeats; but before she did so she always prayed that they might not like them very much.

One day the children were naughty, and she left the schoolroom saying that she should not return, for it grieved her too much to see how little love they had either for God or their duty. As they were very fond of her, they spent the morning in tears, entreating the other teachers to go and fetch Sister Anne, and tell her how sorry they were. At length some one went and, as her heart was tender over the little ones, she relented immediately and returned to them. They flocked around her and she said it was a great consolation to see that they were sorry for their faults, because God forgave those who repented, and it was therefore quite right that she should forgive them also. With this she drew a bag full of sugar-plums from under her mantle and distributed them, saying, that when St. Louis wept as he thought of the Passion of our Lord, he found that the tears which fell upon his lips were sweet like honey; and she gave them the sugar-plums in order that they might remember that when we weep for our faults our tears are sweet. St. Cyran had something of the same compunction in gratifying the childish love for sweet things. He bought a pot of preserved quinces for one of d'Andilly's nieces in Port

Royal, and then did not like to take it to her, lest 'the sweets of earth should destroy her taste for the sweets of heaven.' But his scruples were overcome by hearing that she was ill, and he sent the quinces at once.

Sister Anne had a little, old, battered work-basket, which the children had decided among themselves she must have found in the dust-bin. They used to laugh at it, and protest against it. and call it an old, ugly thing ; whilst she defended it, and praised its peculiar shape and the high antiquity which lends so much value to every object. She spoke in such a bright, merry manner that the children thought teazing the basket capital `in ; and yet in after years they could see that there was earnest feeling in her pleasantry, and that she was teaching them to despise externals, and to look favourably upon the poverty which she loved.

When playtime came, she always remained for some time with them, telling them tales, and joining in games which she invented. She wrote short descriptions of different virtues on slips of paper, and the children drew lots for them ; or she described some virtue or vice under an image or by a simile, and the children guessed until they could discover it. Both these games were very popular, and could not be attempted without Sister Anne.

Her chief aim as a teacher was to make her pupils understand every word they used. St. Cyran had said, that in reading the Gospel we ought to weigh every word as if we were weighing gold ; and she saw that this was impossible without the most careful training as to the use and meaning of words. She had a dread of speaking of religious truths too soon, and used to say that when children are familiar with names and words and dogmas which they do not understand, they are apt to lose reverence for them. •

When she told a child anything from the Bible, she took her apart from the others, and prepared her to listen to a very important truth, and then stated what she had to say in a few impressive words, which often remained engraved upon the memory for life. Thus after one of her nieces had received her first communion, Sister Anne led her away from her companions, and said she had a very serious thing to tell her, and one that she must prepare her mind to hear, for it was very terrible ; and yet it was a thing which all those who had received the

Holy Sacrament ought to know. Then in a grave, earnest voice she continued, 'The Gospel tells us that when the devil has gone out of a human soul he returns again with seven other devils worse than himself, and if they find no resistance they enter in and take up their abode there, and the end of that soul is worse than the beginning.' The child trembled as she listened, and never forgot the pathetic pleading of the voice which uttered this warning.

At first, Sister Anne used to weep over every new pupil, for she distrusted her own power and anticipated the child's faults. But before long she learnt to rejoice at the increase of numbers, and she who had formerly protested against the admission of new pupils now protested against any being refused.

Angélique had yet another sister in Port Royal, Madeleine, the youngest, who took the veil in 1625, the child whose ears she boxed. She is the only Arnauld of that generation who leaves no mark. She suffered from constant ill-health, so that she could not perform any duties. We hear of 'vapours mounting to her brain,' so that she forgot almost everything and everybody ; 'but she never forgot God,' add the Memoirs.

CHAPTER XVIII

RESTORATION.

St Cyran's influence had restored Angélique to herself, and effaced all traces of that period of delusions during which she had listened to the Bishop of Langres. We see once again the Abbess of old days, though with characteristic features a little more strongly marked. Her youthful vigour is developed into vehemence; her denunciations are more keen and incisive than in those early years; and there is a great accession of strength, so that henceforward she goes on her way undaunted by any difficulty that assails either herself or others.

A curious document, drawn up during the previous year, shows both her strength and weakness, and indicates the direction of her faults. It consists of twelve resolutions, among which are the following :—

' I will always speak to the Sisters with great humility; I will never reprove them for a fault at the time when it is committed, nor the first time it is committed, nor before I have prayed to God to enable me to speak, and them to listen, in a right spirit.

' I will no longer persevere in the useless superintendence over all their actions which I have been accustomed to assume, and will put my trust in the guidance of God rather than in my own superfluous precautions.

' I will avoid going to the parlour as much as possible, and when I am no longer Abbess I will not go at all, not even to my relations. When I am obliged to go I will speak as little as possible, will not ask the news, and will prevent its being told me.

'I will speak as little as possible, and will write instead of speaking whenever I can, and make use of signs as often as I can.

'I will write no letters that are not necessary, and will so act that, as far as I can, I may forget all human beings, and be forgotten by them. When I write I will do it as simply as possible, and if ever I put anything that savours of affectation into a letter I will write another.'

The strong, simple sense, and right feeling which can be traced throughout the *Resolutions* contrasts strangely with errors which are inseparable from her belief that the life of a nun, with its superfluous privations and unnecessary incarceration, is a holy life and pleasing to God; and that to forget all human beings and be forgotten by them is in accordance with His will for His creatures.

Angélique, with her large, warm heart, was never forgotten by any human being who once saw her, and she never forgot anyone whom she could help or had helped. She talked and wrote and worked throughout the whole of the long, busy day; exhorting the novices who had been placed under her charge, or expounded the Scriptures in a manner that 'edified the whole community' and drew the nuns to listen to her as well as the young girls who aspired to follow in her steps. Her Resolutions on this point were merely protests which must have pained her by introducing discord between theory and practice. But there is not one that we can entirely condemn, nor one that is not redeemed by some gleam of wisdom, prudence, or kindliness. Moreover, they help us to understand her success as a reformer. She began with herself, never forgot that she needed the discipline she was advocating for others, and did not blind herself to her own faults. She laboured without ceasing to lead the purest and holiest life which she was able to recognize; and whilst she acknowledged the evil in herself she did not shut her eyes to the good in others. This is perhaps the secret of her success; she believed in the *goodness* of women,—not the goodness of individuals, but of the whole sex. She used to say that she never knew any convent, however badly conducted, in which there were not some good women who had escaped the prevailing corruption, and were trying to serve God. She never despaired of any convent, not even of Maubuisson, but believed that the good might be called out in every nun if she were placed in favourable circumstances.

Her opinion of the male sex, more especially of monks and priests, was not so favourable ; she believed in the goodness of certain individuals among them, and in the depravity of the sex. It is characteristic of Angélique that, on her return to Port Royal in 1636, the first evil she wished to remove was the Confessor. He had been appointed by the Bishop, and she attributed, justly, much of the deterioration of the convent to his influence. She applied to St. Cyran for a successor, and he suggested Father Singlin, whom Angélique knew and esteemed, as a disciple of Vincent de Paul. She placed all the novices and such of the pupils as were being prepared for their first communion under his care.

The Bishop of Langres, from the moment that he was excluded from Port Royal, avowed himself the enemy of St. Cyran, and denounced him at court and to Richelieu, saying that at the Holy Eucharist he had hindered the Sisters from partaking of the Holy Communion. St. Cyran had other enemies ; it was owing to his advice that the Cistercian monks, who had won over the Prioress and were still endeavouring to regain a footing in the convent, were banished, and with them the Fathers of the Oratory and the numerous priests and monks who were in the habit of visiting the nuns, listening to their dreams and getting up miracles. All these spoke of him bitterly, and he saw that any connection with him would bring ill-will upon Port Royal. After the appointment of Father Singlin he therefore returned to his abbey near Poictiers, and there was no communication between him and the Sisters except by letter.

As usual much of Angélique's time was spent in undoing the work of the priests. The numerous Directors of Conscience sanctioned by the Bishop had been a fruitful source of evil at Port Royal. The nuns told each other all they knew or could learn about their respective directors, and as many of them had obtained permission to walk out whenever they pleased, and talk to everyone they saw, they were generally provided with abundant topics for conversation.

One of the young nuns was so changed that it was impossible to recognize her. She fell into phrenzies, which were encouraged as manifestations of the Spirit, and it was often difficult

to restrain or control her. This was a fine opportunity for the
visiting fathers, and the nun gave them something fresh to talk
about from day to day. She would conceal herself for days
together, 'led away by the Spirit,' so it was said. When she
returned half-famished she would eat all the food she could beg
or steal. Then followed fits of remorse, in which she begged
to be chained to the fireplace, and wore a muzzle 'like that
put on a calf to prevent it from sucking.' In this condition
she was one of the sights of Port Royal. The fathers appointed
a nun to watch over the possessed Sister, and report all her
sayings and doings. She liked the attention bestowed on her
so much that before long there were no intervals of calmness,
and as the new rulers found that they must not look for im-
provement whilst she remained at Port Royal they sent her to
Tard de Dijon.

Father Singlin, with something of the sternness of St.
Cyran, quietly stamped out all that remained of the exaggeration which had been encouraged for so long. He would have
no saints in the community, not even the Abbess Agnes. One
of the nuns used to watch Agnes when she was praying, never
removing her eyes from her face. She said that nothing made
her so devout, and carried her thoughts so directly to God, as
the sight of her dear Mother in prayer. Father Singlin heard
of this, and forbad her to watch the Abbess.

Agnes was titular Abbess of Port Royal, but Angélique
still ruled, and all important transactions are associated with
her name. It is she who removes the Confessor, restores
obedience to the rules of the Order, reinstates poverty, and
does battle with obstacles and difficulties; always, however,
seconded by Agnes, and taking counsel with her on every
subject, save the debts of the convent; and this heavy burthen
she bore alone.

M. de Langres had quite modern notions as to the advantage
of debt for a charitable institution, and he had plunged Port
Royal into difficulties. The convent owed 140,000 francs, and
paid large sums every year as interest. No one but Angélique
and one nun, Sister Suzanne, knew of this. Angelique told her
nephew, M. le Maître, in later years that she could not rest
for thinking of these debts, and had shed ' millions of tears'
and passed innumerable wakeful nights, through the anxiety
they caused her ; for it was not only the debts that oppressed

her, but the remembrance of her own past conduct. The temptation to receive ladies of fortune probably assailed her, for she consulted St. Cyran on this subject, and he told her, it was not wealthy novices who would pay her debts, but God. She had offended God by her indiscretion and rashness, and must make atonement by repentance : when she had satisfied God, He would satisfy men, and as soon as she had paid her debt to God He would pay all other debts for her.

'This discourse,' she continues, 'did me much good, for he did not flatter me as others had done, and excuse me because in these foolish, rash undertakings my intentions had been good. Still, I had never deceived anyone as to our resources, and once when a man came to offer to lend me money, and asked what security I could give him, I said the only security I had to offer was that of our abbey which was small, and the Providence of God which was great ; and the man seeing my frankness lent us his money upon interest.

'Our creditors often pressed me for money, and when I heard that one of them was asking for me I have often hidden myself, and sent Sister Suzanne. She, poor woman, used to listen to all their complaints, and by her gentleness and tact would induce them to accept her excuses ; and thus she spared me the torture of their applications. But while she was with them I was on my knees before God, weeping bitterly.

'It was so impossible to pay all demands that it came to pass that at length we were 16,000 francs in arrears, and were also deeply in debt. And then God put it into the heart of the Duc de Longueville to redeem an annuity which he had hitherto paid us, and he gave us instead 17,000 francs. I got rid of the arrears for 15,000, and paid off some small debts with the other 2,000. The community did not think I had acted wisely, because I had lost both principal and interest of this money, so I wrote to M. de St. Cyran, who was then in prison. He sent back word that I had done right, and that the hand of God was visible in the matter. About 1640 I sent a carpenter to look at the wood-work in the dormitory at Port Royal des Champs, as I thought of selling it to the nuns of St. Cyr. I wrote to M. de St. Cyran, and told him I could get 6,000 francs for it, and that it was a great useless building, which cost a large sum of money to keep in repair, whilst our creditors were growing importunate. He replied

that we must endure poverty rather than run the risk of destroying a fine building which might some day be of use.'

Angélique had good reason to be grateful for this advice,
and looked back on it as a prophecy.

St. Cyran was upright and honourable in small matters as
well as great, and Port Royal was now under the guidance of
a man who did not think integrity a merely human attribute.

The sister of one of the nuns had promised to send her
fifty crowns, about one hundred and fifty francs, for the use of
the church, but instead of that sum she sent two hundred livres,
or about two hundred francs. The nun, who had entered the
monastery when she was very young, did not know the relative
value of crowns and livres, and said she would rather have
fifty crowns. But Anne Arnauld, who had accompanied her
to the parlour, whispered, 'Take it, take it!' Afterwards,
her conscience reproached her, and when next she went to
confession she began to speak of the matter to St. Cyran.
He interrupted her, saying, 'Sister, say no more. I see what
it is. For the future you must remember that what seems
our loss is in reality our gain. The love of gain diminishes as
charity increases. We must shun avarice and not give way to
it, being assured that God will not leave those who serve Him
to perish, and if He allows them to suffer poverty it is for their
edification.'

Angélique 'took her griefs and debts to God.' On one
occasion she wanted three hundred francs to send to the farm
at Port Royal des Champs, six hundred for Gif, a hundred and
fifty to pay a debt, and two hundred for the butcher. 'I had
not a single sou,' she says, 'so I went to my room and prayed
to God for the money, and when my prayer was ended a widow
lady came to me and said that she had changed her mind as
to the disposal of two thousand three hundred francs which
she had laid by, and instead of keeping them herself, she
wished to give them to me for our immediate use. And after
this people tell me to ask alms of man and not of God.
Indeed I shall ask God. I shall always beg from God and not
from man.'

On another occasion an Irish priest wished to return to his
own country and called on her to ask for help. She had not
seen him for seventeen years, and had only three francs in the
house; it was at a time when they were in great difficulty, and

depended on what they received from day to day to purchase the very bread they required. But she gave the three francs, and prayed for more. On the same day, an uncle, one of Mdme. Arnauld's brothers, who had never bestowed so much as a sou on Port Royal, gave her three hundred francs, saying that by the help of God he had been successful in one of his undertakings and therefore he had brought this sum as a thank-offering.

Worldly friends suggested that she ought to make some provision for the future instead of spending all she received; if not, the nuns of Port Royal would be in danger of dying of hunger, for it was very improbable that they would continue to receive miraculous assistance after her death, and the income of the abbey was not one-third of what they required for bare subsistence.

'If they die of hunger,' she replied with a vehemence which shows her resentment of the flattery implied in this advice, 'so much the better. Hunger could not be put to a better use. Nuns who expect to want for nothing, and who will not trust God to give them their temporal as well as their spiritual food, deserve to be forsaken by God and man, and to be reduced to abject need. I will leave them no other inheritance than our sacred poverty, and with it our trust in Him who has kept us alive by so many miracles to the present hour. If they keep their trust in Him they will want for nothing after my death any more than during my life. If they lose it, I pray God to let them lose everything, and to confound them and bring them low, so that they may no longer put their trust in the treasures of the earth, but in that true treasure which is in heaven, namely, the Providence of God, which is enough for all faithful Christians and all faithful nuns.'

This emphatic protest was called out by the changes in Port Royal, where the poverty she loved so dearly had been lost sight of. She did not immediately and openly attack all that had been done by the Bishop and the nuns of Dijon, but whenever there was an opportunity she gave away, or allowed the Sisters to give away, everything in the convent that reflected the luxury of the court. The common earthenware plates and dishes which she had provided had been replaced by porcelain, the simple crosses by bronze crucifixes of the best workmanship to be had in Paris. There were coverlets of fine grey serge on all the beds, and one room which had been occupied by a young lady of noble birth had a finer coverlet than any other. This room was now used by a nun, to whom Angélique said one day :

'My daughter, I have come to tell you of an act of charity which is required of you. You must give your grey counterpane to make a cloak for a poor gentleman. He is a soldier, and has not got one, so that when he is on guard at night he is nearly frozen to death. Yours is the best in the house and therefore he must have that.'

This was only a beginning, and by degrees she carried them all away and replaced them by others which were coarse and common. The porcelain and the bronze crucifixes had to go also, but no allusion is made to the forks, and we do not know their fate.

In 1630 forks were not generally used,[1] and their introduction at Port Royal may be taken as an evidence of the fashionable habits into which the nuns were falling.

Many of the serge coverlets and all the crucifixes were sent in 1639 to the Ursuline nuns in La Nouvelle France, Canada, which was at that time a French colony. The gifts were received with much gratitude, and the nuns wrote, ' Your charity must extend very far, Reverend Mother, since it has crossed the ocean to reach us.'

Angélique was told that the poor of Port Royal des Champs were in great want, and this gave her an opportunity of selling the silver candlesticks from the altar of the Paris chapel and sending them the money. The Sisters soon took as much pleasure as their Abbess in giving away every article that could be spared, and she further taught them that there is no charity without self-denial, and that we must give what we can *not* spare as well as what we can. Port Royal became once more poor and honest. No debts were incurred for luxuries to be paid for with borrowed money. There were no more delicacies for the refectory, no ornaments in the convent chapel, no purple and fine linen to pain Angélique's heart as she thought of the Lazarus at her gates.

But there was one person in Port Royal who did not approve

---

[1] Even in 1652 forks were a novelty in England, and Heylin says : ' The use of silver forks with us, by some of our spruce gallants taken up of late, came from hence (China) to Italy, and from thence into England.'

of the changes, and that was Mdme. de Pontcarré. She was no longer allowed to receive her friends ; the private door was closed. Everything she saw annoyed her, and she said and did as many disagreeable things as she could. Whereupon the nuns were forbidden to speak to her, and she, as the Memoirs naïvely remark, 'was very much hurt at it.' She scoffed openly ; ridiculed and blamed everyone connected with the establishment, but she was in a house that was deaf and dumb to her. She then spread absurd and exaggerated reports of the conduct of the nuns, and did all in her power to foster the animosity and jealousy which St. Cyran inspired ; she hated him, and attributed to his influence all the changes and restrictions from which she suffered. In 1638 he was imprisoned, and shortly afterwards a printed statement was put up in the convent chapel. It purported to come from the Abbot, and was a petition for the prayers of the community, written by a person who acknowledged his guilt and was overwhelmed by shame and contrition.

The whole community were strangely agitated when they discovered that the author of this outrage was Mdme. de Pontcarré. They resolved to adopt a different course for the future and appointed a nun to be her attendant, who was not to allow her to go anywhere in the house alone. In this matter Angélique showed her usual consideration. She selected a nun of whom Mdme. de Pontcarré was so fond that she had induced her to leave her own convent and go to Port Royal when she took up her own abode there. But Mdme. de Pontcarré did not like the new arrangement ; and one day when she was in a passion she beat Sister Marguerite with a table napkin, and seems to have cuffed her on sundry other occasions.

In 1639, Angélique, who saw that there was no prospect of amendment in the lady's conduct, proposed that they should offer to pay her the interest of the money she had deposited with them, on condition that she left Port Royal. The community gladly acceded to the suggestion. Mdme. de Pontcarré heard it with surprise and annoyance, and did not believe that it was made in earnest. Port Royal was not only poor, but was burdened with debt, and she did not know where they would get the money. As, however, she could not very well refuse to go under the circumstances, she said that she would consent to do so if a deed was drawn up and signed by the whole community, acknowledging her right to return if the interest was not duly paid every quarter. This was done, and she prepared for departure. She carried away everything that could by any possibility be removed, and much that it was necessary to destroy, and which could be of no use to her elsewhere. The orange tubs went of course, and also the wainscoting of her rooms; windows and frames and sashes, and woodwork, even the flooring of the balcony was torn up. The nuns looked on without regret, for they saw that the ruin separated them entirely from her. There was only one catastrophe they dreaded, and that was her return. In order to avert it, her quarterly interest was always paid in advance, and this proof of the manner in which she was regarded seems to have pained her deeply. It is said that some time later she requested to be received again, and was refused. She died at Ivry five years later and now disappears from our pages.

CHAPTER XIX.

MDME. LE MAÎTRE AND HER SONS.

'Oh, how unlucky I am to be the second daughter!' Angélique had said when she was a child, 'for if I had been the eldest I should have been the one to be married.'

Mdme. le Maître was 'the one to be married,' but she had no reason to congratulate herself on her good fortune. She was married in 1605, at fifteen years old, and after ten years, during which the only happy intervals were those which she passed with her parents, she was separated from her husband M. Isaac le Maître, *Conseiller du Roi*, and returned to her father's house, taking with her her five sons. She withdrew from society, and devoted herself entirely to the education of her boys. From time to time, she spent a fortnight ' in retreat ' at Port Royal, and announced her intention of joining the community as soon as her sons were established in the world, and the death of her husband left her free to follow her inclination. She took one of the conventual vows, that of perpetual chastity, in 1619, when St. Francis was in Paris; and he always afterwards wrote to her as ' Sister Catherine.'

When Port Royal was removed to Paris, Mdme. le Maître spent much time with the community. She was Angélique's right hand, and the one who in character resembled her most closely of all the sisters. Angélique and Mdme. le Maître had inherited their father's eager, ardent temperament, whilst Agnes and Anne resembled the mother, and were cold and reserved in manner. Angélique made her plans with Agnes, but carried them out with Mdme. le Maître.

Mdme. le Maître was the constant companion and chief friend of Mdme. de Pontcarré when she was first received at Port Royal, but was deeply grieved by her subsequent conduct, and was one of the first to welcome the intervention of St. Cyran. She did not witness the revolting humiliations and penances to which Angélique submitted, for at that time the Duchess de Longueville had entreated her to take charge of her infant daughter. Mdme. le Maître retained her affection and interest in her pupil through life, and, twenty-five years later, on her death-bed, wrote her a letter which is not only admirable in itself, but valuable as showing her own opinions and character as well as the nature of the influence which the Port Royal Sisters exercised.

'Mademoiselle, I am lying on my death-bed. I have received the last Sacraments and given my last blessing to my children. I cannot forget one whose noble birth will not allow me to presume to call her child, but who has her place with my children in my heart. And therefore since you allow me to take so great a liberty, I desire to write those things which I may never hope to say to you. I know, Mademoiselle, that there are many who can say very pretty things to you, but they care nothing for your soul, which ought to be more precious to you than anything else. . . .

'You are a Christian, Mademoiselle, and God has given you wealth ; therefore you must take all needful care to administer it for the benefit of others. I know that you have good men to counsel you, but I also know that God has not given this wealth to them but to you, and that from you He will demand an account of it. You ought therefore, Mademoiselle, as soon as your affairs are in order, to procure a plan of all your villages, with the houses and land belonging to them, so that you may know the condition of the church, the parsonage, and the priest. If you are the patron of the living, you must seek the advice of wise and good people, so that you may select good pastors, and see that the stipends are sufficient for them. If they are insufficient, you should increase them, so that the curé may have wherewithal to support the burthen of his cure, which is sufficiently great. You ought, also, if you please, to inquire into the condition of the church ornaments, and see in what condition they are, so that all things may be done decently and as they ought to be.

'You should also, may it please you, have a table drawn up, showing the number of inhabitants on your estates, their condition in life, means, and character; also another table, showing the number of the poor who through age or infirmity are unable to earn their bread, and whom you must support until they die; of poor, orphan children who have lost both parents, and for whom you must provide until they are of an age to earn their living. And as to the other poor, over and above these, who are unable to earn their own living all the year round, or who are compelled to ask alms by sickness, a fund should be set apart for their assistance. All this should be set in order at once. . . . You should try to make the acquaintance of some religious and intelligent gentleman in the country, who would inform you of everything that goes on, and especially of the manner in which your steward treats your tenants. . . . And now, Mademoiselle, I have said all that I am constrained to say by that love which will last to the end of my life, and after life is ended. I implore you to weigh my words in the presence of God, who ought to be served by the great as well as by the humble. Before Him you will have some day to appear, and I am summoned to appear before Him now at this very hour. Give yourself to Him, Mademoiselle, for He is the only Lord worthy of the heart of a Princess like you, who are only great in His eyes when you are a Christian, humble, just, and charitable.'

Mdlle. de Longueville, afterwards Duchesse de Nemours, needed the advice of her mother's friend, but did not profit by it.

After her return from the Hôtel de Longueville, Mdme. le Maître lived in seclusion at Port Royal, waiting for the time when she could take the veil. Many of the friends whom she had found whilst she resided with the Duchess visited her frequently; and the great ladies of the court, whom the Bishop had in vain endeavoured to attract by mere outward show, were drawn to the convent by her piety and large sympathy, and attracted by the very simplicity and poverty which the worldly prelate had expected they would find so revolting.

Mdme. le Maître was very liberal, delighting to give to the nuns, to the poor, to everyone who was in want. She had much of Angélique's expansive warmth of sympathy,

so that next to her she was the most beloved member of
the community.   Her husband, one of whose principal faults
seems to have been that he was a persistent Protestant, died in
1640, and she at once entered upon her noviciate and took
the veil in 1644 as soon as all arrangements connected with
her property had been made.

Up to that time her property had been at her own disposal;
she employed it in ministering to the wants of the community,
and, as far as possible, did good by stealth, even to those with
whom she lived.   One Lent the convent was so poor and fish
so dear, that they did not know how to procure it for the infirmary or the boarders.   To supply their needs a basket of
fish was sent by an unknown friend several times a week, and
it was not until long afterwards that they discovered the friend
to be Mdme. le Maître.

She had the same large, motherly heart as Angélique, not the
transient and often selfish instinct which makes a woman affectionate to her own children whilst she is cold and indifferent
to all others; but the larger and more divine motherhood, not
denied even to the childless, which endures through life, and
is tender and compassionate to every suffering, helpless being,
and most of all to young children.   One day a doctor who
visited Port Royal told Angélique he had never been so distressed as at the misery of a poor woman with a baby two
months old, and two or three other young children.   She was
very ill, and absolutely destitute.   She had no food for herself
and nothing for the baby; she used to carry it about to the
neighbours and implore them to put it to the breast for a few
minutes, and thus by the charity of one and another the child
was kept alive; and yet was only just alive, for the mothers
would not rob their own children.

Angélique relieved the mother, but did not know what to do
for the child.   Mdme. le Maître entreated her to send for it,
and put it under her charge.   It was brought to her in its only
garment, a bit of dirty window curtain, within which, covered
with filth and vermin, so that the nuns shrank back from it, lay
the little wasted form.   Mdme. le Maître tenderly took it up,
washed it and dressed it in clothes she had prepared, and laid
it in a little basket which was to serve as bed, and had it with
her day and night, giving it the care 'not of a nurse, but of a
mother.'   Innumerable similar traits are recorded of her as they

are of Angélique. Once, we are told, Angélique remonstrated
with her, saying, that in bestowing charity she should give
nothing more than absolute necessities, and not, as she had
done, pretty fashionable dresses to the child of a lady in reduced circumstances. But Mdme. le Maitre replied that St.
Cyran had taught her that our charity must be regulated by the
condition of the persons whom we assist, so that their hearts
may be gladdened by it, and they may not have the mortification of thinking that we forget what they have been. It seems
unlikely that Angélique should have made the remark, which is
probably attributed to her in error. She did not herself need
St. Cyran's instructions on this point, and was from the very
earliest times Mdme. de *Cœur* Royal, so large and liberal of
heart that she could not humiliate by an unworthy gift, or
urge others to humiliate those who were in misfortune. The
saying deserves record chiefly as showing that the Director
and his followers were already in harmony on so many
points that we need scarcely wonder at his ultimate ascendancy on all.

Shortly before Mdme. le Maitre took the veil she obtained
permission to visit the conventual offices, and ascertain what
was wanting in them. 'My Sisters,' she said, ' tell me all your
little wants, for before long I shall have nothing to give away.'
And then, like a good housewife, she set everything in order,
and provided whatever seemed necessary for the comfort and
convenience of the household.

Mdme. le Maitre's eldest son, Antoine, was born in 1608.
He chose the profession of his father and grandfather, and
was called to the bar when he was twenty-one years old. His
eloquence was considered as great, or even greater, than that
of his grandfather M. Arnauld, and his success as a public
speaker was quite extraordinary. At twenty-six years old he
contemplated marriage with a lady, whom he described as the
loveliest and most virtuous maiden in Paris. He wrote to inform his aunt Agnes, who was at that time Abbess of Tard,
of the project, but she did not approve of it; neither did
Angélique, nor, we are justified in concluding, his mother, who
always prayed that God would draw her sons to Himself, and
take them out of the world. It is worth our while to consider
the views of one of our abbesses on matrimony, and to notice
the reception which M. le Maitre's proposal met with from the

relatives for whom he had so much affection and respect. Agnes writes :—

'MY VERY DEAR NEPHEW,

'This is the last time I shall address you by that title. Just in proportion as you have hitherto been dear to me, you will now become indifferent, for there will no longer be anything in you to call forth remarkable affection. Of course I shall still love you, but it will be with the love which Christianity enjoins, and which is universal ; and as you are about to enter a very commonplace condition, I shall feel no more for you than a very ordinary affection. You are about to make yourself a slave, and you expect to remain a king in my heart. The thing is impossible. You will say that I blaspheme the Sacrament[1] of which you are such a devout worshipper. But do not give yourself any trouble about my conscience. I can quite well separate what is sacred from what is profane, what is precious from what is mean. In fact, I can forgive you as St. Paul does, and you will have the goodness to content yourself with my pardon, and not to ask for approval and praise. But, as I write I read your letter over again, and seem to wake out of a deep sleep, and to discern I know not what light shining through the gloom, and a hidden and mysterious meaning in words, which seemed at first so clear and commonplace.

'I begin to suspect that the story of your love which you tell at such length, forgetting that I have no ears for such a discourse, is only a myth taken from one of the Parables in the Gospel, in which marriages are often spoken of, and where we are told especially of that one wedding to which none but virgins are invited. This little ray of light illuminates my mind, and enables me to try and explain your words, and to look with a more favourable eye upon the maiden who has taken possession of your heart.'

And following out the idea which she has started, the Abbess endeavours to persuade her nephew that *the Church* is the object of his affections, and continues : 'What apology can I offer you, my dear nephew, for the manner in which I wrote at the beginning of this letter ? How was it that my eyes were blinded, so that I could not see the light at mid-day ; for I have

[1] Marriage.

a thousand times more reason to believe that you are seeking the joys of heaven than the joys of earth. Who has ever heard a syllable fall from your lips, except those upon which I put such a coarse interpretation—I am ready to die with shame when I think of it—which breathed any other sentiment than love for that which is holy and pure.'

M. le Maître was not convinced by this letter, nor was he at all inclined to renounce his bride. In fact, he wrote to his aunt, ' The first page of your letter annoyed me so much that I was more than a fortnight reading it ; every line stopped me, and seemed to contain something offensive.' And he proceeds to justify his proposed marriage, and to state that he speaks in a very literal manner and with no hidden meaning. But it is in vain. Agnes, the author of the mystical *Secret Chaplet*, is resolved to find a hidden meaning in his words, will hear of no bride but the Church, and writes back to explain away his explanations. Whether he was altogether influenced in this matter by these protests we do not know, but the project of marriage was abandoned.

The fame of the young advocate increased rapidly. Crowded audiences listened to him, and popular preachers left their pulpits when he was speaking. Friends told him they would rather have the applause bestowed on him than all the glory of Cardinal Richelieu, and through the favour of the Chancellor it was obvious that a brilliant and successful career was before him.

On the death of his grandfather Arnauld, he, together with his brothers and mother, lived with their uncle d'Andilly, and of course made the acquaintance of his uncle's friend St. Cyran. In 1637 his aunt, Mdme. d'Andilly, was seized with a mortal illness. She was a kindly woman, a devoted wife and mother, but worldly and frivolous, and not prepared for the supreme act of renunciation now required at her hands. St. Cyran visited her frequently, and le Maître, who spent much time in his aunt's sick room, was much affected by his exhortations and prayers. He wondered how it would be with himself when death drew near, and how it would be if he was at that very time called upon to appear before God. Mdme. d'Andilly's last hour came. The service for the dying was recited by her bedside. St. Cyran uttered the solemn words, ' Depart, O Christian soul, from this world, in the name

of the Omnipotent God who created thee.'   Le Maître, on
hearing them, burst into tears, and knew not how to contain
himself as he thought of that day when he must listen to such
a command and appear before the presence of God.   But there
was consolation for him in the words of the Liturgy that
followed and told of mercy and pardon, and this fell like
cooling drops upon his heart.   At length all was over, and he
left the chamber of death, and hurried out of the house into
the moonlight.   There, as he paced up and down the long
avenue near the house, he made no attempt to restrain his
grief; he could not stifle his regret for the past, his apprehensions for the future, and he resolved to forsake all that he
had, and by the help of St. Cyran to follow God.

The Abbot heard of this conversion with great joy; but he
saw that it would be fraught with serious consequences to himself and others.   Richelieu was not a man to be trifled with,
and did not approve of the withdrawal of those whom he
expected to find useful.   'I foresee,' said St. Cyran, 'the
direction in which God is leading me when He sends you to
me, but it does not matter; we must follow Him to prison or
to death.'   And he gave no second thought to himself, but
began to make plans for the new convert.   He advised that
le Maître should not abandon his profession until the close
of the annual session of the courts, as he would then be
able to withdraw without attracting so much attention, and
with less injury to his clients than if he suddenly threw up all
his briefs.   He may also have wished to test the sincerity of
the young advocate's convictions, and their durability.   For
some time le Maître attended the court and spoke as usual,
but the applause of the audience sounded in his ears like 'the
crowing of the cock that called Peter to repentance.'   A great
dusty crucifix was suspended in the court, which he had never
previously noticed, but now he could not turn his eyes from
it, and said that it moved him to tears rather than to words.
His speeches had lost their wonted eloquence, and a rival
said that there was a remarkable change in the direction of
le Maître's power, for it no longer produced conviction, but
sleep.   This saying was repeated, and a week later the young
advocate made one great and final effort, uttered one eloquent
harangue, in which he spoke with sparkling eyes fixed on the
author of the sarcasm, arm stretched out, and body bent

towards him, and with no thought, so it seemed, and no look for any other than the man who had for a moment electrified him into life. Then he left the court never to return. The session was at an end, and he was free.

His mother's joy was indeed great ; for as other mothers labour to advance their sons in the world, she laboured to withdraw hers from it. She and St. Cyran thought that the new convert ought to live in strict seclusion for a time ; but there was a difficulty in the way. Her son did not wish to be a monk, and would not join the Carthusians as St. Cyran urged. And then the happy mother proposed to build a lodge in the court-yard of Port Royal, to which le Maître, and perhaps his brothers also, might retire ; whilst she would take the veil, and be always near her dear children. This proposal met with the approval of all parties. The building was begun in October 1637, finished before Christmas in the same year, and as the walls were not dry, they were lined with pine planks. It was close to the church, so that the Recluses could enter and leave the sacred edifice without being seen. Le Maître did not take possession of it alone. His mother's third and favourite son, de Séricourt, was so much impressed by the account of his brother's conversion that he also resolved to leave his pro-fession, quit the army, and place himself under the direction of St. Cyran. The two brothers were installed in the little lodge in January 1638, 'on the day of St. Paul, the first hermit.' In the same month St. Cyran established with them Claude Lancelot, born 1615, a young scholar who had joined a community of priests in the parish of St. Nicholas, at Paris, and who left them to seek a 'more excellent way.' The curé of St. Nicholas warned him against St. Cyran, saying, ' He is a dangerous man, and if you are not careful he will get you into trouble.' In addition to these three, aged respectively twenty-nine, twenty-six, and twenty-three, there were Father Singlin, the Confessor, and four young boys, his pupils, who had spent the previous summer with him at the forsaken monastery of Port Royal des Champs.

We have here the nucleus of the Recluses of Port Royal, and the first germs of the schools which were afterwards so famous. Lancelot was the author of the Port Royal Grammars, Greek, Latin, and Italian, now fallen into disuse ; and he wrote Memoirs, which give a vivid picture of the men with whom he lived, and the holy women whose influence and prayers had helped to withdraw them from the world.

The Recluses began their day with Matins in the chapel at 1 A.M., and had finished by 2 o'clock, when the nuns came. De Séricourt, the former Major, who always retained his punctual military habits, undertook to call his companions in time, and never failed. They chanted the *Te Deum* aloud, and the rest of the service they intoned in a low voice. St. Cyran instructed all those who came to him to chant the services and sing canticles and psalms, even when they were alone. Lancelot says, 'when we went back to our own rooms we all did so, and on all sides there was a soft low sound of singing, so that it reminded me of the early Church at Jerusalem ; for St. Jerome says that even in his time wherever you went, you could hear in the open fields and in the houses the sound of the singing of Psalms and Hallelujahs. But those which we sang were in a very low tone, so that from the neighbouring houses we could not have been heard at all, for our singing would certainly have been misunderstood.'

The reader will remember how Anne Arnauld 'danced for joy' to think that she was a nun. The same enthusiasm of happiness showed itself in a different manner in the Recluses. Lancelot says :

' There was nothing but joy among us, and our hearts were so full of it that it shone out in our faces. And with regard to this, before I proceed I must mention one fact that regards myself. The abounding grace which it has pleased God to bestow on me, and the peace that resulted from it were so great, that I could scarcely prevent myself from laughing at everything that happened. I did not know what could be the cause of this change ; certainly the defect was not one that had troubled me previously.' [Poor fellow, he had abounded in tears !] 'I accused myself of levity, and mentioned this fault frequently in confession. But M. de St. Cyran, who was very clear-sighted, said that this was not really the cause of my exuberant spirits. One day he told me that I need not be surprised, for that sometimes the soul, looking back on the path over which it has travelled, whence it has come, what it has attained, and all that inner life which lies hidden within it, is, as it were, transported and lifted out of its ordinary trammels and restraints ; and he thought that my joy came from this cause

rather than from levity, and that I need not take it so much
to heart.

'I saw that what he said was true, for verily never had I
known such a happy life. God, according to the words of
the Apostle, 'was causing all things to work together for my
good,' so that I knew not how to be grateful enough for His
great mercy. I was deeply impressed by the charity of M. le
Maître, the gentleness of M. de Séricourt, and the humility of
M. Singlin; but that which I admired most of all, and which
edified me most, was the poverty of the nuns. Often they had
not as much as half a franc with which to buy provisions.
They were rich in virtue and in nothing else.

There are few memoirs more charming than those of Lancelot. They still bring before us the fresh gladness of those
early times when the Recluses, bound by no vows, had drawn
apart from the world to worship God, and were waiting to see
what work He had for them to do. The kindly sympathetic
nature of Lancelot gives back in bright colours all the impressions made on it. Men and women live in his pages; we do
not read about them, we know them and love them. It
cannot be denied that Lancelot is diffuse, but then all memoirs
are, and perhaps ought to be, diffuse. They abound in minute
and delicate touches which history cannot give, and without
which human beings are mere abstractions, or virtues and vices
labelled with a name.

In the voluminous memoirs written by sisters, nieces, and nuns
who were her companions, Angélique Arnauld really lives. We
watch her as she holds by her grandfather's sleeves, trots with
him about the house, and shuts out the little brothers and sisters
that she may have him all to herself. We see the handsome
young Abbess having 'whalebone stays' made to improve her
figure, and then sadly turning away and going back to the
gloom of Port Royal. Or in the early days of her conversion
we stand by her as she listens unmoved to the reproaches and
angry commands of her father, but falls fainting at his feet
when he tells her how dear she is to him. We follow her as
she walks through the convent in her paper mask, and know
that her sorrow is not for herself, but for the empty, hollow
show of religion and penitence around her; and we see her on
her knees 'weeping bitterly' for the shame of unpaid debt and
for her blindness to the guilt of incurring it.

In the memoirs of Lancelot, it is St. Cyran who lives before us, a figure as noble as Angélique's, and like her in its mysterious power of attracting others and changing the whole direction of their lives. Angélique and Agnes, Marie-Claire and Anne, Mdme. le Maître and Mdme. Arnauld, have all listened and been convinced; Port Royal is restored to its early piety and simplicity. Priests and bishops and the court have for a time forgotten its existence, but at its gates there is gathering together a little society which is one day to make it famous. One by one St. Cyran is drawing the members of that society from the world; lawyers, soldiers and priests are the first to listen to his voice, physicians and nobles are to follow. We must not tarry with them or forestall that story of the Recluses of Port-Royal which has some day to be written; but we cannot pass on without some notice and some attempt to form a just estimate of their character and influence.

Next to St. Cyran the man most noteworthy is Father Singlin the Confessor. He was born in Paris in 1607, and was at the time of which we speak thirty years old. His father, who was a wine-merchant, had apprenticed him to a linendraper, with whom he remained until he was twenty-two. He was then moved to visit Vincent de Paul, who at once took a warm interest in him and advised him to become a priest. The young man thought this was impossible, for he was uneducated, and knew not a single word of Latin. Vincent de Paul, however, enabled him to overcome all the obstacles in his way, told him of a college where the professors would give him special attention, and, with considerable effort, Singlin contrived to acquire all that was absolutely necessary to enable him to become a priest. Vincent de Paul appointed him Confessor of the *Hôpital de la Pitié*, and it was there that he became acquainted with St. Cyran, who introduced him to Angélique and the nuns at the Holy Eucharist. Many years later Angélique said of him : ' He thinks like one of the Fathers of the Church, and speaks like a linen-draper's assistant.'

Before long, Antoine Singlin resolved to leave all and follow St. Cyran, who had kindled him, so he says, ' like a match held to the fire.' At first St. Cyran was unwilling to receive him, but when he found that the priests had no opportunity of doing good in the *Hôpital*, and that all their efforts were

paralysed by the opposition of the governors, he allowed him
to leave it, and sent him in charge of two of his own nephews
and two other children to spend the summer of 1637 in the
solitude of the forsaken Port Royal des Champs. On his
return he joined the Recluses in Paris, and was appointed
Confessor to the convent.

St. Cyran had, like Angélique, the gift of insight; he
invariably discovered the power and capacity of those who
worked with him, even when they themselves were ignorant of
it. He held Father Singlin to his post in spite of his desire
to leave it and enter a monastery; seeing that his special
power was to speak to the hearts of penitents, and that his
very directness, his blunt unpolished speech lent him a certain
power often denied to finished orators. That and his rectitude, for he was a man upright and honourable, hating lies,
deceit and avarice, never tolerating them anywhere, and least
of all in the service of God. Father Singlin was characterized
also by marvellous tenacity of purpose. He never abandoned
any work which, after mature deliberation, he had resolved to
take up, and was inflexible in what he believed to be right
either for himself or others. St. Cyran saw that the firm,
upright guide must not be allowed to immure himself in a
monastery when there was so much work to be done in
the world.

Le Maître and his brother, de Séricourt, occupied one room,
and their 'retreat' was so strict that they saw their companions
only once in the day, at matins. There was no communication
between the Recluses and the nuns of Port Royal, but they
acted as a stimulus to the fervour and piety of each other,
and St. Cyran's visits formed a bond of union between them.
He saw each Recluse alone, and often went to the schoolroom,
where he exhorted the children and encouraged those who
had charge of them. He used to say that there is no more
important work than education, not only because the whole
future of the child depends on it, but also because it requires
great charity, patience, wisdom, assiduity, and continual effort
on the part of the teacher, who has to turn the child from evil
and lead it towards God. We cannot read many of the hard
sayings that impressed his followers so deeply without pain;
but the life of monk and nun and recluse is only conceivable
for those who accept the doctrine that the world is the devil's

and is under the curse of God, and that living to God means living out of the world and standing apart and loose from all its ties. Lancelot treasures up and records the following anecdote. One day, when St. Cyran entered the schoolroom, he found the little boys busy with their Virgil, and said:

'Look you now at this Virgil. He is damned, yes, he is damned for writing that fine poetry, because he wrote it from vanity and to please the world. But you may be saved through learning it, for you must learn it to please God and to prepare for the service of the Church. And therefore you must offer all study as a sacrifice to God, and be faithful in the employment of your time, for the time which we do not employ in the service of God is the devil's, and he takes it to himself.'

He read St. Augustine with the Recluses, saying, however, to Lancelot that it was not his usual practice to read such advanced works with those who were only beginning to lead a religious life. But he found that milk for babes would not suit le Maître's keen subtle intellect, and thought it desirable to give him something that should task his powers more than any subject he had ever studied. Very often he read the New Testament with them, and would sometimes exclaim in a transport of delight, 'I have discovered a text to-day that I would not part with for ten thousand crowns.'

A few weeks later the three remaining sons of Mdme. le Maître joined their brothers in the little lodge at the gates of Port Royal. The second, St. Elme, returned to the world, had considerable success as an advocate, married, and had daughters, who became nuns of Port Royal. Isaac le Maître de Saci, or de Saci, as he was called, born in 1613, was the fourth son. Two years previously his mother was in great grief, for it was reported that her favourite son, de Séricourt, had been killed at the battle of Philipsburg. St. Cyran called on her and expressed his sympathy. She said: 'I have one son who will, I hope, desire to enter the Church, and the only consolation you can offer me now is to see him and take him under your guidance.' St. Cyran fulfilled her wish, and de Saci, then twenty-two years old, was prepared by him for the Priesthood. He was so ill at one time that his mother said she had lost all hope of his recovery. 'Lost all hope!' exclaimed St. Cyran; 'why do you not know that to lose your son would be the greatest loss the Church could experience!'

Mdme. le Maitre's fifth and youngest son, Charles le Maitre de Vallemont, lived and died a Recluse, but he and St. Elme may be dismissed with the mention of their names, whilst le Maitre the advocate, de Séricourt the soldier, and de Saci the priest, have important parts to play in the future history of Port Royal.

Such a little community of devout men and women in Paris in the seventeenth century, in the very heart of a profligate city, and to some extent in the power of a profligate court and still more profligate priesthood, may well excite our interest and attention. Can they exist together?

The answer to this question is not long delayed.

Two hours after midnight, on the 14th of May, 1638, twenty-two archers surrounded St. Cyran's house, and at six o'clock they knocked and demanded admission. He was reading St. Augustine with his nephew, M. de Barcos, and had come to a passage on contrition. 'That is what we want,' he said. 'Here is something with which to defend ourselves when we are attacked!' At that moment an officer entered and informed him in a low tone that he had the king's orders to conduct him to a carriage which was waiting outside. St. Cyran took him kindly by the hand, and said, 'Well, sir, let us go wherever the king commands. I have no greater pleasure than in obedience.'

They set out, accompanied by several archers who were not in uniform, and, driving through the park of Vincennes, met d'Andilly, who was on his way to Pomponne, his country house.

'Why where are you taking all these people?' he said, laughing, to his old friend. 'I am not taking them, it is they who are taking me,' answered St. Cyran. And then gravely added, 'But I look upon myself as the prisoner of God, and not of man. By the way, they were in such a hurry that I could not even bring a book with me.' Now d'Andilly was reading the Confessions of St. Augustine, so he stretched out his hand, saying, 'Here, this is a book that you gave me long ago, and now I must give it back again.'

D'Andilly was everybody's friend, and was so well known in Paris that the officer allowed the two friends to spend a few moments together in grave and earnest talk; then they embraced, and parted sadly enough, for St. Cyran was on his way to the prison of Vincennes.

CHAPTER XX.

WHEN St. Cyran reached Vincennes, and was conducted to his cell, he fell on his knees, thanked God for this crowning mercy, and implored help to enable him to make a good use of it. In order to show his ready assent to the present dispensation, nay more his gratitude for it, he sent a sum of money to one of his friends, and desired her to divide it into three portions, and procure admission to a convent for one poor maiden, give a marriage portion to a second, and ransom a prisoner.   .

But this state of exaltation was succeeded by great depression. He was placed in strict and solitary confinement; his friends were not allowed access to him, and if any tidings from the outer world reached him, and on this point his biographers are not unanimous, it was that, eight days before his own arrest, Jansen, Bishop of Ypres, the companion of his youth, his faithful friend and fellow-student, was dead. Jansen was dead. Their great work was ended, and who could say that their life-long labours had not been in vain? Jansen had died suddenly, on the very day that his book was completed. So much St. Cyran knew, for Lancelot says he was not told of the death of his friend until he could be reassured on this point. But who could give him any assurance that the work they had begun together would be brought to a successful issue, and lead, as they had hoped, to the reform of the Catholic Church? His own papers were in the hands of enemies who would twist and turn his words to serve their own purpose, and who were ignorant enough to charge St. Augustine himself with heresy. He had no personal fear, but had he not good reason

R 2

to be afraid for his friends and for the nuns and Recluses at Port Royal!

Great gloom fell upon him. He began to ask himself whether he had not been mistaken in supposing that his imprisonment was a mark of Divine favour, and whether it was not rather a punishment and a sign of God's anger. He began to be haunted night and day by the fear of the wrath of God and His judgment. He turned to the Bible for help, but found none. Every denunciation in it seemed directed against himself. He read that ' If the blind lead the blind, both shall fall into the ditch,' and recognized that he was indeed a blind leader of the blind. Or he turned to the passage, ' Every plant which my heavenly Father hath not planted shall be rooted up;' and it seemed to him that his imprisonment was the 'rooting up,' that not man but God was against him, and the ' devil had obtained permission to sift him like wheat.' ' But after the tempest came a calm,' says Lancelot, ' and although God did not deliver him from his chains as He did Peter, yet He delivered him from his fears, and gave him abundant consolation from the same Scriptures by which He had been pleased to afflict him.'

One day, after prayer, St. Cyran had recourse to the chance opening of the Bible, which was at that time considered as asking and receiving a message direct from God. His eye fell upon the words, ' Thou liftest me up from the gates of death, that I may show forth all Thy praise in the gates of the daughter of Zion : I will rejoice in Thy salvation. The nations are sunk down in the pit that they made. In the net which they secretly hid is their own foot taken.' He received these words with reverence and gratitude, and believed that it had pleased God to give him comfort, and put an end to his fears for himself; a few weeks later the anxiety for his friends was also relieved.

D'Andilly was a universal favourite at the French court, and the one subject of his conversation to everyone he met had for some time past been St. Cyran, whose extraordinary piety and wonderful gifts he was never weary of describing. And now everyone pitied d'Andilly quite as much as St. Cyran, and there were many who tried for his sake to use their influence in favour of his friend.

Richelieu's niece, the Duchess d'Aiguillon, appealed in vain

to the great Cardinal for pardon, but she obtained permission to
visit the prisoner at Vincennes and to take d'Andilly with her.
The prisoner was brought from his cell, and after some conversation with the duchess she gave the two friends an opportunity of talking together privately. D'Andilly told him that all
his friends were safe and well. No one had been compromised
by his papers. They had been searched, but his work against
the Calvinists, which had caused him most anxiety, had been
removed before the search began. St. Cyran answered fervently
that a thousand lives would not be long enough to enable him
to thank God for these great mercies.

The duchess was much affected by this interview between
the two friends, and on the way home she said there was no
casket in the world she thought so precious as that which contained the key of St. Cyran's prison, and nothing she would
like so much as to give it to d'Andilly, that he might set his
friend at liberty. It was doubtless through her influence with
the Cardinal that from henceforward d'Andilly was allowed
access to the prisoner whom he visited frequently, and the
Governor of Vincennes often left them alone together. When
d'Andilly was going away St. Cyran would say, ' Why do you
give me the pleasure of meeting if it is always to be followed
by the pain of parting?'

Many friends gathered round St. Cyran, but he called
d'Andilly the friend *par excellence;* not such a friend as Jansen,
who was his equal in character and intellect; not a great man
in any way, but a kindly enthusiast, good enough and clever
enough to appreciate him.

The reassurance which he had received with regard to the
safety of his friends, and probably some alleviation of the
rigour of his confinement, helped to restore the prisoner to
peace and serenity, which he never again lost during the five
years he remained at Vincennes. He was removed to a better
cell than that which he at first occupied, and allowed to take
exercise; but, with the exception of d'Andilly, he was seldom
permitted to see his friends, and was closely watched to
prevent his holding any communication with them. D'Andilly,
however, contrived to supply him with pencil, paper, and sometimes pen and ink. The supervision cannot have been extra-
ordinarily strict, for in addition to a mass of letters, he wrote
during this period two thick octavo volumes of ' Meditations

on Sundays and Holy Days,' and several volumes of ' Meditations on the Priesthood,' ' Poverty,' ' Death,' and other subjects which occupied his thoughts.   D'Andilly conveyed away
these precious documents, and they were carefully deciphered
and copied by his daughter Agnes, who was a nun at Port
Royal, and also by Marie-Claire, his sister.

The Governor of Vincennes showed his prisoner great kindness ; but the wife of the Lieutenant, upon whom St. Cyran
practically depended, treated him very badly.   She robbed him
of his food, and sold his allowance of wood, so that sometimes
in the depth of winter he was left without fire.   Before long
his health showed signs of failing, and he was more than once
believed to be at the point of death, and received the last
sacrament of the Church.   He obtained great influence over
the inmates of the prison, who soon discovered the sanctity of
his life and his zeal for good works.   He was a man who lived
habitually in the presence of God, and thus he was at the same
time humble and strong.   Worldly motives, worldly hopes and
fears he had none ; nor did he form a worldly estimate of the
importance of those around him.   He offered to take charge
of the two sons of the Lieutenant of the prison, and at the
same time taught a poor boy, whom he afterwards sent (one
of many others) to be educated in his own Abbey of St.
Cyran.   The Lieutenant's wife was so angry that his favours
had not been confined to her own children that she treated
him worse than ever.   There were many cases in prison which
excited his special sympathy, and we cannot pass them by
without notice, because they help us to understand not only
his own character, but the affection and reverence with which
the Port Royalists regarded their imprisoned saint.

Perhaps the most characteristic story told of him at this
time is that which relates to the Baron and Baroness de Beau
Soleil.   The Baron was imprisoned in the Bastille, and the
Baroness and her daughter at Vincennes.   They were without
money, and almost destitute.   St. Cyran sold part of his scanty
collection of books to purchase clothes for them.   He gave the
commission to a friend, saying, ' I beg that the material may be
fine and good and befitting their station in society.   I do not
know what is suitable ; but, if I remember rightly, I have heard
that gentlemen and ladies of their condition ought not to
be seen in company without gold lace for the men and black

lace for the women. If I am right on this point, pray purchase the best, and let everything be done modestly and yet handsomely, so that when they see each other they may forget, for a few minutes at least, that they are prisoners.'

Another case that excited his sympathy was that of General d'Enkenfort, who had been taken prisoner in 1638. D'Andilly was always ready to serve everyone whom he met, and it did not need St. Cyran's advocacy to interest him in the German General. Now M. de Feuquières, a connection of the Arnaulds, was a prisoner at Thionville, and in 1640, through d'Andilly's influence, he was exchanged for General d'Enkenfort. The day before the exchange was completed, d'Enkenfort was released on parole, and went to Paris to thank d'Andilly for his good offices, staying all night at his house. In the morning the horses were standing saddled in the courtyard, ready for his departure to Germany, and his foot was in the stirrup, when M. de Feuquières' two sons entered in haste with the terrible news that their father had died in prison before his release. ' We remained motionless,' says the Abbé Arnauld, who recounts the story, ' silent and motionless as if we had been thunder-struck. General d'Enkenfort was no less overwhelmed than we were, but although in this cruel *contretemps* he saw the ruin of all his hopes, and the indefinite postponment of that liberty, the sweets of which he had begun to taste, yet so great was his courage that he overcame his own grief, and began to comfort his friends as if he had not needed any consolation himself.'

That same night he was taken back again to prison, and it was then that he found the true worth of the man who had shown so much interest in his fate. When St. Cyran saw him, he said solemnly, 'Your emperor desired to procure your freedom, and the greatest king in the world consented to grant it, but the King of kings holds you a prisoner still, and it is He who has overruled their action.'

A still more celebrated German prisoner was at that time at Vincennes, and although he did not, like d'Enkenfort, turn for help and guidance to St. Cyran, he conceived great admiration for him, on account of what he knew of his prison life. In the winter of 1640-41, Richelieu gave a series of grand entertainments to the King and court, and the German prisoners of war, Jean de Wert (Johann von Werth) and d'Enkenfort, were

allowed to be present at a magnificent ballet, which represented the triumphs of the arms of France. The subject was
one which must have had a painful interest for them at that
time. At this performance there were reserved seats for the
bishops and abbots of note who happened to be in Paris,
and also for the confessors, almoners, and other priests, who
belonged to the Cardinal's household. Richelieu expected that
the magnificence of the display would greatly impress the
German prisoners, and Jean de Wert was asked what he thought
of it. He replied that it was fine enough, but that which had
astonished him more than anything else in the Most Christian
Kingdom of France was to see the bishops at a theatre and
the saints in prison. This saying was repeated to Richelieu,
but it did not induce him to release his prisoner.

It is difficult to understand the exact grounds on which
Richelieu persecuted St. Cyran. The latter assigns no less than
nineteen causes for his imprisonment. Perhaps they may all be
summed up in this, that Richelieu believed him to be a dangerous adversary, who would neither be silenced by fear or
favour. On the morning after the arrest the Cardinal said to the
Abbé Beaumont de Péréfixe, afterwards Archbishop of Paris :
' Beaumont, I have done a thing which will raise a great outcry.
I have had the Abbot of St. Cyran arrested by order of the
king. Learned people and pious people too will make a great
piece of work about it. But let that be as it will, I am sure
that I have done good service both to Church and State. A
great many calamities would have been averted if Luther and
Calvin had been shut up as soon as they began to dogmatize.'

The dogmatizing which had offended the Cardinal was contained in St. Cyran's opposition to his view of attrition. When
Richelieu was Bishop of Luçon he wrote a catechism, in which
he taught that *attrition* or a fear of God and of punishment,
together with confession, entitled a person to receive absolution, and was therefore all that was necessary for salvation.
Some years later, one Seguenot, a priest of the Oratory,
wrote a book to prove that *attrition* was not enough, unless
it was accompanied by *contrition* or sorrow for sin, arising
from love of God. Now Richelieu was, according to Retz,
' a very great man, but he possessed in a sovereign degree the
weakness of not being able to despise small things,' and
he could not brook opposition to his theology. Seguenot

expressed his regret when he found that he had offended the Cardinal, and retracted humbly ; but he was sent to the Bastille, where he had an opportunity of meditating on the difference between attrition and contrition until the death of Richelieu.   Rumour, however, ascribed the book not to Seguenot, but to St. Cyran ; and although it is certain from internal evidence that he did not write it, yet so far as that particular doctrine is concerned, he might have done so.   After he had been some time in prison, Prince Henry of Bourbon interceded for him, but Richelieu said : ' You don't know the man for whom you are interceding.   He is more dangerous than six armies.   Just look at that catechism on my table ; it has passed through twenty-two editions.   I say in it that *attrition* together with confession is all that is necessary, and he believes that *contrition* is also necessary.   Again, with regard to the marriage of Monsieur (Duke of Orleans), all France agreed with me, and he alone was bold enough to oppose me.'

The Jesuits, and other priests who had their own grievances against St. Cyran, took care, as soon as he was imprisoned, to spread vague reports of grave charges to be brought against him.   The Bishop of Langres found an outlet for his jealous anger in collecting all their denunciations, and forwarding them to Richelieu.   But as a matter of fact no definite accusation was ever brought against him, and it was not until he had been a year in prison that M. de Laubardemont, the Commissioner of infamous memory who presided at the trial of Urbain Grandier, was sent to interrogate him.   He refused to answer anyone except an ecclesiastic, and thereupon Richelieu appointed Lescot, Canon of Notre Dame, and afterwards Bishop of Chartres, who had twelve interviews with the prisoner, extending over a period of three weeks, and tried to obtain from him an admission of heresy and Calvinism.   They contrived to misunderstand each other on every subject they discussed.   Lescot knew very little of the Fathers of the Church, and St. Cyran very little of the schoolmen.   Lescot tried to draw St. Cyran into the meshes of scholastic theology, and St. Cyran in vain referred Lescot to patristic literature.   Each charged the other with ignorance.   Lescot said that much learning had made St. Cyran mad, and he knew nothing of many things he ought to know ; whilst St. Cyran, in spite of his humility and modesty, was eager to prove that Lescot had made a number of gross blunders, some thirty of which he was at the trouble of dictating to his faithful Lancelot.

Lescot tried to draw from St. Cyran condemnation of the doctrine of contrition; but he argued that he had not exercised his private judgment on this matter; his views were sanctioned by the Church, and he could not therefore retract. He offered, however, to write on the subject and dedicate his work to Richelieu, if he was allowed to go out on bail for four or five months. His offer was not accepted, and the following year Lescot again visited Vincennes, and there was a fresh investigation, with no different result.

St. Cyran was at great pains to explain himself to his disciples on this point. He compares *attrition* and *contrition* to sunrise and mid-day, and says that one must follow the other. When the sun rises we are sure of the noon, and God never gives *attrition* which is not followed by *contrition.* If we have obtained mercy in His sight, and are touched by fear, He will also inspire us with love.

The question of the day was, however, not this, but rather whether it is necessary to salvation to love God at all; and whether fear of Him is not enough, or at all events enough until a man is on his deathbed, when perhaps a little contrition may be desirable. Is it enough to turn to the Church in order to escape everlasting punishment, or is it necessary to be moved by genuine sorrow for sin, which implies love of God and a desire to escape not from the punishment of sin, but from the evil of it? It was the latter which St. Cyran asserted; whilst Richelieu, the Jesuits, and the world maintained the former.

His friends were much alarmed when they heard of these examinations. Vincent de Paul hastened to advise him to dictate his answers to the Secretary who was to take them down, and to be sure and verify them afterwards, lest they should be falsified. His friend, M. Molé, the *Procureur-Général,* recommended him to make marginal notes or draw lines over every bit of blank paper on every page, saying that he had to deal with 'curious people,' and it was by no means improbable that statements would 'creep in,' for which he was not responsible.

The examinations, however, were barren of result, and another influential friend, M. de Chavigny, appealed to Richelieu in St. Cyran's favour. The Cardinal promised to 'procure' his pardon if he would adopt the 'ordinary opinions of the Church,' and make a declaration to the effect that attrition, together with confession, was alone necessary to justify the priest in granting absolution.

St. Cyran declined to do this ; but he wrote a long letter to M. de Chavigny, in which he justified both his own view and that of his opponents, and consequently satisfied neither friends nor enemies.

During the five years of his imprisonment attrition and contrition were discussed in every salon in Paris, and the Jesuits were unanimous in condemning St. Cyran.

Port Royal shared both the obloquy and ill-will which the Abbot had incurred. A fortnight after his arrest the Archbishop of Paris informed the Recluses that he had received orders for their removal, as their close vicinity to the nuns of Port Royal was considered unseemly. Father Singlin urged that they had no communication with the nuns, not even seeing them in the parlour or through a grating ; but it was in vain, they were told that they must go ; and, after some deliberation, Port Royal *des Champs*, the Port Royal of Angélique's early days, was fixed on as their future retreat.

For twelve years it had stood empty and abandoned ; but Angélique, Agnès, and the companions of their youth, looked back to it as their home. It was there, on that terrible day when Angélique closed her doors against father and mother, brother and sisters, that she shut out an evil past in order to prepare for a time which, it seemed to her, had now arrived, when mother and sisters could be received within her convent, and brothers and nephews dwell outside the walls. Angélique thought the one a necessary sequence of the other. If she removed abuses she could restore the purity of early times, and allow holy men and women to dwell side by side.

She despatched le Maître and his brothers, together with Lancelot and the young pupils whom St. Cyran forbade them to relinquish, in all some ten or twelve persons, to the deserted monastery. . They found the building almost in ruins, the land around it a wilderness, and vipers and stagnant waters on all sides of them. But the accommodation they required was small, and their diet simple. They spent some weeks as quietly as if they had been in Paris, each following his usual avocations. The only difference was that sometimes in the evening they left the stifling valley, and ascending the hills that surround Port Royal, walked there, and chanted complines in the open air, in order, says Lancelot, 'that the harmony of our voices might bear witness to the joy that filled our hearts, and that we might openly glorify God, even when our enemies thought the truth was held captive.'

A few weeks later Laubardemont, the Commissioner who was afterwards sent to St. Cyran, made his appearance. He had not gone direct from Paris to Port Royal, but had slept at a neighbouring village, and started early in the morning so as to take the Recluses by surprise. He expected to find them in bed, he found them at prayers ; and when he knocked at le Maître's door it was opened by the young advocate himself, wearing a long black coat buttoned the whole way down the front. Laubardemont interrogated all the Recluses and their pupils, even children of eight years old ; but it was against le Maître that the attack was chiefly directed.

Now although le Maître had said farewell to the world, he had not lost the powers which had given him so high a position at the bar, and the result of the examination was by no means gratifying to the Commissioner. It was impossible to entangle the advocate, or draw from him any damaging admissions. He had a way of quietly turning upon his questioner, which was far from pleasant ; and his friends repeated with considerable amusement an answer which was not reported by the Commissioner himself.

Laubardemont asked le Maître in a contemptuous manner if he did not see visions. Le Maître answered coldly, yes, he did : when he opened one of the windows in his room, to which he pointed, he saw the village of St. Lambert, whilst when he opened the opposite window he saw Vanmurier : he had no other visions than these.

Laubardemont next examined his books. They consisted of a Bible in twelve small volumes, four or five little volumes of Saint Augustine, a copy of Paulinus, a New Testament in Greek and Latin, and a translation of St. Chrysostom. The Commissioner gravely wrote that he had not found any book which could be suspected of containing heretical doctrine, and then acquitted himself of the remainder of his task and commanded the Recluses to leave Port Royal.

It was of no use to protest, so they prepared to obey ; and in July 1638 they returned to Paris. As soon as they arrived there de Saci fell ill, and his mother, Mdme. le Maître, had him taken secretly to Port Royal, so that he might be carefully nursed. When he had recovered he joined his brother de Séricourt, who was living with St. Cyran's nephew, M. de Barcos.

It was very difficult to find a home for le Maître, as people were afraid of receiving him lest they should bring ill-will upon themselves. He wished to join the Carthusians in Paris, and asked them to receive him as a boarder, and allow him to attend Matins and the daily Church services. But they replied that they had property to think of, and could not afford to offend the Government. Several other religious houses gave the same answer ; and there was only one that ventured to show a little more courage, and to say to d'Andilly through their prior that they should have been delighted to receive his nephew if it had been possible, but, unfortunately, they had only one suitable apartment for him, and that was occupied by a person who could not be induced to give it up.

St. Cyran had discerned in Lancelot a special gift for the instruction and education of children. He was therefore despatched to La Ferté-Milon, about fifty miles from Paris, with his pupil little Vitart. This boy had been received because he was the nephew of Sister Suzanne, the cellarer of Port Royal ; his father was the Duke de Luines' steward, and resided at La Ferté-Milon, where lived also his wife's sister, Mdme. Racine, and her family.

The Vitarts had heard of the persecution of St. Cyran and the Recluses from Sister Suzanne, and when they learnt still more from Lancelot, they opened their doors to any who chose to come to them, and received le Maître and de Séricourt, who, accompanied by Father Singlin, passed a year under M. Vitart's roof ; but hermits in a lonely cell could not have lived more solitary lives.

The essential point in St. Cyran's system of education was that a pupil must be under constant supervision, and never out of sight of his instructor. Lancelot, therefore, was bound to little Vitart by night and day ; they dined with the family, attended the parish church, and Lancelot could not, according to his own views, lead such a holy life as his companions.

Still, he and his pupil spent as much time in their own room as was possible, and he and the Recluses continued to say Matins together. They had no special place of worship in the house, and did not wish to disturb the inmates during the night, so de Séricourt woke Lancelot by means of a string which passed from one room to the other. They then commenced their devotions, and were 'united in the spirit though not in the flesh.' Lancelot speaks with rapture of the holy secluded life led by his companions. They passed their time in prayer and study, deaf and blind to the world around them, its interests and its cares; and yet they exercised a mysterious attraction over the imaginations of the members of the household. In the summer of 1639 they were ordered to walk every evening on the hills behind La Ferté-Milon for the good of their health, and enjoyed the relaxation of talking together on matters relating to religion. Lancelot says :

'We could not get to the hills without passing through part of the town, but we never spoke to anyone on our way; and on our return, about nine o'clock in the evening, we walked one after the other in silence, telling our beads. It was summer time, and the people would be sitting outside their doors. When they saw us they used to rise and salute us, and were all silent as we passed along; for the holy lives and virtues of these gentlemen inspired great respect.'

Mdme. Racine, little Vitart's aunt, was the grandmother of Jean Racine the poet, who was born this very summer of 1639, and educated in the Port Royal schools. Mdme. Racine had daughters, the poet's aunts, who became nuns at Port Royal; and one of them, under the name of Agnes de St. Thekla Racine, was Abbess from 1691 till her death in 1700.

At the close of this summer, as the storm of persecution seemed to have blown over, the Recluses thought they might venture back to Port Royal, and prepared to take their departure. The Vitart household was strangely agitated, could not part with them, and at last determined to accompany them to the deserted monastery. The Recluses did not object to M. Vitart, who offered to take the charge of the household and look after the buildings and land, so as to leave them free to devote their whole time to study and prayer. But the 'band of pious women,' who insisted on accompanying them, was not so welcome. In vain St. Cyran urged grave objections from

his prison cell, and le Maître entreated; the ladies were resolved to carry their point, and they had a staunch ally in
Angélique, who gave them permission to occupy part of the
building, where they would be completely isolated. They
followed the Recluses to Port Royal, and as long as they
were there together, there was not even verbal communication
between them. Lancelot did not remain at Port Royal. He
went to Paris, to take charge of two boys who had been placed
under St. Cyran's care.

This period of imprisonment is fertile in conversions. They
all took place by means of d'Andilly, who was the medium of
communication between St. Cyran, Port Royal, and the outer
world. Great ladies listened to d'Andilly's accounts of St.
Cyran and his prison cell, of Angélique and her convent. They
visited Port Royal, and what the Bishop of Langres had failed
to effect was brought about in quite another way. Port Royal
became the resort of the court, and might have been, if
Angélique and Agnes had desired it, fashionable and influential. But they spoke of themselves as disciples of an
imprisoned saint, and Port Royal was a stepping-stone to
Vincennes.

The most influential convert made at this time was the
Princess de Guemené. It cannot be said that she did more
than amuse herself with religion, but she was a true friend to
Port Royal, and we may be charitable enough to believe that
her occasional retreat to the convent, and long interviews with
the Abbess, who would talk of nothing but spiritual matters,
show at any rate an aspiration for something more than the life
of vicious intrigue, which she never altogether abandoned.

In the summer of 1639, d'Andilly spent some time at her
country seat, and on her return she paid weekly visits to Port
Royal, and had long conferences in the convent parlour with
Angélique, Agnes, and Anne-Eugénie, who were induced to
break through their rule of silence when they believed there
was an opportunity of winning souls to God. The progress of
this distinguished convert was faithfully reported to St. Cyran,
who knew too much of the world to expect any lasting result
from it : 'The grace of God in her soul,' he wrote, 'is like a
spark kindled upon an icy pavement with the winds blowing
upon it from every quarter.' She was placed under the immediate guidance of Father Singlin, who wrote to Lancelot at

Ferté-Milon and desired him to pray for her, saying, that if the change which had been effected in her was lasting it would be the greatest miracle of that age.

Another of d'Andilly's converts was the Baroness de St. Ange, whose husband was maître d'hôtel to Anne of Austria; d'Andilly made her acquaintance in 1635, and as he never saw a pretty woman without taking an interest in her soul, he begged her to go and see the nuns of Port Royal. She did so in the following year, and on her first visit received a notable rebuff from Angélique.

She entered the little parlour and greeted the Reverend Abbess in the conventional manner, with many compliments and much assumed humility. Angélique in reply drew the curtain before the window of communication, and thus intimated that the interview was at an end. The Baroness was astonished and annoyed, but she took leave in the usual manner, commending herself to the prayers of the community; in answer to which Angélique said :—

'Those who desire that we should pray for them ought to leave us in solitude. The convent parlour is of no use to fine ladies, and their visits do a great deal of harm to nuns.'

The Baroness complained of her reception, but Angélique's sister-in-law, Mdme. d'Andilly, said :

'Do not be deterred from seeking her, for she is like the good angels who terrify at first and comfort us afterwards.'

This account was verified, for when Angélique found that the lady was in earnest, she did all in her power to promote her spiritual well-being, and was not satisfied with the result of her efforts until she had made the Baroness a humble disciple of St. Cyran.

Mdme. de St. Ange was soon promoted from the rank of disciple to that of friend, and St. Cyran had such confidence in her good sense as well as her good intentions, that he used to say if he had fifty thousand crowns to distribute to the poor, he should think it impossible to place them in better hands than hers. During his imprisonment, she and Mdme. le Maitre were his almoners. It is a female friend who is asked to bestow a dowry upon a poor maiden, to purchase suitable garments for a lady of rank, and to buy a black coat for a poor mad prisoner, who could not endure the sight of the grey clothes he was compelled to wear; and the friend was one of the two ladies upon whose delicacy he could rely as confidently as on their charity. The son of Mdme. de St. Ange was one of the boys whom he confided to Lancelot's care.

The influence of this lady led to her husband's conversion; he died in 1651, and she then entered Port Royal, and took the veil in 1654.

The peculiarity of Port Royal is that good and earnest people cannot escape from it. They begin with admiration of the Abbess and reverence for St. Cyran, and are insensibly drawn onwards until the world has no charm, and life offers no brighter prospect than the convent cell, or a lonely hut outside the Abbey gates. One after the other of the great family of the Arnaulds renounces the world, not when they are old and because they are unsuccessful, but in the first flush of youth, whilst the future is bright with promise.

A second generation follows the first; d'Andilly's daughters are nuns in Port Royal, Mdme. le Maître's sons are the earliest Recluses. Before long cousins, uncles, and friends swell this band, until their number and importance overshadow the convent, and the Port Royal Schools and the Jansenist contro-versy cause Angélique, the Reformer, to be overlooked.

Antoine, Angélique's youngest brother, led Port Royal into the troubled sea of theological controversy, and his advent at this period changes the course of action which had hitherto been adopted by our Abbess, and calls out all the combative-ness lying dormant in the Arnauld nature.

Antoine, his father's twentieth child, belongs to the first family, but the second generation of Arnaulds. Born in 1612, he was twenty-four years younger than his brother d'Andilly, and twenty-one younger than Angélique. His nephew le Maître was three years his senior, and de Séricourt and de Saci respectively a year older and younger than himself. He is *Le Petit Oncle* of their boyish days, their companion and school-fellow; so quick, and gifted with such a wonderful memory, that he never had to study his lessons, but used to say them last, and knew them quite well from hearing the two elder boys repeat them before it came to his turn. He chose the law as his profession, but his mother induced him to abandon it for the Church, and after a very distinguished career at the University he proposed to take holy orders and obtain his doctor's degree in the Sorbonne. He already held several benefices

which had been procured for him whilst he was a boy, for
M. Arnauld, as we have seen, did not neglect the temporal
interests of his children. He was wealthy and young, had
attracted considerable attention at court, and Richelieu is said
to have honoured him by an unexpected visit. His youthful
ambition may have led him to contemplate the possibility of
finding such a career open to him as that of the great Cardinal,
but he paused before taking the irrevocable step of becoming
a priest, and began to entertain doubts as to his vocation. His
mother and sisters in Port Royal, his eldest brother and his
three nephews helped to deepen his doubts, and they all spoke
to him of the one man who was alone able to guide him, and
who was now a prisoner for the truth.

To St. Cyran, therefore, Antoine Arnauld referred his difficulties in a letter written at Christmas 1638, and conveyed to
Vincennes by d'Andilly. The prisoner, with considerable difficulty, for he was at that time strictly watched, contrived to
dictate an answer, and ultimately to write a series of letters
which resulted in leading young Arnauld to throw up his benefices, bestow upon Port Royal all that he possessed except a
bare pittance, and prepare for holy orders in a very different
spirit from that which had formerly animated him.

In 1640, Jansen's *Augustinus* was published, and Arnauld's
attention was at once drawn to it. He prepared by careful
study for that defence of the work which St. Cyran said he was
well able to undertake, and in which he spent more than fifty
years of his long life. It was not, however, the defence of
Jansen which first called attention to him, but a book written
in 1643 *On Frequent Communion,* which was called forth in
the following manner :—

A Jesuit priest saw some of the instructions written by St.
Cyran for the Princess de Guemené, and said that they were
much too strict. In a letter which he wrote to prove his asser-
tions, he stated among other things that the less we have of grace
the more boldly we ought to approach the Table of our Lord,
and that those who are entirely engrossed by love of the
world and love of self, ought to communicate very frequently.
Now, in the Romish Church, Communion must be preceded
by Absolution ; and if this doctrine is accepted, hardened and
impenitent sinners may be absolved and receive the Holy Eucharist without repentance. It is the old difficulty of attrition

and contrition over again.   St. Cyran had suffered for his
doctrine.   Arnauld was prepared to suffer and to fight also.
He wrote an answer to the Jesuit's work, entitled, *On Frequent
Communion*, in which he urges the necessity of delaying absolution until there has been sincere repentance for sin.   On the
authority of the Bible, the Fathers, and the Canons, he shows
that this is the doctrine of the Catholic Church, and that
repentance must precede confession ; contrition must go before
absolution ; and communion must be accompanied by penance.
At the time when this book appeared, it was the custom in
France to grant absolution for all sins, great and small, with
extreme facility ; and there was an immediate outcry against
the innovator and his novelties.   The name Jansenist had not
been introduced, but *Arnauldists* and *Cyranists* were declaimed
against from the pulpit.   A Jesuit attacked the book in a course
of sermons, and forbade any of his listeners to look at it.
Their curiosity was excited ; they hastened to procure copies ;
the first edition was sold in a fortnight, and a second was
announced in an advertisement affixed to the doors of the
Jesuit College before the reverend father had finished his
course of sermons.

The Jesuits were undoubtedly alarmed at the number and
importance of St. Cyran's followers, and felt that their supremacy was threatened.   Arnauld's novelty soon became an
established custom throughout France, and absolution was
delayed in the case of flagrant sinners.   It was not, however,
principle the Jesuits were fighting for, but power ; and this
they were resolved to maintain at any cost.

Marshal de Vitri was present at one of the sermons referred
to, and said afterwards he was quite sure there was more than
appeared on the surface in this matter, for the Reverend
Fathers never showed such extraordinary zeal when there was
nothing at stake but the glory of God.

The theological literature of this period is not attractive.
Even the great Arnauld finds no readers in the present day ;
and the work which marked a new era when it appeared, and
attained a sudden popularity almost equal to the *Introduction
to a Devout Life* of St. Francis de Sales, already belongs to
a long-forgotten past.

CHAPTER XXI.

A FEW days after the arrest of St. Cyran the nuns from the Holy Eucharist returned to Port Royal. The small house in a fashionable quarter which the Bishop of Langres had been at such pains to establish, had been a failure and he had ceased to take any interest in it. St. Cyran withdrew from it when he found how much ill-will his visits called forth. Mdlle. de Chamesson had with some difficulty been got rid of, and since that time there had been no incident worthy of record, save a visit from Mdme. de Chantal, who said that she could not pass through Paris without going to see the little community towards which she felt very warmly for the sake of her dear friend the Abbess of Port Royal.

The house was small, inconvenient, without a garden, and overcrowded. Its inmates, for want of air, exercise, and proper dormitories were never well, and at length their ecclesiastical superior, the Archbishop of Paris, would not allow them to remain and die before his eyes. He said they must do one of two things, either purchase a more commodious house with a large garden, or go back to Port Royal. They were strongly inclined to return to the early home from which they had never been entirely separated ; for the Abbess Genevieve referred to Angélique in all her difficulties, Father Singlin was confessor to both convents, and St. Cyran was their spiritual head. Their only fear was lest the unbroken harmony of their little community might be impossible in so large an establishment as Port Royal had become. Father Singlin reassured them by saying that where there is the Spirit of God there will always be peace and union, whether a community is large or small. They could not, however, make up their minds, and in order to enable them to come to a decision, the Abbess put a long pin into the New Testament, and, pricking for a text, fell upon a passage in which St. Paul advocates prayer, charity, and almsgiving; the community saw at once that Port Royal was indicated, and decided unanimously in favour of a return to their very dear mother Angélique.

They were received with great joy; Agnes, who was at that time Abbess, gave them a warm welcome. Angélique was mistress of the novices, and the new comers entreated permission to resume their noviciate, so that they might be under her rule. Their request was granted, they entered upon the duties assigned to them with great zeal, and throughout the whole monastery there was what Angélique especially liked, a revival.

When the little community left Port Royal, the Bishop of Langres was at its head. When they returned in 1638 they scarcely recognized their former home in its new garb of poverty and silence, and were astonished at the complete change that had been effected.

One thing, however, marred their joy. They had hoped to see St. Cyran, and they found that he was in prison. Like all his followers they assigned his persecutions to the ill-will which he had incurred for their sakes. Le Maître thought that his own conversion had drawn odium upon his master, Lancelot attributed the Abbot's misfortunes to the anger of the priests from whose influence he had been withdrawn, and Port Royal traced them to the jealousy of the Bishop of Langres. All these may be reckoned among the causes which helped to make St. Cyran obnoxious, although not one is so important or affords such a complete explanation as the authors of it imagined.

When the Sisters of the Holy Eucharist joined Port Royal the special design of their institution, namely, perpetual adoration of the mystery of the Holy Eucharist, was not abandoned. Angélique, whose tenacity of purpose is one of the distinguishing features of her character, had returned to her original idea and desired to add perpetual adoration to the rules of her own convent.

There were tedious delays in the preliminary arrangements which we need not follow, and it was not until 1645 that the Pope gave permission for the incorporation of the two societies, and the transfer to Port Royal of the funds bequeathed to the Holy Eucharist by Mdme. Bardeau.

The chapel attached to Port Royal was small and inconvenient, and as the community had now the funds, they resolved to build a church. In 1646 the first stone was consecrated by the Archbishop and laid by Mdme. de Longueville, afterwards Duchess de Nemours, and on that day visitors were allowed to enter the monastery. Many who had listened to unfriendly reports which were widely circulated were present on that day, and when they saw Scripture texts painted on the walls of the refectory they said it was just like a Huguenot church; and they were surprised that such heretics as these nuns should have Holy Water and orthodox pictures of the Saints and the Virgin in their convent.

In the following year all preliminary arrangements had been completed, and the Bishop of Langres' new Order which had failed to give him the rank he coveted by the side of St. Francis and St. Charles Borromeo was allowed quietly to subside. When the two monasteries were incorporated a question of vestments arose, as it is apt to do in matters that concern the Church, and this caused Angélique considerable annoyance.

The 'august robes' had been abandoned for many years, but instead of the black scapulary hitherto worn at Port Royal, it was decided that there should be a white one with a scarlet cross to hang over the breast.

Angélique disapproved of the change and would not consent to it, although her sister, Anne-Eugénie, tried to convince her that it was a very simple matter and would do no harm. Whilst the question was still undecided a certain box was opened 'by chance,' or by some one with a good memory, which proved to be full of white scapularies. It had been brought from the Holy Eucharist eight or nine years previously, put away and forgotten. Anne-Eugénie carried all the little capes to Angélique and laid them down before her, saying that God had now decided this matter by a special interposition in favour of the scarlet crosses. Angélique yielded; she liked to feel her dependence upon God's providence, and this manifestation was so very opportune that she could not reject it. A day was fixed in October 1647 for the distribution of the new vestments, and the Grand Vicar officiated at the ceremony.

Possibly it was one of the most distasteful at which Angélique by her own consent had ever presided, and not the less so because she was conscious of a little flutter of excitement in some of the well-regulated breasts on which the red cross was henceforth to repose.

It is thus at least that we interpret the impatience of our Abbess and the manner in which she threw on the capes one after the other so hastily and carelessly that the nuns had to retire and adjust them, before they considered themselves fit to be seen. Angélique, when she was young, would have absolutely refused her consent to any ornamental modification of dress, but at fifty she has begun to see that a cape more or less is of no great consequence, only let there be no nonsense about it.

As for the Grand Vicar he was as glad to hurry through the ceremony as the Abbess, for there were more than eighty nuns to be arrayed, and he was not at all interested in their change of costume.

Genevieve, the Abbess who had been led astray through her sweet submissive nature and the guilelessness of her own heart, and had now resigned her post in order to become a novice, did not live to witness the completion of all the arrangements for uniting her little community with the Sisters of Port Royal.

Shortly after her return she was appointed sacristan. One day she was kneeling down to sweep under a cupboard in the sacristy, and as she rose she struck her eye with such violence against a projecting corner of the cupboard that it was entirely destroyed, and before long she lost the sight of the other eye also. Her blindness was accompanied by incessant pains in the head, and in walking at every step she felt as if she was falling down a precipice ; so that she was never able to go about alone, not even in her own room, but must have some hand to cling to.

It was very touching to see her waiting at a door or standing in a passage until some one passed who would lead her a few steps in the direction she wanted to go.

Sometimes the guide of the former Abbess was an unwilling child, impatient at the delay caused by her companion's timid steps; sometimes it was a nun, who had formerly knelt to receive her commands. She was greatly disfigured by the accident, so that her companions said, 'there was no form nor comeliness' left, and it was almost impossible to recognize the face that had once been beautiful. But her sufferings taught her such patience, humility, and submission, that they began to think she belonged more to heaven than earth, and was only lent to them for a time as a bright example. 'Her death took place in the spring of 1646, and Angélique's niece, who gives an account of it, says :

'I do not know whether I ought to mention one incident which we noticed when she died. . . . The whole of the community was standing round her bed, and we were chanting the *Subvenite*, according to our custom at such a time. A very extraordinary thing happened, which we all noticed ; it seemed to us as if other voices mingled with ours and joined with them in supernatural harmony. Perhaps this may have been merely our imagination ; but we were all certain that the angels rejoiced when they received her soul; and although our senses may have deceived us, our hearts showed us the truth.'[1]

Throughout St. Cyran's imprisonment he was informed of all that passed at Port Royal, and consulted on every matter of importance. During the early years of Genevieve's blindness he wrote her several consolatory letters, and the community turned to him for sympathy and advice in all their difficulties.

After the Commissioner had visited Port Royal *des Champs* and expelled the Recluses, it was rumoured that he was coming to Paris to interrogate Angélique. The nuns expected his arrival from day to day, and feared that he would take their beloved Mother from them. But the friendly Archbishop of Paris averted the threatened danger. He would not hear of an examination by Laubardemont, and said that he would inspect Port Royal himself. His visit was delayed on various excuses, until the excitement caused by St. Cyran's arrest and the dispersion of the Recluses had died out, and there was no further need for it. He adopted this course, not because he sympathised with St. Cyran, but because he entertained a high esteem for Angélique, whom he called a 'holy nun, and a bright

[1] Vies Intéressantes, ii. 13.

example in the Church.' He said she was one of the first who
had set the example of reforming *herself* and leading a holy
life ; that she was perfect in obedience, and had gained his
affection by her respect for her ecclesiastical Superiors. The
storm which threatened Port Royal passed over for a time, and
the incidents of the years that follow are all connected with the
inner life of the convent, from which the shadow of death is
never absent.

Angélique's mother, an old, feeble woman, kneeling at the
feet of her daughters Agnes and Angélique, standing aside
humbly to give precedence to Anne and Marie-Claire and
little Madelon who are her seniors in religion, with dim eyes
almost blinded by her efforts to learn the chants by heart, and
health that fails visibly from day to day, hears in 1639 that her
son Simon, born in 1603, has been killed in battle near Verdun.
It is a terrible blow from which she never rallies, for she had
hoped that some day he would be converted and join the
children and grandchildren who had forsaken the world and
given themselves to God. Two years later, in 1641, death
released her from much suffering, borne without a murmur.

She had at that time six daughters in Port Royal ; for
although Mdme. le Maitre had not then taken the veil, she
had entered upon her noviciate ; and six grandchildren, the
daughters of her eldest son d'Andilly. She refused herself
the gratification of seeing them during her last illness, but
when she was dying they all stood around her. Nature was
stronger than culture, and the Abbess Agnes knelt down by her
side and kissed her, saying, 'My own dear mother, speak to
me, your child, and tell me what God requires of me.'

The dying woman's answer shows even to the last the sub-
ordination of the nun to her Superior, though the mother's love
ultimately triumphs.

'*Ma Mère,*' she replied ; 'my Mother!' and then : 'you must
take care of your health.'

'I know it,' said Agnes.

'Yes,' replied Mdme. Arnauld ; 'but you do not do it. You
must do it faithfully and literally, souls are so dear to God.'

'But my life is not worth caring for,' continued Agnes. 'Of
what use is it?'

'That is not for you to decide.'

And so the conversation ended. All the sixteen years during

which Mdme. Arnauld had been learning to despise the body and mortify the flesh had not sufficed to obliterate the tender solicitude of a mother for her child's health; and, in spite of long repression, it asserted itself as soon as the pressure of silence and obedience was removed.

Ten of Mdme. Arnauld's children died in infancy; of the remaining ten, the six daughters were nuns in Port Royal; her eldest son, d'Andilly, was still in the world; but everyone said that his life there was blameless, and that his only use of it was to draw souls to God. Her second son, Henri, M. de Trie as he was called, was a priest. He had been appointed to one bishopric, that of Toul, during her lifetime; but had resigned it on account of a dispute between the Pope and the King of France as to the right of nomination. He became ultimately Bishop of Angers, but not until after his mother's death.

Her third son, Simon, was dead; killed in battle.

The fourth, Antoine, the twentieth and last child, had gladdened her heart by renouncing the world, throwing up his benefices, and placing himself under the guidance of St. Cyran in 1639. Father Singlin asked her if she had anything to say to her youngest son. She answered that, as God had employed him to defend the truth, she exhorted and entreated him never to relax, but to persevere boldly even though he had a thousand lives to lose.

Once again before her death she was asked, by his desire, if she had any last words for him? 'Tell him,' she replied, 'never to falter in his defence of truth!'

When she died Antoine Arnauld was not in priest's orders, and was still living at the Sorbonne; but he went to Port Royal and stayed there all night. The last Sacrament, Extreme Unction, was administered to her, and he asked Father Singlin to allow him to assist, so that he might be with his mother to the end. But the Father said that de Saci, her grandson, was with him; two assistants were unnecessary and his presence would be *a concession to nature;* his request was therefore refused.

The nuns of Port Royal watched by Mdme. Arnauld, or Sister Catherine as she was called, through the night; and, as it was thought that she would live till morning, they left her to go to matins. Agnes, who was at that time Abbess, said that as her mother's room was immediately over the chapel, she would accompany them and the attendants in the sick room could knock on the floor if there was any change. Soon after the service began she was summoned, and was present when her mother breathed her last. She returned to the chapel and took her place with a calm, sweet expression in her face, so that the nuns thought the sufferer had rallied again; but when they reached that part of the service where the Abbess says the Lord's prayer aloud, and she came to the words '*Thy will be done*,' she burst into tears, and they knew her mother was dead.

Mdme. Arnauld was sixty-eight when she died, and had been twelve years a maiden, thirty-four a wife, six a widow, and sixteen a nun.

Mdme. de Chantal, friend of St. Francis and founder of the Order of Visitation, was now an old woman; her activity was, however, undiminished, and she still went from one city to another and established fresh offshoots from her society wherever there was a demand for them.

In 1641 she visited Paris for the fourth time, and spent two days, before leaving it, with Angélique at Port Royal. It was their last time of communion upon earth; and 'there was a special blessing upon their meeting, and they had great joy of each other.' In November of the same year, a few weeks before her death, Mdme. de Chantal wrote a farewell letter to Angélique, sweet and simple, and breathing the frank and cordial spirit which had been characteristic of their intercourse :—

'MY VERY DEAR AND GOOD MOTHER,

'I cannot help sending this little note to say adieu to you once more. Adieu my very good and very dear Mother, I commit you to God who is unchangeable; we shall meet again in His presence. I cannot tell you what a consolation the pious and cordial union of our hearts has been to me, and I think God in His goodness must have allowed us to live very close to each other in spirit. I send you my books. Alas! can I keep anything back from you? Surely not; I could not bear to do it. When you die let them be sent back here, unless you think it better to leave them to our good Sisters (of Port Royal). It is a great consolation to me to see that our Superiors and Sister Hélène-Angélique desire to live on such cordial terms with you. I salute all our very dear

Sisters and that good servant of God (St. Cyran). Pray for her who is always and altogether yours. Praise the Lord always.'

On the 13th of December, 1641, Mdme. de Chantal died, and Angélique lost in her not only a dear friend but a powerful ally. No shadow of doubt ever rested upon the orthodoxy of Mdme. de Chantal during her life and after death she was canonized. Opponents were silenced when they heard of her approval of Angélique's efforts, her pleasure in Angélique's success, and her protest against the imprisonment of St. Cyran, whom she wrote of as a man 'whose life was quite apostolical, and who was a martyr to the cause of truth and justice.'

If St. Francis de Sales and Mdme. de Chantal had lived, Angélique's course during the period which we are now approaching would probably have been modified. If not she must have forfeited their esteem, and probably have had to reckon them amongst, not certainly her enemies, but her antagonists. Up to this time her course from their point of view had been blameless. She had been the obedient daughter of the Church, reforming abuses but never opposing authority. She had deplored the crimes of the Church privately with St. Francis, but she had not exposed them openly. But a sense of injustice was being roused in her which obedience and submission could not quell. She had begun to ask herself if St. Cyran was a martyr in the cause of truth, what was the Church which persecuted him?

Shortly after his imprisonment the Duchess d'Aiguillon, Richelieu's niece, called to see her, and expressed her sympathy with the prisoner. Instead of entreating her to try and induce the Cardinal to set him at liberty, Angélique was 'carried away by the Spirit of God,' she says, 'and lifted up her voice and said: "There are some who are prisoners in this world who will be free and happy throughout eternity; and there are others who are free and powerful and prosperous in this world, but they will be prisoners and wretched slaves throughout eternity."'

The lady was silent, and Angélique said no more. It was her first outspoken hostile criticism, and it marks the commencement of a new era in her history. Not that there was any immediate change, but the incidents of this period all tended to separate her from the past, and leave her free to take up a new position. She lost dear friends in her mother and Mdme. de Chantal, but a still greater loss awaited her; Marie-Claire died in 1642. Little Marie, at seven years old, had been given to her by their father as pupil, companion, friend, to console her for the loss of all other friends and all dearer ties. She is the child who trembled with fear and yet was prepared to drink the poisonous tisane, who liked nice things but could sacrifice them all if she might live in the desert with her dear sister. In all save one of Angélique's trials Marie-Claire had been with her; she had listened in terror to their father's anger when he was excluded from Port Royal, and accompanied the young Abbess to Maubuisson amongst the insolent 'Ladies;' she had formed one of the little band expelled by the wicked Mdme. d'Estrées, and walked in that silent procession escorted by soldiers with their gleaming swords and flaming torches; she had shared her 'poverty' with the thirty-three novices, and welcomed the advent of the Bishop of Langres, and the increase of ascetic sanctity which accompanied him. After that Marie-Claire was sent to Tard, and on her return she was for a short time faithful to the priest and unfaithful to her sister. Angélique waited patiently until Marie-Claire was convinced of her error. They were reunited, dearer to each other than ever, and then three years afterwards Marie-Claire died.[1] 'I thank God,' said Angélique when she heard that her companions had been desired to write all that they knew of the incidents of her life, 'I thank God that after all people will know very little about me, for that one who knew all my acts and understood me well has taken all with her to the grave.' Other sisters were dear, her brothers and nephews had a large place in her heart, but Marie had been child and sister and friend, trusted even in estrangement; no other could ever fill her place.

Father Singlin said that the countenance of Marie-Claire after death was 'very noble and beautiful,' and made him conscious of extraordinary respect for her. Up to that time one custom introduced from Tard de Dijon had been retained; the dead had been clothed in fine linen; choice flowers were strewn over them, and their bier was surrounded by lighted tapers. But when the nuns looked at the calm, still face

[1] Page 212.

of their Sister, and remembered what her life had been, they felt sure she would have disapproved of these things, and resolved that the last rites should henceforward be as simple as they were in the old times at Port Royal *des Champs*.

Whilst her funeral was taking place, Agnes, who had been ill for some time, was believed to be at the point of death and received Extreme Unction. There was at that time a nun in the Infirmary who was very old and infirm. She had been one of the earliest converts to reform, and had adopted it from love to the two young sisters who were carrying it out. A few days before her death she was told that Agnes was dangerously ill. She said in that case she must get up at once, for this would never do, and she must go and see to it. She insisted on being dressed, made her way to the chapel, and kneeling before the altar offered her life for the life of her Abbess. She then went back happily to bed and died in three days. Agnes, who had by that time recovered from a sudden and sharp attack, was by her side and tended her to the last, and the dying woman looked at her triumphantly, as one who belonged to her and whom she had redeemed from the grave.

Agnes had now been Abbess for six years, and in 1642, when there was a fresh triennial election, Angélique was chosen. It cost her a great effort to resume the office of Abbess which she hoped she had laid aside for ever, but still the change was more nominal than real, as she was and always had. been the head of the community. She was gladdened by learning that St. Cyran's imprisonment was less strict than it had been ; his books and papers were restored, and his friends were allowed to visit him. Richelieu, occupied by other matters and absent from Paris, had apparently forgotten him. On the 4th of December, when the death of the great Cardinal was announced, St. Cyran's friends hastened to inform him of it, and to congratulate him on the prospect of speedy release. Lancelot lost no time in getting to Vincennes, but he found Antoine Arnauld already there, and instead of being engrossed by the news they had just heard, he and St. Cyran were discussing the errors in a book which was intended to refute Jansen's *Augustinus.* Two months later the prisoner was set free, and was allowed to leave Vincennes without any disavowal of the heresy which his enemies had imputed to him. His *ami par excellence*, as he called d'Andilly, fetched him in his carriage, and Vincennes was strangely moved at his departure. The prisoners shed tears of joy for him and sorrow for themselves, the soldiers of the garrison and jailors formed a long line on either side of the road by which he left, fifes were played, drums beaten, and muskets fired off to show their joy. But St. Cyran passed through them all a dying man, aged and broken down by the five years he had spent in that gloomy prison.

The room in which he had been so long confined was looked upon as a sacred spot. In after years his faithful Lancelot used to visit it, and when he found it closed would kneel down and pray outside the door and kiss the locks and bolts.

D'Andilly took St. Cyran into Paris to thank the two friends who had procured his release. They next drove to Port Royal, where information of the prisoner's reprieve had preceded them. Agnes heard it at the time when the Sisters had assembled for the silent meeting which had replaced the gossip of recreation time. She went at once to tell them the good news, and entered with a radiant face, which fixed immediate attention upon her. She spoke no word, but snatched off the girdle which bound her robe and held it forth. Not a sound was uttered; but every heart beat fast, for the Sisters knew that the bonds were broken and the prisoner was free.

It was five o'clock in the evening of a day in February 1643 when St. Cyran and d'Andilly arrived at Port Royal where St. Cyran's nephew awaited them. Father Rebours was also there, a man of whom Father Singlin had formed so high an opinion that he had induced him to enter the Church, and take priest's orders in 1641, at the same time as Antoine Arnauld.

They went to the convent chapel to return thanks, and St. Cyran knelt before the altar whilst the nuns, hastily summoned, chanted the *Te Deum*. Once more he listened to the sweet voices which had been trained to honour as well as praise God in their singing; and the triumphant sounds which called forth his emotion kindled in the nuns an unwonted gladness that somewhat interfered with their usual self-restraint.

The service ended, St. Cyran adjourned to the parlour, and the community was summoned to receive his greeting. And now an unfortunate incident occurred. Father Rebours was an old man, and his sight was failing. In the dim light he could not distinguish the faces of the Sisters so he put on his spectacles, at that time a novelty, and began to peer about him. Some of the younger nuns could not preserve their gravity when they witnessed this extraordinary proceeding. They laughed, laughter is contagious when the heart is very joyful, and it spread. on all sides. St. Cyran, much surprised, asked the meaning of this mirth. It jarred painfully upon him; and he gravely said: 'Truly I had something to say to you; but this is not a fitting preparation for it, and I will wait for some other time.'

The punishment was severe for so slight a fault; but his shattered nerves and suffering condition made him less inclined than ever to tolerate anything that seemed like an approach to levity.

A week later there was a solemn thanksgiving service in the chapel, conducted by Father Singlin, who was assisted by Antoine Arnauld, Father Rebours—without his glasses let us hope—de Saci, and Lancelot. St. Cyran was too ill to take any part in it, though he was present. When the service was ended, he sent to ask Father Singlin if he would select a psalm which he might use every Friday for the rest of his life, in memory of that eventful day.

The confessor and his assistants knelt together in prayer, and asked God to direct their choice; and then the great Arnauld held the psalter, whilst Father Singlin put in a long pin which pricked the thirty-fourth Psalm :—

'*I will bless the Lord at all times: His praise shall continually be in my mouth. . . . I sought the Lord, and He heard me, and delivered me from all my fears. . . . This poor man cried, and the Lord heard him, and saved him out of all his troubles. The angel of the Lord encampeth round about them that fear Him, and delivereth them. . . . The Lord redeemeth the soul of His servants : and none of them that trust in Him shall be desolate.*'

They all felt that this psalm of thanksgiving was peculiarly appropriate, and believed that the method of ascertaining the will of God to which priests and learned men resorted as readily as an abbess and her nuns, had resulted in a divine manifestation in favour of their revered master.

St. Cyran was quite overcome; and begged everyone to leave the chapel, so that he might be free to open his heart to God.   Singlin and Lancelot, however, concealed themselves and watched him; he stood up and intoned the psalm with tears streaming from his eyes; at length, overpowered by emotion, he threw himself upon his face before the altar, and no sound reached them but his sobs.

Although St. Cyran had been set at liberty, he was still suspected and watched.   An attempt was made to suppress and censure a Catechism which he had written; and when this failed, the Jesuits endeavoured to have him summoned before the Archbishop of Paris on a charge of heresy, so that even if they could prove nothing, they might be able to say he had been accused.

Some of his friends wished him to go to the Archbishop and vindicate himself, by explaining his views; but he refused. Angélique urged him to adopt this course, saying that 'humility is always a virtue; and, therefore, when we humiliate ourselves we must be doing right.'   St. Cyran answered:

'It would be right for you because you think so, and you would not by your humiliation compromise truth and honour; but, as for me, I should despise myself before God if I were to do as you say.'   And then he added, cheerfully; 'Don't be afraid.   By God's grace I withstood the great Cardinal, and I certainly need not be afraid of the Archbishop.'

Nevertheless the storm seemed as if it would not blow over.   Arnauld's book *On Frequent Communion* had excited extraordinary interest in its author and the school to which he belonged.   It was all very well for nuns to say that religion and morality, which had been so long divorced, must be united again; but when a learned man, and a priest, asserted such a dangerous doctrine the Church rose in arms against him.   It was rumoured that St. Cyran was to be sent back to Vincennes; that Arnauld would be shut up in the Bastille, and that he and his 'accomplices' would perish on the scaffold.   Port Royal was implicated; the nuns were to be interrogated as to the doctrine they had been taught, and the monastery searched for St. Cyran's papers.

Angélique wrote to her Director, in great anxiety, to ask what she was to do; she had heard that the community was to be dispersed, her nuns placed in other convents, and confessors appointed who would not tolerate *innovations*.   She was still a true daughter of the Church, and thought her duty lay in obedience and submission; she was prepared to yield on all points, but referred to St. Cyran her guardian.

He answered somewhat coldly, that she must do what she thought right; showed clearly that, so far as he was concerned, he did not intend to submit on any point; and added, rather ominously, that, for his own part, he was more afraid of weak people than of wicked ones.

As soon as he could leave Paris, St. Cyran paid a short visit to his faithful disciples, the Recluses at Port Royal *des Champs*. He afterwards frequently expressed his regret that Angélique had left so beautiful a spot, saying that if he had known her at that time he certainly would not have given his consent to the change.

'But, my Father,' she urged one day, 'we were often ill, and sometimes there were not enough of the healthy to wait on the sick, or even to perform the choral services.'

'So much the better,' answered St. Cyran. 'It is quite as good a thing to praise God in an infirmary, if that is His will, as in a church. There are no better prayers than those which we offer from a bed of suffering.'

These words made a great impression on Angélique. She began to look back to the early times, and to ask herself if she had done wisely in leaving her peaceful home for the great city where they had not escaped sickness and death, and had been exposed to far greater dangers than any that had previously assailed them. Doubtless she often discussed the question, . and it may have been in some of her arguments with him on this subject that he was abrupt, almost rude, to her, so that she said:

'My Father, it seems to me that you are only gentle towards those who abuse your confidence and deceive you.'

The reproach was not well merited; but St. Cyran received it well, and was afterwards careful not to hurt her feelings.

D'Andilly's noble converts paid frequent visits to Port Royal, and occasionally spent a week there 'in retreat;' but St. Cyran was not deceived as to the transient nature of their repentance.

'Do you think,' he said one day, to the ladies assembled in the parlour, 'it is an easy thing to turn to God after you have been led astray by the world, and have fallen a victim to its snares? I tell you nay; it is more difficult than you think, and more rare. I scarcely know anyone, except M. le Maître, to whom God in our time has granted the grace of a true conversion.'

So far from thinking that Angélique was doing well in offering an asylum to great ladies who were tired of the world and disappointed with life, he believed it was a doubtful benefit to them, and a step fraught with peril to herself.

It was the theory of St. Cyran, as of other pious Roman Catholics, that the body is an enemy to be tortured and kept in subjection—a snare which the devil has wound about our soul ; but we find traces of a recognition of the opposite belief, that the body is the gift of God, to be used in His service. Monasticism and the celibacy of the priesthood would cease if the former theory were abandoned ; and yet at all times priests and nuns have hesitated to accept and act upon it ; and their treatment of the human body may be described as cruelty tempered by indulgence. They think it a duty to suffer pain, not only without complaining, but often without seeking any alleviation of their sufferings, and at the same time they fall readily into greater sloth and self-indulgence than any other members of the community. Angélique and her nuns found it difficult to reconcile the doctor's visits with their sense of the duty of submission to the will of God. St. Cyran would not allow the Abbess Genevieve to have an abscess opened ; he considered that if such a violent measure was necessary for her relief, it was an indication that God intended her to endure her malady. He could not escape from the fear that the physician to some extent supersedes the decrees of Providence, for when God wills that a man shall suffer, the doctor steps in and says he shall not. In his last illness, the fact that he was attended by an unskilful surgeon was almost a gratification to him. He was urged to call in another, but refused for three reasons. In the first place, his life was in the hands of God and not of man ; therefore it was of no consequence whether the surgeon was skilful or unskilful. In the second place, the poor man was doing his best, and it would be unjust to punish him for what was not his own fault ; whilst thirdly, the medical colleague suggested was one of his own personal friends, whom it would be a great pleasure to see, and he was glad to deny himself this gratification. He was hard to himself, the Recluses, and the nuns, and yet was not only capable of tenderness, but the tenderness lay deeper than the austerity, and was the true source of his power.

St. Cyran lived in an age when false miracles abounded ; his truthful nature revolted against them ; he distrusted visions, and would not listen to marvellous stories. He was told one day of a woman who was surrounded by supernatural light, held communion with spirits, and had received on her own body the *stigmata*—those mysterious marks which represent the wounds of Christ on the Cross. He interrupted the speaker with : 'Ah, yes ; a very extraordinary story—very extraordinary indeed !' and so put an end to the relation. We find the same distrust of visions and miracles in all his followers, Angélique had it all her life, and yet it did not preserve any of them from occasional lapses into gross superstition.

When de Séricourt joined the Recluses he asked St. Cyran to teach him to pray, saying that as he was a soldier he was greatly in need of instruction on this point. St. Cyran put his hands together, bowed his head, and lifted his eyes towards heaven. 'This, sir, is all we have to do,' he replied ; 'we have only to appear humbly before God, and remember that He is looking down upon us.' De Séricourt says that his master's devout look, and these simple words, affected him more deeply and gave him a truer insight into the nature of prayer than all the books of devotion in the world.

St. Cyran advocated mental prayer ; he said that it consisted rather in listening to God than speaking to Him, and in that attitude which prepares us to receive spiritual gifts rather than to ask for them.

He urged his converts not to delay their progress by too much looking back upon their faults ; and St. Francis might have written the pretty fable, that 'To spend time in counting and lamenting little faults, is like a child who has fallen down whilst it is running, and who, instead of getting up and running on again, stops to cry and look at its dirty hands, which delays it far more than the fall has done.' But St. Francis could not have written such a solemn passage illuminated by so vivid a flash of insight as the following : 'The smallest cloud which is in our heart will spread over our pages like an evil breath that tarnishes a mirror, and the slightest impurity is like a worm which will pass into our book and *gnaw the hearts of those who read it to the end of the world.*'

St. Cyran advocated the study of the Scriptures at a time when it was so much neglected, that Lancelot, who had been ten years in the community of St. Nicholas, had never read a word of the New Testament; and there were Cardinals and Prelates, grey-headed men and bent with age, who had not read one syllable of the Bible except what was contained in their breviaries.

When St. Cyran heard that a bull, issued by Urban VIII., was directed against Jansen's *Augustinus,* he said: 'They are going too far. We must show them their duty.' And he warmly approved of Arnauld's proposal to attack the Pope's decree, and take up the defence of Augustinus, saying: 'You are right; and if you were silent the very stones would speak.' He justified his opposition by saying that it was directed against the Court of Rome and not the Church. He was an obedient son of the Church, but refused to submit to the Court; and taught his followers to separate the one from the other, and to be prepared to defend the truth and oppose the Pope, although they acquiesced in all the decrees and accepted all the doctrines bequeathed to them by earlier ages. It is impossible not to acknowledge that the emancipation which he advocated was partial and incomplete, and to suspect that if he had lived longer he would have become the heresiarch which his enemies called him.

The physician who attended him in his last illness belonged to the Jesuit College; one day St. Cyran said to him: 'Tell your Fathers that they have nothing to hope for from my death; they will gain nothing by it; for I shall, in all probability, bequeath them a dozen followers who will give them more trouble than I have done.'

Six months after he left Vincennes he died. The Jesuits spread the report that he had not received the last Sacraments; but his friends were able to prove that this was false. He died as he had lived, a good Catholic; and experienced after death the fate that befalls many good Catholics—he was converted into relics.

He had bequeathed his heart to d'Andilly, on condition that he quitted the world; and Lancelot, who superintended the acquisition of this legacy, speaks in a sickening manner of 'the little treasures' he 'contrived to scrape together;' namely, numerous handkerchiefs dipped in blood, and likewise the stomach and entrails of the deceased. When at length the poor mutilated corpse had been placed in a coffin, le Maître arrived from Port Royal *des Champs* and begged for the hands : ' Those pure and holy hands which had been so often raised in prayer to God ; which had written so many great truths, and were still fighting for the Church when God called him.' His request was at once acceded to. A parish priest, who was deemed unworthy to witness their devotion, was watching by the coffin. He was dismissed on some pretext, and then Lancelot and another ' cut the hands off neatly at the wrist.' They were taken with the other ' relics ' to Angélique, who received them reverently, and kept them with similar treasures which she had been taught to consider sacred.

It is one of those extraordinary contradictions in which this history abounds, and another example of the manner in which a pure and spiritual religion, as Angélique's undoubtedly was, may be degraded by the superstitions of a corrupt Church.

When the Abbess heard of St. Cyran's death, she went about her usual work quite calmly. The Sisters knew that the greatest grief of her whole life had fallen upon their very dear Mother, and watched her anxiously as in silence, with a calm face and tearless eyes, she passed from room to room. Not, however, in absolute silence, for from time to time they heard her ejaculate, ' *Dominus in cœlo ! Dominus in cœlo !*' ' The Lord God is in heaven !' She had no other words with which to express her own loneliness ; and at the same time her profound faith in God, and her certainty that He orders all things both in heaven and on earth.

CHAPTER XXII

ST. CYRAN's death is a landmark in the history of Port Royal. Angélique had been for some time previously more or less undecided as to the attitude she ought to assume. She now sees that it must be one of resistance. No power on earth can make her unfaithful to the dead. She identifies the cause of St. Cyran with that of truth, and is prepared to die for it.

Through the remaining years of her life we see her gradually falling away from her early endeavours. Reform is no longer the great work of her life; it is not less needed than it had been thirty years previously at Maubuisson; her influence had extended far and wide; monks as well as nuns had been affected by it, and much remained to be done for which she was better qualified than anyone else at that time. Age had given her increased authority; she possessed large and valuable experience, and had acquired considerable *prestige*, so that the name of Mdme. de Port Royal was known throughout France. Practically there were no limits to her sphere of usefulness, and yet by degrees she abandons her early labour; Port Royal ceases to be identified with practical work, and becomes the nucleus of a band of men and women, devoted to truth, enduring persecution, affliction, death, winning our admiration by their courage and their fidelity, but occupying the anomalous position of rebelling against a Church every decree of which they assumed to be Divine, and dying in defence of a book which the greater number of them professed to be unable to read.

Doubtless passionate devotion to the memory of St. Cyran

influenced Angélique and her nuns more strongly than any convictions they had imbibed from him, or any doctrine she had inculcated. We see his influence reflected in the character of the women and the intellect of the men who were his disciples ; and although we may regret the deflection of Angélique from her original course, it is difficult to see how she could have armed herself against a man so good, so holy, so wise as St. Cyran, or how she could have resisted personal influence to which men and women, young and old, alike succumbed. No one was better able than she to appreciate the peculiar excellence of her Director, which consisted in the even balance and symmetry of all his faculties. Intellect and heart were alike great ; his moral qualities were as remarkable as his mental powers ; he was truthful in word and deed ; just to friends and enemies ; generous in thought as well as action ; he possessed that supreme charm, a grateful nature, and could not receive the slightest testimony of goodwill from another without desiring to requite it double ; he endured his own sufferings like a Stoic, but was all tenderness and moderation to his friends. Angélique's affection and respect for him were absolute and unbounded, and she could not have acknowledged him to be an unfaithful son of the Church or have joined in the condemnation of his doctrines without becoming an apostate, false alike to the noblest nature and the highest truth revealed to her upon earth.

Almost immediately after the death of St. Cyran, the long-threatened storm broke over Port Royal, and the Grand Vicar and *Grand Pénitencier* paid a formal visit of inspection to the Abbey ; the nuns were interrogated one by one, and the rules drawn up for their guidance by St. Cyran closely examined. The inspectors were not among the friends of the deceased Abbot, but they were compelled to acknowledge that the reports which had reached them were untrue ; that his conduct at Port Royal had been that of a good Catholic and a good Christian, and the convent was the abode of religion and virtue, nay even of sanctity. The Archbishop sent to congratulate Angélique on this result, and assured her that he had not authorized the inspection to satisfy his own doubts, for he had always recognized that God's special blessing rested upon her work, but in order to put an end to the false reports which had been circulated for so many years.

Upon this Agnes wrote to her brother, the great Arnauld, who was at the time in concealment: 'We are such good women, if we will only believe it; but there is another judge who will accuse us before God unless we follow that which we have been taught.'

The result of the inspection was, however, what the enemies of Port Royal had desired. The public looked suspiciously at the Abbey and considered that they had good reason for so doing since the Archbishop had thought it necessary to institute an inquiry into the conduct of the nuns; and the Jesuits made every effort to prevent novices from joining them. Portionless girls who were about to enter the convent were told that they ought not to risk the loss of their souls in order to provide for the body; and noble ladies were informed that they might as well go to a Huguenot chapel as to the church of Port Royal.

Angélique had no reason to fear the hostility which had been aroused, for if Port Royal had influential enemies it had also very powerful friends. But the friends themselves were becoming a source of disquietude. One noble penitent brought another in her train, and not only the Princess de Guemené, but also the Marquise de Sablé and Marie de Gonzague de Clèves, Princess of Mantua, paid frequent visits to the convent.

The Princess Marie came for the first time a few days before St. Cyran's death. She had intended to place herself under his guidance, but was too late and could only be present, an uninvited guest, at his funeral. A few months previously she had been affianced to Cinq-Mars, whose conspiracy against Richelieu had cost him his life. The untimely death of her lover, and the attention directed to her on account of the relation in which she stood to him, were among the causes which prompted her retreat to Port Royal. She was romantic, superstitious, easily affected by the externals of religion, and of a gentle, sensitive nature. Angélique hoped that she might derive permanent benefit from her residence amongst them, and when that hope was destroyed she still maintained a warm affection for her. One day Angélique told her that worldly people treat their conscience as they do their dirty linen, which is washed when it is soiled, and soiled again as soon as it is washed. The Princess answered that this was true and yet there was a difference. for the dirty linen could be made quite pure and clean, but she could not believe that confession and absolution made a soul pure in the sight of God if the heart and its evil courses were unchanged. Angélique thought that this answer was a sign of the grace of God, and it encouraged her to persevere with the noble penitent. A room was assigned to the Princess, which for two years she frequently occupied, coming to it usually every Thursday, and staying some days. She was often joined there by Mdme. de Guemené, and Mdme. de Sablé, who were not so much seeking their own salvation as seeking the desire to undertake the search. Angélique exercised a certain authority over them which gained their respect. Moreover, they saw that she was in earnest about their conversion, whatever they might be. She made rules for the employment of their time when they were in the convent, fixed the hours for their devotion, and named the persons to whom they were allowed to speak. The last was a precautionary measure, as she would not allow the rule of silence to be broken by the Sisters. She did not permit the ladies to spend much time together, saying that they could not help discussing worldly matters and as they had come to Port Royal to learn a new language, it was essential that they should not make use of the old. One day she was told that they had been talking together for a long time after dinner, and exclaimed, ' I must go and separate our ladies, for they do harm to one another. No sooner do they begin to talk than a head-dress, a new fashion, a collar is sure to find its way into the conversation. I must try to put a stop to all these *diableries*, which cannot be tolerated in Christian conversation.'

But her efforts were unavailing. The visits of the Princess de Guemené to Port Royal were, as De Retz says, not so much *retreats* as *escapades*. St. Cyran was right; the 'spark on the icy pavement' was never kindled into flame.

Mdme. de Sablé went to Port Royal in the hope and with the desire of becoming religious. She failed in that respect but she became a Jansenist; not however from conviction, but from that pride of nature which makes tyranny odious, and the side of the oppressed the only possible side to choose. She and the Princess de Guemené were faithful friends of Port Royal in all its persecutions. The Princess offered a home to

the whole sisterhood when they were threatened with dispersion, and concealed in her own house St. Cyran's nephew and
the great Arnauld, when they were summoned to Rome ; whilst
for five years Arnauld and his companion Nicole were hidden
from their enemies by Mdme. de Sablé.

Two years after the Princess Marie paid her first visit to
Port Royal she was demanded in marriage by the King of
Poland, whom she accepted without a moment's hesitation.
She was asked if she would not like to see his portrait, and
replied no it was not necessary, for she was marrying his crown.
Her ambition was fully gratified by the wedding ceremony in
the chapel of the Palais-Royal, where she took precedence of
her former lover the Duke of Orleans, and even of the Queen
of France.   When she reached Poland she carried on an active
correspondence with Angélique, and the replies of the Reverend
Mother—copied without her knowledge before they were despatched from Port Royal—bear witness to the mutual respect
and affection of the Abbess and the Queen, and afford a valuable
insight into the affairs of the convent.

Ladislaus Sigismund, King of Poland, died in 1648, two
years after his marriage.   He was succeeded by his half-brother,
John Casimir, who laid aside his Cardinal's hat in order to
ascend the throne, and married the Queen, his brother's widow.
The second marriage was a very unhappy one ; the Queen saw
all her children die in early infancy ; her adopted country was
never at peace, and never free from civil discord.   Angélique in
her letters does not attempt to give advice on matters concerning which she was imperfectly informed, if informed at all ; but
she wrote as frankly and freely as she would have done to one
of the Sisters, urging upon the Queen attention to the duties of
her position, and above all the necessity of bestowing large
alms upon her distressed subjects.   The Queen was not loth to
follow the advice which harmonized with her own generous
impulses ; and before long her advisers suggested that she had
better moderate her almsgiving and lay by for herself.   She
replied : ' No, I will not save ; for if I am a widow it does not
matter how poor I am ; I shall have enough to go to *la Mère*
Angélique at Port Royal, and she will take me in.

M. le Maître repeated this answer to his Aunt Angélique with
some pride ; but she said : ' I do not know if we ought to wish
for her at Port Royal ; unless a Queen is a woman of excep-

tional piety, it is almost impossible that she should not be the means of relaxing the discipline of a convent. These great ladies are so fastidious that it almost exceeds belief; and I see no reason for expecting that there will be a miracle in her case. Moreover '—and in these words that follow there is a sternness unusual to Angélique, and a bitterness which tells of disappointed hope—' moreover, kings and queens are as nothing in the sight of God, and their pomp and ostentation call forth His aversion rather than His love. They are born doubly children of His wrath, and there is scarcely any princess in whom the spirit and grace of God are to be found.'

Angélique soon discovered that her noble ladies made a pastime of their religion. In Paris she neither sought them nor avoided them; but she turned with longing towards Port Royal *des Champs*, which would not be so attractive as a *retreat* for penitents who wished to spend a few days or weeks in seclusion.

D'Andilly had now renounced the world and joined his nephews, the Recluses. He had been preceded by his second son Charles Henry Arnauld, known as M. de Luzanci who had been converted by St. Cyran. De Luzanci began life as a page in Richelieu's service, and speedily obtained the Cardinal's favour and a commission in the army; but at twenty he left the world and joined his cousins at Port Royal, where also his young brother Jules was at school.

Many years before this time, Angélique, in a dream, saw her sister Mdme. le Maître and her brother d'Andilly coming to her at Port Royal *des Champs;* d'Andilly was on horseback and his sister was riding behind him, and they were both very sad and grave. Her dream was now fulfilled; Mdme. le Maître was a nun and d'Andilly a Recluse. But he was not sad; it would have been impossible to subdue his indomitable gaiety, or to have made him any other than the d'Andilly, whose eager, happy, hopeful nature had for more than forty years surrounded him with friends and converts. 'We used to teaze him,' says Mdme. de Sevigné, 'and tell him that he liked best to save the souls that were in beautiful bodies.' But no one ever doubted that it was the souls he loved; and no shadow of impurity ever rested upon him even in those corrupt times. He was warmly attached to his wife, his children, his sisters, his friends. His wife was dead, and sons and daughters, nephews and nieces, all were congregated at Port Royal; when he joined them he may be considered to have retired into the bosom of his family rather than to have renounced the world.

He took leave of the Queen-Mother, and, alluding to the report that the Recluses occupied their time in making wooden shoes, entreated her Majesty not to believe it if she was told that he was making shoes; but he said that if she heard he was cultivating wall-fruit that would be quite true, and he hoped to send her Majesty some of the produce of his garden. He did so every year, and Mazarin used to laugh and say that the baskets were full of consecrated fruit.

Fontaine, who joined the Recluses in 1644, when he was twenty years old, gives a charming picture of d'Andilly. Fontaine did not write his Memoirs until he was himself an old man, and he makes the mistake of saying that d'Andilly was eighty when he first saw him. He was in reality fifty-seven, for he was born in 1588, and left Paris for Port Royal in 1645 or 1646. The impression which he produced on the mind of the young man is admirably given: 'I confess,' says Fontaine, 'that I am even now carried away by my feelings when I think of the intense vitality of that holy Recluse. Age, which impairs everything, seemed only to have renewed his vigour. I seem to see and hear him now, as he speaks to me with that eager look, those animated words and gestures. His whole appearance gave the lie, as one may say, to his great age; and at eighty years old he had the activity of a youth of fifteen. His bright eyes; his quick, firm step; his voice of thunder; his erect carriage, and healthy, vigorous frame; his white hair which formed such a striking contrast to the bright colour of his face; his grace in mounting a horse and riding it; his marvellous memory; his ready wit; his manual dexterity which was shown as much in his manner of holding a pen as in the way he pruned his fruit-trees—all these were a kind of immortality; they were, as St. Jérome says, a foreshadowing of the future resurrection of the body, and, if one may presume to say it, they were the reward of admirable virtue. Throughout his whole life he combined the most opposite, almost antagonistic qualities; the courtesy acquired in good society, together with great simplicity of manner; a keen penetrating intellect with almost incredible guilelessness; and heroic generosity with profound humility.'

D'Andilly's time was not engrossed by his garden. He caused the marsh, which was the fruitful source of fever and ague at Port Royal, to be drained; made a conduit for the water, and laid out terraces and garden walks. A large unwholesome pond was allowed to remain; but still the place was so much improved that the Recluses thought their ardent wish might now be granted. Angélique and her nuns could return to Port Royal, and they would present to the world such a spectacle as it had not seen for many ages and yet one that was in conformity with the rules of their order; namely, a community of devout men and women, some bound by irrevocable vows and others only seeking a temporary retreat; all united by the bonds of common faith and common worship, and all endeavouring to realize the ideal of spiritual communion. They were to be to each other nothing more than a voice, heard at rare intervals through the grated window of a convent parlour.

In 1646 Angélique revisited her former home for the first time since she had left it twenty years previously. She was accompanied by Mdme. d'Aumont, the widow of Field-Marshal d'Aumont, a lady who lived at Port Royal from this time until her death in 1658, and who earned and well deserved the esteem and respect of the whole sisterhood. She was a compensation to them for Mdme. de Pontcarré; her piety and charity were accompanied by genuine humility, and she was an almost solitary example of a great lady, not bound by any vows, living contentedly in a convent. She identified herself with the interests of Port Royal, and part of her large fortune was devoted to paying some of the debts which weighed so heavily on Angélique's conscience.

Mdme. le Maître, or Sister Catherine de St. Jean, also accompanied Angélique, and so did their younger brother Arnauld—the 'little, dark, ugly man,' who must have formed a striking contrast to the florid, handsome d'Andilly. Father Singlin completed the party.

There was no accommodation for the Abbess and her suite in the deserted convent; and, therefore, M. Pallu, a Recluse who had formerly been a doctor of medicine, gave up his house to them. Angélique stayed three days, and visited every part of her old domain. D'Andilly accompanied her everywhere, pointed out all his improvements, inspected the outlying farms, and made plans for the erection of twelve hermitages to be occupied by as many recluses. He showed that it would be quite easy to secure ample accommodation for them all and also for the schools and tutors to be grouped around the sacred centre, the great heart of their devotion—their very dear and very Reverend Mother Angélique.

The Abbess was convinced that St. Cyran would have approved of her return and had foreseen it when he urged her not to sell the woodwork of the dormitory, still she would not decide on undertaking it at that time without much prayer and the advice of competent persons. On her return to Paris, everything seemed favourable to the enterprise. The Archbishop and the Queen-Regent, who had refused all previous applications, now gave their consent. Anne of Austria was guided in this matter by her Jesuit advisers, who thought that the return of the nuns must, of necessity, scatter the detested band of Recluses. 'There are forty students there,' they said of Port Royal ; 'and forty writers, whose pens are all guided by one and the same hand.'

When Angélique received the Archbishop's permission to return, she summoned the Sisters to the chapter-house and informed them of it. At first they were overwhelmed with sorrow, for they thought she intended to leave them in Paris, and reside in the country with a few companions ; they threw themselves weeping at her feet, and implored her to take them all with her. She replied that she should divide her time between the two monasteries, and take them with her in turns, and added that her conscience had always reproached her for leaving the country convent, and they must rejoice with her at the relief she now experienced.

She made two journeys to Port Royal *des Champs* in 1647, in order to inspect the repairs, and after one of these visits wrote to the Queen of Poland : 'God is served much more faithfully there than He can ever be in Paris. It is marvellous to see the silence, the decorous behaviour and piety of the very workmen ; they are preparing for us with as much reverence as if we were angels.'

On the 13th of May, 1648, all was prepared ; the Recluses had made ready for the accommodation of a small number, and Angélique, accompanied by two lay-sisters and seven nuns, two of whom were d'Andilly's daughters, said farewell to the Paris community. The nuns who were left behind followed her weeping to the convent door, and the nuns who went with her wept also. The first were parting with Angélique, and the last were leaving Agnes and Anne, who remained with the Paris sisterhood. About two in the afternoon they arrived at Port Royal, and as soon as they reached their own domain, the church bells were rung and they saw a crowd of people at the convent gates. These were the poor who had come to welcome them home. Many women had known Angélique twenty-eight years before, when she was the *Good* Mdme. de Port Royal, the young Abbess who fed and clothed the poor, cared for their souls and bodies also. Now they threw themselves at the feet of the worn and aged woman, clasped her round the neck and pressed her in their arms, as if she belonged to them, and they had got their own again. Her joy was as great as theirs; she returned their embraces, although 'many of the women were very dirty, and if one could judge by appearances there must have been plenty of vermin about them.' This was not, however, a point which would have attracted Angélique's attention at any time, for she was in the habit of ignoring what she considered matters of detail. She saw the poor and the aged whom she had cherished in bygone years, and her heart yearned towards them. Behind them stood another band waiting silently at the church-door, a priest in front of them holding a cross. They were the Recluses, Angélique's kinsmen and their companions, who stood waiting to greet her. The Abbess and her companions entered the church, and the Recluses, who were admitted by a different door and occupied the chancel, followed them; the church-bells were still pealing as they all chanted together a joyful *Te Deum*. This was their first and only meeting. Some of the Recluses went to *Les Granges*, a farmhouse on the hill side, and others to private dwellings, which they had erected. The gates of the monastery were closed on the nuns, and the only communication they had from that time forth with the Recluses was in the little convent parlour.

Angélique was very happy. She told her nuns about the good old times when she and her sisters were young, gave an account of their hopes and fears, their prayer and penance, their sacred enthusiasm and zeal in the service of God. Her companions were carried away by her eloquent words, and there was a revival which affected the Recluses as well as the nuns. It was doubtless at this time that the following letter, bearing no date, was addressed by le Maître to the community.

'Although I am only a miserable sinner, overwhelmed by the consciousness of my sins at this very hour, yet I have received too many proofs of the supreme and ineffable mercy of my Saviour, Jesus Christ, not to hope for conversion through His grace and by means of the prayers of His faithful servants. And, therefore, although I am unworthy so much as to speak to the most insignificant nun in this house, and the Reverend Abbess knows that I ought to hide myself in a hole in the earth, and there weep not only for my sins but even for my repentance which has been false and unworthy, yet I do not give up the hope that she and the good Sisters will grant the prayer of one who has resolved to live and die with the name and dress, not of their brother which he does not deserve, but of their servant.

'I should have made this humble prayer to the Reverend Abbess in person, and with her permission should have spoken and not written it to the Sisters; but I am afraid that tears would stifle my voice, and that my reverence for them would cover me with confusion. I have, therefore, thought it better to utter my supplication in these few lines, so that seeing it written they may consider it more attentively and may offer up more fervent prayers for him who, like a beggar and a wretched dog, will consider himself only too happy if God will condescend to feed him with the crumbs which fall from the sacred table which He has spread for the Sisters, and will make him a partaker of the humility, poverty, and obedience which by His grace have been so largely bestowed upon them. And all that I say for myself I say also on behalf of my dear brother de Séricourt.'

The Recluses felt for the nuns an enthusiastic admiration which le Maître's letter does not at all exaggerate, and a tender chivalrous affection shown chiefly in acts but occasionally in words also. Le Maître wrote to Mdme. St. Ange, St. Cyran's friend, urging her to join the community, and saying that if there was a Paradise upon earth it was to be found at Port Royal. He was recovering from an illness, and concludes his letter by saying: 'Pray do not forget poor brother Antoine who is once again on his feet and at your service, and also at the service of the nuns of Port Royal who are our Ladies, our Mistresses, and our Queens.'

Angélique was elected Abbess for the third time, in November, 1648, and frequently visited the Paris community; whilst Agnes returned for a time to Port Royal *des Champs.* She writes enthusiastically of the beauty of this sacred abode and so do the elder nuns whose early associations were connected with it, but the younger Sisters seem to have preferred Paris. There was no relaxation of the rule of seclusion when they were in the country, not even in favour of near relations, and Angélique did not like the Recluses to pay frequent visits to the convent parlour. She was strict in this respect and was faithfully obeyed; but Agnes did not approve of her solitude, and wrote to le Maître :—

'MY VERY DEAR NEPHEW,

' I think you must imagine that I have gone back to Paris or have been excommunicated since you have not deigned to ask to see me for so long a time. Therefore using my authority as aunt and venerable old lady, I desire you to come at noon to-day to the parlour of St. Madeleine, where I intend to reproach you for shutting yourself up; but this does not prevent me from remaining your very affectionate Aunt.'

The peaceful life which to all the Arnaulds seemed a foretaste of the joys of heaven was rudely interrupted. In 1649, the first Fronde broke out and filled Paris and the surrounding country with the miseries of civil war.

It has been impossible within the narrow limits of this volume to dwell upon the political aspects of events connected with Port Royal. In the present instance it is unnecessary. Self-interest drew French nobles and French generals from one side to the other, and whether Marshal Turenne should serve Condé or the King depended not on his principles, his sympathies, or the justice of the cause, but on which side could make him the largest promises. The civil war in England characterized throughout by its profound religious and political earnestness was at an end, and the commonwealth under Cromwell had been established at the very time when Mdme. de Longueville decided in favour of a second civil war in France because she did not wish to join her husband in Normandy. The Fronde was neither an imitation of what had so recently taken place in England, nor a precursor of the French revolution of 1789. Religion and liberty had no part in it, and the people no expectation of advantage from the success of either side. Richelieu had humbled the nobles, and they made one final effort to regain the power which they had lost. Self-interest was their sole motive, and the history of the Fronde is a story not of war but of intrigue.

With intrigue and counter-intrigue Angélique had nothing to do, but the condition of the victims of the war excited her deepest compassion. There was an amount of misery on all sides of Port Royal which taxed even the large resources of her boundless charity.

Abbesses and nuns from neighbouring convents, and ladies who were the wives or daughters of her country neighbours, sought safety in a convent known to be protected by the Recluses. She received them gladly, and encouraged the Sisters to deprive themselves of their simple accommodation in order to offer it to others. But her warmest sympathies were enlisted by the peasants, and her most ardent wish was to save them from robbery and violence. She could not shelter them, but she could at least try to save their stores of provision and their portable property. As soon as this was known they flocked to her with everything they could carry,—corn, peas, beans, cooking utensils, coffers, packets, and even their bread. The house was already full ; there was but little spare room for storing away all that was brought to them, and Angélique, seeing no other alternative, threw open the great doors of the church, offered to the poor the house of God, and received them and their humble treasures within the cloistered precincts. Night and day the door was opened at their demand, and many came daily to take their daily supply of food. The nuns were fairly exhausted by incessant work and watching, but who could show signs of weariness in well-doing when their Abbess was among the first to devote herself to the needs of others ? She received the goods, had them ticketed and arranged so as to avoid disorder and confusion, and when the aisles of the church were filled, she did not scruple to make use of the nave also. 'Our monastery,' say the Memoirs, 'reminded us of Noah's Ark, in which there were all kinds of beasts. For whichever way we turned there was nothing to be seen but horses, sheep, and cows, and our courtyard was full of fowls.'

Angélique was informed that she was incurring great danger; several officers had been heard to say that as they could find nothing in the villages they would certainly go and pillage the monastery. She replied that she did not believe they would do anything of the kind, and even if she did she should not be deterred from doing her duty by fear of the consequences. Besides, did not God listen to the prayers of the poor which were offered up for them daily and hourly?

Some of the nuns entreated her to make a *cache* and hide the few ornaments and articles of value which were in the sacristy and on the altars ; she answered sternly that she would not consent to do anything of the kind. Certainly Angélique Arnauld looking after her property would offer a new and unexpected spectacle. She explained to the timid Sisters that their suggestion was not even prudent, for if the soldiers found no valuables where they had a right to expect them, they would be sure to pillage the monastery; and she added that if they came she should give them everything worth having with her own hands, so that they might go away the sooner.

Only a few of the well-to-do peasants had money or stores to conceal ; the greater number of them were reduced to absolute destitution. Angélique caused enormous quantities of bread and soup to be prepared and supplied daily to those who were in the greatest need. From time to time throughout the day she went to the kitchen to inspect the huge cauldrons, and if the soup was not good she made the cooks taste it in her presence, and asked if they could eat it themselves like that, and how they had the conscience to give it to the poor. Then she would have onions fried and added to give it flavour, and would see that it was not only good but appetizing. The expense was great and Port Royal poor, but this was not a time to think of ways and means, her only concern was to give away as much as possible. Thanks, doubtless, to d'Andilly's care, the abbey gardens had been very productive. There was a large stock of apples and pears for winter use, as well as of beetroot, which, with peas and milk, formed the food of the nuns during Lent. Angélique first of all distributed large baskets of apples and pears, giving them out after the soup ; when they were all consumed she bethought her that, if she gave away the beetroot which took up considerable space, there

would be more food for starving wretches, and she could take
charge of additional property for the peasants.

It is not merely what Angélique does, it is the manner in
which she does it which is so charming ; not only her dauntless
courage in the face of difficulties, but the happy brightness
with which she encounters them.   She astonished her companions by indefatigable activity, but still more by the ' marvellous joy' which animated her.   When she ehhorted the
poor to have courage and take patience for God was looking
upon their sorrows and their suffering and would have compassion upon them, it is no wonder that they believed her to
be inspired, and that the help she gave them seemed nothing
short of miracles wrought in their favour.   All her letters
written at the time contain vivid pictures of the scenes she
witnessed.   In April 1649, when the worst was over, she wrote
to Port Royal in Paris : ' We will do the utmost we can, my
very dear Sister, to hire a horse and send you the rest of the
dresses ; our own horses and asses are dead.   It is a sad thing
to reflect on all our misfortunes ; war is a horrible scourge.   It
is a marvel that men and beasts are not all dead from having
been so long shut up together.   We had horses in the room
beneath us, and horses opposite us in the chapter-house,
whilst in a cellar there were forty cows belonging to us and
some of the poor peasants.

' All the courts were full of fowls, turkeys, ducks and geese,
and when we could not take in any more they said : ' Keep
them yourselves if you like, we would rather you had them
than the soldiers.'   Our church was so full of wheat, oats, peas,
beans, pots, kettles, and all kinds of rags that we had to walk
over them to get into the choir, and when we reached it the
floor was covered with books piled up, belonging to our hermits.
Moreover there were ten or twelve nuns who had taken refuge
with us.   All the women servants from Les Granges were inside
the abbey and the men out : the farm buildings were full of the
halt and maimed and wounded, and the outer courts were full
of cattle.   In fact if it had not been for the great cold we
must have had the plague ; still the cold itself added to our
discomfort for our fuel failed, and we dared not send to the
woods to fetch more.

' And yet with all this God was so present with us and helped
us so mightily, that in one sense we were not sad ; and the

extreme misery of the poor who were hiding in the woods to escape butchery made us see that God had been only too good to us. There is nothing now to be had at any price, for every place has been pillaged and ravaged. Indeed it is a terrible thing to see our poor country. I did not intend to tell you all this, but my heart is so full of pity and sorrow that I write on without knowing it.'

During this period the Recluses were the 'guardian angels' of the nuns. They left Les Granges to which they had retreated the previous summer, and came down to the valley to guard Port Royal. ' Our good hermits,' writes Angélique, ' girded on their swords again for our defence, and they also threw up such strong barricades, that it would have been difficult to take us by assault.'

The Paris community was even worse off than the country sisterhood. Their chief danger was from famine. With considerable difficulty a store of provisions was from time to time forwarded to them, conveyed by a strong guard of Recluses. Before long it was manifest that so large a number of women, many of them quite young, were not safe in an outlying faubourg of Paris. Angélique proposed to send for them to the country, and have them all under her own charge, but this plan was quite impracticable. A charitable friend offered the loan of a house in a safe part of the city, and it was decided that Agnes, who was the Prioress, Mdme. d'Aumont and some thirty or forty of the younger nuns and pupils, should be sent thither on the 11th January, 1649. But when they were about to set out the inhabitants of the neighbourhood, who considered the presence of these holy women a security to them, refused to allow them to leave the convent. On the following morning, therefore, M. le Nain—father of the historian le Nain de Tillemont—and M. de Bernières who lent the house, wearing their robes as magistrates, were obliged to escort them through the streets ; the nuns formed a procession, in which the white scapulary and scarlet cross of their Order would form a striking feature. They walked on in silence and quite calmly, although many of the Sisters thought they were setting out on foot to join Angélique in the country !

It was difficult to contrive accommodation for so many in a small house, and there was but little comfort or convenience for them. They were liable to all the alarms of war, and had good cause for anxiety when they thought of the friends and companions from whom they were separated, and the difficulty of procuring their supplies. The present and future must have been dark enough, but Agnes Arnauld was at their head, and her courage animated them all. She thanked God daily for the opportunity He had granted them of making a sacrifice of all that had hitherto conduced to their comfort, rebuked all selfish fears and hopes, found employment for all in cutting out and making clothes for the poor, and three months later led back her little band in a higher state of discipline than when they left the gates of Port Royal.

The older nuns who had remained in the convent were under the care of Marie des Anges,[1] who had returned from Maubuisson the previous year, and of Anne Arnauld. There was no relaxation of discipline among them, although they were exposed to continual alarms, and incurred considerable risk. They had recourse to 'extraordinary penance' in order to try and appease the anger of God, but in other respects their rules and customs were unchanged during this troublous time.

The result of Angélique's noble charity during the war, of the self-sacrifice of the Recluses, the piety of the Sisters, and the protection of the Archbishop, was to fill Port Royal to overflowing. In May 1651 there were two hundred and twenty-eight persons in the Paris and country houses, including pupils and Recluses, and the numbers increased from day to day. The Recluses received as many accessions as the nuns, and their rank and acquirements made them as formidable in the eyes of the Jesuits as their numbers.

But death was already diminishing the number of the Arnaulds. Magdalen Arnauld, little Madelon, Angélique's youngest sister, had been a great sufferer for twenty years. In February 1649 she died, 'deprived of the great consolation' of seeing Angélique. In 1650 de Séricourt died, the gallant young soldier, brother of le Maître, who had given up all that he had to follow Christ. He was his mother's favourite child, and his death affected her deeply. Three months later she also died, and Angélique lost the sister, who in the world and the convent had been her faithful friend and trusted adviser. Mdme. le Maître, or Sister Catherine as she was called after she took the veil, was in the country house with Angélique during

[1] See page 141.

the war, and her tender compassion and boundless charity
gained all hearts. On her death-bed she wrote the letter to
Mdme. de Longueville previously inserted,[1] and she was consoled by the ministrations of her fourth son, de Saci, who had
two years previously received priest's orders and been appointed
Confessor of Port Royal *des Champs.*

Our Abbess was re-elected for the fourth time in 1652, and
she then resolved to build new dormitories for the country
house and raise the pavement of the church, which was many
feet below the level of the ground. This work which provided employment for a large number of destitute labourers
was commenced and completed in troubled times. War had
again broken out, and the country was so unsettled that it was
thought necessary to remove the Sisters to Paris. They were
guarded by a strong escort, and Angélique and fifty nuns
reached the Faubourg St. Jacques without any adventure. A
few of the aged nuns courageously remained at Port Royal, in
order to distribute alms to the destitute, and to keep open the
soup kitchen, which supplied two hundred peasants with food.

The second Fronde affected the Sisters very differently from
the first. It was no longer the peasantry who thronged around
Angélique seeking help, but nuns from all the convents in the
neighbourhood of the capital who, on the approach of the rival
armies, sought refuge in Paris.

The Sisters in a convent at Etampes received notice that
they were in danger. They set out immediately for Paris, and
reached it about nine o'clock at night. Some of them had
friends in the city but knew not where to find them, others
were friendless. It was quite dark, they had no guide, no
guard, and did not know where to seek shelter and safety.
Worn out with fear and fatigue they could bear up no longer,
and began to weep bitterly. They were in the Faubourg St.
Jacques, and as they passed Port Royal one of them remembered
that her sister had known Mdme. le Maître, and had often told
her of the good Abbess Angélique. She bade her companions
be of good cheer, Mdme. de Port Royal would take them in.

When Angélique heard that a whole community of poor
terrified women stood at her gates, not knowing which way to
turn nor how to escape the dangers of the night, her heart
yearned towards them as if they had been her own flesh and

---

[1] See page 229.

blood. This was no time for considering the rules and regulations which forbade an Abbess to receive members of another community without the permission of her Superior. 'Charity is above law,' she said and took them in. The house was already overcrowded, her own two communities more than filled it, and there were also many strangers who had obtained leave to stay at Port Royal until the war was at an end. Angélique's first consideration for the twenty-five new comers was to give them their supper. Now, fortunately, the nuns had prepared their next day's dinner over night; a novice, Jacqueline Pascal, was going to take the veil, and they all wished to be present at the ceremony and the sermon. There was food, therefore, for the tired Sisters and they were urged and encouraged to eat. Next came the more difficult task of finding beds for them. Nearly all the Port Royal nuns were already in bed and asleep, but when they heard voices and quick steps in the dormitory they were soon out of their cells, for they were living in the midst of dangers. 'When we found that it was not a troop of soldiers in the house, but a band of nuns worn out with fatigue for whom there were no beds, we turned back again and began to gather together all that we had. There was nothing to be met in the passages and on the stairs but Sisters dragging their beds, pillows, coverlets, mattresses, and doing it with the heartiest good-will.'

When the Archbishop was informed of what had taken place he expressed great satisfaction at Angélique's conduct, and gave her a general permission to receive all and any nuns who applied to her. This was noised abroad and numerous were the demands upon her charity and hospitality. On the 15th of September, 1652, she wrote to M. de Barcos, St. Cyran's nephew: 'More than four hundred nuns, of different orders, sought refuge with us during the war, which seems to me a special mark of God's providence. It has given us a little work but not, thank God, too much excitement and distraction. On the contrary, what we have seen has given us good reason for recognizing our great obligations towards God, and those whom He has pleased to send to instruct us in our duties (chief among them the author of all our happiness, M. de St. Cyran, our good Father who is now with God). The spiritual destitution of these poor nuns has been something terrible to witness, and many of them were strongly prejudiced against us.

They are now undeceived, and even think more highly of us than they ought to do ; for they judge us by our rules and maxims and well-regulated household. Many have been converted, and eight of the number have remained with us altogether. We have sometimes had as many as fifty in a day, and yet have had no difficulty in supplying them with food ; and although our total number in the convent has sometimes amounted to a hundred and eighty, there has been no confusion or irregularity. Never have the Sisters maintained more profound silence, and never have we experienced less difficulty in procuring the means of subsistence, although provisions have been a third dearer than in any previous year. I humbly entreat you, my father, to ask God to make us truly grateful for all His mercies. . . . I tremble to think how unworthy we are of the special favour God has shown us.'

One day a Sister came to demand shelter and hospitality who wore a tight-fitting scapulary with a busk, which may have recalled to Angélique the whalebone corset of her youth. The sister also had gloves, and her demeanour was quite unlike that of a nun. Angélique looked at her, and immediately reprimanded her severely ; then saying : 'Daughter, I cannot allow our Sisters to see you in this condition,' she took away the busk and the gloves, and flung them down. The poor nun stood speechless, and could not regain her equanimity even when the Abbess brought food and spoke kindly to her.

On another occasion she noticed that a Sister who entered the room wore her hair in curls. She made her take off her coif, comb out the curls and arrange her hair simply ; then with a stern rebuke bade her, when she next went to confession, tell the Father that she was a hypocrite.

One day at the conference there was a nun from Poissy who said that in her convent they had cut off part of the chants as a mortification.

' You would have done much better,' said Angélique, ' if you had cut off the tails of your gowns.'

Many of her sayings in later years show stern impatience with the vanity and foolish affectation which had excited her compassion when she was young, and she not unfrequently inspired awe rather than affection. ' I assure you, sir,' said Mdme. d'Aumont to le Maître, ' that I get on better with la Mère Agnes ; la Mère Angélique is too severe for me.' Le

Maître himself acknowledged that he was afraid of her. But her severity was shown to folly and vice, and she never lost her compassionate tenderness for misfortune or suffering. One day she was talking to the novices somewhat sternly about the performance of their duty, and the difference between a halting and a vigorous performance of them, when looking round she saw the sad expression of a lame nun's face. 'Come, come, daughter,' she said, 'don't make yourself unhappy, for the lame walk as quickly in Paradise as any others.'

When the war was at an end she prepared for a return to Port Royal *des Champs* for she had been in exile in Paris, and in January 1653 she returned with an increased number of Sisters to her early home. The Recluses retired to Les Granges and their respective dwellings. During the war they had resided at Port Royal, which they defended by means of intrenchments, and towers built on the walls. The old soldiers among them had resumed their swords, the men of peace and the labourers had been drilled and trained, and military zeal bad fair to rival religious ardour.

But de Saci, the young priest and Confessor, looked on at first in silent and before long in open disapproval. The Recluses yielded, resumed their peaceful avocations, and wielded no other weapons than the hoe, the spade, and the trowel. Still there was a division among them which threatened grievous results. Owing to the overcrowded condition of the house—for there were, including the labourers employed upon the dormitories and church, some three hundred men—an epidemic broke out, of which a considerable number died. M. Hamon, a retired physician, resumed his lancets and was in most cases fatal. The Duke de Luines and d'Andilly thereupon each introduced an unauthorized practitioner, one of whom treated every malady with pills, and the other with powders, and there was a division amongst the Recluses as to whether they ought to die at the hands of the faculty or the quack. De Saci again found it necessary to interfere, and he did so in favour of M. Hamon's lancet. The empirics disappeared, and there was peace in Port Royal; but the Memoirs say that the position of de Saci was something like that of Moses in the midst of the children of Israel whom he had led into the wilderness.

CHAPTER XXIII.

THE Bull of Pope Urban VIII. dated 1641, but not promulgated until 1643, interdicted any resumption of the dispute on grace and had therefore prohibited the publication of Jansen's *Augustinus*, though without naming it. It was in reference to this bull that St. Cyran said : ' They are going too far ; we must teach them their duty.' The prohibition came too late ; the *Augustinus* had been already brought out at the Fair of Frankfort in 1640, and received with acclamation by the Calvinists in Holland. It reached Paris in 1641, and speedily excited the theological world. A second edition was published at Rouen in 1643, and the Paris pulpits began to resound with attacks on Jansen, who was called a Calvin 'warmed up.' Perhaps no book so famous as the *Augustinus* has ever been so little read. Sainte-Beuve compares it to an overloaded cannon which bursts within the fortress, and does more injury to friends than enemies. Under no circumstances could it have become popular since it is written in Latin, and it may well be doubted whether it would have excited so fierce a controversy if it had not been identified with Port Royal, which the Jesuits detested and were determined to crush ; and it is more than probable that its doctrines would not have been so well known if Pascal had not defended them in his immortal Provincial Letters.

The *Augustinus* consists of a selection from the works of St. Augustine, passages chosen and arranged so as to form a complete theological system. Jansen thought St. Augustine's works contained those true and pure doctrines which had been lost sight of in later times,[1] and he spent his life in discovering

[1] See page 188.

and preparing to promulgate them.   The whole system rests upon the belief that man since the Fall has been lost in sin, and can only be redeemed by the grace of God.   No man has a right to claim or expect this grace ; for all have fallen.   God gives it to whom He will, and withholds it from whom He will.   Predestination is the eternal decree by which God has resolved to withdraw and except certain persons from their just doom, whilst He leaves others to perish.   We know nothing of the motives of this preference, and can simply refer it to the Divine will.

These doctrines in our own times are distinguished as Calvinistic or Evangelical, and in the seventeenth century the Jesuits pointed triumphantly to the fact that their enemies at Port Royal were guided by a man whose doctrines were identical with those of the arch heretic of Geneva.   Some of the Arnaulds were Huguenots, and le Maître's father had lived and died a Protestant, so that the charge of Calvinism was once more urged against them.

The Jesuits protested against Jansen's works but Rome was silent, for, though unwilling to favour Calvin, she was equally unwilling to condemn St. Augustine.

The Jesuits accused Port Royal of despising the Sacraments of the Roman Catholic Church and being in alliance with Geneva.   Arnauld replied by learned apologies in defence of Jansen.   Father Brisacier, who had failed to procure the condemnation of Arnauld's book *On Frequent Communion* returned from Rome more bitter than ever in consequence of his defeat ; he now attacked the nuns of Port Royal, calling them ' Foolish Virgins, deriders of the Sacraments, impenitent, devoid of religion and morality.'   Mdme. d'Aumont and Angélique wrote to the Archbishop of Paris in 1651, called his attention to Father Brisacier's *Jansenism unveiled*, and appealed to him for protection.   The Archbishop prohibited the sale of the book, and ordered a copy of his censure of the Reverend Father to be fixed against the doors of every church in his diocese.   He also imitated the policy of Rome, and forbad any further mention of the controversy on Grace.   But in 1649 Nicholas Cornet, Syndic of the Faculty of Theology at Paris, had asked that seven abstruse propositions referring to Grace should be examined, and their orthodoxy or heresy decided.   Seventy doctors protested against any reopening of the discussion, but ultimately the propositions, reduced to five, were submitted to Pope Innocent X. and a congregation of Cardinals and Assessors, and condemned by a bull issued in 1653. All the propositions were declared heretical, and the first and fifth were also called impious and blasphemous.[1] It was not directly asserted that these propositions were to be found in the *Augustinus*, though the Pope's bull attributed the dispute to its publication and certainly implied that they were extracted from it.

The triumph of the Jesuits was almost complete; their enemies were heretics in the eyes of the Church; they were resolved that they should be heretics in the eyes of the people also. On the frontispiece of an almanac, of which Angélique says that 16,000 copies were sold or distributed, Jansen was represented with his bishop's robes and the devil's wings, hoofs, and horns, flying before the Pope, who hurled thunderbolts at him and his followers. A farce was performed in the Jesuit College in Paris, in which Jansen was carried off by devils; whilst in a public procession of students at the Jesuit College of Mâcon, Jansen was represented in chains, and led prisoner by 'saving grace.' Before long the words *saving grace* and *predestination* were considered suspicious.

The Jansenists revenged themselves on the Jesuits for the almanac and the farce by recounting how a certain bishop who was visiting an abbey in his diocese, entered the refectory at meal-time and heard the words: 'For it is God which worketh in you, both to will and to do of His pleasure.' He sternly bade the reader be silent and bring him the book. To his

---

[1] These propositions were as follows :—

1. Some of God's commands cannot possibly be obeyed by just men; they desire and strive to keep them, but have only their own strength and not the grace of God, by which alone it is possible to obey Him.

2. In the state of fallen nature there is no resistance to the action of internal grace.

3. In a state of fallen nature imputed merit and demerit do not depend on free will exempt from the necessity of action; it is enough if there is free will exempt from constraint.

4. The Semi-Pelagians admitted the necessity of preventing grace in every action, even the first beginnings of faith; they were heretics because they said that this grace was of such a nature that the will of man had power to accept or reject it.

5. It is a Semi-Pelagian error to say that Jesus Christ died or shed His blood for all men without exception.

great surprise he found that it was one of the Epistles of St. Paul!

All good Catholics accepted the Pope's decree, and acknowledged that the Five Propositions were heretical, but the Jansenists had still a point in their favour. There had been no indication of the page or chapter of the *Augustinus*, in which the propositions were to be found, and they said it was a mistake to attribute them to Jansen, since the words were not his nor the meaning either. And thereupon arose the celebrated dispute concerning the *droit* and the *fait*. The *droit* was the justice of the Papal censure of the propositions, which all Catholics admitted; and the *fait* was the existence of the propositions in Jansen's *Augustinus*, which the Jansenists denied. The great Arnauld was an untiring controversialist : letters of 250 pages, pamphlets, volumes, were poured from his ready pen in defence of Jansen's doctrines, and to prove that the heretical propositions were not contained in his works and did not represent his true meaning. It was necessary therefore to silence Arnauld also; and in 1656, he was censured. expelled from the Sorbonne, and all his writings declared heretical and placed in the Index. Whilst the Doctors of the Sorbonne were deliberating on his sentence, the Recluses at Port Royal were urging Arnauld to defend his views : ' Are you going to let them condemn you like a child, without saying a word and without letting the public know what are the points in dispute.' He accordingly drew up a reply, doubtless very long and learned, and read it aloud to his friends. They listened in silence. No one praised it. Arnauld said : ' I see that you don't like my paper, and I think you are right.' Then he turned to Blaise Pascal, who had recently joined them. ' Now you,' he said, ' who are young, why don't you do something?'

Pascal set to work at once and wrote the first of his ' Letters to a Provincial from one of his Friends;' or, as they are called, ' The Provincial Letters.' On the following day it was read to the Recluses. ' That is excellent!' exclaimed Arnauld. ' that's exactly what is wanted! We must print that.' And on the 23rd of January, 1656, nine days after Arnauld's condemnation, it was published.

Blaise and Jacqueline Pascal had been attracted to Port Royal in the first place by a disciple of St. Cyran, and there could be no more important acquisition than a man whose scientific eminence was at that time unrivalled. On the death of their father, Jacqueline entered Port Royal during the Fronde, and took the veil in 1653, whilst her brother Blaise joined the Recluses in 1655. The excitement produced by Pascal's first letter was very great, and increased with each one that succeeded it. The first three letters are occupied with the subtle disputes on grace and free-will, and the all-absorbing questions of *droit* and *fait*. But in the fourth Pascal leaves these subjects in order to expose the corruptions of Jesuit morality and attack the writings of the Casuists; and from these attacks, which were the first of their kind, the Jesuits have never recovered. In the sixteenth letter the author refutes the calumnies so persistently uttered against Port Royal, and recurs in the seventeenth and eighteenth to the subjects discussed in the first. All the later letters cost him much time and labour. He apologizes for the length of the sixteenth, excusing himself on the ground that he had not had time to make it short. He worked at many of them for twenty days; writing and rewriting them six or seven times, and he is said to have rewritten the eighteenth no less than thirteen times. Those wonderful letters clear, eloquent, and incisive, so brilliant and playful and yet so earnest, hindered for a time, but could not avert the ruin of Port Royal.

All Paris listened and waited for their appearance, talked of the Five Propositions, Jansen's *Augustinus* and the question of *fait* and *droit*. But it is doubtful whether many of the nuns of Port Royal knew the *Provincial Letters* even by name.

Their lives were once more flowing on smoothly and in the old channels. Father Singlin's preaching, with its rugged power, was producing more effect than the most finished discourses. Their church was crowded every Sunday, and numerous were the converts who testified to the sincerity of the change which his words had wrought.

Angélique had been chosen Abbess at four successive triennial elections, and in 1654 she finally resigned her post. Her successor was that Marie des Anges, who had returned to Port Royal after twenty years' absence as Abbess of Maubuisson. Angélique was never again the nominal head of the community, and was relieved of some of the cares of office, but she occupied a place in the eyes of the Sisters, the Recluses, and the world, independent of title or office.

She had up to this time deserved the praise bestowed upon her by the Archbishop of Paris as an obedient daughter of the Church. She had submitted and was prepared to submit to all its decrees; but the events of the years that follow tended to draw her earnest mind away from the Church of Rome and assuredly in the direction of Protestantism. By slow degrees she began to exercise an independence of judgment which is incompatible with the intellectual and moral attitude required of a devout Catholic. She asked herself if a decree was right and not if it was ordained by the Pope, and she resolved to be faithful to the truth at the risk of imprisonment and excommunication.

But in 1654 she had not begun to contemplate the possibility of resisting the decrees of the Court of Rome.

When the bull of Innocent X. condemning the Five Propositions was promulgated, Port Royal deliberated as to the course to be adopted. St. Cyran's nephew M. de Barcos, who was now the Abbot de St. Cyran, urged that there must be no signature of the formulary of submission with which France was threatened, le Maître agreed with him, and it was decided that the Recluses must refuse to sign any condemnation of Jansen's writings, but that the nuns might submit to whatever was required of them.

In a letter written at the time, Angélique says that she does not pretend to understand the Five Propositions and therefore can neither receive nor reject them; moreover, submission is the duty of all and more especially of nuns who cannot dispute and argue: 'All we can do is to serve God in silence and by obedience to our rule, so that we should be doubly guilty if we did not submit. I can assure you that except myself, who by reason of my office am sometimes obliged to speak with persons not belonging to the convent and thus to hear what is going on, none of our sisters know anything of this matter.'

Agnes writes even more strongly: 'Don't give yourself any trouble about the bull any more than we do who are not at all uneasy about it. We condemn whatever it condemns without knowing what that may be. It is enough for us to know that it is issued by the Pope, and that as daughters of the Church we are bound to respect all the decrees of the Holy See.'

But before long ominous rumours reached the convent. The

opposition of the Recluses and their refusal to acknowledge
the decisions of the Pope were attributed to Angélique's influence, and it was asserted that she was to be sent to the
Bastille.   Her nephew le Maître told her of this report, and
said it was very unlikely that her enemies would do more than
send her to some distant monastery.   She replied, that this
would not trouble her; she had always desired to end her
days alone and apart.   She would take spectacles and lancets
with her; spectacles that she might study the Truth, and
lancets that she might be of some use in the world.

Her ascetic spirit led her to desire that the monastery to
which she was banished should be under Jesuit government:
'Nothing,' she says, 'would be such a trial as to have them
coming to convert me.'

It was suggested that even in such a convent the nuns would
be good to her, but she said she thought not; they would
believe they were doing God service if they got rid of an old
heretic.

Her time was spent chiefly at Port Royal *des Champs*, and in
interviews with le Maître and Arnauld she often urged them to
translate into French St. Bernard's treatise on grace, and the
works of any of the Fathers who held the same views as St.
Augustine, and this shows that she wished not merely to defend
Jansen's views but to promulgate them.   And then she would
suddenly exclaim, 'We must amend our lives, we must amend
our lives, that is the right way of rendering truth victorious!'

All her life she had been learning and teaching obedience,
and the habits of a lifetime clung about her and could not
easily be discarded.   St. Francis de Sales had required absolute submission, so had St. Cyran, so had every Director to
whom she had submitted her conscience, and it had been
granted.   She had recognized that obedience to a Director
implies a far more profound and humble submission to the
Pope, the Father of the Church; throughout her whole life
she had received those doctrines sanctioned by the Pope and
rejected those which he had declared to be contrary to the
Catholic faith, without any reference to the dictates of her
own intellect or conscience.   Now she was gradually drifting
into an attitude of opposition, and learning to uphold those
who ventured to assert the rights of their own individual
judgment.   When Arnauld was about to be condemned

by the Sorbonne and went into hiding to escape imprisonment, she wrote: 'I cannot help telling you, my very dear
brother, with what calmness and joy I saw you leave us to
suffer whatever it may please God to ordain for you whilst
you assert His Grace.   Indeed, so complete is my resignation,
that I have lost the fear with which natural affection and the
tenderness I have always felt for my poor little brother had
filled my heart.   I no longer dread the evils to which you are
exposed, they will turn out to be real advantages. . . . If your
name is struck out from among the doctors of the Sorbonne,
it will only be written the more plainly in the book of God.
. . . Whatever happens God is with you, and you will serve
His sacred cause better by your sufferings than by your writings.'

In the years between 1653 and 1656 she gradually learnt
to identify the cause of Jansen and St. Cyran with the cause
of Truth.   There is no further mention of submission to the
Pope, that is of absolute, unconditional submission, but only
of assent to decrees which do not imply any censure of the
great teacher of Port Royal.

The position was one of daily increasing danger, to which
Angélique was not blind.   The Recluses had made known
their decision not to sign any condemnation of Jansen's works.
She had taken up her position on their side.   The ranks of the
enemy received fresh accessions day by day.   Even Vincent
de Paul protested strongly against the Jansenists, and was
amongst those who urged their suppression.

The friendly Archbishop of Paris was dead.   His nephew
and successor Cardinal de Retz had been proscribed for his
conduct during the Fronde, and as Port Royal was faithful to
him it was accused of disloyalty as well as heresy, and denounced as a nest of traitors.   Mazarin's fears were aroused
when he was assured that it was a centre from which political
as well as religious disaffection was disseminated ; he espoused
the cause of the Jesuits and resolved upon the suppression of
the Jansenists.

The Recluses were the first to suffer, and Angélique wrote to
the Queen of Poland in 1656: 'The preparations for our dispersion are making rapid progress from day to day.   They
are only waiting for *water from the Tiber* to submerge our
monastery.   At one time we thought that it would be better
for the hermits to withdraw before they were turned out, but

they have entreated to be allowed to remain until the last
moment and until they are driven away from a spot which grows
dearer to them daily now that they see how short a time they
have to stay in it.'

But d'Andilly's influence was still considerable with the
Queen-Mother, and she could not be induced to consent to the
harsh proposals of her advisers. 'The Queen's behaviour,'
said Mazarin, ' is really admirable in this affair of the Jansenists.
When they are spoken of in general, she says they must all
be exterminated, but when it is proposed to root out two or
three, and begin with d'Andilly or some other, she cries out at
once, and says they are too good and too faithful to the King,
and she won't have it.'

However, her scruples were so far overcome, that in March
1656, although the formulary of submission had not been promulgated, she consented to the dispersion of the Recluses and
the breaking up of their schools. Even then she did not forget
d'Andilly, but informed him of what had been decided. He
wrote at once to the Queen and Cardinal Mazarin, saying that
it was not necessary to employ force, he and his friends would
submit and leave Port Royal at once. The Order in Council
was therefore revoked, and on the 27th of March, 1656, Angélique wrote to tell le Maître, who was in concealment with
Arnauld, that the pupils were scattered, the Recluses dispersed,
and d'Andilly, who was the last to go, had just set out for his
country seat at Pomponne. A few days later the *Lieutenant-Civil*
appeared to interrogate Angélique, and ascertain if any of the
Recluses still remained. As it was supposed that the proscribed Jansenist literature was issued from Port Royal, he
searched the buildings for printing presses ; but as they did
not exist he could not find them. He then tried in a long conversation with Angélique to induce her to acknowledge that the
Recluses formed a regularly constituted religious community,
and were amenable as such to established laws. This she denied ; they were hermits and solitaries, bound by no vows, free to
come and free to go, and to live apart or together as it might
seem good to them. During the conversation there was some
reference to Laubardemont and his visit, and the first dispersion
of the Recluses in 1638. 'Oh, Madam !' exclaimed the Lieutenant-Civil, ' for whom do you take me ? I am not Laubardemont, the butcher of Loudun !' He left her with expressions

of regret for the duty he had been compelled to perform, and of admiration for all that he had seen and heard in Port Royal.

There were rumours that this inspection was only the precursor of still more severe measures ; and it was asserted that the confessors of Port Royal were to be dismissed, and the nuns, both in Paris and the country, dispersed.　On the 6th of April, Angélique wrote to the Queen of Poland : 'At last the Queen has commanded the Assembly of the Clergy to treat us with the utmost rigour, and has said that she looks upon the matter as one that concerns herself.　I have no angry feeling against her Majesty ; I know that she believes she is doing a very good work, and that she is constantly told it would be impossible to do a better.　Our Saviour said that those who persecuted His servants would think they did God service. All that we have to desire is that we may suffer because we are His servants, and not because we are evil-doers.'

Angélique was prepared for the worst that could befall when unexpectedly there was a respite ; the persecution ceased, and the Port Royal nuns, from being denounced as heretics were in a fair way of being worshipped as saints.

A certain great-uncle of Angélique's, M. de la Potherie, a priest living in Paris, had a passion for collecting relics, and, among other treasures, believed that he had obtained possession of a thorn from the crown which our Saviour wore at His crucifixion.　When it had been placed in a fitting shrine he sent the thorn to Port Royal, that the nuns might behold and adore it.　Accordingly, on Friday, the 24th of March, 1656, the very day on which the Recluses were compelled to abandon Port Royal *des Champs*, a solemn procession of nuns, novices, and scholars, chanting appropriate psalms, moved along the choir to the altar, on which the sacred relic was deposited.　Each in turn kissed the Holy Thorn, first the nuns, then the novices, last the scholars.　Among the scholars was little Marguerite Périer, niece of Jacqueline Pascal, a child of ten years old, who for three years and a half had been afflicted with what was supposed to be *fistula lachrymalis* of the left eye, and the bones of the nose were said to be diseased.　As a last resource the operation of cautery had been resolved upon, and the child's father was on his way from Auvergne to be present when it was performed.　As this afflicted child in her turn approached the relic, Sister Flavie, who had taken the place of

Anne Arnauld as schoolmistress, said to her : ' Commend yourself to God, my child, and touch your eye with the Holy Thorn !'
and with this Sister Flavie herself took up the sacred relic and
pressed it to the child's face.

The ceremony ended, the Holy Thorn was restored to M. de
Potherie. But at night Sister Flavie overheard the child saying
to a companion, ' My eye does not hurt me now, the Holy
Thorn has cured it.' Sister Flavie approached, and could discover no difference between the diseased and the healthy eye.
She at once informed the Prioress, Agnes Arnauld, of the
miracle, who on the following day told the child's aunt, Jacqueline Pascal. It was not until five days later that M. de la
Potherie, the proprietor of the Thorn, was informed of the
miraculous cure ; and the doctor, who had not seen the child for
more than two months before the event, did not visit her again
until the 31st of March, a week after it. She was brought to
him without a word being said, and he began to press, and
probe, and examine ; he was asked if he did not remember
what a sore eye she had, and answered, ' That's what I am
looking for, but I see no traces of it.' Thereupon Sister Flavie
told him what had happened, and he asked if the cure was
instantaneous. She replied that it was and the child, when
appealed to, confirmed this statement. Upon which M. Delancé,
the doctor, said that he was ready to affirm upon oath that
such a cure could not have taken place without a miracle.
On the 14th of April seven physicians and surgeons drew up a
statement, in which they asserted that it was impossible the
child could have been instantaneously cured without a miracle ;
and the miracle began to be noised abroad.

M. Périer, Marguerite's father, was delighted to think his child
was spared a painful operation which he had most unwillingly
authorized. He spoke everywhere of the miracle, and soon
Paris and the Court were ringing with it. The Queen was
very unwilling to give it credence, the Jesuits said it was all
a trick, and that another child had been substituted for Marguerite Périer, whose eye was in the same condition it always
had been. The Queen therefore sent M. Felix, first surgeon
to her son Louis XIV., to report upon the case. He inquired
and examined, and said the child was undoubtedly cured,
that such instantaneous relief could be nothing else than the
work of God. Next appears upon the scene the Grand Vicar

of the Archbishop of Paris, who inquires, and approves, and verifies, and lends the sanction and approval of the Church to the miracle. Six months later, on Friday, October 27th, there is a solemn ceremony in the church of Port Royal in Paris. It is crowded with people although the rain falls fast. The Grand Vicar and numerous priests and deacons with lighted tapers and clouds of incense carry the Holy Thorn to a little altar which has been prepared for it. The nuns kneeling in the choir sing : 'Loose thyself from the bands of thy neck, O captive daughter of Zion ;' and little Marguerite, neatly dressed in grey and wearing a coif, kneels on high cushions, so that all the people who are pressing forwards and climbing to every point of vantage may be able to see her. There is a lighted taper before her, and a little chair behind, so that she may sit down when she is tired. As the ceremony proceeds the rain ceases, and soon the sunlight streams down upon the kneeling nuns, the little motionless figure in grey before the altar, the outstretched heads of the spectators, the gorgeous robes of the priests, and the heavy clouds of incense.

As the miracle had received the sanction of the Church, all devout Catholics were convinced that the nuns of Port Royal were holy women, and the reports spread against them wicked slanders. The Holy Thorn was begged by other communities. It was lent to the Ursulines and the Carmelites and worked no wonders with them ; but when it was sent back to Port Royal it yielded a harvest of miracles. Nuns came from all parts of France to touch the Holy Thorn, and more than eighty cures were effected, all of them upon women. It was the work of one nun to apply the sacred relic to rosaries, medals and linen which were brought to her. The Princess Palatine, sister of the Queen of Poland, was restored to health by the application of linen which had been touched by the Thorn ; and Henrietta Maria, widow of Charles I. and exiled Queen of England, made a pilgrimage to it. Every Friday crowds thronged to Port Royal to adore the sacred relic. Masses were said on that day from five o'clock until noon ; the congregations were so large that seats had to be secured months beforehand ; and soon the streets outside the church were full of people, watching the long string of carriages and their occupants, and the windows of houses which overlooked the

Faubourg St. Jacques were let to sight-seers who were afraid
of the crowded streets.

Protestant readers will consider it equally unprofitable to enter
into any discussion as to the genuineness of the miracle or of the
Thorn. And yet on behalf of the miracle it must be urged
that Pascal, Arnauld and le Maître, the man of genius, the great
scholar, and the learned advocate, all believed it ; that Angélique, whose integrity and truth we dare not presume to doubt,
received it ; and that it was attested by surgeons and physicians
who, although not very able men, were probably honest. In
fact, there is such a mass of overwhelming evidence in its
favour that it is only when we discover that Sister Flavie, on
whom so much depended, was, by her own confession seven
years later, a liar and an impostor, that we get an inkling of
the manner in which the deception was practised. It is not impossible that a physician's diagnosis should be incorrect, and
that there was a mistake as to the nature of the disease from
which the child was suffering.

Sister Flavie had every opportunity for carrying out a deception, because she was the child's mistress and only attendant.
Granted the faulty diagnosis, and parents, friends, physicians,
to some extent even she herself, had some grounds for believing
that the child had been miraculously cured of a malady, which
would otherwise have necessitated a painful operation. Sister
Flavie herself may have been led on almost unconsciously to
exaggerate and invent all the details that were necessary to
show that there was extensive disease of the parts affected.
When she told Agnes Arnauld of the miracle, Agnes quietly
went to bed and did not repeat the story to the child's aunt,
Jacqueline Pascal, until the following morning. After that,
the Abbess, Marie des Anges, heard it, and the nuns began
to hope that their petition in the service of the previous day
had been heard. 'Shew me a token for good,' they had sung,
'that they which hate me may see it, and be ashamed.'

Angélique was slow to believe the miracle, and we may be
allowed to doubt whether we should have heard anything of it
if she had been Abbess instead of Marie des Anges, or even if
she had been in Paris. It was not until a month afterwards
that she wrote an account of it to the Queen of Poland, telling
her in a simple natural way exactly what she had heard. She
accepted the miracle as a Divine manifestation, and was grate-

ful for it. But in another letter she writes : 'If I were to desire and ask for miracles, they should not be worked upon the body, but upon all the wretched souls which languish under miseries a hundred times worse than any bodily evils.' Again when she was consulted respecting the account that had beer. drawn up of the miracles at Port Royal, she replied : ' I cannot approve of these investigations ; God knows why He performs these miracles, and He will manifest His own glory in them in such a manner as He shall see fit. It is not necessary that we should interfere or do anything except adore His Divine Provi-dence, and bless Him, with all humility and gratitude for His good gifts. . . . I believe it to be the will of God that the world should speak of the miracles, and that we should be silent —and not we only, but all our true friends.'

But the true friends were not all silent, and Pascal, in the celebrated sixteenth letter, alludes to the 'holy and terrible voice which astounds all nature, and consoles the Church.' He apostrophizes the Jesuits :

' Cruel and cowardly persecutors ! cannot even the most secluded cloisters afford a refuge from your calumnies ? Whilst these holy virgins, according to their rule, day and night adore Jesus Christ in the Holy Eucharist, day and night you do not cease to state publicly that they do not believe He is either in the Eucharist, or even at the right hand of the Father ; and you cut them off openly from the Church, whilst they pray in secret for you and for the whole Church. You calumniate those who have no ears to hear you, and no mouth to answer. But Jesus Christ, in whom they are hidden, and with whom they will one day appear, listens to you now, and answers for them. We hear His voice at this very hour—that holy and terrible voice which astounds all nature, and consoles the Church ; and, I fear, my Fathers, that those who harden their hearts, and obstinately refuse to listen to Him when He speaks as their God, will be condemned to listen in terror when He speaks as their judge.'

Pascal's impassioned appeal, and the popular belief in the authenticity of the miracle, averted for a time the ruin of Port Royal. The conscience of the Queen was touched ; she would proceed no further in the matter. It was in vain that the Jesuits urged that the miracle might just as well have happened in a Protestant chapel as in the church at Port Royal ; and that it only proved that God would work a miracle wheresoever and whensoever it seemed best to Him, and often more readily in the midst of unbelievers than of the faithful.   No one heeded their words, not even the Queen.   She gave d'Andilly permission to return to Port Royal; one by one the Recluses followed, the schools were re-opened, and the persecution ceased.   Cardinal Retz was still in exile; but he appointed Father Singlin Superior of Port Royal and Angélique wrote : ' I have now obtained my chief desire upon earth, for I can see nothing more likely to lead us to heaven.'

CHAPTER XXIV.

For three short years there was peace at Port Royal; years of plenty the nuns called them, that preceded famine. Port Royal in Paris was crowded with nuns, novices, postulants, and school pupils; so was the house in the country. The Recluses had all returned; their schools were again in full activity and threatened to become formidable rivals of the Jesuit schools and colleges; the pupils trained in them were taught to reverence the life of St. Cyran, the work of Port Royal and the writings of Jansen.

Angélique, the very Reverend and very dear Mother of the whole community, is failing fast. Her mental vigour is unimpaired, but her physical strength is almost gone. 'My life,' she wrote, 'is one long languor.' Her threescore years and ten are almost accomplished, and her work upon earth is finished. Her old age was honoured, as it deserved to be; and two short letters, in the Memoirs, give a picture of her which is well worth dwelling upon. On her way to Paris in 1655 she stayed at Gif, and one of the nuns who accompanied her wrote back to the Prioress of the country convent:

'We arrived at Gif, where our Reverend Abbess was received just as we should have received her ourselves; that is, like a saint; and with all the respect, submission, and joy that daughters owe to a true mother. The Abbess of Gif was the first to welcome her, and spoke to her alone; and then all the community came and talked to her with the greatest possible frankness. There was not one single secret kept back from our very dear Mother; and I can assure you that this was no small satisfaction to someone who accompanied her and whom I need not name. I wish you could have seen for yourself all that I tell you, for our reception throughout was of the same kind. Our only trouble was that there seemed no bounds to the hospitality, affection, and delight of our hosts. In short, they did everything that love and respect can do under such circumstances. Our dear Mother held two conferences with the community, at which she spoke in a manner worthy of her. She gave images to all the Sisters, who prize them very highly; and she read to each one a sentence from St. Theresa which gave them great satisfaction.'

Angélique also wrote to the Prioress. giving an account of this same journey:—'We paid a very happy visit to Gif, thank God. Everything passed off well except that I made an unfortunate speech which I am afraid vexed a person who had previously seemed touched with what I said to her about devoting the whole of her life to God. I entreat you very humbly to pray that my fault may be repaired. With that exception there was nothing but joy and affection; indeed, it would have been impossible for them to show more; but the old lady cried more than she laughed. Nevertheless they treated her very well and with great civility. . . . I think fatigue must suit me, for although I slept little and talked much at Gif, I am not too tired this evening.'

The young Abbess, with her eager, ardent appeals to the nuns whom she visited, has now become the Reverend Mother, venerated even by those who do not agree with her views, keeping watch and guard over her words, and reproaching herself for an inconsiderate speech. Before setting out on this journey she wrote to le Maître expressing her fears lest her 'brusque, imperious, indiscreet nature and habit of command' should lead her astray; and undoubtedly the old fire does leap forth, but it does not burn steadily as in the old time, and 'the old lady cries more than she laughs.'

One last trait of her disinterestedness deserves a place here. A stranger to the community, who knew her by report, bequeathed a valuable property in Bazas to the Sisters of Port Royal. Angélique induced them to renounce it in favour of a poor Ursuline convent in that town, of which she heard a very favourable report. She told the widow of their benefactor that he would gain by the change, because he would have the prayers of the two communities instead of one. 'Believe me,' she said to one of the Sisters, 'this house shall never be rich as long as I live ; for after the wants of the community, who are the first poor we are bound to assist, are supplied, all that comes in at one door shall go out by the other.'

When she was a girl, she resolved that her vow of poverty should be a reality ; and she has at seventy the same noble improvidence which characterized her at seventeen. These last years brought her many sorrows and many losses. Her sisters, Mdme. le Maître, Anne, Marie-Claire, and Madeleine were all dead ; only Agnes remained from whom she was of necessity separated, for one was in Paris when the other was in the country. She looked forward to her own death, and frequently spoke of it to her nephew le Maître, entreating him not to let there be any nonsense and 'grimacing' at her funeral, but to let her be buried simply. She showed him one of the medals which Sister Flavie, she of the Holy Thorn, had made of the 'blood, hair, and veil' of her sister Anne, and expressed her fear lest a similar fate awaited her. He reassured her, and promised that there should be nothing of the kind. But the nuns were already collecting materials to show that she was a saint, and had worked miracles. A Sister attempted one day to persuade her that she had miraculously caused some heavy bread to become light : 'Go about your business, and hold your tongue !' replied the Abbess, with her usual swift common sense. She said mournfully one day : 'They are too fond of me ; and after I am dead, if they are not kept in check, they will invent a hundred fables about me. I know them. It is a point on which they are not to be trusted.'

Le Maître was not able to fulfil his promise, for in 1658 he died. His death had been preceded by that of his friend M. de Bagnols, a Recluse who was highly esteemed by the whole community and of whom Angélique said, when she heard that he also had passed to his rest : 'It seems as if there was no one left in the world.' In 1658 her faithful pupil, novice, and friend, Marie des Anges, who had been elected Abbess of Port Royal in 1656, died in Paris. On her death-bed she spoke with a shudder of the twenty years she had passed at Maubuisson, but added : 'Ten years ago God brought me out of the house of bondage.'

Angélique requested that the heart of her deceased friend

might be sent to her at Port Royal *des Champs*, and this was done. Nine days later Mdme. d'Aumont died, also in Paris. And then, in both these overcrowded houses, there was a terrible mortality. In Paris it was measles, always a more serious disease in France than in England, and malignant fever to which the nuns fell victims ; whilst in the country it was inflammation of the lungs, of which five died in a fortnight. D'Andilly lost another daughter at this time.

Meanwhile, though the nuns said that these were years of plenty which preceded the famine, they added that they ate their bread in anxiety.

In the year 1656, Pope Alexander VII. declared that the Five Propositions were to be found in Jansen's *Augustinus*, and had been condemned in the sense in which Jansen propounded them ; and, therefore, a synod of the clergy of France, at the request of Louis XIV. and the Queen-Mother, drew up a formulary of submission to the Pope's decree and condemnation of the 'Five Propositions of Cornelius Jansen,' which not only all the ecclesiastics of the realm were to be compelled to sign, but also all the nuns and schoolmasters. The last clause was aimed at Port Royal, and it was well known that to enforce it would secure the suppression of the hated monastery and its attendant schools. From various causes, however, the signature of the formulary was not enforced until after Mazarin's death in 1661. At that time the Queen Dowager no longer possessed any power, and Louis XIV. had placed his conscience in the hands of the Jesuits, who ruled him for sixty years.

The final dispersion of the Port Royal schools took place in 1660. They had existed for fifteen years, and had been dispersed three times ; they had, probably, in no year received more than fifty boys, and sometimes less ;[1] but the names of masters and pupils—Nicole, Fontaine, du Fossé, de Saci, le Nain de Tillemont, Racine, and many others—have made them illustrious.

After the dispersion of the schools, the *Lieutenant-Civil* and a troop of soldiers returned to expel the Recluses. But they had already abandoned their homes, and Arnauld, de Saci, and Father Singlin had thought it prudent to go into concealment ; indeed, Arnauld was scarcely ever out of it. 'I am looking everywhere for M. Arnauld,' said Louis XIV. at a later

[1] Port Royal, par C. A. Sainte-Beuve, iii. 478.

period. 'Your Majesty has always been fortunate,' replied
Boileau ; 'you will not find him.'

Volume after volume, pamphlet upon pamphlet, issued from
the untiring pen of the great controversialist. 'For God's sake
keep M. Arnauld quiet!' said the King on another occasion
when there was an illusive promise of peace between Port
Royal and the Jesuits.

The schools and the Recluses were scattered, but the Sister-
hoods remained. The first step taken by the King at the
instigation of the Jesuits was to command the Grand Vicar of
Paris to depose the Director Father Singlin, and the confessors
of Port Royal, and to submit fresh names for the royal approval.
This he refused, saying that as Singlin had been appointed by
the Archbishop, it was not in his power to remove him.

The King, therefore, gave orders that on the 23rd of April,
1661, the *Lieutenant-Civil* should visit Port Royal, and see
that within three days all the boarders were sent to their
homes.

When Angélique heard of the impending blow she felt that
her place was in Paris ; and, on the 22nd of April, said farewell
to the community and the house she loved so well, knowing
that she should see them no more. D'Andilly was waiting for
her in the courtyard outside the abbey.

'Farewell, brother,' she said ; 'be of good courage whatever
happens.'

'Sister,' he replied, 'don't be afraid, I have plenty of courage.'

'Ah! brother, brother, we must be humble. We must remember that humility without firmness is no better than
cowardice, but courage without humility is presumption.'

When they reached Paris, the Sisters met her with sad faces
and in tears. She said cheerfully and calmly : 'Why, I think
I see tears ! My children, what does this mean ? Have you
no faith ? And why are you amazed ? Is it because men are
plotting against us ? Well, they are flies ; are you afraid of
them ? You hope in God, and yet there is something you are
afraid of ! Believe me, that if you fear Him and Him only, all
will be well.' And then she raised her eyes to heaven and said :
'My God, have pity on Thy children ! My God, Thy holy will
be done !'

She returned amongst them as their true Mother, inspiring
fortitude and resignation. But this first blow was indeed a

heavy one. There were thirty-three boarders in Paris, and about as many in the country. Many of them were orphans, and knew no other love than that which the kind Sisters lavished upon them. They could not keep back their tears at the thought of separation, and when the time came, and one after the other was removed, their sobs and cries resounded through the convent. The nuns could scarcely restrain their sorrow as they saw that they were to be deprived for the future of the children to whom they were tenderly attached,[1] and who gave so much of brightness and interest to their lives. Angélique was the strength and consolation of all around her. Anxiety and excitement prevented her from sleeping, and she spent the night in writing letters, making arrangements, and giving orders. Father Singlin came to take leave of her and of the community, and that farewell seemed the greatest trial she had experienced. She begged the nuns to leave her in the parlour alone that she might confess to him for the last time, for she was so weak she thought that she must die.

But there were more trials for her still. An order came for the removal of the postulants. Among them were two girls to whom she stood in the place of a mother. One was the daughter of the Duchess de Luines and the other of M. de Bagnols. They had been confided to her by the parents, and had been under her care since they were infants. They also must go, and it was she herself who led them to the door, spoke words of comfort to them, and dried their tears. The Duchess de Chevreuse, who was waiting to receive them, was astonished at her calmness, but she replied : ' Madam, when there is no God I shall lose courage, but whilst God is God I will put my trust in Him.'

Agnes, who had been elected Abbess on the death of

---

[1] There were at that time English girls in the convent school, whose parents had sought refuge in Paris after the execution of Charles I. Among those expelled were daughters of Lord Hamilton and Lord Muskerry. The eldest of the Ladies Hamilton, *La belle Hamilton* as she was called, married the Count de Grammont, and as Countess de Grammont was one of the beauties of the Court of Charles II. Louis XIV. one day desired his favourite, the Count de Grammont, to read Jansen's book and find the celebrated Five Propositions. When he was asked the result of the study, he said that if they were there they must be *incognito.* The Countess was rather proud of her husband's *bon-mot,* and often repeated it.—*Mémoires de Port Royal,* ii. 389.

Marie des Anges, had allowed seven of the postulants to enter
upon their noviciate and assume the dress of novices after the
order of dispersion had been received.   When the King heard
this he commanded that the dress should be taken from them,
that they should be expelled with the other postulants, and
that no fresh members should be allowed to enter the community.   To this Agnes could not submit, and she wrote a
letter to the King, in which she pointed out very respectfully
that such a course would involve the extinction of a monastery which had done nothing to forfeit the favour of his
Majesty.   She explained that the seven postulants had been
long destined for a conventual life, and one of them was
Marguerite Périer, the object of a special Divine manifestation
in favour of Port Royal.   She professed entire submission to
the King's commands, but implored him to reconsider his
decision.

The King praised the letter, but sent the *Lieutenant-Civil*
to remove the seven novices, with orders that the Abbess was
to take away the religious and restore their secular dresses.
This command she refused to comply with.   It was against
her conscience.   It was not she who had received the postulants, but the Church.   She had neither will nor power to
revoke what was done.   It was in vain that the *Lieutenant-
Civil* threatened to break open the convent doors, and to
make her answerable in person and in her own name for
setting the law at defiance.   She would not yield ; and the
seven young girls were removed wearing the dress of novices.

Day by day matters assumed a more threatening aspect :
seventy-five persons had been removed, the gates were guarded,
the courtyards full of archers ; the Grand Vicar of Paris had
yielded to the King's wish, and nominated a hostile Superior
in the place of Father Singlin.   The Abbess again protested,
but in vain ; she was compelled to accept the new Superior and
the confessors whom he appointed.

The nuns fasted and prayed, and strove by extraordinary
penance to 'appease the anger of God ;' and then it was
decided that there should be a solemn procession, and the
whole community, barefooted, should carry their sacred relics
and implore the intercession of the Saints at the throne of God.
Among the relics there was a 'fragment of the true cross,' small
and light, which was assigned to Angélique.   On the 10th of

May, a fortnight after her arrival in Paris, she took her place
in the procession, bearing this fragment. As they entered the
choir she sank to the ground and could not rise again ; with
great difficulty she was so far restored as to be carried to her
own room. For two days she remained in a state of insensi-
bility and then, rallying, was attacked by the malady to which
after three months of suffering she succumbed. The Sisters
said God had shown them that she was to 'bear the cross with
them, but to sink under its weight.'

Fresh troubles awaited them daily. The novices were torn
from them, and both the Paris and the country house were now
stripped of all except the professed nuns. 'At length our
good Lord has seen fit to deprive us of all,' Angélique wrote
to Mdme. de Sevigné. 'Fathers, Sisters, disciples, children—
all are gone. Blessed be the name of the Lord.'

There was still one step which she thought might be attended
with advantage to the community, and at every moment of
respite from pain she dictated at intervals, sometimes of days,
a long letter to the Queen Dowager, Anne of Austria.[1] There
is no anger in it, and no trace of weakness. She pleads her
cause and that of her household dispassionately, without
reproaches or complaint ; she exposes the wrongs they have
suffered and the injustice of their persecutors.

'I should be afraid of offending God,' she says, 'of whose
justice I stand in awe, if, while your Majesty to some extent
represents Him upon earth, I should neglect to justify myself
before you, and fail to give my Sisters, who are borne down
by affliction, the testimony which I owe to God and to their
integrity. And I believe that, at the peril of my life, I should
give this testimony to any house, however alien from me, if I
saw it persecuted as this is, and was convinced of its innocence.'
The whole letter is an appeal for justice—an appeal which
passed unheeded. 'Now my earthly business is done !' she
exclaimed, when it was ended.

On the 12th of July, the Grand Vicar and **the** new Superior
visited Port Royal by the King's order, to inspect and
examine the convent, and report to him upon its condition.
It was a humiliation which Angélique felt keenly, and against

---

[1] Sainte-Beuve suggests that Arnauld and Nicole furnished Angélique
with memoranda for this letter, and they probably corrected and revised it
for publication after her death.

which she uttered a spirited protest. When the inspection was over they went up to her room, and the Grand Vicar, sitting down by her bedside, said :—

'And so you are ill, Reverend Mother ; what is the matter with you ?'

'Dropsy,' replied Angélique.

'Jesus!' exclaimed the Grand Vicar, 'you say that as if it was nothing remarkable. Why, does not such an illness startle you?'

'I am incomparably more startled at what I see taking place in this house. For, in fact, I came here to die, and therefore I was bound to be prepared for it, but I did not come here expecting all that I now see, and had no reason to look for such treatment. Oh sir, sir, this is man's day, but the day of the Lord is at hand which will disclose many things that are hidden, and avenge all.'

She spoke with all her old energy, and with an outburst of righteous indignation at the cruel persecution to which she was subjected. And then, as if she desired to plead for those whom she was so soon to leave, she added : 'I am sure, sir, that there are very few convents in which, if you were to search them as strictly as you have done this one, you would not find many more books and much more knowledge of the world and passing events than there is amongst us. For I am certain, sir, that you will find in our Sisters nothing but a very true and simple faith.'

She passed to her rest through great suffering, bodily and mental, with a fear of death upon her, and an anguish which she knew not how to put into words. 'Believe me, my children, believe what I tell you. No one knows what death is. No one realizes it. I have been afraid of death all my life. My thoughts have always been full of it, and yet all that I have imagined is less than nothing compared to what it really is, to what I feel and what I understand now. . . . Now all the world is nothing to me. I am set alone and apart; and it seems as if all that I hear and all that I see cannot enter into my mind, or occupy my attention, or divert it from the one thought that engrosses me. And now I know what death is.'

Again she said : 'I have never understood as I do now that saying of the Scripture, that as the tree falls so it must lie ; for truly in sickness the tree has fallen, and there is nothing more to be done.'

But the dark clouds passed before sunset; hope returned, peace and joy were again granted to her, and with the removal of all those to whom she had turned for help upon earth, her soul sought and found comfort in God. ' I shall never see you again,' she said to Father Singlin, who had come by stealth to visit her once more; ' but I promise never again to be afraid of God.'

Her nephew de Saci had paid her frequent visits. At length the time came when he could no longer do so without danger to the community. They hesitated to tell her, and she guessed it, saying, 'Ah, my poor nephew, he is not to come again; I shall never see him more. It is the will of God. I have nothing to do with it. My nephew without God can do nothing for me, and God without my nephew is all in all.' And again she said : 'It does not distress me that I cannot see Father Singlin. I know that he is praying for me and that is enough. I revere him greatly, but I do not put a man in the place of God.'

On one point she was unchanged. 'Bury me in the grave-yard,' she said, ' and pray don't let there be so much nonsense after my death.'

For some days before the last she was scarcely conscious, but from time to time she rallied, and then the same words were repeated : 'Adieu, my children, adieu, adieu, adieu.' And at the last, 'Jesus, oh Jesus, you are my God, my justice, my strength, my all.'

And thus on the 6th of August, 1661, in the midst of the storm and tempest of persecution, she sank calmly to her rest. We may truly say that her work was finished. And what was the end of it? Her labours in the cause of conventual reform had been abandoned, and she and all her nuns were clinging desperately to the one shred and particle of truth that they had discovered. They would not sign a formulary stating that five propositions were contained in a book written in an unknown tongue, which they never had read and never should read. They would not condemn a man as a heretic whom they believed to be a saint, and whose pure doctrines were capable of regenerating the world.

This was what Angélique's death taught the devoted women

who stood in silence round her grave. They, too, would be faithful to the end ; they would not shrink from bearing the cross, although like her they might fall beneath the burden.

'Pure as angels,' said the angry Archbishop of Paris, M. de Perefixe, 'they are proud as devils.' This was the judgment of the Church, and their reward on earth was persecution, tribulation and privation.

Agnes survived Angélique ten years. Upon her refusal to sign the formulary in 1664, she was torn from Port Royal and imprisoned in a convent of the Order of Visitation, where her treatment is a remarkable comment on the farewell letter in which Mdme. de Chantal rejoices at the friendly feeling of those of her Order for Port Royal.[1] Agnes was imprisoned ; the Last Sacraments were refused when she was believed to be dying, and finally she was threatened that her dead body should be thrown out unburied if she did not submit. It was in vain ; she did not yield, and never signed. After ten months she was released, and died at Port Royal *des Champs*, in 1671, at seventy-eight years of age.

Before long there was a division in the monastery. The nuns not trained by the Arnaulds, or influenced by St. Cyran or his successor Singlin, readily yielded to the wishes of the new Superior and confessors. Port Royal *de Paris* soon became all that they could desire, and was the abode of intrigue and revelry. The Abbess gave brilliant entertainments, and made application to the sister house for funds to defray her expenses. Whereupon the King said, 'No, no. If Port Royal *de Paris* dances, Port Royal *des Champs* shall not pay the piper.' There was a final separation between the two monasteries, and those who were faithful to the tradition of their house and the memory of Angélique, retired to the now scantily endowed house in the country.

All the after history of Port Royal *des Champs* is a tale of bitter relentless hostility to the Recluses, of mean unmanly persecution of the nuns. There were Arnaulds among them still,[2] and they not only did not yield, they fought nobly for

---

[1] Page 267.

[2] Notably Angélique de St. Jean, d'Andilly's second daughter : 'a prodigy of talent and goodness,' as the Memoirs not unjustly say. All the best accounts of Angélique are from her pen.

every inch of ground, and by protests, petitions, and remonstrances, held the enemy in check. But the end came at last.

Fifty years after Angélique's death there were still twenty-
two nuns at Port Royal *des Champs.* They were old and feeble
women; bedridden, paralytic, dying. They had been shut up
within the convent, without confessor, without priest, without
sacraments for the dying; they had been excommunicated, and
yet they had not yielded, nor set their hands to the detested lie.

Mdme. de Maintenon, a hard, narrow bigot, ridiculed their
sufferings; and she, as well as the Jesuit confessors of Louis
XIV., had always exasperated him against Port Royal. He
was now urged to take the final step—disperse these old
women, and raze their monastery to the ground.

On the 26th of October, 1709, the decree of the King in
Council was granted. D'Argenson, with a troop of three
hundred soldiers, was appointed to carry it out. He had also
twenty-two *lettres de cachet*, numerous carriages, and permission
from Cardinal de Noailles to enter all the cloistered parts of
the abbey.

When he reached Port Royal and seated himself on the
throne of the Abbess, the nuns, whom he had summoned,
appeared before him veiled and silent. He deprived them of
papers, property, title-deeds, all that they had, and made
known to them the King's decree of exile: they were to be
immediately sent one by one to different convents out of the
diocese of Paris. The Prioress asked if they might not go
two by two, as many of them were so infirm. The answer
was 'No.'

Might they have time to prepare for their departure and take
a few necessaries with them? Ten minutes were granted.
They were re-assembled, and placed one after the other in the
carriages waiting to convey them to their destinations. Many
of them were between seventy and eighty years old; the
oldest was eighty-six, the youngest more than fifty. Many
were too infirm to walk; one was borne away in a litter. Some
died on the journey; others as soon as they reached their
destination. They were imprisoned in cells without window-
light or fire, deprived of sacraments and their dying or dead
hands guided to obtain a signature which no persecution had
previously been able to draw from them. At length the
Church was able to assert triumphantly that their obstinacy

was vanquished, and that its faithful efforts had been rewarded by the signature of these formidable enemies.

Even this was not enough. The monastery where the nuns had dwelt, and the farmhouse of the Recluses, the church in which they had worshipped together, and the quiet graveyard in which so many were buried, were a memorial and a protest. They must be destroyed and overthrown. They were laid low to the foundations; and then a band of workmen, prepared for their task by drink, broke open the graves of Recluses and nuns, tore the bodies from their graves, threw them together in heaps, and allowed the dogs to feed on them. The lacerated remains were heaped up in carts, and conveyed to a large pit near the churchyard of St. Lambert, into which they were cast.

When Louis XIV. lay on his death-bed, he thought of this scene, and of the dying women whom he had tormented. He turned to the Jesuits by his side and said—

'If indeed you have misled and deceived me, you are deeply guilty; for, in truth, I acted in good faith. I sincerely sought the peace of the Church.'

All was over; and at length in the name of right and truth and for the sake of the 'peace of the Church' one of the noblest efforts of the seventeenth century had been utterly and finally trampled out.

Angélique had striven to substitute order for disorder, virtuous self-denial for vicious indulgence, and charity for spoliation. Far and wide stories of the good Abbess of Port Royal found their way into convents and monasteries, and roused monks and nuns from the sloth of self-indulgence. Her great courage carried her triumphantly through all the difficulties she encountered. She was never daunted, never discouraged; the thing that seemed to her right she must do at any cost to herself or others. Nuns were weak and foolish, and priests wicked; the same difficulties met her again and again. All the tricks of dream, and vision, and miracle, she knew and hated, and was on her guard against them. She tried to make the religion of her house pure and undefiled, and when she failed, with unshrinking courage she was ready to begin again, and to try once more. There was nothing small or mean about her, no petty jealousy, no pride: 'My Order is that of all the Saints, and all the Saints are of my Order,' as she said.

We cannot wonder that her personal purity and active philanthropy exercised such marvellous influence over others; that into the magic circle of which she was the centre, she drew mother, sisters, brothers, cousins, nephews, and nieces. The 'eloquent family,' Balzac called the Arnaulds, they were also the earnest family; having put their hands to the plough, not one of them ever drew back. They were undaunted by hardship, poverty, persecution, death, and not one Arnauld was faithless to the example of heroic endurance and lofty courage which the great Angélique had set. It would be an easy and a thankless office to point out Angélique's mistakes, to call attention to her sordid humiliations, penance, and childish superstitions. They are here faithfully recorded. If such a woman, with high aims, exalted morality, and vigorous intellect, could not free herself and her household from them, the fault lies with the system and not with the individual. She did all that would be possible for any woman, and more than is attainable by the majority.

Angélique Arnauld is nothing more than a name, but a name which those who have once known it can never forget. Her influence survives though not her work. Her heroism may kindle our hearts, but we search in vain for any traces of that Port Royal *des Champs* she loved so well, of the church in which she worshipped, and the chapter-house in which she spoke. The Roman Catholic Church has rejected her, and yet the truth remains that she is of 'the Order of all the Saints, and all the Saints are of her Order.

THE END.

www.ingramcontent.com/pod-product-compliance
Lightning Source LLC
Chambersburg PA
CBHW030921050726
47498CB00003BA/845